'Scared?'

Randal allowed his gaze to roam over her delicious form. 'I didn't think you were scared of anything, Katharine!'

Kate blushed at the teasing warmth in his deep voice. 'There are several things I find disturbing,' she murmured sweetly. 'Thunder happens to be one of them, although I would not rank it half as irritating as impertinent questions!'

'Touché!' A crack of laughter escaped his lordship. 'Why do I bother attempting to cross swords with you?'

'Perhaps you like to live dangerously, my lord,' Kate retorted.

Gail Mallin has a passion for travel. She studied at the University of Wales, where she gained an Honours degree and met her husband, then an officer in the Merchant Navy. They spent the next three years sailing the world before settling in Cheshire. Writing soon became another means of exploring, opening up new worlds. A career move took Gail and her husband south, and they now live with their young family in St Albans.

THE ELUSIVE HEIRESS

Gail Mallin

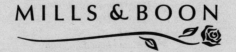

MILLS & BOON

First published in Great Britain 2000
Harlequin Mills & Boon Limited,
Eton House, 18-24 Paradise Road, Richmond, Surrey TW9 1SR

© Gail Mallin 2000

ISBN 0 263 82302 4

Set in Times Roman 10 on 11¼ pt.
04-0005-87000

Printed and bound in Spain
by Litografía Rosés S.A., Barcelona

Chapter One

1811

The house lay drowsing in the afternoon heat. Mellow with age, its sturdy black and white timbers gave it the appearance of a queerly striped fantastic beast bred from and nourished by the rich soil in which it stood.

Peaceful silence reigned. A flock of geese, preening in the sunlight, paraded solemnly across the sweep of greensward that fronted its ancient walls. They paused for an instant by the massive oaken door before disappearing in the direction of the ornamental lake, but nothing stirred behind the diamond-leaded window panes.

Suddenly, the dreamlike silence was shattered by the sound of approaching carriage wheels. Moments later a chaise rounded the final curve of the driveway and slowed to a halt before the main entrance.

The steps were let down and a fashionably clad young woman descended. She surveyed the rambling structure of Crawford Hall for a long moment and then, lifting her chin, trod purposefully forward.

'A visitor for you, my lord.'

Randal Crawford suppressed a groan. Who the devil wanted

to disturb his peace? It was too damned hot to be paying social calls.

'Tell 'em I'm not at home!'

'I'm afraid the young woman was most insistent, sir,' his butler murmured apologetically.

Scenting a mystery, Randal carefully closed the volume of Baron Denon's *Voyages dans la Basse et la Haute Egypte* that he had been studying. Egyptian antiquities could wait!

'Who is she, Blake?'

The butler sniffed. 'She would not give her name. However, I would judge her to be a lady.'

Knowing that his efficient retainer had a keen eye for the niceties of speech and dress, Randal dismissed the fleeting notion that his unknown visitor might be one of the Cyprians who had accompanied Nick and Harry north to Chester for the recent Spring Meeting.

A shudder of distaste ran through him.

His horse, Golden Boy, had won the City Plate and his former comrades-at-arms had invited him to dine with them to celebrate. Flown with champagne, Harry's little blonde piece had sat upon his knee and plied him with amorous kisses!

Luckily, Harry, full of good food and wine, his pockets well-lined from backing Golden Boy, had merely laughed. Randal's own amusement had rapidly dissipated when the girl continued to throw out lures in his direction. In the end, he had been almost glad to see Race Week draw to a close. The friendship formed with Harry when they had both served in the 12th Light Dragoons was too strong to be damaged, but an unwelcome note of constraint had been introduced, not helped by the wench's brazen hints on their last evening that she would like to remain in Chester when the rest of the fashionable world deserted the ancient city and returned to their usual haunts.

Randal frowned at the memory. He had ignored her, of course, but early the next morning a scented *billet-doux* repeating her offer to become his mistress had been delivered to the Hall. Throwing it away, the cynical thought had occurred to him that Harry must have let slip the extent of his fortune.

'Shall I send the young person away, my lord?'

Recalled to the present, Randal considered the matter. It was unlikely that this present weather would last much longer, which, since he enjoyed the heat, was one reason for not going back on his decision to spend a well-earned, idle afternoon in the shade of the great oak that overlooked the Knot Garden. On the other hand, he was aware of a niggle of curiosity. Situated in the depths of the Cheshire countryside, Crawford Hall rarely received unexpected visitors. Even patrons of the arts desirous of admiring its well-known Tudor architecture usually had the forethought to ensure that they would be welcome before venturing so far.

'Did she say why she wished to see me?'

Blake shook his head, his disapproval plain.

Randal handed him the book he had been reading and came lithely to his feet.

'Show her into the library. I'll see her in ten minutes,' he announced briskly, his irritation at being disturbed vanishing at the prospect of action.

'Very good, my lord,' Blake replied woodenly.

Randal laughed and strode away into the house, where, true to his word, he swiftly exchanged his informal shirtsleeves for more decorous attire.

With a minute to spare, he headed for the library, a handsome double cube room which lay beyond the oak-beamed front entrance hall.

'Good afternoon.' Randal paused on finding a stout middle-aged dame seated upon the old carved wooden settle by the main door.

She rose swiftly to her feet in response to his greeting and bobbed a silent curtsy.

'I take it you are waiting for your mistress?' A lady's maid, if he was any judge. Clad in black bombazine, she was the image of respectability.

She nodded, but vouchsafed no further answer.

A fleeting smile touched Randal's well-cut mouth. 'Then I shall endeavour not to keep you waiting too long,' he said pleasantly.

Hearing the note of steel underlying this remark, a look of alarm flashed over the woman's somewhat heavy features. It was swiftly veiled, but Randal realised she was extremely nervous.

His interest quickened. Now, why should she be scared of him?

With a nod of dismissal, he turned away towards the library, a sense of anticipation filling him.

She was standing over by one of the long sash windows, which had been inserted some twenty years ago on his father's orders. Apparently intent upon the view, she did not turn round.

However, Randal thought he saw her shoulders tense; certain she had heard him enter, he experienced a flicker of affronted surprise. It was not the usual habit of young ladies to ignore him!

Coxcomb! Recovering his sense of humour, his mouth twisted in a wry grin. Instead of behaving like a puffed-up popinjay, he ought to take advantage of the situation.

The lady's excellent figure was certainly worth studying. She wasn't very tall but, clad in a dashing travelling costume of pomona-green, she possessed enticing curves. He preferred brunettes, too, and the ringlets escaping from the confines of that frivolous little bonnet were very dark.

'I see you admire our view, ma'am,' Electing to make the first move, Randal strolled across the thick Turkey carpet towards her. 'It is generally regarded as one of Repton's finer prospects.'

Slowly, with a panache Randal found himself admiring, she turned to face him and made a graceful curtsy. The lace veil on her hat was down, obscuring her features, but as she straightened she lifted up her hands and flung it back.

Randal caught his breath in an involuntary gasp of surprise. She was a regular little beauty!

Framed by the bonnet, her face was a pure oval with a straight little nose and a softly rounded chin, but her mouth was no pink rosebud. Randal stared at her soft full lips. Could that rich inviting colour be as natural as it seemed?

Her eyes were even more striking. Long, slanting and as black as midnight, they held a faintly mocking smile as they met his gaze.

'Lord Redesmere, I presume?'

Her voice was low and sweet…and faintly amused.

Recalled abruptly to his senses, Randal bowed. The movement lacked his usual grace, but his voice was perfectly steady when he answered.

'You have the advantage of me, ma'am.'

She smiled. 'Don't you recognise me, sir?'

Randal shook his head, trying to ignore the sudden fierce surge of attraction that twisted through him at her smile.

'Should I?' he enquired, concealing his perturbation and gesturing politely towards one of a pair of comfortable leather-padded armchairs that stood before the richly carved Tudor mantelpiece.

'No. I suppose not. After all, I dare say you couldn't have been more than fifteen when we last met.' She moved towards the chair. 'And I was still in swaddling clothes,' she added, glancing back over her shoulder, her expression provocative.

Randal's brows shot up, but he waited until she was comfortably settled before seating himself and taking up the challenge.

'May I ask the circumstances surrounding this momentous occasion?'

There was a note of amusement in his attractively deep-toned voice that told her he was enjoying their banter and his visitor experienced a flutter of satisfaction. No matter how Mary protested, she *knew* this roundabout approach was exactly what was needed!

It was essential to engage Lord Redesmere's interest and support if their plan was to succeed, but it wasn't going to be easy. Gossip painted him a strong-minded and intelligent man who went his own way careless of public opinion. Since he was as rich as he was well connected, this eccentricity was forgiven him, particularly by matchmaking mamas who eagerly sought him as a husband for their daughters.

He was also said to be a dangerous man to cross!

'Actually, sir, it was my christening,' she answered, still managing to keep her tone light in spite of the sudden chill which feathered down her spine.

'I attended your christening?' A puzzled frown banished the admiration in his eyes.

They were very blue eyes. Set in a strong-boned face, they justified all the flattery she had heard. He *was* handsome, although she didn't care for the way he wore his wheat-blond hair in a Brutus crop.

She could imagine how devastatingly attractive he would be if he ever bothered to smile with genuine warmth.

'I'm told you declined the honour of becoming my godparent, but I understand we were formally introduced.' She allowed a hint of mischief to creep into her tone. 'To be honest, I believe I possetted all down the front of your best coat.'

'Good God! Are you saying that you are *Kitty Nixon?*' Randal ejaculated the name in astonishment.

Gratified by his thunderstruck expression, his visitor nodded, setting her luxuriant sable ringlets dancing.

'Indeed, sir. I am your long-lost cousin. And you must know why I am here.'

'Do I?'

A moment ago, he had fallen for that dramatic trick she'd played with her veil, but it seemed he was not quite as bedazzled as she had hoped!

'Oh, come, my lord!' She gave him a roguish smile. 'It is not kind of you to tease me when I have travelled all the way from America to see you.'

'To see me or lay claim to John Nixon's fortune?'

Nettled by this reply, her thin black brows flew together. 'Surely you did not think to inherit *everything*?'

All trace of amusement fled Randal's face. 'I think, ma'am, that you are impertinent,' he countered icily.

'Then I pray you will excuse me.' Reining in her temper, she adopted a conciliatory expression. 'I didn't mean to impugn your honour. My grandfather would not have named you as his executor unless he trusted you.'

She dropped her gaze to her lap and let a convincing sigh escape her. 'Forgive me. It has been a long journey and I fear my wits are somewhat addled with fatigue.'

Ninnyhammer! Where was the sense in antagonising him? Even if he had hoped to inherit the old nabob's fabulous wealth, he was hardly going to admit it!

To her relief, he acknowledged her apology, adding smoothly, 'May I offer you some refreshment? A glass of ratafia, perhaps?'

She accepted with a pretty show of thanks, hiding her disappointment. Devil take the man, was that all the hospitality he was going to offer her? After such a heavy hint she was sure he would feel duty-bound to proffer an invitation to stay to dinner at least. Where was his family feeling?

Swallowing her resentment at this setback to her plans, she watched him rise to summon one of his servants.

He moves very well for such a big man, she admitted grudgingly to herself. Although she had known he was once a major in an elite cavalry regiment, she hadn't expected him to be quite so tall and broad-shouldered…or to exude such an aura of powerful virility!

It was rather disconcerting!

Randal pulled the bell, but did not immediately resume his seat. Instead, he took up a position standing by the wide stone hearth.

'When did you hear of John Nixon's death?' he asked, fixing his gaze attentively on her face.

'Last November,' was the prompt reply.

'He died in July.' Randal pointed out the fact gently.

'So we were informed, but the letter you instructed the lawyers to write took a long time to reach us.'

'May I ask why?'

She clenched her teeth. Until this moment, she wouldn't have thought it possible to dislike such a velvet-toned voice!

'It went astray, sir.' Realising she had fallen into the error of sounding sharp again, she produced a pretty smile. 'They sent it to our previous address.'

His expression remained polite, but she sensed he was sceptical.

It was very annoying! She hadn't expected to find him so difficult to convince.

'Did you know that my grandfather quarrelled with my mother when she wrote to inform him that she was to marry again?' she asked abruptly.

Realising she was endeavouring to explain, Lord Redesmere dipped his blond head in acknowledgement. 'That would be… what…three, four years past?'

'In 1807. Four years ago. He had some fustian notion that she ought to remain true to Papa's memory and wear her blacks forever!'

'Very old-fashioned,' Randal agreed smoothly. 'Whereas I imagine she wanted the protection of a husband?'

'America may be a young country, sir, but we are quite civilised. Mama didn't *need* a husband. She simply fell in love with a kind and honourable man.'

'I stand corrected, ma'am.' No trace of his amusement at being put so severely in his place appeared in Lord Redesmere's meek reply.

His visitor gave him a suspicious glance, but returned briskly to the point.

'Even though her marriage to Mr Ashe came a full two years after Papa's death, the minute Grandfather heard of it he stopped the small allowance he had been making us and refused to answer any of our letters.'

An expressive shrug dismissed this act of petty spite. 'He and Mama had never been close, of course. He had disapproved of Papa marrying her and made things so very uncomfortable that she was glad to leave England.'

Randal nodded. If memory served him correctly, Charles Nixon had fled to America to escape his father's baleful influence. They had initially quarrelled over his refusal to become a merchant. John had made his spectacular fortune in India, but Charles was not interested in trade. He wished to become a scholar and, being as stubborn as his father, finally managed to persuade John to let him go up to Cambridge, where he had promptly fallen in love with the daughter of one of his tutors.

John, who had wanted a grand match for his only child, had been furious, but Charles had stuck to his guns and married his Lydia as soon as he turned twenty-one. Since John refused to receive his new daughter-in-law, Charles would not return home to the magnificent house in Chester but had sought employment.

He had obtained a position in the household of a rich London cit who aspired to become a gentleman. His secretarial duties were light but well paid, and the young couple's happiness was crowned when a daughter was born to them almost a year to the day after their wedding.

Randal reflected that a grandson might have inclined the old nabob to seek a reconciliation, but Kitty's birth did not soften him. Instead, hating to be crossed and too proud to consider he might be in the wrong, he had schemed to have Charles removed from his post. Unfortunately, his son discovered the real reason why his employer no longer required his services.

When the same thing happened again a few months later, Charles's anger had been so great he decided to remove himself and his family to a place where his father's influence could not affect them. It was almost inevitable that he should choose America, a land which cherished freedom and the country which John Nixon, an ardent supporter of King George, disliked above all others.

Hearing that another Cambridge existed in Massachusetts, Charles announced his plan to emigrate. Piqued that his meddling had achieved the exact opposite of what he had intended, John Nixon swore never to speak to his son again.

It was a vow he was to keep, but the price of his pride was high. With every year that passed he became more reclusive and eccentric, refusing to see all but a few favoured visitors. On his deathbed he had been a lonely and embittered man.

'My great-uncle was a difficult man,' Randal commented in a carefully neutral tone. 'He liked to get his own way.'

'It must be a family trait, sir.' A sugar-sweet smile accompanied this remark.

Randal's blue eyes narrowed and, realising she was skating on dangerously thin ice, she hurried to conclude her explanations. 'The people who bought our bookshop kindly forwarded your letter on to us in Amherst as soon as they found someone willing to act as a carrier.' She paused to make sure he understood. 'It is a considerable journey. Amherst is in western Massachusetts.'

He ignored her helpful geography lesson. 'You owned a bookshop in Cambridge?'

She nodded. 'Papa used all his savings to open it soon after we settled there. He had worked very hard to make it a success. You may disapprove of trade, my lord, but the miserly allowance my grandfather made us after Papa's death was insufficient to keep us. Mama refused to beg for more so we had no choice but to continue with the business. We both worked long hours to keep it thriving and I am proud to say that we were successful.'

Admiring the way her eyes flashed, he said mildly, 'I meant no criticism. I see nothing demeaning in earning one's own living. Honest toil must be preferred to charity.'

Deciding he was sincere, her stern expression relented. 'I am pleased to hear you say so, sir. My steppapa warned me that I would encounter silly prejudice if I mentioned my background. Not that I care. I have no regard for the opinion of idle fops.'

Her disdainful tone amused him. Intrigued, he would have enjoyed hearing more, but a tap at the door announced the arrival of a footman and she fell silent.

Randal gave instructions concerning their refreshment and waved her to continue as the servant left the room.

'Pray do go on, ma'am.'

She shrugged lightly. 'I have no wish to bore you with my opinions on society, sir. Let it suffice to say that my recent mode of life was different to that enjoyed by the young ladies of your acquaintance, but I am not in the least ashamed of having to work for my living.'

Her attractive contralto voice held a note of utter conviction.

Randal owned himself puzzled. Every answer she had given accorded with the report Messrs. Hilton, Tyler and Dibbs had submitted for his scrutiny. His great-uncle's papers having revealed little—he must have destroyed Lydia's letters—Randal had ordered Hilton to write to America.

Many months later they had finally received a reply when Lydia wrote to explain that she and Kitty had moved to Amherst following her marriage to Henry Ashe, a widower with three sons. Her new husband was the owner of a successful boarding-school and well able to provide for them. Kitty had no need of John Nixon's money. However, she would permit her daughter to accept the legacy if she wished to do so.

It all tied in. And yet...

'May I enquire why you waited so long to claim your inheritance?' Randal allowed no hint of his inner conflict to show in his expression. 'Surely my letter explained how awkwardly matters had been left?'

With one elbow resting on the mantelshelf, his pose was casual, but she was uncomfortably aware that he was watching her very closely.

A mouse must feel like this, waiting for the cat to pounce!

She lifted her chin and met his gaze without flinching.

'My mama and steppapa did not wish me to run the risk of encountering winter storms at sea.'

He nodded. It was a reasonable precaution.

'I assume from your attitude you think my Mama and Mr Ashe should have accompanied me to England.' She threw out the challenge boldly. She did not understand what had prompted him to question her in this suspicious manner, but it was imperative she still his doubts and gain his trust.

'The thought had crossed my mind.'

'Naturally, they wished to do so, but circumstances forbade it. Mr Ashe is the headmaster of a school and could not easily leave his post. Mama helps him teach and she looks after the boarders and my three young stepbrothers.'

She paused, willing a shy little blush into her cheeks as she smoothed her skirts in an embarrassed manner. 'And she has a new baby to tend.'

She looked so very lovely with that wild rose colour accentuating her high cheekbones that Randal had to force himself to concentrate. 'There was no mention of a baby in her letter of reply.'

'I dare say Mama didn't realise she had to relate every detail of her private life.'

Touché! A wry grin twisted his mouth as he absorbed the justice of this rebuke. It could be true, of course. Lydia was barely forty, not too old to have given birth to another child.

'My half-sister was only a few days old when we first heard from your lawyers, sir,' his unusual visitor continued in a softer voice. 'Even if the weather had been better, I could not have left home then.' Her gaze dropped modestly. 'Mama needed my help.'

'I see.' Randal's tone was dry. 'You are to be congratulated on your sense of duty, particularly in view of the temptation on offer.'

The dark head came up sharply and she eyed him suspiciously for an instant before continuing. 'Mama arranged an escort for me, of course. I travelled in the company of a respectable married couple who wished to visit relatives.'

'Perfectly proper, ma'am.'

Lord Redesmere noted that his visitor had stopped pleating her skirts. Had she been fidgeting merely to make him think she was a demure and retiring young miss? He wasn't certain—perhaps she was genuinely nervous, but he didn't believe she was shy. Her obvious enjoyment of their earlier banter suggested a more robust nature.

He *was* mocking her! Resisting the temptation to glare at him, she concluded her explanation. 'Mama allowed me to make up my own mind whether I wanted to fulfil my grandfather's last request. I must apologise if the delay while I made my decision caused any inconvenience, but, as you can see, I am here in good time.'

John Nixon's will had stated that, unless his granddaughter came to England within a twelvemonth of his death to claim her inheritance in person, she would forfeit everything.

'There are almost two months still in hand,' Randal agreed, his deep voice as smoothly bland as cream.

Two months before all that fabled wealth would pass automatically to the man standing before her. With a sudden start of dismay, she wondered if the gossip was accurate. What if he were not as rich as she had been told? Perhaps he led an expensive life.

For the first time she truly understood that her arrival must change things for him, too. The realisation made her uncomfortable. She didn't want to hurt anyone!

And how must he feel, seeing his chance of gaining a fortune shrivel into dust? Did he hate her?

A flash of amusement lit up Randal's face as he read the thoughts flickering in her wonderfully expressive eyes.

'Pray do not look so worried, ma'am! I have no intention of throwing you into the lake to drown.'

At his words she turned so white that he thought she would faint. Good God, surely she hadn't taken him seriously?

She jumped to her feet, looking as if she wanted to flee, and every last vestige of remaining colour faded from her creamy complexion.

'Sit down!' Biting back a worried imprecation, Randal swiftly crossed the room and pushing her into the chair, dropped on to one knee besides her.

'Permit me!' Without waiting for an answer, he took her by the shoulders and forced her head down into her lap.

'Keep still for a moment and the dizziness will pass.' Randal contained her brief struggle with ease and then, to his relief, she relaxed against him as the sense of what he was saying penetrated her distress.

At length, judging the danger to be over, he slowly drew her upright. 'There, that's better! You have a little more colour now.'

His hands were warm. He was holding her gently, but she could feel their heat penetrating her thin summer gown. Her dizziness had gone, banished by his efficient treatment, but a curious languor was stealing over her, replacing the momentary panic his ill-timed jest had induced.

With a little spurt of shock that set her heart racing anew, she realised what she was experiencing was the slow burgeoning of desire. Appalled, she tried to tell herself it wasn't true, that she was just imagining the sexual tension spiralling between them, but from the expression on his face she knew he felt it, too.

She was so close Randal could see the pulse fluttering at the base of her slim throat. Her breathing was shallow and rapid, stirring her bosom. The slight movement drew his gaze like a magnet. Discreetly revealed by the fashionable neckline, her breasts were beautiful. High and firm, they were deliciously rounded.

Randal couldn't tear his eyes away. He felt his loins react as desire surged in him. Her skin was like satin with a creamy sheen that made his fingers itch to explore...

Involuntarily, his hands tightened their hold on her shoulders.

A tiny gasp reached his ears and he lifted his gaze to find her great dark eyes fixed on him. He stared into their mysterious depths and felt his heart begin to hammer.

'Thank you. You may let me go now, sir.'

Her voice was a breathless whisper, but it was enough to make Randal release her as if he had been struck.

What the devil had got into him? For one insane moment all he had wanted in the world was to rip that gown off her and carry her up to his bed!

He rose abruptly to his feet, glad that the physical evidence of his attraction had died an instant death with the return of common sense. 'Pray excuse my rough-and-ready treatment, ma'am,' he said, controlling his voice so it did not betray his disquiet. 'I thought you about to swoon.'

She managed a shaky smile. 'There is no need to apologise, sir. I did feel a little faint.'

That was true enough!

'Please accept my thanks for your prompt action,' she added, searching for an acceptable excuse. 'I think the heat must have overset me. I had not expected to find England so warm in May!'

He acknowledged her thanks with a punctilious bow and moved away to resume his previous seat.

An inaudible sigh of relief escaped her. She felt safer with him at a distance!

It had been stupid of her to panic. The situation was enough to strain the strongest of nerves, but she should have realised he was merely joking. Unfortunately, she found him too thoroughly unsettling to be able to think straight!

God knows, she hadn't expected it to happen—it had been a long time since a man had managed to affect her so! Yet a moment ago when his hands had tightened their hold, a frightening urge to respond to his touch had leapt within her. She had wanted to wind her arms round his neck and abandon her-

self to the desire she could see mirrored in his burning blue
eyes.

Heaven help her, she must be going mad!

The arrival of the footman bearing a silver tray on which
reposed a moisture-beaded jug of fresh lemonade broke the
awkward silence.

The tension still lingering in the air was dispelled and Lord
Redesmere became the perfect host, seeing to it that his guest's
glass was filled and tempting her to try a sample of his cook's
excellent baking.

Randal was glad of the diversion. He had been on the point
of behaving like an absolute fool and he didn't care to think
on it!

'If my clumsy attempt at humour upset you, I apologise,' he
announced gruffly once the footman departed. 'I did not mean
to alarm you with a threat of violence.'

She murmured a slightly incoherent denial, assuring him that
she had known he was speaking in jest.

Randal set his empty glass down on a nearby kingwood tri-
pod table and, determined not to relax his guard a second time,
said, 'In that case, if you are feeling restored, may we return
to the subject under discussion?'

A nod of her sable curls answered him.

Steepling his fingers together in a thoughtful gesture, Randal
stared at the brass trellage bookcases lining the wall. 'My great-
uncle had precise views concerning the disposal of his fortune.
When he asked me to be his executor, he stipulated that I must
adhere strictly to his instructions. I was not entirely happy with
all of his conditions, but I agreed and promised him I would
do my best to see that his wishes were carried out.'

Abandoning his air of contemplation, he gave her a direct
look. 'Naturally, I am prepared to relinquish my own claim to
the rightful legatee, but honour demands I ensure the terms of
the will are met before I hand over a single penny.'

Fright restored her wits. What did he mean by *rightful*?

'I commend your vigilance, my lord,' she said crisply.

'However, I will not deny it is a relief to hear that you do not intend to dispute my claim, for, frankly, I have no desire to stay in England. The sooner the details are settled and the money is mine, the sooner I shall be able to return home.'

'Don't you mean to visit your Irish connections first?' he asked softly.

She could feel the colour rushing into her cheeks; to give herself time to think, she took a slow sip of lemonade.

'Or perhaps you have already been to Dublin, eh, ma'am?'

His deep voice held a note of silken mockery that set her teeth on edge. Damn him, how much did he know or was he just guessing?

'What…what do you mean?' She strove for composure, but apprehension sent a chill shivering down her spine.

Randal did not immediately answer her, but instead rose to his feet and, crossing to the handsome oak library table set in the centre of the room, picked up a letter which lay upon its polished surface.

'This came two days ago.' He leant back, propping his lean hips against the edge of the table. 'Shall I read it to you?'

'Your correspondence can be of no interest to me, sir,' she retorted with a frown of faintly irritated puzzlement, but her heart was thumping.

'Not even when it comes from Mr Gerald Sullivan and his wife?'

The blood drained from her face, leaving her pale once more, but, rallying quickly, she gave a scornful laugh.

'If my uncle has written to you, then I'll wager it is to censure me and I most certainly have no wish to hear any more of his complaints!'

Thrown off balance, Randal frowned. 'Why didn't you tell me earlier that you had been to stay with the Sullivans?'

She raised her thin brows. 'I was not aware I needed to account to you for my every move.'

'Believe me, it is necessary,' he said grimly.

'Oh, very well!' She gave an impatient shrug. 'If you must

know, the ship on which I sailed was Irish-owned. The captain wished to make landfall in Dublin and it seemed logical to visit Papa's relatives before proceeding on to England.'

'There were no children from my great-uncle's second marriage,' Randal intervened. 'Ellie Sullivan was already a widow with a young son when they met. He agreed to treat Gerald as his own, but he never adopted him formally.'

'Nonetheless, Papa regarded Gerald as his brother!' She allowed her annoyance free rein for an instant. 'Mama wanted me to pay my respects. Unfortunately, my visit to Ballyhad House was not a success.'

The vivid blue eyes narrowed. 'Pray explain, ma'am.'

Deciding she did not dare risk taking affront at his brusque tone, she complied. 'It is simple, sir. My arrival came as an unpleasant surprise. Perhaps you can afford to be philosophical about losing a fortune, but it appears that my uncle Gerald is not a rich man. I had no idea his finances were in such a sorry state or I might have realised how much he would resent me.'

She sighed. 'I suppose things might have been easier if Grandfather had left him a more generous bequest instead of a mere hundred pounds.'

Randal silently agreed with her shrewd observation. He had tried to persuade his great-uncle to change his mind, but the old man had thought Gerald a frippery fellow.

'Nay, lad, I don't trust that rogue,' John Nixon had gasped, wheezing for breath as his last illness had tightened its hold. 'Many's the time I had to rescue him from his gambling debts to dry his mother's tears and I warned him he'd had the last penny off me when I packed him back to Ireland after her funeral. I paid him off handsomely to stay there and trouble me no longer. He's no cause to complain.'

All that he would agree to was Randal's insistent suggestion that a codicil be added to the will, stating that if Kitty Nixon failed to collect her legacy, then Gerald Sullivan was to be paid a further sum of £10,000 out of the estate before it passed to Randal.

'Call it a sop to my conscience, sir,' Randal had insisted with a wry smile. 'I don't want the fellow to think I abused my position to cheat him.'

A silvery laugh penetrated Lord Redesmere's recollection and he saw that his visitor's mood had lightened and her enchanting countenance now wore a rueful grin.

'It was an excessively uncomfortable situation, sir! I was made to feel my grandfather's peculiar will was all my fault! What with Aunt Moira lamenting that they would end in debtors' prison and my uncle's sulks, I hardly knew where to look!'

She turned a limpidly innocent gaze on him. 'I couldn't wait to leave!'

In spite of himself, Lord Redesmere's finely moulded lips twitched. 'You paint a masterly picture, ma'am.'

She laughed, a low throaty chuckle of wicked amusement, and Randal had to steel himself against her charm.

Blister it, why did he have to find her so attractive!

'Well, sir, are you satisfied now?' She tilted her head at him enquiringly. 'I dare say Uncle Gerald is miffed about my sudden departure from his house. It was unforgivably rude of me to run off without so much as a goodbye, but he must take his share of the blame.'

The pure line of her jaw hardened. 'I never meant to raise false hopes in anyone, but I *am* here now and, if you are finished with your questions, I should like to get on with the business. I assume the lawyers have papers for me to sign?'

He shook his fair head, the last traces of amusement fading from his expression. 'I'm afraid you go too fast, ma'am. There is something else we must discuss first.'

The grim note in his voice caused her heart to skip a beat, but she forced a smile. 'Heavens, not more questions, my lord! Haven't I explained everything already?'

'Not quite.' Randal straightened to his full height and walked back across the room. Halting before her chair he looked down at her. 'I do have one final question.'

Searching her lovely face, he looked deep into her dark eyes. 'Who are you?'

'My lord? I...I don't understand. Is this another of your strange jokes?' In spite of her best efforts, a little quaver shook her voice.

Hearing it, Randal knew his suspicions were correct.

'I do not find this funny, sir!' Worried by his silence, she broke into rapid speech. 'You know I am your second cousin. We share the same great-grandparents and—'

'Stop!' He made the demand with an abrupt authoritative gesture of his hand and she reluctantly obeyed.

'This game has gone on long enough. You have been well schooled, ma'am, but it is pointless to continue.'

'Game? I think you have run mad, sir!' Fighting off the terrifying nausea which threatened to overwhelm her, she struggled to marshal her wits.

Ignoring her protest, Randal tossed the letter he was still holding into her lap. 'Read it.'

Sheer willpower enabled her to break free from his authority and disobey this command. Flinging the letter down on to the rich carpet, she glared at him angrily. 'No! I've told you, I'm not interested in what he has to say.'

'You should be.' Randal's voice was grim. 'You see, Gerald Sullivan didn't write to complain of Kitty Nixon's behaviour. He wrote to inform me that she is dead. She drowned in the River Liffey three weeks ago.'

Chapter Two

'Detestable man! Leading me on in such an odiously under-hand fashion! I swear he enjoyed every minute of my discomfiture!'

Kate Devlin threw herself back against the dingy squabs of the hired chaise, a frown distorting the exquisite beauty of her face.

'Not one single shred of mourning to warn us. Does the man lack all sense of family feeling? If he thought Kitty dead, why didn't he display at least a modicum of grief?' Her rich contralto voice crackled with rage.

'Perhaps he thought it would seem hypocritical,' Mary Porter suggested quietly. 'Him not having seen her since she was a baby, I mean.'

'It would suit him if she was dead. He stands to inherit her fortune! Come to think on it, I wouldn't be surprised if he was in league with Sullivan.'

'Calm down, Kate. You know you shouldn't make such wild accusations without proof.' Mary's broad face creased into disapproving lines.

'Bah!' Kate snorted inelegantly.

Mary hid a smile. It was no use scolding the lass. Kate Devlin was wholehearted in everything she did. Without her enthusiasm, their plan would never have got this far, but it was a pity she had decided to take his lordship in dislike.

'We ought to be deciding our next move,' she reminded her young companion gently.

Kate emerged from her brooding and took a long, calming breath. 'You're right as usual, Mary,' she sighed. 'But it goes against the grain to let him think he has won!'

'I reckon Redesmere is as shrewd as he can hold together.' Mary scratched her chin thoughtfully. 'Maybe we ought to abandon the attempt?'

'No! I'm damned if I'm going to let that…that interfering oaf prevent us from helping Kitty.'

Wisely, Mary said no more. She had argued against the whole crazy scheme from the beginning, but Kate's soft heart had been touched by Kitty Nixon's plight and once she got an idea into that stubborn head of hers then Old Nick himself couldn't shift it.

A silence fell between them. Kate stared blindly out of the dusty window, too preoccupied to notice the bone-shaking of the old chaise as it rattled down the narrow country lane.

She had told the coachman to convey them away from Crawford Hall with all possible speed. Unfortunately, she couldn't shake off the memory of her interview with Randal Crawford so easily.

How she had longed to slap that mocking expression off his handsome face! She hadn't been able to think of a single thing to say after he had dropped that bombshell in her lap. The tide of embarrassed colour which had flooded her cheeks hadn't helped.

By the time she had recovered her nerve he was ringing for the footman to escort her out.

Rising to her feet, she had met this reversal of fortune with dignity.

'You will find, sir,' she had informed him coolly, 'that my uncle is mistaken. I am Kitty Nixon and I can prove it.'

'You will have to.' His expression had hardened, the blue

gaze raking her up and down with obvious contempt. 'But I would advise you not to try.'

Ignoring the *frisson* of alarm that made her knees quake, Kate tilted her chin at him defiantly. 'Is that a threat, my lord?'

'Consider it a warning,' came his silky reply.

Forgetting her haughty pose, she glared at him. 'You, sir, are a bully,' she declared hotly.

To her fury he had burst out laughing.

'And you, ma'am, are an adventuress,' he riposted with a smile that dripped mockery.

'How dare you—'

'No. Don't bother to deny it.' He silenced her protests with an easy gesture of one well-kept hand. 'Accept your *congé*, gracefully, m'dear. Otherwise...' He gave a significant shrug.

Kate understood him perfectly. 'Don't worry. I will go quietly,' she snapped back with vicious irony. 'But you needn't imagine this is the end of the matter. I intend to take my claim to the lawyers.'

His brows drew together in a quick frown at her reply.

Stupidly, Kate found herself noticing how much darker they were than his hair. They were a tawny brown, like the long thick lashes that framed his vivid eyes.

'That, ma'am, must be your choice.'

The cold anger in his voice immediately put paid to Kate's wool-gathering and she tensed.

'But be sure you understand the consequences. Next time I might not find your impudence so amusing.'

The arrival of the footman to escort her to the waiting carriage had been timely. Another moment in Randal Crawford's company and Kate might have exploded!

Fiend seize the fellow! What was it about him that could set her all on edge? He was very handsome to be sure, with those strong, well-cut features and that tall, lithe body, but she was hardly a green girl whose head could be easily turned. Once, perhaps...but that was a long time ago.

A little shiver ran through her slender frame. Her nerves

must be in a worse state than she thought. Recalling the past was an idiotic waste of time. Her folly was best forgotten. Dead and buried like Francis.

'Are you all right, lass?' Mary asked anxiously. 'You look as if you've seen a ghost.'

Kate swallowed down the bitter mixture of regret and sorrow that threatened to choke her whenever she thought of her late husband and, turning back to her companion, managed a slight smile.

'I'm sorry. I'm behaving like a fool!' A faint sigh escaped her. 'I should have guessed Gerald Sullivan would try something. No wonder Redesmere was suspicious!'

'Now don't go falling into the dismals!' Mary reached out to give the small white hands that lay clenched in her young friend's lap a comforting squeeze. 'You weren't to know that blackguard would write to his lordship.'

'*He* called me an adventuress,' Kate seethed. Then, drawing a calming breath, she asked in a much more hesitant tone, 'Do you think he could have guessed what I really am? Perhaps I betrayed myself in some way.'

Mary shook her greying head. 'Never,' she said firmly. 'Why should he suspect? You *are* a lady. You were gently born and bred and nothing can change that fact, even if you've come down in the world since.'

Her heavy features softened into a smile. 'Bless you, lass, you mustn't blame yourself for failing to convince him! It was just bad luck that Sullivan's letter arrived before we did.'

Reassured, Kate settled herself more comfortably on the somewhat lumpy seat and began to contemplate their next move.

Money, as usual, was the problem. It was in scarce supply and providing a suitable wardrobe for her new role had been expensive. None the less, they would have to stay at a better kind of inn tonight, one which catered for the gentry. A well-bred young lady like Kitty Nixon couldn't stay anywhere else!

At least they could dispense with the carriage once they returned to Chester. As soon as the stage had set them down outside the White Lion this morning they had sought a means of conveyance to Crawford Hall. The inn was one of the busiest and most popular in the city and the landlord had treated their request with scarcely veiled impatience once he realised that they did not possess a long purse.

His brusque attitude made it plain that he found their desire for economy as peculiar as their lack of male escort. However, when Kate employed her sweetest smile and fluttered her impossibly long eyelashes at him, he'd relented.

Unfortunately, the chaise eventually provided wasn't quite the bargain it had seemed on first sight. The showy paintwork couldn't disguise its neglected interior or its abominable springing. Before they'd gone a mile Kate was regretting that they'd been forced to deplete their slender resources on hiring such an uncomfortable vehicle.

Her generous mouth twisted. For all the good it had done, they might as well have saved their money. The visit to Crawford Hall had been a disaster!

What would his high-nosed lordship think if he knew the real truth of her identity? If he knew that she was a professional actress, paid to parade herself on the public stage? Without a doubt, he would despise her! Good God, even her own father had cast her off and refused to have anything more to do with her!

'Do you know, Mary,' Kate said abruptly, forcing herself to eject the detestable Lord Redesmere from her thoughts and concentrate on more important matters, 'I think that the Sullivans probably *do* imagine Kitty to be dead. They certainly intended she should drown.'

'Aye, she would have done, too, if Ned Gillman hadn't picked that particular stretch of the river-bank for a moonlit stroll.' Mary let out a cackle of mirth. 'Right unlucky he was, if you ask me!'

'Mary! You know I have no romantic interest in Ned. I like him and find him easy to work with, but he is just a friend.'

A flush of rosy colour stained Kate's cheeks, betraying he embarrassment.

Fearing her outspoken colleague would argue that the actor manager of their small company wanted to play a much large role in her life, Kate hastily brought the conversation back to the problem in hand. 'We shall have to seek out Lady Edge worth and try to engage her support. If Kitty's godmother i seen to accept me, it will lend weight to my claim. She migh even have some influence with the lawyers.'

Mary nodded. It was worth a try.

'I wish John Nixon hadn't left everything in Redesmere' control.' Kate's slim fingers drummed against the cracke leather seat. 'The lawyers will be very reluctant to go agains him, even if I can persuade them to acknowledge me.'

'Maybe Lord Redesmere will change his mind when he see that letter and the locket Kitty gave you,' Mary suggested hope fully.

Kate shrugged eloquently. 'I doubt he is the vacillating type He'll probably say I stole them!'

Her dark gaze fixed itself upon the campion and lady smock rioting in the passing hedgerows, but all she saw was a pair o bright blue eyes narrowing with contempt. It was strange hov much it had hurt.

Her gloomy expression suddenly brightened. 'Still, there i one thing even Randal Crawford must take into consideration Gerald Sullivan claims Kitty is dead, but he cannot prove i not without producing her body.'

Mary began to chuckle. 'I'd like to see him try!'

Kate grinned back at her. 'So it is his word against mine an everyone knows that he is desperate for money.'

Her rich laughter soared to fill the coach.

'Onwards to Chester and Lady Edgeworth! The game is stil afoot!'

The sun was already hot when Kate emerged from the Hop Pole Inn in Foregate Street the next morning. Unfurling he blue silk parasol to shade her delicate skin, she had the satisfaction of knowing it set off her demure outfit to perfection.

She had taken a great deal of care with her appearance for this meeting with Lady Edgeworth. A wealthy widow in her mid-forties, Kitty's godmother was one of the leaders of local society and said to be a generous hostess.

'But I don't really know much about her,' Kitty had informed them apologetically. 'She and Papa were childhood friends and she wrote a very kind letter to Mama after he died. She even offered to give me a London Season once I was out of mourning. Mama refused—we could not afford it—but when it was decided I should claim my inheritance Mama wrote, asking her if she would house me while the business was settled. She thought such a course would be more suitable since Cousin Randal is a bachelor, but we did not receive a reply before I left home.'

Given the difficulties of sea transport, Kate was not daunted by this silence on Lady Edgeworth's part. She had sent a note round to Abbey Square as soon as she had removed her bonnet in the Hop-Pole's best bedchamber. In spite of Mary's gloomy prediction that her ladyship might be away from home, a page-boy had brought round a reply within the hour.

Kate was invited to call after breakfast and, correctly deducing that Lady Edgeworth would not expect her before eleven, she partook of coffee and rolls in a leisurely fashion before beginning a toilette designed to impress her supposed godmother. Once she had bathed, she sat patiently in her wrapper while Mary brushed her dark curls until they gleamed to rival seal's fur and dressed them in a simple chignon, leaving just a few loose tendrils to frame her face.

'Nearly ten o'clock. Time you was dressed. We don't want to start off on the wrong foot by being late.'

'Oh, no!' Kate let out a mock groan. 'Dearest Mary, you aren't going to make me wear all those? Can't I just wear the petticoat?'

Mary ignored Kate's plea. 'Proper young ladies always wear

drawers and stays,' she said inexorably, handing Kate the pair of flesh-coloured pantalettes she held.

'I had forgotten what a restricted life I used to lead. Heavens, I shall be baked alive!' Smothering a sigh, Kate slipped the long drawers on and then allowed Mary to lace her into the corset *à la Ninon*, which was at least soft and lightweight enough to be fairly comfortable.

Mary had ironed her gown while Kate had breakfasted; it lay on the bed waiting for her, a snowdrift of pure white muslin, its only ornamentation a narrow row of pale blue embroidery about the flounced hem.

Kate had refused to wear it yesterday.

'I don't care if it makes me look demure. The green is more eye-catching and I want to make an impression!'

Well, she had certainly made Randal Crawford sit up and take notice! The only trouble was, he'd decided she was an adventuress!

Damn the man! She hadn't been able to stop thinking about him. Last night she had lain awake for hours, going over their interview again and again, trying to decide where she had gone wrong.

Had she really just imagined that insistent tug of attraction?

'Thank you, Mary.' Annoyed at not being able to exercise more self-control, Kate took refuge from her thoughts by scrambling into the white gown with a haste that made Mary mutter in protest.

'I look hideous!' she complained, regarding her reflection with distaste.

'Fiddlesticks!' Mary retorted. 'You would look good in sackcloth and ashes, Mrs Devlin, and well you know it!'

Kate grinned at her and flung up the palms of her hands in an extravagant gesture of defeat. 'All right, I admit I was fishing for compliments but, truly, I don't believe white to be my colour.'

'Be that as it may, just you remember what Miss Kitty told us. That dress is an exact copy of the one she described to me.'

Kitty had been forced to leave Ireland with nothing but the gown she stood up in. Kate was tempted to think it was no great loss after hearing the younger girl describe her wardrobe, but Mary's talented fingers had been able to recreate the same modest style.

Kate's own tastes ran to something more sophisticated. She liked rich fabrics and glowing colours to set off her exotic looks and, at the advanced age of four and twenty, she felt entitled to discard virginal muslins. It was going to be distinctly irritating to have to wear the pastel shades deemed appropriate for a young unmarried girl again.

Mary handed her a pale blue spencer to put on.

'I dare say Lady Edgeworth will find nothing to cavil at in my appearance at least,' Kate consoled herself, picking up her parasol.

This knowledge gave her fresh confidence as she stepped out across the flag-way. Mary, clad once more in her respectable black bombazine, took up a correct position a few paces to the rear and, declining the services of a pair of idle chairmen, they set off on the short walk to Abbey Square.

Armed with comprehensive instructions from the landlady of the Hop-Pole, they made their way down the street and passed inside the well-kept city wall.

Eastgate Street was crowded. Kate looked about her with interest, her attention caught by her first proper sight of the famous Chester Rows. Yesterday's travels had afforded them nothing more than a brief glimpse of the town, which she had never had the opportunity to visit before, but she had already heard of these unique two-tiered streets.

Continuous covered walkways had been built into the ancient buildings at first-floor level and Kate noted that, at intervals, steps had been provided to allow access. There were shops on both levels of the Rows, but those on the upper gallery seemed to house a better quality of merchandise.

'It must be pleasant to be able to go shopping and stay sheltered from any bad weather,' she remarked to Mary.

'Aye, but I expect those shopkeepers charge higher prices,' Mary answered.

In addition to these shops, stalls selling butter, poultry and cheese had been set up on the uneven cobbles of the street and a great number of waggons and carts were struggling to pass along the busy thoroughfare. Kate began to look for the short-cut mentioned by their landlady, but the thronging crowd made the task difficult.

'Watch out!'

Mary let out a warning and Kate narrowly avoided stepping into the mucky channel running down the street as she dodged a heavily laden basket wielded by a busy housewife.

'Perhaps I should have taken a chair,' Kate commented wryly, inspecting her skirts for damage.

Luckily, the white muslin was not splashed and they walked on.

'I think this is the place,' Kate announced a moment later and they proceeded to climb up the steps that led to the entrance of Godstall Lane.

This narrow passageway led towards the Abbey and Kate was glad to find it quiet, if somewhat gloomy.

'I shouldn't fancy coming down here at night.' Mary gave a shudder.

Kate instantly understood her meaning. Although pictur-esque, this ancient lane, like the Rows themselves, must be shadowy and dark after sunset. A perfect backdrop for danger and violence!

Nearing the end of the lane, they spotted the decaying bulk of the Abbey.

''Tis a pity to see a great church going to ruin,' Mary commented as they drew closer.

Kate agreed. 'If there is money enough to ensure the Wall is fit for use as a promenade, you would think the good citizens could spare a few coppers to keep St Werburgh's in decent repair.'

An astringent smile touched her lips for an instant.

'I hear they don't stint themselves when it comes to secular pleasures. Ned says all the leading actors from Garrick onwards have played here at the Theatre Royal. Mrs Siddons, Mr Cooke, Mrs Jordan, even Master Betty.' Her smile broadened. 'I wonder what they would make of the Gillman Players?'

'Oh, hush, do!' Mary implored. 'You never know who might be listening!'

Kate laughed, but, as they turned into the handsome square they sought, obediently let the subject drop.

'Heavens, how grand!' Kate exclaimed, catching sight of the tall stone obelisk which dominated a central green, which was neatly separated from the cobblestones by iron palisading.

To one side of them stood a long, rather low building which she guessed must be the Bishop's Palace from the description given to them by the mistress of the Hop-Pole. It was unexpectedly plain, but the elegant terraces which made up the rest of the Square were as fine as any she had seen in Bath.

Lady Edgeworth's house was in the centre of the west terrace and Kate's heart was hammering as she ascended the shallow stone steps to the classically modelled front entrance.

A footman answered her knock and they were swiftly shown into the morning-room, a large sunny apartment panelled in cherry-coloured silk and filled with a rather overpowering quantity of expensive boule-work furniture.

'Ah, Kitty, my dear! How delightful to see you here at last!'

The middle-aged lady, sitting on an inlaid ebony sofa set in the centre of the room, rose to her feet at their entrance, a smile of welcome wreathing her plump face.

Standing, her figure was revealed as a little too buxom to be elegant, but her morning gown of striped gauze was the latest mode and she wore a smart lace cap trimmed with ribbon perched upon her elaborately dressed blonde hair. There was a slight hint of brassiness about the golden curls, indicating that Lady Edgeworth's hairdresser was helping nature along, but her complexion had retained its girlish bloom.

Kate decided she looked good-natured, a first impression reinforced by the kindly way in which she instructed the footman to take Mary along to the kitchen, where Kate knew her friend would be regaled with tea and gossip while she waited.

'Come and sit here beside me, Kitty, and let me have a proper look at you.' Lady Edgeworth patted the cream-satin upholstered sofa invitingly.

Kate obeyed, hiding her nervousness behind a polite murmur of appreciation for her surroundings as she moved across the room.

Lady Edgeworth beamed. 'How kind of you to say you like my furniture. It is new, you know. Gillow and Sons, the cabinet-makers, made it for me specially when I asked them for something in the French style.'

Kate sat down next to her and she paused, peering more closely at her visitor.

'Why, Kitty, you have grown up into a beauty!' she exclaimed.

'Thank you, Godmother,' Kate replied demurely.

'Lud, pray call me Alicia, my dear! Godmother makes me feel positively ancient.' A twinkle appeared in Lady Edgeworth's somewhat protuberant hazel eyes. 'And, although it is several years since I was left a widow, I hope I'm not in my dotage yet.'

Kate smiled, liking her cheerful humour. 'I'm sure no one would think so, ma'am.'

'Well, my figure is not what it was and my eyesight is getting worse, but at least my health remains robust.' Alicia gave a little chuckle. 'To be honest with you, Kitty, I should be very unhappy if I were truly invalidish and could not go about and enjoy all the events society has to offer.'

She beamed at Kate. 'I was delighted to receive your dear mama's communication. Nothing could please me more than having Charles's daughter to stay. I love to entertain!'

Kate's heartbeat quickened. 'I am happy to hear Mama's letter arrived safely,' she murmured. 'When we did not receive a reply, we were a little worried that my visit might not be welcome.'

'I expect you had set sail before my answer was halfway over the ocean, but indeed there was no need for your mama to ask. I have been longing to see you again!' Lady Edgeworth reached out and touched Kate's shoulder in a little gesture of affection. 'Oh, I shall enjoy taking you about with me and introducing you to all my friends! My marriage was not blessed with children, but having you here will almost be like having a daughter of my own.'

A faint tinge of colour crept into Kate's cheeks.

'Oh, dear, I hope I have not embarrassed you?' Anxiety shook her hostess's rather high-pitched voice. 'I dare say I must seem sentimental, talking in such a vein when I scarcely know you, but I was extremely fond of your papa. Not in any romantic way, I hasten to add, but he took the place of the brother I always wished for.'

Kate hastily reassured her, wishing it was not necessary to deceive such a transparently nice woman.

'It was a great shock when he quarrelled with your grandfather and, although I suppose I ought not to speak ill of the dead, I believe their rift was entirely old Mr Nixon's fault. Your mama was a charming girl.'

Lady Edgeworth stared hard at Kate. 'Strange, when you were a baby I thought you resembled her, but now…'

'Memory can play some odd tricks, can it not?' Kate said quickly.

'Indeed. I could have sworn your hair and eyes were a much lighter brown.'

'I believe my hair was,' Kate responded airily. 'Mama says it became darker with every year I grew older.'

Lady Edgeworth nodded, her faint frown fading as she mentally dismissed the subject. 'Now, am I right in thinking that you are presently at the Hop-Pole?'

Kate confirmed it.

'A very good sort of place, but, and you may call me old-

fashioned an' you will, my love, I cannot altogether approve
of your staying there. In fact, I wonder at those friends of your
mama's! Why did they not escort you to me immediately?'

Kate hesitated. She had made the mistake of assuming Lord
Redesmere would not get to hear of Kitty's Irish sojourn. Her
carelessness had rebounded on her head with a vengeance!

'Actually, ma'am, you must not blame Mr and Mrs Hogan.
They did as Mama asked and gave me their escort to my Uncle
Sullivan's.'

'You went to *Ireland*?'

Kate launched into explanation and, without appearing vulgar, managed to thoroughly condemn Kitty's Irish relatives before concluding with a rueful, 'So you see, ma'am, I thought
it best to leave. Naturally, I should have preferred to travel
with an escort. However, since my presence was so plainly
unwelcome, I didn't care to linger until a suitable person could
be found, but departed with great haste.'

A vigorous nod of approval greeted this statement, embold-
ening Kate to continue. 'Frankly, ma'am, their lack of courtesy
angered me and I fear I spoke my mind a little too freely.' She
sighed softly. 'I am sorry for it now. I did not wish to be on
bad terms with my uncle.'

'You must not blame yourself, my dear. I have heard it rumoured Gerald was furious over the terms of your grandfather's will. It doesn't surprise me in the least that he behaved
uncivilly towards you. He was always a hot-head and I dare
say he is eaten up with jealousy.'

There was warm sympathy in Alicia's tone and, for an instant, Kate was tempted to confess the whole, but caution held
her back. Even if Alicia disapproved of the Sullivans, it didn'
mean she would be willing to lend her support to Kate's daring
plan to save Kitty's inheritance.

All I can do for now is play the situation by ear, she thought
And pray that oaf Crawford doesn't interfere!

As she remembered the steely glint in those vivid eyes, this
seemed extremely unlikely!

Kate squashed the panicky flare of apprehension suddenly curdling her stomach. She was behaving like a ninny to let that man impress her so!

All you have to do, she told herself sternly, is drop a few hints about his atrocious behaviour. Alicia knows he stands to lose a fortune. Let seeds of doubt grow in her mind and his claim that you are an adventuress will lose its credibility!

'I applaud your action, but how did you manage to find a ship on your own?' Unable to curb her curiosity, Lady Edgeworth broke into Kate's silent meditation. 'Docks are no place for a young lady!'

Kate answered that her maid had undertaken this task. 'She managed everything wonderfully.'

'How fortunate she accompanied you from America! I suppose she has been with you for many years?'

Kate nodded, glad that Alicia had made this assumption. Pretending that Mary was an old family retainer was a little risky, but it was the best way to explain her presence and it seemed unlikely that any one would bother to check the credentials of a mere servant.

'I've always been very glad of Mary's company. She is completely trustworthy and is very skilled at dressing hair and every kind of needlework,' Kate added with perfect sincerity.

It was true. She had regarded Mary Porter as a friend ever since the first day they'd met nearly seven years ago. Kate could still remember it vividly. She and Francis had just joined the Gillman Players. It was only a few weeks after their elopement and, still trying desperately to come to terms with the fact that her new husband was a completely different man to the gentle, ardent suitor he'd so recently been, she had been totally bewildered by the strange environment into which she'd been pitchforked.

Mary took pity on her and Kate was grateful for her cheerful help and advice. Barely seventeen, Kate still missed her own mother who had died just two years earlier and, in a way, Mary had taken her place, giving Kate the support which Francis never bothered to offer.

The nature of their friendship had changed over the years as Kate had matured and grown in confidence. She had eventually risen to be the company's leading lady while Mary had begun to concentrate on backstage work, but Kate would always be grateful for Mary's kindness and encouragement.

Not that she could mention a word of such matters to Alicia, of course!

'On our arrival in England,' she continued instead, 'I felt I ought to present myself first to Lord Redesmere. He is, after all, my blood relation.'

'Very proper, my love.'

Kate gave her a shy smile. 'I must also confess that I did not want to appear on your doorstep practically a pauper. Getting to England has taken most of the money my steppapa generously gave me. I thought that, as the custodian of my fortune, Cousin Randal would agree to advance me immediate funds against my inheritance.'

A sigh escaped her. 'Sadly, it appears I was mistaken.'

Lady Edgeworth frowned. 'Trust the lawyers to make a hash of things, but don't worry. I am sure Randal will sort out whatever it is that is causing them to delay.'

'I don't think Messrs Hilton, Tyler and Dibbs can be blamed.' Kate paused delicately and dropped her gaze to her skirts. 'The money is apparently available, but Lord Redesmere refuses to loan me a penny.'

'What? I don't understand! What can he be thinking of?' Lady Edgeworth exclaimed, her surprise metamorphosing into indignation.

Kate shrugged, her expression a picture of demure confusion.

'Now I consider it, his behaviour seems entirely reprehensible. Why didn't he ask you to stay overnight at the Hall, instead of letting you go rushing off to an inn?' Lady Edgeworth demanded. 'I know he has no one to act as his hostess, which makes things a trifle awkward, but in the circumstances

I'm sure not even the highest stickler would object. You are family, after all.'

'The connection is quite distant,' Kate murmured, staring modestly at the tips of her neat half-boots.

'That signifies nothing!' The golden curls shook in agitation. 'Really, I am surprised at him! He should have brought you straight here to me if he was concerned at what people might think, though Heaven knows, it would be the first time he has ever let such a consideration weigh with him!'

Kate permitted herself a small mirthless laugh. 'I very much doubt either such thought crossed Lord Redesmere's mind. To put it plainly, ma'am, I was not welcome and he couldn't wait to be rid of me. Not that I minded having to leave straightaway. I found his manners just as atrocious as Uncle Gerald's.'

Alicia goggled at her and demanded to know the whole.

Adopting an air of puzzled disappointment, Kate quickly sketched in the broad outlines of her visit to Crawford Hall.

'Lord Redesmere obviously felt I should not have run away from my uncle.' Kate's lovely face suddenly darkened. 'He even said my behaviour was not that of a lady!'

'Lud, that don't sound like Randal at all!' Lady Edgeworth looked astonished. 'Are you sure you understood him aright?'

'He practically threw me out of the house, ma'am!'

Alicia let out a small sound of shocked dismay. 'How…how very dreadful for you, my love.'

Kate quickly reassured her. 'I am quite recovered, although I must admit it was distressing at the time. I had not expected to be greeted with such ill-tempered hostility.' She paused. 'Not twice.'

Alicia threw her a startled look. 'Oh, you must not compare Randal with Gerald!'

Kate shrugged. 'As you will, ma'am.'

'I'm sure there must be a simple explanation.'

Delighted to hear a note of uncertainty in her tone, Kate pressed on. 'If Lord Redesmere has no interest in hanging on to my fortune, then I can only assume he took my person in dislike.' She could feel her teeth clench as she strove to produce a regretful expression.

'I doubt that, my love.' Alicia chuckled and shook her head. 'He has an eye for a pretty woman.'

Kate barely prevented herself from making a very rude remark.

'I take it that you know him well, ma'am?' she asked after a moment.

'Oh, since he was in leading strings! The Crawfords are one of Cheshire's foremost families, you know. What's more, Godwin Crawford was my husband's oldest friend.'

Kitty had told her that Randal had two sisters, but she had never mentioned that particular name. Panic tore along Kate's nerves for a few seconds before she decided to bluff it out. 'I'm sorry, ma'am, but I'm afraid I cannot quite place the gentleman,' she murmured, surreptitiously crossing her fingers within a concealing fold of her skirts.

Alicia looked faintly surprised. 'Godwin is Randal's uncle,' she enlightened her. 'On the paternal side so no connection of the Nixons, but surely your papa mentioned him? They were quite friendly. Indeed, I believe they were at school together.'

'You must forgive me, I'm afraid I don't know all the ramifications of the family tree.' Kate hastened to repair the damage. 'My parents rarely spoke of their past.'

'I dare say their memories of England were tainted by your grandfather's spite.' Alicia sighed and then her expression brightened. 'Still, I vow you'll like Godwin immensely. All the ladies do, even though he is the most confirmed bachelor.' She laughed. 'He has a roguish twinkle in his eyes that charms us all and the most beautiful manners!'

Unlike his nephew, thought Kate sourly as she asked if Mr Crawford lived in Chester.

'Indeed he does. He has a very pretty house in Stanley Place.'

'Does Lord Redesmere ever visit Chester, ma'am?' Kate's

voice was perfectly level as she put this question, but her heart-beat quickened when Alicia nodded.

'He has many acquaintance here in the city and often attends parties and entertainments.' Alicia coughed slightly. 'In fact, he sometimes pays a call on me when he is in town.'

'Then in that case, perhaps I had best stay at the Hop-Pole.' Kate smoothed her skirts in a brisk gesture. 'Our dealings seem likely to be fraught with difficulty and I have no wish to cause any unpleasantness in your house.'

'Fudge! I won't let you escape me so easily, my dear. Randal's opinion has no bearing on the matter, although I cannot imagine why he should believe a word the Sullivans say. Gerald was a rogue as a young man and by all accounts his son is worse! Your information that they are heavily in debt does not surprise me in the least.'

Lady Edgeworth shook her head. 'Randal's motive for being so uncivil remains a mystery, but I pray you will not let any thought of a possible quarrel influence you. I'm sure your bad beginning will resolve itself, but even if it does not you needn't fear censure from me.'

She reached out to take Kate's hand in her own. 'You are my goddaughter. Losing your company before we have had a chance to get to know one another would upset me far more than any quarrel with Redesmere could.'

Her conscience hurting, Kate forced herself to smile back. She was beginning to wish that she had never conceived this plan to help Kitty!

'There!' Alicia gave her hand a final pat and let it go. 'I do not mean to embarrass you, my dear, but truly I cannot think of anything which would give me greater pleasure than to have you as my guest.'

'I, too, should like that above all things.' Kate's unease was chased away by a sense of triumph. Let Randal Crawford chew on the news that she was accepted in Abbey Square! With any luck, he might choke on it!

* * *

'Shall I remove the covers, my lord?' Blake enquired with a discreet cough.

'What? Oh, yes. Thank you.' Roused from his brown study, Randal Crawford sat back in his carved chair, pushing it away from the long oak dining-table.

The butler bowed and waved the footman who accompanied him to begin clearing the table. Most of the dishes served for his lordship's dinner were untouched. Even one of his favourites, a harrico of lamb cooked to tender perfection, hadn't tempted his appetite.

Blake's expression creased with concern. His lordship had made poor work of his breakfast, too. It wasn't like him. He didn't look ill though. A mite troubled, perhaps...

Blake brought a crystal decanter of port over to the table and, setting it down, cleared his throat in a preparatory fashion.

'Light the candles before you go, there's a good fellow.'

There was an implacable note of dismissal in that request! Deciding discretion was the better part, Blake took the hint. Whatever it was that was bothering him, his master plainly didn't want to discuss it.

Speedily, Blake completed his tasks and, ushering his minion before him, quit the room.

Light spilled from the tall candelabrum which his butler had set on the table. Randal poured himself a glass of port and lifted it up to survey its deep colour before conveying it to his lips. Its taste was rich upon his tongue, but his mind wasn't on wine.

How long had he sat here lost in thought? Dusk had crept unheeded into the room and he hadn't even heard his butler enter. Randal frowned. Such careless inattention would have cost him his life once upon a time, aye, and on more than one occasion that he could remember!

'Blister it!'

He wasn't in the army now, but still it irked him that he seemed to have lost control over his thoughts. His mind kept spinning off, returning endlessly to that strange encounter yesterday with the woman who had pretended to be his long-lost cousin Kitty.

Her dark beauty had touched off a chord of response in him, awakening desire and a memory which had never died. Once, years ago when he had been campaigning in Egypt, he had been offered a small painted alabaster figurine. The *fellah* selling it had sworn it was that of an ancient queen. Enchanted by the delicate perfection of the little statuette, Randal had bought it.

Later, it had been stolen from his lodgings, but every detail of its rare beauty remained clear in his mind. His unknown visitor had the same elegant swan-neck and the same long eyes as that ancient queen. They slanted above those marvellously sculpted cheekbones, as black as a Stygian night and as mysterious!

Who the devil was she?

Randal shrugged his shoulders impatiently. Her name scarcely mattered. She was an adventuress and a damned clever one. If he hadn't had that letter from Gerald Sullivan he would have been taken in by her poise and confidence.

The thought rankled, but Randal strove to ignore it.

'What will she do now?'

He spoke the words aloud, but found no answer in the quiet silence. Would she really dare approach his lawyers as she had threatened?

A reluctant grin touched his well-cut mouth. Unless he missed his guess, that little baggage had the nerve to try anything! And if she had the proof she claimed, their office must be her next port of call.

Draining his wine, Randal decided it behoved him to alert Messrs Hilton, Tyler and Dibbs. It was time he paid a call on Godwin and he could look in on the lawyers and save them the journey out here.

He set down his empty glass and rose to his feet.

If the wench chose to persist in spite of his warning, he supposed he would have to put an end to her game. An unsavoury public dispute over Nabob Nixon's fortune would distress his sisters.

However, as he strolled from the room, Randal was aware of a vulgar hope that she wouldn't give up so easily. He would enjoy the chance of another encounter with his dark enchantress!

Chapter Three

Kate was surprised to find herself the sole occupant of the breakfast-parlour when she made her way to this smartly furnished apartment shortly before ten on her first morning in Abbey Square.

'Beg pardon, Miss Kitty, but there's no need to wait on her ladyship,' announced Thorpe, the elderly butler. 'She always breakfasts in her room.'

Kate thanked him and he indicated the laden sideboard.

'Can I help you to some of this gammon, Miss Kitty, or perhaps you'd prefer kippers? Should you fancy something cold, I can recommend the beef. Cook has a nice touch with roasting.'

Surveying the vast array of silver chafing-dishes laid out in readiness, Kate repressed a shudder.

Allowing him to shepherd her forward to inspect their contents, she chose a small slice of ham and a very modest helping of buttered eggs and sat down at the breakfast table. Thorpe then brought her a pot of coffee before withdrawing with a kindly admonition to ring for him the instant she required anything further.

Left to consume her breakfast in peace, Kate made a mental note to tell Alicia that she couldn't face gargantuan feasts at this hour. Theatre life had destroyed her early morning appetite, but she didn't want to hurt Thorpe's feelings or Cook's.

Apart from the fact she didn't want to upset anyone, Kate was shrewd enough to realise it would be stupid to risk setting the servants against her. Gossip flew fast belowstairs and there was going to be talk enough. It was too much to hope for that her appearance in Chester would meet with universal approval, but things would be easier if Kitty was deemed to be a proper young lady.

Forking up the last mouthful of her unwanted eggs, Kate ruefully reflected on how the rest of the company would envy her current luxury. Their usual bed was to be found in cheap lodging-houses or even in the waggons alongside their props and costumes. What's more, they had often gone hungry when the takings were poor.

Kate laid down her knife and fork with a sudden clatter. Guilt was extremely bad for the digestion, she was discovering!

It was all Redesmere's fault. If he had not been so disobliging, she need never have troubled Kitty's godmother. Now, as a result of his stupid objections, she was forced to make shameful use of Alicia, who deserved better.

Kate squirmed in her seat, remembering how Alicia had summoned Thorpe yesterday and ordered him to send George, the young footman, to the Hop-Pole to fetch her bags and settle her account.

'You don't wish to return to the inn, do you, my dear?' she had added, turning to Kate who had quickly answered,

'Only to pay my shot, ma'am.'

Alicia had looked puzzled. 'There is no need. George will take care of everything.'

'I cannot allow you to foot my bills,' Kate had insisted, every instinct protesting that it was bad enough pulling the wool over Alicia's eyes without letting her fund the deception.

'Lud, child! We shall not argue over a few shillings, surely?' Laughing, Lady Edgeworth had wagged a scolding finger at her.

Kate had continued to protest, but had been forced to drop her objections for fear of hurting Alicia's feelings.

The incident had left a bad taste in Kate's mouth and reinforced her desire to get the whole business over and done with. I shall go and see the lawyers today, she resolved.

She had meant to discuss her plans with Alicia last night, but her hostess had been engaged to dine with friends.

'I think I should cry off,' she'd fretted. 'It seems so inhospitable, leaving you to a solitary supper on your very first evening.'

'Actually, I'm quite tired and would like to go to bed early,' Kate had fibbed and, reassured, Alicia had allowed herself to be persuaded.

Kate had been glad of the chance to be on her own. Being plunged back into the kind of life she had once known was much more unsettling than she had anticipated. Alicia's beautiful house was more luxurious than the small country manor on the shores of Lake Bassenwaite in which she had grown up, but it was still familiar territory.

She had forgotten how pleasant it was to have servants on hand to fetch and carry!

For an instant Kate allowed herself to imagine what her life might have been like if she hadn't attended that fatal performance of *Romeo and Juliet* while visiting her grandmother in Carlisle.

It had been the first time she had ever been inside a theatre and she was thrilled by the performance which, in truth, had been no more than average, although she had been too inexperienced to realise it. When Francis had walked on stage and begun to speak in his caressing voice, her heightened senses had reeled. With his long elegant legs displayed to advantage in tights and his romantically disarrayed black curls, he had seemed the perfect hero.

Caught up in the magic of the night, Kate had immediately tumbled headlong into a deep infatuation, which she mistook for love.

Stop daydreaming, my girl, Kate admonished herself sharply, forcing herself back to the present. You can't afford to get too used to being a young lady again. When this charade is over, it's back to work for you!

Kitty had promised her £500 in return for her help. It would allow her to pay off the last of Francis's creditors. The prospect of being clear of debt for the first time since her marriage was delightful, but the fee wasn't enough to free her of the need to earn her living.

And what respectable household would employ her? Unless she lied about her past she would never obtain a genteel position.

You went through all these arguments three years ago when Francis died, she scolded herself. Nothing has changed today, except that you are feeling nostalgic!

In her mind Kate could hear the echo of Mary's advice after his funeral, when Kate had told her friend that she was thinking of leaving the company to go into service.

'Why give up your friends and a profession you've learnt to enjoy to drudge in some kitchen? You'd probably earn even less than you do now and, while it might be a more respectable way of life, you would still be a fish out of water. I think you would be lonely and, worse, you are too pretty to avoid trouble!'

Kate remembered how she had protested, but in her heart she had suspected that Mary might be right.

'Francis made you miserable, but now that he's gone things will be different,' Mary had declared. 'He wasted your talent and stopped you getting the roles you deserve, but I'll wager that if you stay you'll be the company's leading lady within a year.'

Her friend's prediction had come true. She'd become a successful and popular actress through sheer hard work and effort. She had even managed to forget Francis and learnt to be happy again. So why then did she suddenly feel so depressed?

Could it...could it possibly have something to do with that

look of contempt on Randal Crawford's handsome face as he had dismissed her?

Kate gave herself a little shake. She was being foolish beyond permission!

Fiend seize Crawford! He could think what he liked of her. She was no adventuress, although her youthful folly had put an end to her claim to respectability.

No amount of regret could change matters. Instead of dwelling on what might have been if her father had been more kind and her grandmother less self-centred, she ought to be concentrating on thinking of a way to discredit Kitty's supposed drowning before his interfering lordship spread the news all round town!

Filled with a fresh determination to win Kitty's fortune for her, Kate made her way to the morning-room, where Alicia presently joined her.

'Ah, my dear! You are down already. I hope you slept well?' Alicia greeted her with a smile.

'My bed was wonderfully comfortable, thank you,' Kate responded politely.

In point of fact, she hadn't experienced a restful night. To her annoyance, a pair of vivid blue eyes had haunted her dreams.

Lady Edgeworth sat down and Kate asked her if she had enjoyed her dinner-party.

After a full description of this event, Alicia continued, 'I announced your arrival, my love, and everyone was desirous of an early introduction. Once word of your visit gets out I dare say we will have the whole town calling.'

Kate tried to look pleased.

'In fact, I thought I would make a list of all the people you ought to meet, Kitty. It wouldn't do to leave anyone out...now, where did I put my tablets?' Lady Edgeworth broke off her discourse, her expression distracted. 'I was sure I left them in here.' She peered shortsightedly around.

Kate spotted the little writing-set on one of the side-tables. 'Is that the one you mean, ma'am?'

Alicia nodded and made a move to rise from her seat.

'Allow me.' Kate quickly jumped up to get it.

'Thank you, child.' Alicia accepted the set of tablets from her. 'I see you have your mama's pretty manners. I did wonder whether, living at such a remove from civilisation, you might…' Realising that her remark might be construed as criticism, she hastily amended what she was going to say. 'Well, it was doubtless very silly of me, but I did worry that you might speak with a…a coarse accent.'

Kate, who was a gifted mimic and could abandon her own ladylike tones at will to ape a large number of convincing accents, looked suitably shocked. 'Papa would never have permitted it. He maintained a cultured person must always avoid slipshod speech.'

In truth, Kitty didn't sound like a foreigner—her gentle voice was as refined as her godmother might wish!

'You know, my dear, nothing can be so fatal to a girl's chances as an ugly voice,' her hostess continued earnestly. 'I think it more off-putting a fault than a bad complexion or graceless figure for a man may close his eyes, but it is not so easy to stop one's ears.'

Kate nodded dutifully, concealing her amusement at this sage pronouncement.

'Only a lack of dowry is more prejudicial.' Lady Edgeworth shuddered at the very thought. 'Not that we have to contend with such a disaster in your case, thanks to your grandfather finally deciding to make amends for his atrocious behaviour. I could wish he had relented sooner, but at least he saw sense in the end.'

She beamed at Kate. 'Why, we might even contrive a brilliant match for you!'

'Mama needs me at home so my visit cannot be extended once the business of my legacy is concluded,' Kate exclaimed, her amusement rapidly vanishing.

'All the more reason not to waste time, my love!' Alicia gazed at Kate with obvious satisfaction. 'Youth, beauty and a fortune! You will be besieged by admirers!'

The sinking feeling in the pit of Kate's stomach grew worse.

'It's very kind of you to offer to introduce me to your acquaintance, ma'am,' she said firmly. 'However, I have no desire to find a husband.'

Disappointment flickered over her hostess's plump features. 'Your mama might not like the notion,' she agreed after a moment's silence. 'Never mind. At least you can enjoy an agreeable flirtation or two while you are here.'

'I don't think it would be a good idea for me to become too much of a social butterfly,' Kate said hastily.

'But why ever not, Kitty?' Surprise rounded Alicia's eyes. 'I remember your mama telling me how disappointed you were when you could not take me up on my previous offer to give you a Season.'

Kate shifted a little in her seat, trying to think of some good reason for Kitty to have changed her mind.

'I was younger then, ma'am, and more inclined to frivolity—' she began, but Alicia swiftly interrupted her.

'Lud, child, you are only one and twenty now! Hardly a greybeard, or don't you like parties and dancing, eh?'

Kate did.

'There! I knew it!' Triumph coloured her hostess's pronouncement. 'Your face betrays you, my love! You would enjoy cutting a dash.'

Kate nodded reluctantly, suppressing her irritation at her own lack of self-control.

'You have too lively a manner to fool me into thinking you a quiet mouse, my dear.'

Abandoning that tactic, Kate tried another.

'My purpose in coming here was to secure my legacy, ma'am, nothing more. I know it would cost a great deal to launch me into society and I could not impose on you by putting you to such expense.'

'But I should enjoy sponsoring you!'

'I cannot allow you to do so.' Kate smiled to take the sting out of her words, but her tone was firm.

Alicia played with the little pencil attached by a gold cord to her writing-set. 'You will be in possession of your own fortune soon,' she murmured. 'I'm sure a bank loan or some such could be arranged to tide you over.'

Kate shuddered.

'Surely your mama wouldn't begrudge you spending a little money on enjoying yourself?'

Kate refuted this objection. 'Mama would not, but the very notion of debt is abhorrent to *me*, ma'am. I will not spend a shilling which isn't my own,' she announced, conveniently ignoring the fact that she had hoped to persuade Lord Redesmere into advancing some money.

He, damn him, hadn't been open to persuasion!

'Your prudence in waiting until your legacy is handed over is admirable, my dear.' Alicia's tone was politely doubtful.

It was obvious to Kate that her companion did not hold the same views on finance, but it was unlikely Alicia had ever been physically threatened by duns. If she had, she would be wary of incurring debts she could not repay!

'All the same, it seems a pity to waste this opportunity and there is another solution, if you will agree to it.' Alicia leant forward eagerly. 'My husband left me very handsomely provided for and I can easily afford to act as your banker myself until this silly delay is cleared up.'

'But, ma'am—'

'I don't want to press you, but pray consider, my love! You lost most of your wardrobe fleeing Ireland. Surely you wish to replace your gowns?' Alicia's tone was gently persuasive. 'Please, Kitty. Let me loan you some money if you won't accept it as a gift.'

'I know you mean well, ma'am.' Kate bit her lip, wondering how to reject the offer without hurting the older woman's sensitive feelings. 'However, I did manage to bring one valise away with me from Uncle Gerald's; as for the rest, I have guineas enough for my needs if I'm careful.'

'You are much too young and pretty to have to worry about economising!'

'I shan't go into a decline for the lack of a few new dresses.' Kate essayed a cheerful shrug.

Alicia sighed. 'You mustn't think I am offering my help merely for your benefit, Kitty, my dear. If you were to sit at home all day, I would feel obliged to stay at home, too!'

In other circumstances Kate would have been amused by this artless confession, but there was genuine distress in Alicia's hazel eyes.

'I do so want you to enjoy this visit, Kitty. I should feel I was failing in my duty to you and letting your mama down if I didn't provide you with proper entertainment.'

Her heart sinking, Kate knew she was beaten. She could think of no convincing reason to refuse Alicia's help and, without a good excuse, it was ungracious to go on protesting.

'I should not wish to cause you any inconvenience, ma'am.' Kate swallowed her pride, mentally resolving to repay Alicia out of Kitty's £500 the instant the charade was over. 'I shall be happy to accompany you wherever you wish to go, if that is what you desire.'

'Then you will accept my offer?' Alicia clapped her hands together. 'Oh, famous! We shall have such fun, I promise you!' She smiled happily at Kate. 'I think we must start with the Leghs' drum tomorrow night, and then there is Lady Massey's rout on the seventh of June. I shall hold an evening-party for you, of course, and there are events such as the musicale at the Royal Hotel next week, which I'm sure you will enjoy.'

'I only managed to pack two evening dresses,' Kate murmured, wondering what the devil she had let herself in for.

'Then we must go shopping without delay! Oh, I shall enjoy taking you to Celestine's! You have the perfect figure to carry off her creations. I saw a lovely spider gauze there last week which I long to buy for you.'

Alicia's smile faded at the look of reluctance which spread over her guest's features. 'You will allow me to spoil you a little, won't you, Kitty?' she asked uncertainly. 'I am your godmother after all.'

'I should be happy to accept any *small* token of affection, ma'am,' Kate answered, hoping Alicia would take the hint since the idea of taking expensive presents from a woman she was deliberately duping revolted her.

There was a tense little silence.

'Very well. I promise not to buy anything without your approval since I can see that you do not like being beholden to other people,' Alicia said at last. 'I admire you for it, but I must say your attitude surprises me. Is it usual in America for girls to be so independent?'

This piece of unexpected shrewdness startled Kate and she realised that she must not relax her guard and confuse Alicia's frivolous nature and open-handed kindness with stupidity.

'I cannot speak for other families, but I was brought up to stand on my own two feet,' she replied carefully. 'Few restrictions were placed on my freedom.'

'You will find matters arranged rather differently here,' Alicia warned. 'Girls are expected to conduct themselves with decorum, not to assert themselves.'

'After the way Lord Redesmere reacted to the story of my escape I suspected as much, ma'am!' Kate replied tartly.

Alicia coughed. 'Randal is inclined to be forthright,' she murmured uneasily.

'He obviously thinks I am a silly, underbred female who has no notion of how to behave.' Kate's tone was deliberately scornful. 'I expect he will tell you to send me packing before I cause you trouble,' she added, seizing the opportunity to strengthen her position.

Lady Edgeworth bridled, as Kate guessed she would.

'If he dares say such a thing to me, I shall show him the door!' she exclaimed indignantly.

Satisfied, Kate gave a tiny shrug. 'I do not care if Lord

Redesmere holds a low opinion of me,' she said with less-than-perfect truth. 'My conscience is clear and that matters more to me than what other people think.'

'That was always your papa's attitude, too.' Her hostess smiled reminiscently. 'You remind me of him very much, you know. Lud, he could be so stubborn! Why, I could tell you a dozen tales—'

She came to an abrupt halt and blinked rather mistily. 'Oh, dear, I think we had better change the subject or I shall disgrace myself by becoming a watering-pot!'

'Shall we get on with your list, ma'am?' Kate suggested gently.

'The very thing, my dear!' Lady Edgeworth banished the sentimental tears that threatened to overwhelm her. 'And when we are finished we shall visit Celestine's. That is, if you are agreeable, Kitty?'

'I should also like to pay a call upon Messrs Hilton, Tyler and Dibbs,' Kate said. 'Would that be possible?'

'I don't see why not. But let's go to Celestine's first, yes?'

Bowing to the inevitable, Kate dipped her glossy head in graceful acquiescence.

'Miss Kitty Nixon, sir.'

With a nod of thanks to the young clerk who had announced her, Kate swept into the inner sanctum of the solicitors who had acted for old Nabob Nixon.

Given that the building was an ancient half-timbered edifice in Watergate Street, she wasn't altogether surprised to find the senior partner's office was somewhat small and cramped. Although one narrow leaded casement had been thrown open to admit what little breeze the warm afternoon afforded, it was also dark, an impression intensified by heavy oak panelling and the numerous bookcases which crowded the room.

More books and papers littered a large mahogany writing-table behind which sat Alan Hilton. He rose to his feet at her entrance and Kate saw that he was a thin, middle-aged individual who wore a plain neckcloth and a neat, white-powdered bag-wig.

Kate gave him her best smile as she stepped forward to greet him, but the words died on her lips as she suddenly realised that they were not alone.

A man was standing in the shadows by one of the corner bookcases. As he moved towards the centre of the room and into the light his fair hair gleamed gold.

'Good afternoon. I must apologise if I startled you. However, ma'am, I cannot say *I'm* surprised to see you here.'

The sound of Lord Redesmere's deep musical voice sent a shiver down Kate's spine, although she couldn't have said whether it was from fear or a swift involuntary pleasure at his unexpected appearance.

He was just as tall and broad-shouldered as memory painted him. Elegantly garbed in cream pantaloons and a single-breasted coat of blue superfine worn open over a pale lemon waistcoat, he also looked annoyingly handsome!

Hastily rearranging her features to conceal her perturbation, Kate dipped an icily polite curtsy. 'My lord.'

'Shall we sit down?' Mr Hilton gestured hastily to a pair of square-backed mahogany chairs arranged in front of his desk.

Kate took the nearest one and settled herself with an angry swish of her cambric skirts. She had dressed for this meeting with the greatest care, choosing her almond green walking dress with the vandyked hem and a pretty chip-straw hat. Both her mirror and Alicia had told her that she looked sweetly demure, but from the wary expression on the lawyer's face it seemed her efforts might have been wasted.

He looked at her as if he thought she might bite!

To her further annoyance, she was very conscious of Redesmere seating himself next to her. Within the confines of this cramped room he seemed larger and more threateningly virile than ever!

Determined to ignore him, she fixed her gaze firmly on Mr

Hilton. 'Am I to apprehend, sir, that my cousin has already told you I am an imposter?' she demanded coolly.

'My dear Miss Nix…my dear young lady!' Taken aback, Alan Hilton glanced helplessly at his noble client. 'Er…there does seem to be some confusion. Pray do not take offence.'

Kate raised her brows at him. 'To be called a liar is not pleasant, sir.'

'You…you still insist that you are Kitty Nixon?'

'Of course I am!' Kate let impatience flood her tone. 'It is nonsense to suggest otherwise.'

An expressive snort of derision from the man at her side greeted this statement and she turned to glare furiously at him.

It was a mistake.

Their gaze met like a clash of steel and locked in combat. Kate sucked in her breath, her pulse quickening as they stared at each other. God, but his eyes were blue!

'Ahem!' The lawyer coughed delicately, breaking the tense silence.

The spell shattered and Kate managed to drag her gaze away, but a queer little shiver feathered slowly down her spine and it was all she could do to concentrate on the lawyer's rather monotonous voice.

'Mr Gerald Sullivan has written to inform us that his niece suffered a fatal accident. While out for a stroll one evening she fell into deep water and drowned.'

'Rubbish,' snapped Kate, recovering her composure. Fell, indeed! What would they say if she told them what really happened, that Kitty had been knocked on the head and pushed into the river! 'My uncle is lying. He is heavily in debt and wants to grab what he can of the Nixon fortune.'

'And you don't?'

Kate ignored his lordship's smooth interruption. 'Let me ask you this, Mr Hilton—what proof does my uncle offer? Can he name you witnesses to this tragedy?'

The lawyer shook his head.

'No, I thought not.' Kate's lip curled. 'And what of the body? Has he produced it for inspection?'

Mr Hilton consulted his papers. 'He says that Miss Nixon's mortal remains have not been recovered as of yet.'

'I see.' Kate let out a scornful laugh. 'No witnesses and no body. How very convenient!'

'You present a clever case, ma'am.'

Kate flicked at wary glance at his lordship.

'There is no question that Sullivan would benefit from my cousin's death,' Randal continued in the same cool tones. 'However, although he is a greedy man, he is not a fool and I hardly think he would claim that Kitty was dead unless he had reason to believe it true.'

'I agree, my lord,' Mr Hilton chimed in. 'To attempt such a deception would be fruitless. The instant Miss Nixon reappeared he would be exposed as a liar and his reputation damaged beyond repair.'

Kate bit down hard on her tongue. She longed to shout out that the Sullivans had never intended Kitty to be seen again. They had plotted murder!

'It may be that he does think me dead.' Kate decided it could do no harm to concede this point. 'I did leave in extreme haste without furnishing any explanation.'

'But why should you act in such a rash manner, my dear young lady?' exclaimed Mr Hilton in a shocked voice.

Kate began to explain how matters had stood. 'In the end, sir, I began to feel so very uncomfortable at Ballyhad House that I simply had to get away.'

Randal eyed her pure profile thoughtfully.

She didn't sound as if she was lying. In fact, he would have sworn to her sincerity. And yet...

'You spoke of Gerald having no proof. Can you offer us any proof, ma'am, that you are the person you claim to be?' he asked as soon as Kate finished speaking.

Although she had been expecting this question, Kate's pulse still gave a little flicker of alarm.

'Of course,' she responded coolly, inwardly grateful for the years of training which enabled her to keep her voice level and her hands perfectly steady as she opened the knitted silk reticule she had brought with her.

Withdrawing a slightly crumpled letter, she leant forward and laid it on the desk in front of Mr Hilton. 'This is for you, sir, from my mama. You may compare the handwriting to her earlier missives if you wish.'

Mr Hilton picked it up rather gingerly and, breaking open the wafer, perused it carefully before handing it over to Randal.

'The content tells us nothing.' A small frown creased Lord Redesmere's tawny brows. 'However, the hand does appear to be that of Mrs Nixon.'

'Mrs Ashe, if you please,' Kate reminded him crisply, relief welling up in her.

Thank heavens Kitty had been right! She had promised them that her handwriting was virtually identical to her mother's when she had offered to make a fresh copy of Lydia's letter for Kate to use.

'Mama insisted on writing a formal letter of introduction. She didn't want anyone to think us backward in the proper civilities. I can remember exactly what it said for I helped her to compose it,' Kitty had told them earnestly.

The original letter, which Kitty had taken to keeping on her person after finding evidence that the Sullivans were prying into her belongings, had been stowed in the pocket of her cloak, but it had not survived their mutual immersion in the river. The ink had run, adding to the water stains, and everyone in the Gillman Players agreed that Kate could not offer such a sorry object as a credential to Messrs Hilton, Tyler and Dibbs, particularly as to do so might arouse the very suspicions they were trying to avoid.

'This is scarcely conclusive. Do you have any official papers?' Lord Redesmere laid the letter back on the desk.

'Not on me, no. My uncle insisted on taking my certificate of American citizenship into his care. He said he would keep it safe for me.' Kate shrugged lightly, praying that they wouldn't guess how tension was knotting her stomach. She could feel Crawford watching her like a hawk.

'Why didn't you ask for it back?'

'I was scared of him! Why else do you think I ran away?' Kate glared at him. What was the matter with the man? He must have a heart of stone!

'I see.' Apparently unimpressed by her plight, his lordship flicked an imaginary speck of dust from his immaculate sleeve. 'In that case, can you offer us any other proof?'

Kate's temper slipped its tight leash.

In a swift gesture she pointed to the gold locket which she wore around her neck. 'I suppose I also forged these,' she snapped, flicking it open to reveal two miniature portraits.

With a slow deliberation Randal raised his quizzing-glass and proceeded to stare intently at the locket lying upon her creamy bosom.

Her cheeks flushing, Kate reached up to undo the chain, meaning to hand the locket to him, but in her agitated haste her fingers fumbled the task.

'Allow me.' Before she could frame a protest, he rose swiftly to his feet and came to her aid.

She had washed her hair with jasmine. He could smell the delicate sweetness as he gently moved the heavy, shining ringlets aside. How soft they felt, like the finest silk!

A quiver of unexpected pleasure shot through Kate at the touch of his warm hands, quenching her anger. She sat very still, acutely conscious of his strong, well-muscled thighs brushing against her shoulders. To her horror, she suddenly realised that she wanted to turn round and clasp him in her arms.

'Please bend your head forward a little.'

In a daze Kate obeyed the quiet command and felt his fingers move to the clasp. Her heart began to thump. She knew she ought to have more sense, but it made no difference.

Randal undid the clasp and the chain fell away. For an instant he remained motionless, staring down at the tender curve of her bare nape. Mastering the crazy impulse to press a kiss upon her satiny skin, he turned away and sat down again.

The locket had fallen into her lap. With an effort, Kate pulled herself together and picked it up. Avoiding his gaze, she held it out to Randal. 'My father gave this to my mother on their wedding day. I believe it originally belonged to his mother.'

Her hand was trembling. Why? Was it guilt, or had she too felt something at his touch?

And why should that particular thought please him so much?

Randal sternly quelled his irrational speculations and took the locket. He stared down at the twin portraits. Charmingly executed in watercolours, they depicted a young man and woman clad in the styles of some twenty years ago.

Silently, he handed the locket over to the lawyer.

'Mama commissioned a travelling artist to paint them soon after their arrival in Massachusetts. Do you recognise my father, sir?' Kate asked, fixing her great dark eyes on Alan Hilton's face.

'Indeed. The likeness is excellent.' The lawyer paused. 'That is to say, I recognise this as an accurate portrayal of Mr Charles Nixon.' He shifted uneasily in his seat. 'The locket is also known to me. I was present when Mr Charles received it from his father. However, my dear young lady, in itself this locket does not prove that Charles Nixon is your father.'

'Oh, come, sir!' Kate gave him her most charming smile. 'Is it likely that an imposter would possess such a family heirloom? And what about Mama's letter? How do you account for that?' She shook her head coquettishly, setting her sable curls dancing. 'Surely it is more logical to accept that this sorry confusion has arisen solely because my uncle made a mistake?'

'Are you claiming that Gerald allowed optimism to cloud his judgement when you vanished?' Randal demanded.

Kate reluctantly turned to face him. How she wished she only had to deal with Mr Hilton! The lawyer might be cautious, but she sensed a growing sympathy behind his dry manner.

'I cannot think of any other explanation, my lord.' Kate opened her eyes wide in an expression of limpid innocence and smiled at him sweetly.

Randal stared back at her. Hellfire, why did she have to be so damned attractive! It made it difficult to think!

'Perhaps our first reaction was too hasty,' Mr Hilton murmured, giving a dry little cough.

Kate flashed him a look of gratitude. 'Oh, I am relieved to hear you say so, Mr Hilton! It is dreadful to be thought a liar!'

Whipping out a lace-trimmed handkerchief from her reticule, Kate applied it dextrously to the corners of her eyes and gave an artistic little sniff. 'You cannot imagine how upset and worried I have been,' she sighed, risking a tiny sob.

'Pray do not disturb yourself, my dear young lady,' Mr Hilton squeaked, his voice rising in alarm.

Risking a peep over the edge of her handkerchief, Kate saw him leap gallantly to his feet. 'Let me procure you a restorative.'

Satisfied that he had fallen for her damsel-in-distress ploy, Kate was about to refuse his offer and press home her advantage when Lord Redesmere forestalled her.

'A glass of sherry would be an excellent notion, Alan. I shall keep Miss…Nixon company while you fetch it.'

Somewhat offended at his client's assumption that he meant to act as his own errand-boy, Mr Hilton almost failed to note the accompanying slight jerk of his lordship's fair head.

'Ah, yes. Of course.' Belatedly realising that he wanted a chance to speak to the girl in private, Mr Hilton edged towards the door. 'I…I don't know if we have anything to suit a lady's palate so I may be a few moments.'

Kate stared at his retreating back and had to struggle not to curse.

'Yes, I know. Very shabby of him to abandon you like that.' Randal's tone held mock sympathy. 'Still, you can take comfort from the fact that his desertion has proved a miraculous cure for your tears.'

Realising that her unguarded expression had betrayed her, Kate returned her handkerchief to her reticule. 'I cannot imagine what you mean,' she said primly.

Randal grinned. 'What, no protests, ma'am? Not even a complaint at being left alone with me?'

Kate's black brows winged upwards in haughty disdain. 'I believe my virtue to be safe, sir,' she said coolly, indicating the door which Mr Hilton had carefully left open as convention demanded.

Randal's grin broadened. Blister it, but he couldn't help admiring her panache!

'Since you have engineered our privacy I assume you have something you wish to say to me?'

He nodded, his smile fading. 'We appear to have reached a stalemate. I don't believe you are Kitty Nixon, but I can't prove it. Nor can I explain whence you got that letter and locket… unless you stole them, of course.'

Ignoring the gasp of indignation which greeted this remark, Randal continued calmly. 'It is equally obvious that you aren't going to give up your claim without a fight. Therefore, the only logical way forward is to organise further investigations.'

He paused, giving her the opportunity to comment, but, somewhat to his surprise, she merely nodded agreement.

'I shall suggest Hilton begins by writing to Ireland. If necessary, he can contact Mrs Ashe in due course, but I do not want to cause her any needless worry. Sullivan may well have other engagements, but once he is free to travel we should be able to get to the bottom of this matter quickly enough.'

'You want him to identify me?' Kate managed to put the question calmly, hiding her shocked alarm. She had never imagined such a hideous complication!

'Just so, ma'am.'

'You believe he will speak the truth?' Kate asked, rallying.

'Sullivan has the reputation of a rogue, but I doubt if even he would dare to deny you if you are who you claim to be. Honour aside, he is intelligent enough to realise that I won't let this matter drop. One way or another, I mean to find out what really happened in Ireland.'

There was a grim note in his deep voice and, hearing it, Kate experienced a *frisson* of despair.

The instant Gerald clapped eyes on her the game would be up!

Her thoughts whirling as she tried frantically to work out the implications of this new development, Kate was scarcely aware at first that Randal was speaking again.

'Unfortunately, given the distance involved, any investigation is going to require time. It may take weeks to discover the truth.' Randal shrugged. 'Therefore, although it grieves me to do so, I propose we agree to a truce.'

'A truce?' Kate's attention snapped back into focus. Was he trying to trick her? What had he to gain from a truce? 'May I ask why you want us to be on cordial terms?'

'I don't give a fig for gossip, but my sisters would be distressed if word gets out that we are fighting over the Nabob's fortune.'

'I didn't have you down as a man of such sensitivity.' Kate's rich contralto voice held a note of sarcasm.

Randal acknowledged the justice of this remark with a slight inclination of his head. She had a right to feel angry...if she was the real Kitty.

When she had produced that locket, his conviction that she was an imposter had suffered a distinct knock. Could he be wrong? Discounting Gerald's damning letter, all he had to go on was instinct. Somehow, and he couldn't for the life of him say why, he just didn't believe she was his little cousin.

'You may think me unfeeling, ma'am, but please believe me when I say that my opposition to your claim is based upon a desire to execute my duty rather than a wish to cause you distress.'

Innate honesty forced Randal to admit that his memory of Kitty was hazy. It was a long time since he had seen her. He swallowed his pride. 'I am willing to admit that you might be my cousin.'

'Is this an apology, sir?' Kate demanded saucily.

'Only time will tell if I have anything to apologise for, ma'am,' Randal retorted drily. 'However, if you are willing to overlook the harsh things I said to you on your visit to Crawford Hall, then I am prepared to set aside my doubts and act in a more civilised manner while we wait for Sullivan.'

'You will acknowledge me as your cousin?'

Randal heard the challenge in her tone and his instinctive reaction was to damn her impudence, but the words died unspoken on his lips. If he did not acknowledge her, her position would be extremely awkward and there would be gossip. An imposter might deserve to feel such anxiety, but if he was wrong it would be a needless cruelty.

'I shall treat you as I would the real Kitty.'

Kate's face lit up in a brilliant smile. 'Thank you.'

'Don't mistake this concession for weakness,' he warned her. 'It doesn't mean that you have convinced me. I am merely following one of the first principles of warfare.'

'My lord?' Kate was puzzled.

'Know your enemy.'

If Mr Hilton was surprised to find his visitors in apparent harmony on his return, he was sensible enough to conceal it.

Lord Redesmere was known to have an eye for a pretty woman and Miss Nixon, if indeed that was her name, was a beautiful creature.

Mr Hilton, who was by no means averse to a pair of fine eyes himself, hoped her story was true. He had been saddened to hear of Kitty's supposed accident. It was always upsetting to hear of anyone so young dying and he'd regretted that Kitty's demise would benefit a rogue like Gerald Sullivan.

That Sullivan might have tried to take advantage, he didn't doubt. But his lordship wouldn't let him get away with it. A very strong sense of duty his lordship had. He would see there was fair play and no mistake!

'I believe that's all for now, Alan,' Randal said crisply, drawing the ensuing discussion to a close. 'Let me know the moment you hear from Sullivan.'

'Of course, my lord.' Mr Hilton turned to Kate. 'If you do think of something later that you wish clarified, I should be pleased to advise you, ma'am,' he promised.

His visitors rose to take their leave.

'Thank you, sir.' Kate dipped a neat curtsy. 'And thank you, too, for your hospitality. I have seldom found a glass of orgeat more refreshing.' She smiled at him sunnily. 'It was kind of you to go to so much trouble.'

'Not at all.' Mr Hilton, who had sent out for this beverage, flushed with pleasure and hurried to open the door.

Randal hid his amusement. The little baggage certainly knew how to turn a man up sweet!

He politely gestured Kate to precede him. 'Don't bother to see us out, Alan. I'll escort Miss Nixon downstairs.'

Kate was glad that the stairs were too narrow for him to offer her the use of his arm. She needed to think and his nearness seemed to have an unfortunate effect upon her wits!

The interview hadn't gone as well as she had hoped. Hilton had been sympathetic, but Crawford's presence had blocked her plan to enlist the lawyer's aid.

How was she going to avoid Sullivan accusing her of fraud? She might have known Crawford would suggest an identity check. Too fly by half was his lordship!

At least the truce he had suggested would give her a little breathing space; maybe if they spent some time together his opposition would soften. Kate ignored the inner voice which whispered delight at the prospect of his company.

They reached the outer office.

Randal frowned. He had expected to see the middle-aged dragon who had accompanied her to the Hall, but the room was empty save for clerks. 'I see you didn't bring your maid. May I escort you home?'

'Thank you, but there is no need.' Kate glanced at the fine lacquered longcase clock which stood against the far wall. 'I agreed with Lady Edgeworth that she would collect me at four and it wants only a few minutes to the hour.'

'Alicia?' Randal's frown deepened. 'Are you staying with her?'

Kate nodded warily. 'She invited me to be her guest when she learnt I was putting up at an inn.'

He continued to frown and Kate hurried on. 'She wanted to come with me this afternoon, but I felt it was better if I spoke to Mr Hilton alone. I told her that I could easily walk home afterwards, but she wouldn't hear of it.'

'No doubt she scolded you for your independence.'

Kate wasn't sure what to make of his tone. 'She was scandalised,' she agreed cautiously. 'I told her I was used to my freedom and that I liked walking.' A tiny gurgle of laughter escaped her. 'I suspect she thinks me quite mad, but I don't intend to become a milk-and-water miss, even to please her.'

Randal stared down into her enchanting countenance.

'Your behaviour is your own concern,' he said roughly, steeling himself against her dangerous charm.

Devil take the wench! Her laughter was as warm and rich as molten honey. If he didn't take care, he'd find himself as bedazzled as Hilton!

'What does concern me,' Randal continued in the same hard voice, 'is that Alicia is not cozened. Does she know what Gerald is saying?'

Kate, who had been taken aback by his sudden change of mood, realised he was going to be difficult and sought for a soothing answer.

'Well? Are you going to explain how you inveigled yourself into Abbey Square? What have you told her?'

'I told her the truth,' Kate snapped back, irritated into forgetting her good intentions. 'That you are a rude and overbearing bully!' She tilted her chin up to glare at him. 'I wouldn't surprise me in the least to discover you were the most disliked man in Cheshire!'

'Why, you little—' Anger washed over Randal, darkening his bright eyes, and Kate took a hasty step backwards.

Suddenly remembering the clerks, Randal reined in his temper.

'This is no place to discuss what I have to say to you ma'am,' he said with chilling formality. 'However, be assured that I shall call on Lady Edgeworth at the first opportunity to acquaint her with my suspicions.'

Kate felt herself pale, but, refusing to give him the satisfaction of seeing her cowed, she inclined her head with regal grace and said, 'I shall look forward to your visit,' in the most insolent tone she could muster.

For an instant murder flickered in his gaze and then, with stiff bow, he turned silently on his heel and walked out of the room.

Chapter Four

'So there you have it, Mary. The shortest truce in history!'

Kate tossed her hairbrush on to the dressing-table with an impatient sigh. 'All evening Alicia spoke of nothing but her plans for me. She is going to be terribly hurt when Crawford blabs his suspicions.'

Mary continued in her task of laying away Kate's evening clothes, but her expression was thoughtful. 'Maybe you can persuade him to keep silent,' she said.

'Hah!' Kate gave an inelegant snort of disbelief. 'The sun will rise in the west before that man changes his mind... unless...' She paused as a new idea struck her.

'What is it, lass?'

'Maybe nothing.' Kate yawned suddenly. 'Let me sleep on it.'

It had been a long evening. There had been no opportunity to discuss Crawford's threat with Mary before dinner and an angry anxiety had churned within her, ruining her appetite. She had been glad when it was bedtime and she could retreat to her room.

'Into bed with you, then.' Mary turned down the bedcovers. 'And no fretting, mind. If I know you, Mrs Devlin, you'll soon think up a clever plan to foil his lordship.'

Kate jumped up from the dressing-table stool and, crossing

the room, gave her old friend a hug. 'Thank you, Mary. You do wonders for my confidence.'

With a chuckling admonition not to be so daft, Mary took herself off.

Kate climbed into bed and blew out her candle. The quiet darkness lapped itself around her, but sleep wouldn't come. In spite of her exhaustion, she couldn't relax, but it wasn't worry about what the morning might bring that was keeping her awake.

Damn that man! She could still feel the touch of his fingers against her skin, feel the warmth of his body next to hers. Even the memory was enough to set her blood racing.

It had been so long since she had wanted a man to touch her. Francis's selfish behaviour in their marital bed had quickly destroyed her innocent yearning to be held in his arms. His love-making shamed the name for there was no love in it. Greedy for his own swift satisfaction, he had treated her no better than a whore.

After his death, her favours had been sought by other men, but she had firmly rejected them. Even Ned, who was a good, kind man, had not been able to touch her frozen heart. Francis had shattered her dreams and she had never thought to feel desire again.

She had tried to pretend to herself that her reaction to Randal's touch that first time at Crawford Hall had been an illusion, which owed more to tension and overwrought feelings than attraction. Today's incident had blown that convenient theory out of the water.

She wanted Randal Crawford to touch her, wanted to know what his lips would feel like against her own! God help her, but she wanted to lie in his arms and discover if the romantic dreams she had entertained before her disastrous wedding night could become reality at last.

Kate pressed her hands against her hot cheeks.

What a fool she was! Surely she wasn't going to allow herself to make the same mistake twice! She had fallen for Francis's looks and flattering manner and never stopped to think what lay beneath the surface of his charm. What did she really know of Randal Crawford beyond his handsome face and dry wit? He seemed an honourable man, but her instincts could be wrong and the stakes in this game were too high to take the risk.

'For all you know, my girl, he might even be in league with Sullivan,' she warned herself aloud. 'That amount of money could tempt a saint.'

For Kitty's sake, as well as her own, she would have to keep herself on a tight rein and resist the deep attraction Randal held for her.

But it was going to be hard to carry off a pretence of indifference when the least sight of him reduced her to a quivering flawn!

The sun was shining in a cloudless sky when Lord Redesmere arrived in Abbey Square the next morning.

He was greeted warmly by Thorpe, who knew him well, but the elderly butler shook his white head apologetically when Randal enquired after the mistress of the household.

'I'm sorry, my lord. Her ladyship is still abed.'

Randal experienced a stab of annoyance. He had forgotten Alicia was a late riser.

'Would you care to step inside and wait, sir?'

Randal was about to refuse and tell Thorpe he would return later when the butler said, 'Maybe you'd like to talk to your cousin, sir, while I send a message up to her ladyship?'

'An excellent idea.' Deciding not to take the risk of asking whether Miss Nixon would receive him, Randal stepped into the marble-flagged hallway. 'In the morning-room, is she, Thorpe?' he asked, doffing his high-crowned hat and handing it to the butler. 'Don't bother to announce me. I know the way.'

The door to the morning-room was ajar. Randal pushed it open. She was sitting on the sofa, her dark head bent over what looked to be a bound volume of some ladies' journal.

Randal paused involuntarily, his gaze absorbing the charming picture she made in her simple white muslin dress. By God, but she was a beauty!

'Good morning.'

The dark head jerked up at the sound of his voice and the volume slid from her lap to the thick Aubusson carpet as she jumped to her feet with a little gasp of surprise.

'Forgive me, I seem to be in the habit of startling you.' Randal had himself well in hand now and was able to meet her shocked gaze with an imperturbable smile. 'However, I hope you will permit me a few moments of your time?'

'Of course.' Kate tried to ignore the traitorous delight which insisted on welling up at the sight of his tall figure. 'Please, do come in.'

Regaining her composure, she waved him towards a chair and resumed her own seat. 'May I offer you some refreshment, sir?' she enquired politely.

'Thank you, but this is not a social call.' Randal shook his head firmly.

Apprehension flickered in her lovely eyes.

'I see that you understand me,' Randal murmured.

Swallowing hard, Kate adopted an air of calm. 'Your concern for my godmother is wholly admirable and I applaud your desire to spare her grief. However, have you considered, sir, that you may be doing more harm than good by revealing your suspicions to her?'

Randal's brows shot up. What was the little baggage up to now? 'Pray explain yourself, ma'am.'

'I don't know if you realise it, my lord, but Alicia was greatly looking forward to my arrival.' Mary had agreed this idea was worth a try. 'She has already spoken to many of her acquaintance of her intention to introduce me to Cheshire's *haut ton*. I fear she would be extremely disappointed and embarrassed if you force her to give up her plans.'

'Possibly,' Randal retorted, his tone dry. 'However, I think she would feel a far greater embarrassment if it turned out she had foisted an imposter upon society.'

Kate bit her lower lip. Trust him to misunderstand her meaning! 'There is more to it than that, sir. She treats me like a daughter and I think she would be dismayed to learn that I am under suspicion.'

'Are you saying that she has grown fond of you?' Randal allowed his disbelief to show. 'In such a short time?'

'She was already fond of me for my father's sake,' Kate replied simply.

Randal frowned. 'I have no wish to upset her, but if you are right then her hurt will be all the greater the longer she is kept in ignorance.'

'Assuming, of course, that my claim is proved false.' Kate managed to sound cool.

The objection he'd raised had already occurred to her and she hated the thought. However, if she abandoned her masquerade now, Kitty would lose her fortune by default. She had given Kitty her word. Breaking it would not save Alicia pain. It was already too late for that.

Randal acknowledged her protest with a curt inclination of his head. 'My assumption may seem unfair, ma'am, but in view of the circumstances I cannot afford to relax my guard.'

'In plain words, you don't trust me.' Kate knew it was foolish to feel disappointed, but she did. 'Yet yesterday you offered me a truce.'

'That was before I knew Alicia was involved.'

'Her involvement does not alter my position, sir. I will still have to wait for Uncle Gerald to arrive whether or not you succeed in persuading Alicia to throw me out.' Kate tilted her head on one side and gave him a quizzical smile. 'Are you no longer worried about possible gossip?'

'*Touché.*' Randal laughed mirthlessly.

Was he being too hard on her? Admittedly, he was worried about letting her powerful allure influence his judgement. A part of him longed to trust her. She looked so heart-stoppingly

lovely and innocent in that white dress it was almost impossible
to believe she was an adventuress. A strange urge to protect
her was growing in him, struggling for supremacy over caution
and the knowledge that he could not abandon his duty.

'Pray, won't 'you reconsider your decision to speak to Alicia?' Kate sensed his unease and pressed on, aware that Lady
Edgeworth might come in on them at any moment. 'I know it
is a lot to ask, but you must admit that you are partly responsible for my dilemma.'

Did she imagine he wanted to keep the old man's fortune?
'Do you censure me for taking heed of Gerald Sullivan's letter?'

'Not at all.' Kate smiled easily, wishing she was as confident
as she sounded. 'However, you cannot deny that without your
opposition everything could have been sorted out quickly and
I should not have needed to accept Alicia's hospitality.'

'You lack funds?'

Kate nodded, glad of his perspicacity. 'I did not anticipate a
long stay in England.' She paused delicately. 'If Alicia asks
me to leave it will be…difficult.'

He stared at her in silence and Kate wondered what he was
thinking. His handsome face was impassive, but her instinct
told her that his rigid opposition was beginning to weaken.

Conscious that there was no time to waste, she fluttered her
eyelashes demurely in a gesture she had perfected for the role
of Lydia Languish in *The Rivals*. 'Won't you at least agree to
wait until we have an answer to Mr Hilton's letter?' she begged
softly. 'I swear I don't want to hurt Alicia.'

Guilty until proven innocent? In his determination to prove
himself impervious to her beauty, was he in danger of forgetting justice? 'What of my family? Do you expect me to deceive
them, too?'

'Of course not!' Kate schooled her patience. 'I do not expect
you to tell lies for me. All I am asking for is a little forbearance.'

He steepled his fingers together, obviously deep in thought, and Kate caught her breath. Let him say yes and she would do all she could to make it up to Alicia once Kitty had won!

'Very well. I shall keep my doubts from Alicia until further evidence presents itself.' Randal smiled at her suddenly. 'You have my word on it…cousin.'

'Thank you!' Kate's eyes lit up. Their truce was on again!

Randal ignored the faint disquiet which tugged at the edges of his mind and told himself that she really was much too beautiful a girl to be consigned to some inn with only a maid to protect her. Any buck might ogle her or offer her worse insult! Liar or not, she had obviously been bred a lady and it went against the grain to subject her to that kind of discourtesy while they waited for her fate to be decided.

'May I ask if you have seen much of Chester yet?' he asked, abruptly changing the subject and consigning his doubts to the Devil.

'Not a great deal so far, I'm afraid.' Kate smilingly accepted the olive branch he held out to her. 'My wardrobe is limited and Alicia insists that I cannot wear the same clothes too often. So I must contain my impatience until the dressmaker has completed my new gowns.'

She bent down to pick up the journal she had dropped earlier. 'Luckily, Madame Celestine doesn't deem it necessary to trim bodices with sable or use bejewelled fastenings,' she said with a little chuckle, holding the volume open so that he could see what she meant.

Randal looked at the willowy goddesses depicted in the fashion sketches and grinned. 'Very fetching, but not exactly practical.'

Kate felt her spirits lift. It was reassuring to know that they shared the same sense of humour. When he came in she had been engrossed in trying to work out the cost of the elegant toilettes sketched in *The Ladies' Monthly Museum*. It had depressed her to think how much money she was going to owe Alicia, even though she had insisted on the plainest styles.

But when he smiled at her with that warmth in his brilliant eyes, she couldn't continue to feel anxious or low-spirited!

'Ah, Randal! Thorpe told me you were here.' Lady Edgeworth sailed into the room, a militant expression on her face. 'Come to apologise, have you?'

Kate winced. However, to her infinite relief, Randal showed no sign of taking affront at this cavalier greeting.

'How do you do, Alicia,' he said calmly, rising to his feet and making her a polite bow.

Lady Edgeworth eyed him uncertainly, rather regretting her belligerence. For all that she had known him since he was in short coats, he was a man who commanded respect. 'Why are you here?' she asked in a less hostile voice.

'I came to see how Miss Nixon was getting along.' Randal's tone was bland. 'Obviously, I needn't have worried. I perceive you are taking excellent care of her.'

'An odd way you have of showing your concern!' Alicia retorted. 'Why didn't you invite the child to stay at the Hall, eh?'

Kate decided it was time to step into the breach.

'Dear Godmama, don't be cross! Lord Redesmere has explained everything to me and we have agreed to settle our differences.' She turned to Randal. 'Isn't that so, my lord?'

'Indeed.' Randal inclined his head in her direction.

'Oh, well, in that case, I shall say no more!' A delighted smile broke out on Alicia's plump features and she waved him to resume his seat.

Sitting down next to Kate on the sofa, she patted her hand. 'There, didn't I tell you there must be some mistake,' she whispered behind her raised fan. 'I knew he would apologise.'

Kate's soul burned with embarrassment. It was only natural Alicia should be pleased at what she imagined to be a happy reconciliation, but Kate prayed she would say no more.

Risking a glance at Randal, she saw that he had overheard. His finely moulded lips had tightened, but as their eyes met his expression softened.

A strange little quiver danced down Kate's spine and she couldn't drag her gaze from his face as he and Alicia began to exchange small talk.

'Do you intend to honour the Leghs' drum with your presence tonight, cousin?'

Becoming aware that he was speaking to her, Kate dismissed her absurd desire to run her fingers through his thick blond hair and forced herself to concentrate.

'I do, sir. Unless you have changed your mind, ma'am?'

Thus appealed to, Alicia laughed heartily. 'Of course we are going, child. Why, Celestine has promised to deliver your new gown this very morning!' She paused and then shot their visitor a crafty look. 'Are you going, Randal?'

Guessing what was coming, Randal hid a smile. 'I have accepted the invitation.'

'Excellent. Kitty won't know a soul there save for us. You can introduce her to a few of your friends.' Lady Edgeworth chuckled. 'Maria Legh has held out the lure of cards and dancing so I expect we'll see plenty of you young gentlemen there.' She threw out another broad hint. 'You're still keen on dancing, ain't you, Randal?'

Knowing what was expected of him, Randal agreed and, directing his gaze at her young companion, continued, 'Will you do me the honour of standing up with me, cousin?'

Guilt warred with her longing to accept as Kate sought for an answer. In all her plotting, it hadn't occurred to her that she might want to dance with the man she was intending to deprive of a fortune!

'Did you get much opportunity to attend parties in Massachusetts?' Randal asked, feeling ridiculously disappointed at her silence and hoping to find an alternative reason for it than the one which immediately sprang to mind.

Kate wondered if she ought to deny it and then remembered just in time that she had already told Alicia she knew most of the popular steps when her hostess had asked her if she would like to have dancing lessons.

'I attended a few, sir, but they were small events and I'm not sure if my skill is equal to that of the ladies you know,' she prevaricated.

'You are too modest I'll be bound, Kitty dear.'

Randal was inclined to agree with Alicia. He'd wager that a girl who possessed the proud deportment of a queen was certain to be a good dancer.

'I should like the chance to begin again,' he said softly, knowing that she would understand even if Alicia did not. 'Say you will consent to save the supper dance for me?'

Torn between delight and alarm, Kate could only nod silently.

The gown promised by Celestine had still not arrived by the time Lady Edgeworth arose from an afternoon nap taken to recruit her energies for the evening ahead. Kate had declined to rest before the party and was engaged at the handsome little rosewood escritoire which graced her bedroom when Alicia came hurrying in to see her.

Quickly concealing her letter to Ned, she set herself to soothing Alicia's alarm. Fortunately for her nerves, the older woman was soon interrupted by a knock at the door.

'There, ma'am,' Kate said cheerfully. 'That is probably Mary come to tell us the delivery-boy is here.'

To her surprise it wasn't Mary who entered, but Susan, the parlour-maid, who was carrying a box much too small to hold a dress.

'For you, miss.' Susan bobbed a curtsy and handed the box over to Kate. 'Just been delivered.'

It felt very light and Kate suddenly knew what it must contain.

'Do open it, my dear,' Lady Edgeworth encouraged.

From the broad smile on her face Kate knew she had also guessed that the box contained flowers.

'How charming! From Crawford, I assume?'

Kate stared down at the exquisite bouquet and her heart did a peculiar flip-flop as she discovered the accompanying card.

She held it out to Lady Edgeworth, who scanned it with satisfaction.

'And tied up with pink ribbons too!' Alicia smiled happily. 'They will match your new gown.'

Her smile faded abruptly as she remembered what had brought her post-haste to her goddaughter's bedchamber. Ordering Susan to remove the posy, she exclaimed, 'I shall send to Celestine directly! It is too bad of her to keep us waiting when she knows that this is your very first evening-party!'

In the event it did not prove necessary to badger the modiste, for the dress arrived before Alicia had completed her angry note and Kate had plenty of time to prepare for the drum.

'And remember to watch your tongue, Kate! Don't forget you are supposed to be a shy young miss,' Mary warned when Kate was at last ready to go down for dinner.

Kate grinned at her. 'I dare say that there aren't many American ladies in Chester. If I overstep the mark, let's hope they think me an eccentric foreigner!'

'Very pretty, my love!' Alicia gazed at her in approval when she entered the drawing-room. 'Celestine may be a very irritating woman, but she certainly can sew! You will outshine every other girl present!'

'Thank you, ma'am,' Kate laughed.

Alicia beamed at her, conveniently forgetting that she had been doubtful when Kitty had first explained how she wanted the modiste to alter a dress that had caught her fancy amongst the shop's stock of ready made-up gowns. The dress would need only minor alteration for a perfect fit, but the colour was unusual for a debutante and it seemed to her that it would be very plain once the trimmings Kitty disliked were removed.

She had allowed herself to be overruled, giving way to Kitty's determination and Madame Celestine's discreet urging, but she had feared the result might not show off her goddaughter to advantage. Fortunately, she had been wrong! Nothing could become the girl's exotic beauty more than that deceptively simple sheath of deep rose satin!

Another quarter of an hour passed and Alicia glanced anxiously at the cloisonné clock which stood upon her white marble mantelpiece.

'I do hope Godwin isn't going to be much longer,' she said. 'Or I shall have complaints from Cook!'

Mr Crawford was to be their escort to the Leghs' and had been bidden to dine in Abbey Square beforehand.

'If he is half the trencherman you told me of, I'm sure he will be here soon,' Kate replied soothingly.

She had barely finished speaking when they heard the sound of the front door opening and then voices in the hallway.

'My dear Alicia, pray forgive my tardiness! An unfortunate problem with one of the carriage lanterns, but all is now well and here I am at last!'

Kate surveyed Randal's uncle with interest. He was a tall, well set-up man who was just beginning to run to fat, a tendency his elegantly cut dark brown coat helped to disguise. His fair hair was receding from his forehead and it was liberally streaked with grey, but his blue eyes were alert and his smile lively. She judged him to be around fifty.

Alicia performed the introductions and Godwin bowed over Kate's hand with a graceful flourish.

'Enchanted to meet you, my dear! I remember your father well. You have a look of him, you know.'

Kate suppressed a smile.

Dinner was a protracted meal. Mrs Hibbert had excelled herself, producing a delicious mulligatawny soup for the remove, followed by two elaborate courses which included several of Mr Crawford's favourite dishes.

'Pray give my compliments to Mrs Hibbert, Alicia,' Godwin begged as he sampled the splendid haunch of venison roasted to perfection. 'I swear her cooking gets better every time I dine with you.'

Kate could only marvel at the amount of food he managed

to put away while at the same time conducting a thoroughly entertaining conversation with both his neighbours.

'Let me help you to some of this syllabub, Miss Kitty.' Godwin waved his spoon at the large glass dish set in the centre of the table. 'It is extremely good.'

Kate, whose appetite had been satiated long before the second course had been set before them, thanked him prettily, but shook her head. 'If I eat another mouthful, sir, I fear I shall not be able to dance one single step tonight.'

He laughed jovially. 'I see I must not tempt you, then, else all the young fellows will be out for my blood.'

When he had at last eaten himself to a standstill, Alicia signalled to Kate and they rose to their feet and left him to his port.

'Godwin enjoys his food, but he is not a heavy drinker. I doubt if he will keep us waiting long,' Alicia said as she led the way back to the drawing-room.

Kate perched upon the edge of a chair and let out a restless sigh. She hoped Alicia was right. Dinner had lasted almost three hours and it was now well after nine. They were going to be late.

'Do not worry, my love! The Leghs won't expect us before ten.'

Kate was sorry that her impatience had been so obvious. 'I meant no criticism of Mr Crawford,' she murmured.

'No need to apologise, Kitty. It is only natural that you are nervous.' Alicia smiled at her reassuringly. 'None the less, I'm confident you have nothing to fear. Now, why don't you run along and have Mary refresh your toilette before we leave?'

If only she knew, thought Kate as she obeyed this sensible suggestion. She wasn't feeling nervous about the drum. Playing the debutante and meeting Alicia's friends was something she had prepared herself for. It was no more alarming than embarking upon any other new role.

The prospect of dancing with Randal Crawford, on the other hand, made her pulse race!

When Kate came downstairs again her companions were ready to leave. Godwin ushered them out to his comfortable carriage and, on the short journey to the Leghs' substantial mansion in Brook Street, Kate's initial liking for him grew. No one could have shown greater concern for their comfort or been more attentive in seeing that they were not jostled as they joined the throng queuing to crowd into the house.

Conscious of curious eyes, Kate kept her head held high as they ascended the fine oak staircase and she was introduced to her hosts.

Maria Legh was a small, bird-like woman wearing a showy profusion of Venetian lace and too much jewellery, but her smile was kind as she greeted Kate.

'Welcome to Chester, Miss Nixon,' she said. 'I trust you had a good journey from America?'

Kate murmured something appropriate and then they moved on into the first of the elegant drawing-rooms.

'I don't see Redesmere,' Alicia declared after directing a sweeping glance over the crowd.

'M'nevvy is always inclined to arrive late. Don't think the boy really enjoys these kind of gatherings.' Godwin let out a rich chuckle. 'Too many matchmaking mamas out on the catch, if you follow my meaning!'

Realising that she had been holding her breath in anticipation, Kate gave herself a mental shake. She wasn't here to dangle after Randal Crawford, she was here to establish herself so thoroughly that Gerald Sullivan's revelations would not be believed. The sooner she got on with the task and stopped behaving like a greensick ninny the better.

'Charming girl, your goddaughter. Spoke to her earlier. Frederick was very taken with her, too. She made him laugh! Thinks she's got style. He can't abide these namby-pamby misses who haven't a word to say for themselves.' The stout elderly woman bedecked in diamonds who had stopped by Lady Edgeworth's chair let out a gruff chuckle of amusement. 'Shouldn't wonder if she sets a new trend!'

Alicia felt a tiny flicker of alarm mingling with her satisfaction as she thanked Lady Massey for her compliments. Kitty had a great deal of self-confidence for a girl of her age and, scorning the coy submissiveness currently in vogue, made no attempt to hide her intelligence or her opinions.

'She's a beauty, too. You are going to be kept very busy, Alicia, if I'm not mistaken. But you'll make time to bring her to our rout, eh?'

Pride overcame Alicia's anxiety and she assented to the influential old lady's demand with a happy smile.

Lady Massey moved away and Alicia surveyed the impromptu dance floor, which Mrs Legh had created by the simple expedient of removing most of the furniture from her second drawing-room. The carpet had been taken up and the oak boards polished to a high shine while small groups of chairs had been set out at intervals around the edges of the room to enable watchful mamas to keep an eye on their darlings.

A cotillion was drawing to a close and she watched Kitty's graceful figure with satisfaction. The child danced beautifully, an opinion she was sure Tom Egerton, her current partner, shared. One of the most notable young bachelors in Cheshire, he had made haste to obtain an introduction the minute he had clapped eyes on her goddaughter and had managed to secure two dances before her card was filled.

A smattering of applause accompanied the end of the set and the dancers began to leave the floor. Tom's auburn head bent close to Kitty's and Alicia felt sure that he was asking her for another dance. For a moment gratification outweighed all other considerations and then a *frisson* of apprehension penetrated her haze of delight.

Had Kitty's mama warned her of the impropriety of bestowing more than two dances on any gentleman? Even at a small private party like this, a girl who did so would be considered fast. Perhaps the unwritten rules of polite behaviour were different in America? She should have thought to check!

To her relief she saw the sable curls shake in refusal and

they began to thread their way back towards her. Tom's expression showed his disappointment, but by the time they reached her little gilt chair he was smiling again and laughing at something Kitty had just said.

'Thank you, Lady Edgeworth, for inviting your goddaughter to stay with you,' he remarked enthusiastically. 'And thank you, Miss Nixon.' He made an extravagant bow. 'I have never enjoyed a dance more.'

Kate responded with a curtsy, glad of the chance to drop her gaze and hide her amusement at his boyish raptures. Although her own age, he reminded her of an overgrown puppy, all bounce and enthusiasm, but she had no wish to hurt his feelings.

Somewhat to her surprise, Alicia did not encourage him to linger.

'He is a very personable young man, but I would be failing in my duty to your mama if I allowed him to make you an object of gossip,' she murmured in explanation when he had moved away to rejoin his parents on the other side of the room.

There was a lull in the dancing and Alicia seized the opportunity to introduce her to more of the company.

Trying to remember each new name and sparkle, Kate could feel a headache coming on. Her face ached from smiling and her throat was dry and she couldn't help wishing that the rooms were not so hot. The atmosphere was heavy with the scents of candle wax and too much perfume.

None of which would matter a button, of course, if the one man she wanted to see had been present!

The dancing resumed. Kate stood up for a reel with Godwin and accepted his offer to fetch her a glass of lemonade when it was over. Seeing her temporarily deserted, Tom Egerton made a beeline for her side and launched into a request that she join him over supper.

'I know you can't dance with me again. My mother gave me a scold. Told me I shouldn't have asked you to,' he muttered, colouring. 'Nothing to offend propriety, though, in letting me escort you into supper, is there?'

'I'm sorry, sir. I am already promised to Lord Redesmere.'

'But dash it, Miss Nixon, Redesmere ain't here!' Tom's round face was wreathed in protest.

Kate, who happened to be facing the door, suddenly saw that he was wrong.

Her unexpected smile dazzled Tom, who was at a loss to account for it until a deep voice behind him bade them both good evening.

He spun round to behold Lord Redesmere, attired in a superbly cut black coat. A plain white waistcoat, black pantaloons and an intricately tied neckcloth completed the elegant picture. Tom, who was wearing his new blue coat with its wadded shoulders and wasp-waist and a bright flowered waistcoat, had a sudden uneasy feeling that he was over-dressed.

Kate held out her gloved hand and Randal raised it fleetingly to his lips. 'How do you do, Miss Nixon.'

Kate's skin burned beneath its thin covering of white silk. Trying to ignore her rapid pulse, she frowned at him with mock severity. 'You are very late, my lord. Had you forgotten we were engaged for the supper-dance?'

'I would never forget so pleasant a prospect, cousin.'

Tom eyed the older man with disfavour. 'Using your family connections to steal a march on the rest of us, I see, Redesmere,' he muttered sulkily.

Randal looked down on him from his superior height. 'Why, Tom, you amaze me! I should have thought everyone would approve of the rift in the Nixon family finally being healed,' he retorted with a silky mockery that brought a tide of hot colour into Mr Egerton's cherubic cheeks.

Mortified by this set-down from one whose style he secretly admired, Tom mumbled something, bowed stiffly to Kate and hurried off.

'That was not kind,' Kate said sternly. 'The poor boy is not up to your weight.'

'I know. Unforgivable of me, wasn't it, but I wanted to talk to you,' he replied promptly.

Disarmed by his impudence, Kate let out a little chuckle.

'How are you enjoying the party? Does it live up to your expectations?'

Kate, whose headache had completely vanished, nodded enthusiastically. 'I think it a very elegant assembly, sir.' An impish grin lit her face. 'I suppose I ought not to have said that! Alicia tells me it is fashionable to appear bored, which seems a strange notion to me. At home we expect guests to try to appear pleased with their entertainment. It would be thought most impolite to complain of a *sad crush* as I have heard several people do tonight.'

'Such ill-nature deserves a flogging,' Randal agreed solemnly.

Amusement glinted in his brilliant eyes and Kate wasn't sure whether he had swallowed her fiction or not. She hadn't the least idea whether American society held such views since Kitty had not mentioned the subject but, convinced he would not be able to contradict her, it had seemed too good a chance of underlining her supposed nationality to miss.

'You are bamming me, I think.' Kate peeped up at him demurely through her lashes. 'You must consider me a complete rustic.'

He laughed. 'Not in that gown! Celestine has excelled herself.'

His gaze was admiring as he took in the way the fluid satin flowed over her shapely curves. Its lack of ornamentation and the very plainness of the style with its low round neck, high waist and tiny puffed sleeves merely emphasised the excellence of her figure.

Happiness bubbled up in Kate. 'Take care, my lord, or I shall consider that as a compliment,' she warned.

'Please do,' he responded promptly.

'Then I stand in your debt twice over.' Kate lifted her posy up to her face and inhaled the delicate fragrance of the pink blooms.

'You honour me by wearing my roses. They are a poor homage to your beauty, ma'am.'

'Oh, please don't call me that!' Kate exclaimed involuntarily.

He raised his tawny brows in enquiry and Kate blushed.

'It reminds me of all the times we have quarrelled,' she murmured, feeling flustered.

Randal understood. 'In that case, to continue its use would be a violation of our truce,' he agreed softly, knowing that he had previously hurled the epithet at her in icy contempt.

A contempt he no longer felt, he suddenly realised. Whether or not she proved to be an adventuress, he had begun to like her.

She was very beautiful, of course, but it was more than that. He had desired other beautiful women and he knew the difference between lust and liking. This unknown girl had spirit and intelligence. A lively sense of humour, too, which was another attribute he admired. Best of all, she did not toad-eat him!

Randal was not vain, but he was under no illusions about the power of his wealth and status. Too many young women had thrown themselves at his feet for him to think otherwise. Beauties hopeful of wedding his fortune had tried every trick known to the female imagination to lure him into the parson's mousetrap.

It was rare in his experience to meet a girl who made it clear that she didn't give a snap of her fingers for his good opinion. And yet he did not think she was indifferent to him. On the contrary, he would have wagered a goodly part of his inheritance that the sensual attraction which plagued him whenever she was near disturbed her as well.

Made nervous by his continuing silence, Kate blurted the first thing that came into her head. 'How did you guess I would be wearing pink tonight?'

'I asked Celestine,' he confessed, his serious expression

lightening. 'I wanted to be sure, you see, that you would carry my flowers.'

'You are a complete hand, sir!' Kate grinned back at him, relieved that her impetuous remark had not spoilt their harmony.

At that moment Mr Godwin Crawford hove into view. 'Ah, nevvy! Decided to show your face at last, have you?' He handed her glass of lemonade to Kate and shook Randal's hand. 'Might have known I would find you talking to the prettiest girl in the room.'

Randal's grin broadened. 'You pipped me to the post, as usual, O most revered uncle.'

Kate sipped her lemonade and listened to their banter. It was obvious that they shared a strong affection as well as a distinct family resemblance.

A fleeting sadness touched her. She would have dearly liked to have been part of a close-knit family, but only her mother had ever shown her any real affection. Her father had always been cold and her grandmother's fondness had been a shallow thing, shattering at the first frost of misfortune. As for her stepmother…! Lucy had positively disliked her, no doubt due to the fact that they were almost of an age and Kate's presence embarrassed her.

The trio of musicians hired by Mrs Legh began to tune up their instruments for the final dance before supper, snatching Kate from her gloomy thoughts.

Randal held out his arm to her. 'It would serve me right if you gave this dance to some more deserving candidate, but I hope you won't.'

Kate smiled at Godwin. 'What do you think, Mr Crawford? Shall I punish your nephew for his tardiness?'

'Jupiter, no, Miss Kitty! He is staying over at my house tonight and I cannot abide long faces.' He took her empty glass from her. 'Be merciful to the wretch, I beg you.'

'In the face of such eloquent advocacy, how can I refuse?' Kate laughed.

She placed her fingers upon Randal's sleeve. Beneath the smooth black broadcloth she could feel the hard strength of his arm and a delicious shiver went through her.

They joined the set for the quadrille and Kate strove to control her wanton thoughts and concentrate upon the dance. Some of the figures were complicated and she did not want to make a mull of it and create a bad impression.

'You are very quiet, cousin.' Randal directed a teasing glance at her as they touched hands. 'Is that because you are minding your steps?'

'Certainly not,' Kate replied brightly.

They parted and when their paths crossed once more, she tilted her chin at him and demanded to know if he thought she talked too much. 'Otherwise why should you think me troubled when I am silent?' she quizzed.

He smiled at her. 'I did not mean to accuse you of being a chatterbox. However, I do think you are a woman of decided opinions.'

Parted by the dance before she could ask for further clarification, Kate thought this remark over. Had he meant to criticise? She didn't think so. His tone had sounded almost admiring.

A spurt of pleasure shot through her at the thought that he might not deem it necessary for a woman to be an empty-headed doll.

The music ceased and Kate fanned herself vigorously, hoping her cheeks weren't as pink as they felt.

'Would you care to take a turn about the terrace before going in to supper? It will be cool.'

Kate hesitated. She was hot and his thoughtfulness pleased her, but was it safe to lay herself open to temptation? The idea of being alone with him in an unchaperoned darkness was quite unnerving! 'Alicia might not approve,' she murmured.

Randal smiled. 'I promise to behave myself.'

The colour in Kate's cheeks deepened. Heavens, what must

he think of her! A proper young lady would never have made such a betraying remark!

Taking pity on her mortification, Randal suggested they ask Lady Edgeworth for her permission.

'Of course, you may go, Kitty. It is quite *comme il faut.*' Alicia beamed approval but, turning to Randal, added a gentle warning not to stay out too long.

The terrace was wide and surrounded by a handsome stone balustrade which came up to Kate's waist. She could see three other couples out for a stroll and it wasn't as dark as she had feared. The moon was up and lanterns had been arranged at intervals to give light to those who sought the air.

'Better?' Randal asked as they wandered over to the edge of the terrace and stood looking out at the dark garden below.

'Much, thank you.' Kate lifted up her face to better appreciate the gentle breeze which was wafting over the balustrades. 'What a lovely new moon.'

Randal stared at the pure lines of her profile and felt a surge of tenderness which surprised him.

It is the moonlight, he told himself sternly. You are just imagining she looks fragile and in need of your protection.

Kate became aware of his intense regard and panic fluttered along her nerves. Oh, heavens, why didn't he say something!

The silence stretched on and, desperate to break it, Kate blurted the first thing that came into her head.

'Do you like gardening, sir?'

Shaking off his idiocy, Randal laughed. 'To be honest with you, cousin, it is not a subject that I know much about.'

'I just wondered,' Kate improvised. 'The grounds at Crawford Hall are exquisite.'

'You must thank my gardeners for that. If it is a pastime you esteem, you might enjoy talking to Lady Massey. She is something of an expert.'

'I made her acquaintance earlier. Alicia hopes to secure me an invitation to her rout next week. I understand it is one of the highlights of the summer.' Kate played with the sticks of her fan in what she hoped was a casual manner. 'Shall you attend, my lord?'

Randal, who until this moment had no intention of doing so, nodded.

A wide smile turned up the corners of her generous mouth in response, straining Randal's self-control.

Kate saw his broad shoulders tense. He wants to kiss me, she realised and, torn between delight and dismay, her heart started to thump in a dizzying fashion.

'I shall be pleased to see you there. It is always pleasant to encounter old acquaintance when venturing somewhere new,' she murmured, knowing she sounded inane but desperate to defuse the tension spiralling between them.

'Then I hope you will save a dance for me, little cousin.' Randal could hear the husky catch in her voice and his gaze was drawn to the rapid rise and fall of her bosom. Partially exposed by the low-cut neckline of her gown, her breasts were full and enticing, the smooth delicate skin gleaming like pearl. He longed to draw her into his embrace and discover more.

In the moonlight his brilliant eyes glittered with desire and Kate sucked in her breath, knowing that it was only his earlier promise which was preventing him from making the first move.

She dropped her gaze in confusion. 'Perhaps we should go back,' she whispered. 'I think we must be the last ones here.'

Randal took a step closer. 'Not quite. There is one other couple over there at the other end of the terrace,' he said quietly.

Slowly he reached out his hand and gently tipped up her chin so that he could look down into her face. Her velvet dark eyes met his and he could see his own passion mirrored in their depths. 'Won't you stay a moment longer?'

The blood drummed in Kate's ears and she trembled at his touch. Just a few feet away there was a pool of shadow. No one would see them there. All she needed to do was give him the slightest signal of encouragement and she would be in his arms.

Waiting for her answer, Randal realised he was holding his breath. God, but he hadn't felt such an intense carnal longing since his youth! He wanted her so much that his pulse was racing. All he could think of was kissing her delectable mouth!

A loud burst of laughter from the other couple on the terrace made Kate flinch, startling her back to reality.

She stepped away from him quickly. 'I think we should go in now, sir.'

'Of course.' Randal acknowledged her request with a rueful smile.

The moment was lost, but, alleviating his disappointment, was an utter certainty that another opportunity would soon arise to find out whether her mouth was as kissable as it looked.

Chapter Five

The presence of Lord Redesmere at Morning Service at St Peter's on the Sunday following the Leghs' rout caused something of a stir.

'What a nice surprise to see you here, Randal,' Lady Edgeworth said, greeting him as she emerged from the old church which had been her preferred place of worship for many years.

'I had business in town,' he murmured, aware that his decision to attend St Peter's would attract curiosity. The congregation contained many members of the *haut ton*, but none had travelled so far for the sermon.

Alicia's mouth dropped open a trifle, but she was too polite to ask what kind of business demanded attention on the Sabbath.

Watching him greet Kitty, she realised she didn't need to enquire. Elation surged in her plump breast. She was a simpleton not to have realised before now that Kitty had caught his interest!

It had troubled her a little that Kitty's arrival had deprived Randal of an inheritance which had looked set to become his. He was a very likeable young man, and heaven knows that unpleasant old misanthrope had been demanding. Not that Randal had ever complained. He was not the kind of man to shirk family responsibilities.

What was more, he possessed a strong sense of honour and she was sure he didn't begrudge Kitty her windfall. But if they were united in matrimony, the money would stay in Cheshire and so would Kitty. She would not lose her after all.

Glowing with satisfaction, Alicia invited Randal back to Abbey Square. 'Come and eat a nuncheon with us. It is a long drive back to the Hall and the wind has turned chilly today.'

Randal accepted with alacrity and Kate shot him a quizzical look.

She would lay odds that he had planned this outcome all along! 'Tell me,' she said softly. 'What have you done with your carriage?'

'Stabled it at the Falcon Inn,' Randal replied promptly. 'I could hardly bring a curricle and a pair of greys into the churchyard, now could I?'

His expression was so innocent she couldn't help chuckling.

'I shall take a chair home, Kitty,' Alicia announced, capturing their attention. 'Shall you do likewise? You may walk back with his lordship if you prefer.'

Kate was happy to walk. It was only a short distance back to Abbey Square and she would have Randal all to herself.

They saw Alicia off and then Randal tucked Kate's arm into the crook of his elbow. 'Let's not stand dawdling about,' he said cheerfully. 'Look at those clouds. I think it is going to rain.'

'I hope not,' Kate replied. 'I like sunny weather.'

Randal glanced down at her. She was looking particularly pretty this morning in a pale jonquil coloured muslin worn with a neat little bonnet in white Italian straw. 'Do you? I thought the climate in Massachusetts was cold?'

'Only in the winter, sir,' Kate answered, devoutly relieved that she had taken the trouble to ask Kitty a few simple questions on the subject. 'We have hot summers.'

'Then for your sake I hope I'm wrong and this fine spell lasts.'

Kate dimpled up at him and thanked him prettily and Randal's flicker of suspicion faded.

He hadn't meant to test her knowledge. He had made the remark on the spur of the moment, although he supposed he ought to be laying traps to catch her out. It would be the sensible thing to do, but such behaviour seemed shabby. He had given her his word to wait for news from Ireland and he meant to keep it.

Blister it, be honest, his conscience protested. It's got naught to do with your promise. You don't want her to let slip that she is an imposter because you want to keep the present status quo.

Maybe in a few weeks' time he would be glad to see her go, but for now he was deriving a great deal of pleasure from her company and he didn't want the idyll to end.

'Am I walking too fast for you?' He slowed his long stride to match her pace.

'You have the advantage of wearing breeches, sir. Skirts are so restrictive.'

His eyebrows lifted in astonishment and Kate realised her mistake. She had been thinking of the freedom of movement she had enjoyed strutting about the stage in her favourite breeches part as Sylvia in *The Recruiting Officer*.

Frantically cudgelling her brains, she remembered Kitty saying what little ruffians her stepbrothers were. 'No doubt you will think me shameless, but when we first moved to Amherst I often used to borrow my stepbrothers' clothes,' she explained brightly. 'They were much more comfortable for exploring the woods.'

'Your mama approved?' Randal did rapid mental arithmetic. She would have been sixteen or so, a little old to be playing the tomboy.

'Not at all.' Kate essayed a bright laugh. 'She put a stop to it as soon as she found out. I have never forgotten that sensation of freedom, though. You men don't know how lucky you are!'

'Ah, but I do.' Randal smiled at her lazily. 'You might have been born a boy instead of merely liking to wear breeches.'

This unexpected compliment silenced Kate and her rosy blush was still in evidence a few moments later when they reached Abbey Square.

Lady Edgeworth had arrived before them. She offered them an excellent sherry and announced, 'Our meal will be ready shortly.'

Kate's eyes widened at the size and magnificence of the nuncheon laid out in the dining-room. Up to now she and Alicia had always partaken of a simple, informal meal, just a few cold meats and some fruit and cakes taken to bridge the gap between breakfast and dinner, which Lady Edgeworth liked served at the fashionably late hour of six.

She could understand Alicia ordering additional dishes. What surprised her was the sheer scale of the offerings. Poor Mrs Hibbert must have been run off her feet to provide so much extra food at such short notice.

Kate glanced across the table at her hostess, curiosity nibbling at the fringes of her mind. Even allowing for Alicia's desire to appear hospitable, this show of lavish bounty was excessive. After all, it wasn't as if Randal was a stranger.

Then another thought struck her and she almost choked on a piece of cold roast chicken.

'Are you all right?' Randal threw back his chair and leapt up as she began to cough and splutter.

'Pat her back, dear boy!'

Randal willingly obeyed this advice until Kate begged him to desist.

'I'm perfectly well now,' she gasped.

Randal poured a glass of water and handed it to her.

'Thank you.' Kate sipped it and hoped her reddened cheeks would be excused by her fit of coughing.

Nuncheon finished, Randal made a move to leave.

'Oh, do stay a while longer,' Alicia invited. 'We shall be sadly bored if you go, shall we not, Kitty?'

Kate managed a weak smile of assent. Torn between her own wish for him to stay and the suspicion that had raised its head during their meal, she didn't know whether to be glad or sorry when he agreed to remain.

They repaired to the drawing-room and after a while, when it was evident that his lordship was again poised to say his farewells, Alicia commanded Kate to play the pianoforte. 'You must hear her, Randal. She puts all our local damsels to blush.'

'I'm sure his lordship isn't in the mood for music,' Kate demurred, her suspicions hardening at Alicia's fulsome praise.

'On the contrary, Miss Nixon. It would be delightful.'

Convinced he was merely being polite, Kate continued to shake her head.

'Please, indulge me, my dear,' Alicia trilled with an inexorable smile and Kate reluctantly got up and went over to the pianoforte.

'You will turn the music for her, won't you, my lord?' Alicia demanded with an arch smile that made Kate's blood boil.

'I should be happy to do so.'

There was a note of amusement in his deep voice and Kate wondered if he thought her reluctance to play was based on nervousness.

Does he think I lack skill? she conjectured indignantly.

In fact, she had been well taught in her youth and had kept her natural talent honed. When not required on stage, she had often helped provide music for performances given by the Gillman Players.

'I can manage without your help, sir,' she answered waspishly, a determination to prove herself overcoming her intention to appear a demure miss.

Flexing her fingers and hoping her memory would not let her down, she launched into a vigorous rendition of 'Heart of Oak', a song that was always popular.

'Bravo!' Randal joined in Alicia's applause, stifling the small voice in his head which whispered that it was odd that an American girl should know Boyce's patriotic tune off by heart.

Kate tilted her chin at him, her eyes sparkling with mischief. 'And you, sir, will you not reveal your own talent?'

'Alas, I cannot play the pianoforte.' Randal's finely moulded lips twitched. Unless he was very much mistaken, that was a challenge!

'Then perhaps you will sing for us?' Kate asked sweetly.

Somewhat to her surprise he agreed and she discovered that he had a very fine voice. Her initial chagrin fading, she offered to accompany him when Alicia begged him to sing 'Piercing Eyes', one of her favourite Haydn canzonettas.

'Thank you.' He smiled down at Kate when the song was finished. 'You play as beautifully as you dance.'

Kate inclined her head in a demure fashion as she accepted the compliment, but her appearance of calm belied her inner delight at his praise.

Her mood was so elated she forgot her earlier misgivings, and when he offered to take her out for a drive she gladly accepted.

'Then I shall bid you farewell until Tuesday, cousin.' Randal bowed over her hand with exquisite grace.

His kiss still tingling upon her skin, Kate watched his elegant figure depart.

She began to collect up her music, but her busy hands stilled as Lady Edgeworth, who had escorted him out into the hall, came hurrying back into the room.

'Oh, my dear! I am so pleased for you!' she exclaimed, her voice rising in excitement. 'He is quite smitten, I vow!'

Her broad smile revived all of Kate's earlier suspicions and she stared at the older woman, her heart sinking.

'Just because he asked me to go driving with him, dear God-mama?' She shook her head airily. 'I think you are mistaken. Lord Redesmere is merely being polite.'

'Fiddlesticks! Randal Crawford wouldn't waste his time on mere politeness.' Alicia tapped the side of her nose significantly. 'Believe me, Kitty, I know him! He is a man who goes after what he wants. Why, I hardly need have bothered trying to encourage him for I swear he has made his mind up already to have you!'

'Indeed!' Kate's eyes flashed dark fire. 'And am I to have no say in the matter?'

Alicia blinked at her in startled dismay. 'Whatever is the matter, Kitty? I thought you liked him.'

Kate bit her lip. 'I do,' she muttered at last, knowing it was impossible to deny it.

What girl wouldn't find him attractive? In the prime of life, he was handsome, intelligent and extremely virile. He was also overbearing and far too fond of getting his own way, but his arrogance was tempered by a self-depreciatory sense of humour and an innate kindness.

'Well, then, what is troubling you, my dear?' Alicia asked. 'He is a great catch, you know—'

'I did not come to England looking for a husband,' Kate interrupted hotly.

'I realise that, Kitty. However, it is time you were thinking of marriage and your mama could not possibly object to an alliance with Lord Redesmere. Indeed, she could not find a better match in America.' Her plump face took on a beatific glow. 'You would have everything, an ancient lineage, fortune, title. No mother could wish for more.'

Knowing her words to be true, Kate was silent.

Puzzled by this lack of response, Alicia sighed. 'Oh, my dear, surely you can see that marriage to Lord Redesmere would be the perfect solution?'

Kate's fingers clenched upon the sheet of music she held, crushing it. 'Solution, ma'am? I'm afraid I don't know what you mean.'

But she did. If Kitty married Lord Redesmere, then the rift between the two branches of the Nixon family would be finally healed and all the difficulties caused by the old Nabob's will would be smoothed away.

Unfortunately, much as Kate found the man attractive, she couldn't allow her impersonation of Kitty to go that far!

As predicted by Lord Redesmere, a change in the weather took place. Watching the rain fall all during Monday morning Kate's spirits were as gloomy as the downpour.

Her plan had seemed so simple. Poor Kitty had been terrified after the attempt on her life in Ireland and she had jumped at Kate's offer to take her place. Ned hadn't been keen on letting his best actress go, but Kitty's plight had touched his kind heart and he had allowed himself to be persuaded after Kate had promised to return quickly.

'After all, Ned, how long can it take to sign a few documents?' she had declared cheerfully. 'I'll be back with the money before you know it.'

Well, she had been wrong. Claiming the Nixon fortune had turned out to be more than just a formality. She had already been away from the company for a week and had made no real progress. All she had done was to embroil herself in a web of lies and deceit that made her nights uneasy.

'Give over moidering, Kate. It ain't like you to look on the black side,' Mary scolded on their way home from posting Kate's letter to Ned that afternoon.

Lady Edgeworth had offered to send a footman with this missive, but Kate had been wary of curious eyes noting its destination and in any event had felt a need to get out of doors even though the sky was grey and still spitting drizzle.

'I'm sorry, Mary, I know I'm as blue as a megrim,' Kate apologised. 'But I feel that I've let both Kitty and the company down.'

'Aye, lass.' Mary gave her a sympathetic smile. 'Still, maybe Gerald Sullivan will take fright at that lawyer's letter. I reckon he's a coward and won't dare show his nose in Chester.'

Kate nodded thoughtfully. From what Kitty had told them Gerald had taken care not to get his hands dirty. It was Sean who had carried out the attack and pushed her into the river.

'If he doesn't come, Mr Hilton won't believe he is telling the truth.' Kate's face brightened. 'And then the locket and letter might be proof enough.'

'What about Crawford? Do you think he will throw another rub in your way?'

'I'm not sure.' Kate's dark eyes took on a dreamy expression. 'I think his opposition to me is weakening.'

Mary sniffed. 'You'd best watch out then, Kate, that your own feelings don't change. He's an *oaf*, remember?'

Kate had told her all about the Leghs' drum and his lordship's affability. Mary wasn't sure she'd liked that note of happiness in her young friend's voice. She had never seen Kate behave this way before. Usually, she ran a mile if a man showed interest in her. Now she seemed eager for Crawford's company.

It was worrying, particularly as Mary could see no reason for his lordship to have had a change of heart, unless, like many another man before him, he had fallen victim to Kate's beauty. In other circumstances, Mary might have encouraged Kate to toss her cap over the windmill and take him for a lover. She deserved a taste of happiness, God knew, but, given the situation, how could a liaison with Crawford end in other than disaster?

'I was overhard on him that day.' Kate shrugged awkwardly. 'He had reason to mistrust me, but we are getting along famously now.'

'He has a fancy to you, lass, but it won't last.' Mary shook her head dolefully. 'Lust never does and there can be naught else between the pair of you, not unless you tell him the truth.'

'How can I?' Kate's voice was unsteady. 'He would despise me.'

Alarmed by the regret in those dark velvet eyes, Mary exclaimed, 'Don't let him touch your heart, Kate!'

'I'm not such a fool, I hope!' Kate swerved to avoid a puddle of rainwater, her colour high. 'I know he isn't serious and I don't intend to let his compliments go to my head.'

A disbelieving snort answered her, but to Kate's relief Mary held her tongue.

This conversation was still at the forefront of Kate's mind when Lord Redesmere arrived to take her driving on Tuesday afternoon. Combined with a desire to make it clear to Alicia that she was only interested in a polite friendship and nothing more, it rendered her greeting to him as cool as the overcast weather.

Randal, who knew perfectly well what Lady Edgeworth was about, suspected that embarrassment lay at the root of this aloofness and did not allow her lack of enthusiasm to ruffle his temper.

'Are you warm enough? Would you like a rug for your knees?' he asked after handing her up into his curricle.

'No, I am quite all right, thank you.'

Randal gave his greys the office to start. 'It is fortunate, is it not, that the rain relented?'

'Indeed.'

Abandoning this unprofitable topic, Randal none the less continued to confine his conversation to similar innocuous small talk and was rewarded by a gradual relaxation of her stiff formality.

'I had thought to drive out to Broughton,' Randal remarked as they proceeded down Northgate Street. 'There are pretty views of the river and the countryside is pleasant. However, since the day is somewhat inclement, a shorter excursion seems preferable.'

He glanced at her stylish carriage-dress of fine French cambric. 'It would be a pity to risk spoiling such an elegant outfit.'

That deep amber colour was striking and he thought it suited her extremely well. She had, it seemed, the courage to rebel against the conventional pastels deemed suitable for girls of her age.

Now he came to think on it, she was surprisingly mature in other ways, too. Unlike most young fillies let loose on society she didn't giggle or hang her head shyly or simper in that arch manner he detested. Her poise and confidence equalled his elder sister Milly's and her conversation was a great deal more sensible.

Admittedly, she was slightly older than the average debutante, but he had a feeling her self-assurance owed its origins to a different explanation, to something in her past.

'Tell me,' he asked, apropos his musing. 'Do you miss working for your living?'

For one horrible moment his unexpected question turned Kate cold all over. Then, thankfully, she remembered she had told him that Kitty had worked with her mother in their bookshop. 'Sometimes, yes, I do,' she answered, her heart still thumping.

Deciding it might be dangerous to probe his motive for asking, she continued lightly, 'Of course, it is pleasant to have the leisure to enjoy myself, but I don't believe I should like to be a social butterfly forever. A constant round of parties must become boring in the end.'

Randal was intrigued. He had formed this same opinion years ago, but he had never heard a woman share it. 'What should you like to do instead?'

Kate gave him a quizzical look but, reading nothing but genuine interest in his expression, allowed herself the luxury of being completely honest. 'I should like to marry a man I could love and have his children.'

Randal smiled. 'Somehow I expected you to declare a more extraordinary ambition.'

Kate shook her head firmly, setting the feathers on her frivolous hat dancing. 'I have no desire for adventure, sir,' she said, hiding a wry amusement.

She could hardly confess that, having been a vagabond for seven years, the idea of a settled life in her own home seemed like heaven.

'You surprise me.' Randal's tone was so dry that Kate laughed and forgot her vow to stay aloof.

'Do you believe domesticity to be dull, my lord?' she teased him with a saucy look of challenge in her dark eyes.

'I imagine it depends on one's partner.'

Kate grinned. 'Is that why you have never wed?'

His shout of laughter caused heads to turn in their direction. 'You, cousin, are a minx!'

She dimpled at him innocently. 'Plain speaking is much favoured in America, sir.'

'Then to give you a plain answer, I am a bachelor because I have never found a woman I liked enough to want to marry.'

'What? No lost romance that has blighted your life? No dark secrets of the soul?'

'Not one,' he agreed mournfully. 'You must think me a very boring fellow.'

Kate thought nothing of the sort, but she didn't dare admit even to herself what her true feelings regarding Lord Redesmere might be.

Randal saw the shadow pass over her enchanting face and wondered at it as he was forced to break off the conversation and give his attention to the busy traffic.

Were her ambitions really so simple? With her looks she could aim high, but she had said nothing about wanting to marry a rich man. She appeared to value love above wealth.

Somehow, against all the odds, he found himself believing she meant it.

'Besides, I am sure that marriage need not mean one's brain must wither,' Kate announced thoughtfully, breaking her silence.

Randal cocked one eyebrow sceptically at her.

'I know many ladies do become immersed in their own domestic sphere, but surely marriage does not automatically preclude an interest in wider affairs,' Kate persisted. 'If my circumstances were affluent enough to allow me the leisure to cultivate pursuits outside the family, I do not believe I should forget my interest in music, architecture and the theatre.'

Kate had been hesitant whether to include this last. It seemed like tempting Fate, but, luckily, Randal did not question her taste in plays or actors, but asked instead how she came to be interested in architecture.

'America is a young country. There is always construction work going on. I enjoy watching how buildings take shape,' she replied, hastily adapting her own feelings to suit Kitty's experience.

'Then, in that case, I know where we should drive today,' Randal said. 'I shall show you Harrison's work at the Castle.'

In response to her look of enquiry, he explained that Thomas Harrison, one of England's greatest exponents of the Greek Revival style, had won a competition to rebuild the county hall and gaol at Chester Castle in 1785. 'He's been hard at it ever since and I dare say it will take several more years yet before he has finished, but it is a magnificent achievement.'

'I should like to view it.' Kate's eyes sparkled with enthusiasm. 'We don't have such a wide variety of architectural styles at home. Chester is quite fascinating. There are so many old houses here.'

She chuckled. 'Yesterday when I was out for a walk I saw a most curious house in the Rows. It was one of the old timbered sort and it had *God's Providence Is Mine Inheritance* carved into one of its front beams.'

'Ah, I know the house you mean,' Randal replied, without taking his eyes from his team as he negotiated a narrow space between another carriage and a stationary waggon full of barrels. 'There's a story to it.'

'Will you tell me?'

Bright interest animated her face and he thought she looked even lovelier than usual.

'As you can imagine, an old city like this one with its narrow airless streets and tightly packed dwellings has often been subject to terrible outbreaks of disease. Certain parts of the town are still unhealthily crowded, but in 1605 there was a particularly virulent attack of plague. Only one house was spared.'

'That one?'

'Aye. In gratitude, the owner had that legend carved into the front of his house.'

'A charming story, sir.' Kate smiled to herself. Maybe she should take it as a reminder to look on the bright side even when there seemed no grounds for hope.

'You mentioned that you were out walking yesterday,' Randal changed the subject as they neared the end of Bridge Street. 'Didn't Alicia object to the exercise?'

'Oh, I didn't go out with Lady Edgeworth.' Kate heard the amusement in his deep voice. 'She likes to stay at home by the fire when it is raining. Mary accompanied me.'

'I salute your fortitude.'

'You are gammoning me again!' Kate laughed. 'Actually, I might not have ventured forth had I not wanted to post a letter.'

'You need not have troubled. I would have franked it for you.'

'Thank you, I shall remember your kind offer next time,' Kate replied easily, although her pulse quivered at the thought of letting him see her correspondence to Ned. Hardly a suitable acquaintance for the respectable Miss Nixon!

They had reached Castle Street and the conversation lapsed while Randal manoeuvred the curricle through the confusion that surrounded the building works.

'Let's find a good view point. Ah, over there, I think,' he announced and once he had brought the carriage to a halt, Kate began to fire a stream of questions at him.

'What is that central block constructed of?'

'An ashlared Manley stone,' he replied, happy to satisfy her boundless curiosity.

'It is very handsome. And you say those wings contain a barracks and an armoury?' Kate stared at the workmen scurrying to and fro. 'What are they working on now?'

'The gateway. It was begun last year. I understand that Harrison intends it to be of the Doric order with two pedimented lodges. He said he was inspired by the Propylaea at Athens.'

Randal saw her eyes widen and grinned. 'Impressive, ain't it? But if you have seen enough, I think we should move on.'

'Oh, yes, of course. We shouldn't keep your horses standing too long,' Kate said quickly, hoping she hadn't chattered too much.

Randal announced that he would drive her home a different way. 'If we go via Nuns Lane, we shall avoid the congestion in Bridge Street and it is a prettier route,' he explained.

It was also a much longer way home, as Kate discovered.

'I hope this lengthier journey will not inconvenience you, sir,' she murmured, gazing out at the greenery of Nuns Gardens without really seeing it.

Could he have wanted to prolong their outing? Worried she had bored him back there at the Castle, she hardly dared hope her conjecture might be right.

'I wish it was twice as long.'

There was a note of sincerity in his deep voice which sent a ripple of excitement fluttering along Kate's nerves.

'Then you didn't mind answering all those questions?' she asked shyly. 'I thought you must be wishing me at Jericho.'

'Goose!' Randal shot her a quick smile. 'This outing has been more enjoyable than any I've undertaken in a long while.' He returned his gaze to the road, but his voice was full of warmth as he continued. 'You are very good company, cousin.'

Kate decided that he wasn't just being polite. He meant what he said. A feeling of happiness welled up in her. She had been apprehensive about being alone with him, but they hadn't exchanged a single cross word all afternoon. In fact, she'd experienced a harmony she had never known before with a man, not even with an old friend like Ned Gillman.

An inner voice warned her not to be harebrained. She had no business encouraging him to form any kind of friendship with her. Her deception, no matter how innocent, made close acquaintance dangerous.

Relaxing your guard might lead to the discovery that you are a fraud, she scolded herself silently. The consequences would be disastrous. Not only herself and Kitty would suffer. There was Alicia to consider and how would Randal feel to realise that he had given his trust to a liar?

Kate glanced across at him. It wasn't fair on either of them to let herself become involved. She liked him too much already.

A sensible woman would avoid his company. But how was she to be sensible when her self-control splintered as soon as he came near? For years she had wrapped her feelings in ice and now it seemed that Nature was having her revenge.

It was so hard to resist the appeal he held for her! It wasn't just his looks or his deliciously dry humour. On some deeper level, she had felt drawn to him from their very first meeting.

If she had been inclined to fanciful extravagance, she might have claimed that they were destined to be soul mates. As it was, she couldn't explain the phenomenon. All she was certain of was that it wasn't infatuation. She had suffered that kind of mindless obsession with Francis and her feelings for Randal were totally different.

The only similarity was Randal's physical effect on her. He had the power to awaken her senses, and the feeling of being alive again after so many barren years was intoxicating!

I can't seem to help myself, she thought. I want to control my emotions, but my will-power simply isn't strong enough.

Just then, becoming aware of her regard, Randal turned his head and their eyes locked.

Unable to tear her gaze away, Kate could feel the colour blooming in her cheeks and knew that her thoughts must be showing on her face. Desperately, she sought to protect herself by raising a polite mask, but her acting skills had deserted her.

Slowly, Randal reached out a hand towards her and gently touched one of the sable ringlets which curled upon her neck. 'Do you know how beautiful you are?' he asked softly, his deep voice unsteady.

Kate managed to force a trill of laughter. 'You are too kind, sir,' she replied lightly.

'I wish you would call me Randal,' he exclaimed impatiently, letting his hand fall away.

'I don't think that would be appropriate,' she murmured. Her attempt to defuse the moment had failed miserably. She might have known that he would guess she was trying to fend him off!

'Why not? I stopped calling you ma'am days ago.'

Acknowledging this hit, Kate reluctantly agreed to his request. 'But I would rather you didn't call me Kitty,' she added sharply.

It was irrational, but she didn't want him to call her by another woman's name. It was bad enough to have to deceive him about everything else. At least let her have one tiny crumb of honesty to assuage her guilt!

Randal's tawny brows drew together in a frown and she realised her demand had sounded unwittingly churlish.

'It is a name I no longer like,' she blurted in swift explanation. 'I think it sounds childish. Unfortunately, it is difficult to shake off old family nicknames.'

'What would you prefer me to call you?' Randal's frown eased.

'Katharine.' It was her real name, but no one used it nowadays. Francis had christened her Kate and the company had followed his lead. 'I should like you to call me Katharine.'

There was a note of passionate sincerity in her rich contralto voice which startled Randal. For an instant he wondered if he had inadvertently stumbled upon a clue to her real identity before he swiftly crushed suspicion into oblivion.

'If that is your wish, then I am happy to comply... Katharine.'

His reward was a smile so dazzling that, thinking of nothing but his need to kiss her, he allowed his hands to drop preparatory to drawing her into his embrace.

Instantly his greys shot forward and he bit off a curse as he steadied them.

Opening his mouth to apologise for this alarm, he spotted a

glint of amusement in her dark velvet eyes. Good God, he was behaving like a veritable schoolboy! 'You must think my approach lacks finesse,' he murmured with a rueful chuckle. 'I ought to know better than to attempt to make love to a lady while in charge of a curricle!'

Kate caught her breath. 'Am I to assume that you want to kiss me, my lord?' she asked, recovering. The urge to flirt with him was irresistible.

The laughter died in his bright eyes and was replaced by an altogether different emotion. 'I don't think there is any doubt about that.'

Kate shivered deliciously as she watched him set the carriage in motion again.

'Does this mean that my virtue is safe for the moment?' she teased wickedly as they bowled away.

Randal nodded. 'For the moment, sweet Katharine.' His gaze flicked across to meet hers and there was a steely determination in his smile. 'But I will make you no promises for the future.'

The rest of the week flew by on swift wings. Lady Edgeworth's determination to introduce her protégée to her friends kept Kate so busy she scarcely had time to draw breath. Everywhere she went she was fêted and, although she told herself that the Nixon fortune was responsible for this flattering reception, she was human enough to enjoy all the attention.

Her only disappointment was a failure to encounter Lord Redesmere at any of these functions. Telling herself it didn't matter was no use. She missed him and could hardly wait for Friday, the day of Lady Massey's rout, which he had promised to attend.

'It is to be quite a grand affair,' Alicia informed her as they partook of a dish of tea on their return from a shopping expedition to buy an ell of gold embroidered ribbon, with which Kate intended to dress her hair that evening. 'Some two hundred guests have been invited and you may be sure that Lord Massey will serve only the best champagne.'

A pleasurable shudder shook her ample frame as she contemplated the astronomical costs of holding such a large party. 'I dare say it will be a shocking squeeze, but you will enjoy it, especially if Eliza Massey throws open her garden again. Last year it was turned into a positive fairyland with hundreds of coloured lanterns and she invited anyone who wanted to do so to enjoy a refreshing stroll after supper.'

A little chuckle escaped Lady Edgeworth. 'A few high sticklers thought it a shocking idea, but it was a great success, particularly with you young ones.'

'It sounds delightful, ma'am,' Kate murmured, trying to ignore the wicked voice in her head which whispered that a moonlit garden would make a perfect setting for Randal to fulfil his vow and kiss her.

'Indeed it was.' Alicia smiled reminiscently for a moment and then added briskly, 'Tonight, of course, any repetition will depend on the rain keeping off.'

The weather had been as unsettled as Kate's heart, with sunshine one minute, showers the next; her rioting emotions caused her spirits to see-saw giddily as she struggled to knock some sense into her reluctant head. Knowing she ought to behave sensibly, she had even tried to persuade Alicia that she did not want to go to the rout, but Alicia had been horrified at her refusal and Kate had hastily relented.

She was still in two minds about whether she could claim to have developed a last-minute headache when she went upstairs to dress for the evening.

Mary was waiting for her. A hip-bath filled with hot water steamed before a newly lit fire and her clothes had been laid out in readiness on the bed.

Taking one look at the ivory spider-gauze which Alicia had insisted on buying for her, Kate came to a sudden halt. 'I don't think I can go through with this,' she announced shakily.

Mary stared at her in surprise. 'Why ever not? You had no trouble handling that drum last week. I know there will be a lot more people there tonight, but you've no reason to think anyone will doubt you.'

'It's not my ability to carry off my role that is bothering me,' Kate confessed, sinking into the velvet-upholstered elbow chair by the window.

'It's Crawford, isn't it?' Mary shook her greying head. 'I thought you had more sense, lass.'

Kate shrugged wearily. 'I don't think I've got any sense at all where he is concerned, which is why I ought to try and keep away from him.'

'Aye, you should, but you can't cry off from this party,' Mary said emphatically. 'You can't afford to. If you do, you'll offend Lady Edgeworth.'

'She will forgive me if I apologise hard enough.'

'It ain't like you to be cynical, Kate.' Mary frowned and then relented as she saw the look of misery on her young friend's face. 'He's a very attractive man,' she sympathised, 'but he ain't for you. Keep on like this and you're bound to get hurt.'

Kate's hands clenched together convulsively in her lap. 'I know,' she said bleakly.

Sensing that further sympathy might provoke a storm of tears, Mary changed tack. 'Anyhow, it ain't just her ladyship you've got to worry about,' she said firmly. 'We don't need to set tongues wagging about the pair of you.'

Kate shuddered. 'Please, you've said enough. I swear I will try harder to ignore him, but don't ask me to go out and playact tonight, Mary. I don't think I've got the strength.'

'Damn it, Kate, the whole town must know you are promised to the Masseys after the way her ladyship has been puffing you off.' Mary balled her fists on her hips and stared at her friend, shock evident in every curve of her sturdy body.

If she hadn't heard it from her own lips, she would never have believed that Kate Devlin would run from a challenge. Why, the lass had dealt with every blow that Fate had dealt over these last seven years with the courage of a lioness! It must be the fault of that blasted man! His effect on Kate was greater than she had realised. He had made her want to be a lady again, to belong to the world she had lost, but all the time the poor girl knew her fantasy could only be temporary. The conflict within her was ruining her usual confidence and ability to concentrate on her work.

Anger at her own blindness in failing to spot what was happening made Mary's voice sharp. 'You can't skulk at home. You've got to show your face or they'll wonder at your absence. You owe it to Kitty.'

'I wish I'd never laid eyes on the wretched girl!' Kate shouted, perilously close to losing her temper.

'It's a bit late for that,' Mary retorted laconically.

Kate glared at her and then slowly a faint smile appeared to curl up the corners of her generous mouth. 'I suppose so.'

Realising that they both needed a moment to calm down, Mary moved away and began to needlessly rearrange the towels she had put out earlier.

Kate remained as she was, staring blankly into the fire. At length, Mary turned back to her.

'Come on, lass,' she encouraged softly. 'Never say die.'

Kate's hands clenched together so tightly that her knuckles showed white. 'I don't know if I'm up to it any more, Mary,' she whispered. 'I didn't expect to have to play the role for more than a few days. And now...well, now it's even more complicated.'

Her voice trailed away, but Mary understood. She, too, had felt the strain of sustaining her own part in this charade. It must be a hundred times worse for Kate. And the poor lass hadn't bargained on Randal Crawford messing up her concentration. No wonder she was having second thoughts!

'I know you're scared, but you can do it if you try,' she said gently. 'You're a bloody good actress and, besides, what other choice have you got, eh? We've both got to carry on as normal or give the game up. There's no road betwixt.'

'All right, all right.' Kate threw up her palms in weary surrender. 'I'll go to the Masseys'.'

She had been through the same arguments in her own mind and she knew that it was essential she behave in the manner society expected of Kitty, who had no reason to be afraid.

Rising to her feet, Kate began to remove her clothes.

'Maybe there is a way to solve the problem,' Mary suggested hopefully as she got into the bath. 'You must convince him you are indifferent to him. Crawford is a proud man and I reckon his pride will make him leave you alone if you pretend you don't find him attractive any more.'

Kate threw her a look of despair. 'I'm not that good an actress, dear friend!' she muttered and, reaching for the cake of rose-scented soap, scrubbed at her skin as if her life depended on it.

Chapter Six

One cause for satisfaction was granted to Kate later that evening. When she entered the Masseys' drawing-room on Tom Egerton's arm, heads swivelled in their direction as if pulled round on a puppeteer's strings.

'Said you'd be the belle of the ball,' Tom declared smugly.

He had encountered Lady Edgeworth's party as they had been making their way into the house and had begged the favour of being allowed to join them. Sir Richard Fitton, an elderly admirer of Alicia's, was their escort tonight, but Lady Edgeworth cheerfully consented to Tom's request.

Kate scarcely heard Tom's comment. Randal was already here and he was coming towards them!

She was tempted to whirl around and pretend she hadn't seen him but, taking a deep breath, she stood her ground.

'Good evening, Katharine.'

Kate's pulse bumped unevenly. How lovely her name sounded when spoken in those deep velvety tones!

'Evening, Redesmere.' Tom's hand tightened possessively on Kate's.

Randal acknowledged him with a brief nod, his gaze returning instantly to Kate.

Putting aside the impulse to snatch her hand away from

Tom's grip, Kate summoned a bright smile. 'Hello, Randal. Are you enjoying the party? We've only just arrived.'

'I know.' Randal continued to smile, but a flicker of irritation tensed his broad shoulders. Why the devil didn't she send that young puppy to the right-about instead of letting him paw her arm?

'Tom met us on the way in,' Kate said in the same frivolous tone. 'Particularly fortunate, don't you think, seeing as he is my partner for the first dance.' She patted Tom's arm with her free hand and gave a tinkling little laugh. 'It might have taken him an age to find me in this crush.' She fluttered her gold-spangled fan. 'I swear I never saw so many people all together in my life!'

Randal's brows lifted in surprise. For the first time in their acquaintance she was behaving like one of the empty-headed young women he found so boring.

'If you'll excuse us, Redesmere,' Tom broke in portentously. 'I think we ought to make our way to the ballroom, Miss Nixon.'

'Oh, yes, of course.' Kate forced a note of careless gaiety in her tone. 'I shall see you later, Randal.'

She allowed Tom to lead her away, firmly resisting the temptation to look back.

Randal stared after her, a frown creasing his brow.

Was he imagining it or had her manner towards him cooled?

Randal's suspicion grew as the evening progressed. Far from seeming pleased to see him, his elusive heiress fluttered out of reach whenever he tried to get near.

By the time the country-dance she had promised him arrived, Randal's patience was wearing thin.

'Have I offended you?' he demanded abruptly as they walked on to the gleaming floor of the Massey's resplendent gold and white ballroom.

Kate opened her eyes wide and denied it, but her heart was hammering.

Experience had taught Lord Redesmere not to pursue any

subject worthy of serious discussion on a dance floor. However, the moment the music ceased and they were embarked upon their journey to find her chaperon, he renewed his attack.

'Is something wrong, Katharine? Have I upset you in some way?'

'No!' Kate shook her head so hard that the glittering golden ribbons entwined in her high-dressed curls trembled.

'I wish you would tell me the truth,' he replied in a low voice.

Kate's footsteps faltered. How she longed to do so!

'You are imagining things, my lord.'

Rebuffed, Randal gazed at her, feeling half-perplexed, half-irritated by her denials.

In that delicate, fairy-tale gown she was as lovely as a dream and Randal felt something stir in his heart beyond mere desire.

He had told her the truth when he had confessed he had never liked any girl enough to think of marriage. He knew that his unknown bride must possess qualities beyond a pretty face and charming ways. Such attributes would soon pall, but exactly what it was he was looking for in his life's companion he didn't know.

Then, a few days ago during their drive out to the Castle, his blithe conviction that he was destined to remain a bachelor like his Uncle Godwin had undergone a severe disturbance. Telling himself that he was too old to be caught by a pair of laughing eyes, he had none the less been unable to shake off a feeling that he might have met the right woman at last.

The whole idea was absurd, of course. He didn't know a thing about her life before she had turned up here claiming to be his long-lost cousin. She could be anybody! Her manners were those of a lady, but that was no guarantee of good blood. He didn't give a fig about seeking out a rich wife and he was more interested in a woman's character than her pedigree, but he owed it to his father not to bring disgrace upon their name.

None of these sensible reflections had succeeded in banishing Katharine's image from his mind and he had hurried here

tonight, arriving early for once, full of an excitement he
couldn't suppress. But the girl he had longed to see had vanished into thin air. Instead, he was faced with a stranger. There
was no spark of animation in her midnight eyes, no hint of
wicked amusement in her alluring voice.

'No doubt you are right. My imagination is to blame.'

Kate detected a faint note of bitterness in his reply and cast
him a worried look before she could stop herself.

It was a difficult tightrope she was attempting to walk. She
wanted to prevent their relationship from developing, but she
couldn't afford to alienate him and lose his support.

'Don't look so alarmed. I have no intention of forcing a
quarrel on you.' Aware of numerous eyes watching them, Randal decided a strategic retreat was in order.

His cool reply made Kate's heart sink like a stone.

Idiot! This is what you wanted, she scolded herself silently.
Remember, you are Kitty, his little cousin! It was a mistake to
give free rein to your own feelings and be yourself the other
day.

Even leaving aside the business of her impersonation, Kate
knew the situation was hopeless. The gulf between an impe-
cunious widowed actress and a peer of the realm was too vast
to be breached. She had no right to dream!

They found Alicia in one of the salons.

'Ah, Kitty, there you are. Young Tom Egerton has been
tormenting me the last ten minutes past!' A flick of her ivory
fan indicated that young man, hovering a few yards away. 'You
are promised to him for the next dance, he tells me.'

Kate nodded, but offered to forgo the pleasure if Alicia required her company.

'Lud, child, you don't want to sit out one single dance at
your age!' Alicia chuckled at the very idea. 'Besides, my love,
Godwin has asked me to partner him in a game of whist.'

She signalled to Tom, who came bounding forward.

Kate forced a warmly welcoming smile to her lips and took
a few steps forward to meet him.

Jealousy raised its ugly head for an instant in Randal. He crushed it quickly. 'Pray excuse me, Lady Alicia. I am engaged to partner Miss Legh for the next dance,' he remarked stiffly.

'Of course, but don't forget you are promised to us later,' Alicia reminded him with a roguish smile as he bowed farewell.

'I shall look forward to it, ma'am.'

He nodded curtly to Kate and Tom and moved away, but not before Kate had caught the glint of annoyance burning in his blue eyes.

No one observing Miss Nixon as she danced indefatigably until the supper interval would have guessed how little she was relishing her evening.

'You are looking quite pale, my dear,' Alicia announced as Kate rejoined them. 'Don't you think so, Richard?'

Sir Richard, a notoriously shy man, murmured an evasive reply.

Alicia persisted. 'Are you feeling tired, Kitty? We can go home if you have the headache.'

Kate denied it and declared her enthusiasm for the party, but Lord Redesmere also noted that she seemed subdued when he entered the long salon where supper was being served.

There was a place reserved for him next to hers and he slipped into it.

'We meet again at last, fair Katharine,' Randal said with deliberate cheerfulness. 'How are you enjoying the evening?'

Kate managed a convincing smile. 'Very well, everyone is so kind!'

A footman appeared at her elbow and poured wine for her. Kate took a large sip, hoping for Dutch courage.

'Have you ventured into the yellow drawing-room yet?' Randal enquired. 'There is a very fine Canaletto above the mantelpiece, a view of the Doge's Palace in Venice.'

She had told him that she admired Italian art, but to Randal's amazement she merely gazed at him in a bored fashion and murmured that, no, she hadn't seen it and would he be so good as to pass her that dish of green peas. 'I do so adore them when they are fresh and tender.'

Nonplussed, Randal addressed himself to his own wineglass.

Supper progressed and Kate skilfully deflected his lordship's further attempts to draw her into meaningful conversation. The moment he attempted a remark which strayed beyond the bounds of trivial politeness she withdrew, treating him to a display of monosyllabic insipidity.

His tawny brows had tugged together in a frown by the time Lady Massey's well-trained servants brought in the last of the refreshments and Kate felt sick. As a rule, after all that dancing, she would have had a good appetite and enjoyed her supper, but tonight even the almond cheesecake, a particular favourite of hers, tasted like dust in her mouth.

Randal was struggling to contain his rising temper. Why the devil wouldn't she talk to him! Even when he tried to pay her a compliment she quickly changed the subject, making it very clear she had no desire to flirt. She had denied she was annoyed with him, but he couldn't think of any other reason for her abrupt *volte-face*.

After supper ended he asked her if she would stand up with him again.

'I'm afraid I cannot. My card is full,' she murmured.

'In that case, may I escort you for a short turn about the garden before the dancing resumes? It is a warm evening and Lady Massey has had the grounds prepared.' A persuasive note entered his deep voice. 'I think you would enjoy it.'

Kate shook her dark head. There was nothing she wanted more, but she knew she had to resist the temptation. She didn't trust herself to keep up her pretence of indifference alone with him in the moonlight. 'I'm sure it is a very pretty garden, but I think I shall wait for an opportunity to view it in daylight.'

'Katharine, I want to—' Randal bit off what he had been about to say and cursed in silence as a very foppishly dressed dark-haired young man came up to them, hesitant admiration written all over his thin face.

'Pray don't apologise, Mr Hewitt,' Kate said gaily in reply to his murmur that he was sorry for interrupting them. 'We weren't discussing anything important, were we, Randal?'

Good manners forced Randal to agree.

Jack Hewitt glanced at the taller man uneasily. For some reason he couldn't quite name, he felt sure that Lord Redesmere could cheerfully strangle him!

'I know our dance isn't due to start for some time yet, Miss Nixon, but would you do me the honour of coming to meet my sister?' Nervousness shook Jack's voice, reminding his listeners that he was still several months short of his majority. 'She's just over there.' He turned to indicate a plump brunette in a white dress on the other side of the room.

'I shall be happy to make her acquaintance,' Kate agreed with a glowing smile. 'Excuse me, Randal.' Dismissing him with a cavalier haste, she allowed her youthful admirer to whisk her away.

Randal stared after her retreating figure, anger overcoming his puzzlement.

Perhaps he had been wrong to think she was attracted to him. She could have been pretending to like him merely because she needed his blessing. Now that he had given her his word not to express his doubts to Alicia and they had been seen together several times in public she might have decided her position was secure enough to dispense with his sponsorship.

Was she just a calculating little cheat using her lovely body to blind him?

Doubt flickered through Randal. He could have sworn her reaction to his touch mirrored his own!

Reluctantly he acknowledged that he didn't want to believe ill of her. Stupid, no doubt, but he had grown to like her. Whether or not she was his cousin, she had humour and a lively intelligence which he found deeply attractive.

His pride rebelling at the thought that she might have been using him for her own ends, Randal frowned grimly.

Damn the wench! She had the power to unsettle him in a way no other female could.

He stared at her across the room. She was talking to Sophy Hewitt with all her usual animation, her face alight with laughter. Even at this distance he could see her eyes sparkling and the soft rise and fall of her lovely breasts.

Desire tightened his loins and the hunter in him awoke.

By all that was holy, he was going to discover what her true feelings for him were!

Too experienced a hunter to pursue his quarry too closely, Randal resisted the temptation to attend St Peter's on Sunday. He directed his energy instead into formulating a plan which would allow him to fathom the intricacies of Miss Nixon's mind and Monday morning found him back in Chester.

'Great Jupiter, boy, this is an unconscionable hour to be a-calling!' Mr Godwin Crawford favoured his nephew with a jaundiced look as Randal was shown into the breakfast-parlour.

Although it was almost noon, Mr Crawford was still seated at the table clad in his banjan, a loose silk dressing-gown of such startling hue it made Randal blink.

He surveyed the remains of an ample meal still littering the table. 'Haven't interrupted your breakfast, have I?' he enquired solicitously.

'Hah! Much you'd care if you had, you undutiful rogue!' Godwin grinned back at him. 'As a matter of fact, I've finished.' He picked up a sheaf of letters from the crumb-strewn surface and waved them. 'I was just about to read my post.'

'Shouldn't bother if I was you. Probably all bills.' Randal's eyes twinkled.

'Impudent dog!' Godwin frowned at him severely and then spoilt the effect by adding gloomily that he was bound to be right. 'Never see anything other than damned bills these days.'

'Are the dibs out of tune, O revered uncle?'

'Just a trifle, dear boy.'

'If you need a loan—'

'Nay, it's not as bad as all that!' Godwin exclaimed. 'Besides, I don't hold with sponging off my relatives.' He shot his nephew an artful look. 'Dare say you wish Milly felt the same. Her three brats must have cost you a pretty penny since Robert was injured and lost his ship.'

Randal shrugged. It was no secret that his elder sister, who had married a naval officer of sadly improvident habits, had generous access to his purse. 'Harold is my heir,' he pointed out.

'That poisonous little toad should have been strangled at birth,' Mr Crawford stated bluntly, his mouth curling in distaste. 'Time you wed and got yourself a son of your own.'

Randal put up his brows. 'That's rich coming from you, a confirmed bachelor if ever there was one.'

'Ah, but I wasn't the eldest son,' Godwin retorted. 'You are head of the family, m'boy. It's high time you settled down and provided for the succession.'

'Do you know, you are beginning to sound just like Milly.' Randal threw down his hat and gloves on to a side-table, his expression irritated.

It was something of a sore subject. Even his younger sister, Emma, had read him the same sermon before departing for Wales last month. The fact that she was joyously embarking upon her honeymoon and had meant the advice most kindly had tempered his desire to tell her to go to the Devil.

Heeding the note of boredom in his visitor's tone, Godwin abandoned his lecture. 'Well, I dare say you didn't come here to talk about marriage. Here, stuff these into that drawer for me—' he thrust the pile of letters at his nephew and indicated the mahogany sideboard '—and sit yourself down.'

Randal obeyed and, thrusting his chair back from the table, Godwin crossed his legs and made himself more comfortable.

'What brings you here?' he asked genially.

'I've come to ask a favour.'

Mr Crawford eyed his nephew suspiciously. 'That's a new one. Boot is usually on someone else's leg.'

In spite of his acerbic response just now, Randal took his position as head of the Crawford family seriously. Why, even as a young lad he'd possessed a strong sense of responsibility and duty. Too strong in some ways for his own good. Otherwise he would have ignored Cedric's foolish demands to give up his career in the army.

Godwin pursed his lips. His late brother had been an odd fellow! Surly and tight-lipped, a more imperious man he had never met. It had sometimes crossed his mind to wonder if his sister-in-law had played Cedric false for he could see no trace of his brother in Randal. Not that Harriet would have played such a low trick. She'd been a sweet little thing, so perhaps Randal inherited his good nature from her.

Gladly dismissing his stiff-rumped brother from his mind, Godwin said, 'Well, spit it out, lad. What do you want?'

'I want to become your lodger.'

Randal grinned at the look of amazement on his uncle's face. 'Just for a week or two, I hasten to add.'

'But damme, why? Are you planning on refurbishing the Hall? I thought you had the workmen in last year.'

'I did,' Randal concurred. 'Everything is in order, which is just as well since I promised Emma I would host a ball for her and Matthew when they get back from Wales. It might be some considerable time before we see them again and they deserve a good send-off.'

Godwin nodded approval. His favourite niece had married a young lieutenant in Lord Wellington's army and was going back to Spain with him when his current leave was up. 'A splendid idea, but it doesn't explain your request.'

'Don't you fancy my company, Godwin?'

Mr Crawford guffawed. 'Bone-head! You know you are welcome any time. But I still don't see—' He paused abruptly. 'This ain't got anything to do with that delicious creature Alicia has got staying with her, has it?'

Randal smiled. His uncle liked to give the impression of being a genial old buffer, but his wits were shrewd. 'Exactly so, O revered uncle.'

'Admire your taste, my boy. I suppose you want to see more of her?'

'Much more.' Randal's mouth twisted in wry amusement. 'In fact, I'm thinking of offering her a *carte-blanche*.'

'What?' Godwin gaped at him open-mouthed. Feeling in need of sustenance, he made a long arm to reach the bottle of claret which stood at the near end of the sideboard and, locating two clean glasses, poured a generous measure of wine into each. 'Here, have a drop of this and stop trying to bamboozle me, for God's sake.'

Randal took a swallow of the wine. 'This is excellent. Where did you get it?'

'From Williamson's. I'll let you have a dozen bottles if you like,' Godwin, who prided himself upon his palate, was distracted for a moment. Then, recovering himself, he fixed his nephew with a stern look. 'But never mind that now. You cannot offer such an insult to the chit. She ain't one of your Paphians, she's a respectable girl!'

'Is she?'

Godwin glowered at him. 'Damme, you may look sober, my boy, but you must be as drunk as a wheelbarrow! Of course she is, she's Charles Nixon's daughter and your cousin to boot!'

'I have my doubts about that, too.'

Nonplussed, Godwin could only stare at him and, taking a deep breath, Randal began to explain.

'Not a word of this to anyone, mind,' he concluded. 'I gave my word that I would not discuss the matter outside the family.'

Godwin poured himself another glass of wine and drained it. Then, recovering his usual rather florid colour, he let out a low whistle. 'Jupiter, there's going to be a dust-up if the tabbies get wind of Gerald's rantings.'

'I'll deal with Sullivan,' Randal replied. 'No matter the outcome, I'll see to it that he doesn't create a scandal.'

Looking at the grim set to his nephew's mouth, Godwin was quite sure Gerald would indeed favour discretion. 'Aye, but what if this wench does turn out to be an imposter? What are you going to do then?'

'My first duty must be to find out what has happened to the real Kitty.'

'Do you think this chit might know something?'

Randal nodded. 'It seems likely. If she is a cheat, she must have had contact with Kitty at some time in order to obtain that letter and the locket.'

'Aye.' Godwin chewed his lower lip reflectively. 'Do you think there's foul play involved?'

'Not on Katharine's part, I'm sure of it.' The quick denial sprang instinctively to Randal's lips. Recovering himself, he added more mildly, 'However, I wouldn't care to vouch for Sullivan.'

Godwin eyed him thoughtfully. His nephew was a good judge of character as a rule, but he had admitted to a fancy for the wench.

'I know what you are thinking,' Randal said ruefully. 'The same doubts have crossed my own mind.' He shrugged. 'I'll own I'm finding impartiality difficult. She's too damned beautiful!'

'A gorgeous creature,' Godwin agreed. 'Hard to imagine her a villainess.'

Randal's brow creased in a frown. 'Maybe my instincts are wrong and she really is my long-lost cousin. At the moment, all I can do is try to keep an open mind. On all points.'

Godwin poured more wine for them both, his expression ruminative. 'You can tell me to go hang if you wish,' he said after a long moment of silence, 'but it seems a damned fool idea to get romantically involved with the chit. At least until you know how the land lies.'

'You are perfectly correct, uncle.' Randal's deep voice was

as smooth as cream. 'Unfortunately, I'm afraid your advice is too late.'

'Here, you ain't fancying yourself in love, are you?' Godwin demanded in alarm.

'Nothing is further from my thoughts.' Randal shook his head.

A thin smile twisted his fine lips. 'However, I do think she deserves to be taught a lesson.'

Godwin cocked an enquiring eyebrow. 'What sort of lesson?' he asked a touch uneasily.

He had never seen such a sour expression on his nephew's face before. As a rule the lad took his *amours* lightly, but this wench had managed to get under his skin. Somehow or other, she had hurt him and, unless his instinct was very much at fault, Randal intended to have revenge!

'Humility,' Randal replied softly.

Godwin choked on his wine.

'Whoever she is, she is mistaken if she thinks she can abuse my trust to further her own ends,' Randal continued in the same steely tone. 'I dislike being played for a fool.'

There was a wicked glint in his brilliant blue eyes. 'What's sauce for the goose, eh, O revered uncle? By fair means or foul, I intend to fix my interest with our mysterious heiress and then we shall see who has the last laugh!'

The days following the Masseys' rout seemed the longest Kate had ever known. Thanks to Alicia's social ambitions, she was kept busy, but each event she attended struck her as more tedious than the last. Even a concert of music at the Royal Hotel failed to engage her interest.

'I wish Sullivan would answer Mr Hilton's letter!' she complained to Mary as she changed her plain morning-gown ready to accompany Lady Edgeworth on an outing to the Groves, a fashionable promenade spot near the river. 'I hate all this waiting. It is driving me insane!'

Mary unfolded the Paisley shawl Kate was to wear—it was

a warm sunny afternoon—and smoothed out its creases as she debated a reply.

She knew what was really bothering Kate. The lass had a sore conscience. Thankfully, the ploy of treating Redesmere badly seemed to have worked—he hadn't been near all week. Kate hadn't uttered a word of regret and yet, if Mary was any judge, she was missing him something shocking.

But it would do no good to say so!

'Happen you'll feel better when we hear from Ned,' Mary murmured soothingly. 'It's been ten days since we posted that letter.'

Kate sighed. 'He is probably cursing me. The company can't afford to lose us both.' She hesitated. 'Perhaps you ought to go back.'

'Nay, I'll not leave you.' Mary gave her a wry grin. 'We're in this together, lass. Sink or swim!'

Kate smiled back. Dear Mary, what would she do without her unfailing support!

'There. You'll do.' Mary gave the shawl one last tweak into position and stepped back to view her handiwork. By God, but the lass repaid proper dressing! In that eau-de-nil jaconet she looked as fine as a queen. No one would ever dream she was other than a lady.

'You know, it's a crying shame you can't accept an offer from Mr Egerton.'

Kate winced, her face twisting into an involuntary grimace.

'Sorry! I spoke without thinking,' Mary apologised. 'Go on. Be off with you and try not to fret.'

Kate thought about Tom as she descended to the hallway. He had paid a morning call yesterday and had secured Alicia's permission to speak to her in private. Guessing he meant to propose, Kate had managed to head him off. Skilfully implying she had a sweetheart back home in America, she hinted that any serious attentions were unwelcome.

To do him justice, she didn't think Tom was a fortune-hunter. He was a nice boy who had simply tumbled into love with the unreal image he had formed of her in his own mind. She had seen the same symptoms before in the young men who flocked into the green-room to pay shy homage to Mrs Devlin after a performance. Unless she had read him completely amiss, Tom's feelings ran no deeper than theirs and his infatuation would fade soon enough once she left Chester.

There was no need to wound his pride with a sharp rejection.

Kate shuddered. She didn't think she would ever be able to forget the look of amazed disbelief in Randal's eyes when she had spurned his company at the Masseys' rout. Her act as a silly selfish flirt was one of the hardest roles she had ever played. He had swiftly veiled his feelings, but she knew she had hurt him.

The ache of it still echoed in her own heart.

Preoccupied with her thoughts, Kate rounded the final bend of the stairs. For an instant her brain refused to recognise the tall figure standing in the hall and then she had to clutch at the polished bannister to support herself as her knees almost gave way with shock.

'What…what are you doing here?' she gasped.

'Waiting to escort you to the Groves.' Lord Redesmere gave her a calm smile. 'Alicia is feeling indisposed.'

'But I thought—' Kate bit off what she had been about to say and substituted an excuse. 'I…I don't think I should go out if she is feeling unwell.'

'A slight headache only. She specifically charged me with the task of ensuring that you did not sacrifice this lovely afternoon out of a mistaken sense of duty.'

Randal walked to the bottom of the stairs. 'You are free to leave, Katharine. Let's not waste any more time.'

Kate hesitated, fighting the incredulous joy which battered her resolve to stand firm and refuse.

'Come,' he said firmly, holding out his arm to her and Kate found herself meekly obeying.

On their way out to the carriage Kate allowed her starved senses to drink in his immaculate appearance. He was wearing a dark green coat she hadn't seen before and a very smart waistcoat in pale lemon. She wondered if he had been out in the sun; his wheat-blond hair had acquired lighter streaks and his face was bronzed.

He looked even more handsome than her memory had painted him and Kate's heart twisted within her. She knew she was a fool, but she didn't want him to think badly of her!

'Tell me when you are ready,' Randal said, patiently steadying his pair while she unfurled her silk parasol to protect her complexion against the hot sun.

His thoughtfulness aroused a flicker of hope in Kate. Why was he being so nice to her? Indeed, why did he want to take her out driving at all? Was it possible he had forgiven her coldness?

'I'm sorry I have not been to call on you,' Randal said easily as they set off. 'I've been lending a hand with haymaking.'

'That explains your colour,' Kate exclaimed unthinkingly.

Randal brushed off her hasty apology. 'You should have seen me when I came home from Egypt,' he joked. 'I was as brown as a cobnut.'

Kate's spirits bubbled upwards. Impossible as it seemed, he *was* extending an olive branch to her! Ignoring the warning voice of caution which screamed that nothing in their circumstances had changed, she smiled back at him, the last remnants of her constraint dissolving in a rush of happiness.

'I do believe you are gammoning me again,' she declared, instinctively abandoning her role as Kitty and slipping back into her own skin. 'Why on earth should you wish to travel to Egypt of all places? No one goes there.'

Hearing her quicksilver laughter, Randal experienced a surge of exultation that had nothing to do with the success of his scheme.

He had set out today determined to force her to accompany him. He hadn't given her a chance to refuse his company and he wouldn't have been surprised if she had reacted angrily. However, instead of resenting his high-handedness, she was treating him with all her old camaraderie. Had she regretted her abominable behaviour?

Ignoring the tiny voice which whispered in his mind that she might just be as pleased to see him as he had been to see her, he continued in the same bantering tone, 'You may laugh, Miss Nixon, but I swear to you that I enjoyed my time there more than most countries I've visited, in spite of a French hussar who had an ambition to separate my head from my neck and came close to succeeding.'

'You were there to fight Napoleon?' Kate suddenly remembered he had been in the army.

He nodded, his gaze flicking away to survey the road. 'My regiment was ordered to Egypt with Abercromby.'

The Egyptian campaign had taken place some ten years ago. Kate wasn't sure how much Kitty might have heard of it, but she could recall how *The Cumberland Pacquet* and the other news-sheets her father subscribed to had been full of stories about Sir Ralph Abercromby's brave heroism and his successful attempt against all the odds to prevent Napoleon from adding Egypt to his conquests.

'The General was killed at the Battle of Aboukir, was he not?' she said cautiously, reckoning that Kitty might know this simple fact at least.

'He died of his wounds. A very brave and able man.' Randal's expression was sombre as he recalled the fierce fighting that had taken place in that hot dry land. The casualties had been heavy. They had been badly outnumbered and had lacked siege guns, but the men had been determined to do their duty and show the world that the French were not invincible.

'Under his successor, General Hely-Hutchinson, we took Cairo,' Randal continued. 'That was at the end of June, but the French garrison in Alexandria managed to cling on until October. They were only saved by the signing of the Peace Treaty.'

A frown suddenly marred his features and Kate understood why. Her own father, although weary of war and like everyone else in the country longing for it to end, had fulminated against the government for throwing away the fruits of recent victory in their haste to appease Napoleon's threat of invasion. The Peace of Amiens had proved a false dawn and given the French eighteen months to re-arm before the fighting had begun all over again.

Randal shrugged, his grim expression lightening. 'Napoleon may have pulled off his bluff and frightened Addington and Hawkesbury witless, but, by God, Lord Hutchinson was made of sterner stuff! He absolutely refused to let the French keep any of the valuables they had looted during their stay in Egypt. He appointed Sir Tomkyns Hilgrove Turner to organise the transfer of everything except small personal items into our keeping. Knowing I was interested in antiquities, Turner requested my assistance.'

A grin split Randal's tanned face. 'I must confess that I had a wonderful time! The French tried every kind of trick to hide things from us. Old Menou was furious when we discovered where he had hidden the Rosetta Stone and snatched it back.'

Kate blinked at him, struggling to absorb this unexpected information. She hadn't known he had scholarly interests. Kitty had never mentioned anything of the sort!

'I remember hearing something about the Rosetta Stone,' she murmured. 'Papa was interested in the discoveries Napoleon's scholars made. Some French soldiers found it, didn't they?'

'Aye, in the ruins of Fort St Julien, which stands on the mouth of the Nile near the town of Rosetta. It was a slab of black basalt, a damned—I mean dashed—heavy lump of a thing carved with three parallel inscriptions.' Randal chuckled. 'We had to take a detachment of artillerymen and a devil-cart to carry it off back to Turner's house. Mind you, he had the decency to allow French scholars to make a cast before it was packed up to be sent home.'

Kate inclined her head to one side in thought. 'But why was it so important?' she asked. 'I recall that scholars were very excited at its discovery, but I never really understood why.'

Randal glanced across at her. Her lovely face had taken on the glow of animation he remembered from the day they had visited the Castle.

'It is important because one of the three inscriptions it bore was in Greek. It translates as a decree praising the King Ptolemy V and we think that the other two inscriptions in the hieroglyphic and demotic of the ancient Egyptians say the same thing.'

'I see! You hope that by comparing them with the Greek that you will be able to decipher them.'

'Exactly!' Randal threw her a glance of approbation before returning his attention to the road.

The busy traffic silenced their discourse for a few moments and then Randal said, with a casualness he was far from feeling, 'If you are interested, perhaps you would like to view the collection of oddities and small items of ancient art I amassed during my travels? It isn't a splendid hoard, I can't claim to have emulated Lord Elgin or my father in that respect, but you might find it worth viewing.'

'I should love to see it!' Kate's eyes began to sparkle. He *must* have forgiven her!

'Good.' Randal smiled at her warmly. 'We must arrange a date for you to visit the Hall one day next week.'

It would never had occurred to him to woo her with such bait, but her unexpected interest had brought him one step nearer to achieving his aim!

For once Kate and Alicia were to enjoy a quiet dinner at home that evening and Kate decided to broach the subject of Randal's invitation when the dessert had been set upon the table.

'Lord Redesmere suggested I stay overnight so I shall require a chaperon,' she concluded. 'He thought next Monday, if that suits you, ma'am?'

'I shall be happy to accompany you.' Alicia gave her a delighted smile. 'And not only for your sake, Kitty. I adore the

Hall, it is such a wonderfully romantic house! There is even a ghost!'

Kate grinned. That was one problem solved at least. Not that she had expected Alicia to refuse. Her hostess had questioned her closely about her afternoon and made no secret of her satisfaction on hearing that the outing had been a success.

Mary's reaction to the plan had also been predictable.

'You are a damned fool if you go, Kate,' she had said bluntly. 'It's too risky.'

Kate hadn't asked her to clarify this statement.

She had tried being sensible and it hadn't worked! For whatever reason of his own, Randal had ignored her attempt to rebuff him. Short of telling him she disliked him and didn't want him near her, there was little else she could do. Such rudeness might backfire—she still needed his consent for Kitty to gain her fortune and, besides, she didn't think she could carry it off.

Lying in bed that night, Kate knew the time had come to confront the truth of her feelings for Randal Crawford. She had tried telling herself that it was just a physical attraction, but it was more, much more, than that.

Kate had sworn she would never fall in love again. Her heart had been so bruised by her experience with Francis that she was too scared to trust any man. Randal had broken down the barriers she had erected to cage in her emotions. When she was with him her whole being came alive.

She had only known him a few weeks and yet it felt as if they had been friends for years. They laughed at the same things and their minds were in tune.

What of his feelings? Did he care for her at all or was it merely desire that held him in thrall? Kate didn't know. All she knew was that it was too late for her to wish she had never met him.

Mary thought she was a fool. And she was probably right. Nothing could come of it, but she *wanted* to go to the Hall.

It could be only a matter of days now before the situation

came to a head. If Gerald Sullivan turned up and denounced her as an imposter, they would have to flee Chester in a hurry. If that happened, it was unlikely she would ever see Randal again.

This might be her last opportunity to spend a day with him. Surely, if she kept her emotions in check, there could be no harm in allowing herself to enjoy his company?

Chapter Seven

Everywhere Kate went in the next few days she encountered Lord Redesmere. At a picnic hosted by Mrs Egerton at her home on the banks of the Dee, she finally asked him if he had taken up residence in Chester.

'In a manner of speaking, you could say I had.' There was a gleam of amusement in Randal's gaze. 'I've been staying temporarily with Godwin, you see.'

Kate's mouth formed a circle of surprise.

'I shall, of course, be returning home tomorrow night in readiness for your visit,' he reassured her with his most charming smile.

Kate vaguely noticed that he hadn't mentioned why he was staying at his uncle's house, but was distracted by him saying that his sister was expected home from her honeymoon.

'Emma wrote to tell me that they would be arriving around four o'clock.' Randal took out his gold verge watch and glanced at it. The Egertons lived near Shotwick, he would have to ride hard to return to Chester in time. 'So I'm afraid I must leave in a moment.'

Kate hid her disappointment. 'I understood Alicia to say that Lieutenant Lattimer's family live in Cornwall,' she remarked, fanning herself idly. It was another hot afternoon, although it felt a little cooler here by the river. 'Is he going to take your sister to pay them a farewell visit before they leave England?'

Randal shook his fair head. 'They said their goodbyes at the wedding.'

'I suppose his parents are used to him being away. Alicia said he has been in the army since he was sixteen.' Kate had heard all about Randal's new in-law from Lady Edgeworth, who had attended Emma's wedding and thought it a very good match. 'However, I dare say you will miss your sister.'

Randal agreed. He was some fourteen years Emma's senior, but they were close. 'I had hoped that they would stay at the Hall for the rest of their leave, but Emma declined my offer. I think she wants to prove she is now an independent married woman. They are to put up at the White Lion until they take ship for Spain.'

Randal had been somewhat disappointed, but now realised that Emma's decision to assert her new status afforded him a useful privacy.

Rising reluctantly to his feet, he said, 'Shall I see you at Godwin's party tomorrow?'

Kate stood up, too. 'Try keeping me away! I love strawberries!'

Randal grinned at her. 'You had better wear an old dress then. Godwin takes his strawberrying very seriously!'

Kate chuckled. Alicia had told her that Godwin's strawberry party was an annual event. 'It is a very informal occasion. Everyone has the greatest fun,' she'd enthused.

Randal raised Kate's hand to his lips. 'Don't forget your sunbonnet,' he murmured softly. 'It would be a pity to spoil so perfect a complexion.'

Kate could still feel a tingle of excitement from his kiss even after she had returned to Abbey Square.

She went upstairs to remove her hat and when she came down she discovered that Alicia had ordered some orgeat to be served.

'This came for you, Miss Kitty, while you was out.' Susan

set the tray holding the cooling beverage down on the ornate boule-inlay table which decorated the morning-room before presenting Kate with a letter.

Kate thanked her. 'Is Lady Edgeworth still upstairs?'

'I heard her say she was thinking of taking a bath, miss. Ever so hot she looked.'

'Perhaps you had better take a glass of orgeat upstairs for her,' Kate suggested.

The minute Susan departed, Kate ripped the missive open. It was from Ned, which was no surprise to her as she had recognised his handwriting. The contents were much as she expected too.

'Damn!' she muttered, chewing on her lower lip in frustration.

Ned wanted them home.

Kitty has been making herself useful, he wrote. *She is very handy with her needle and right willing to do anything to pay her way, bar helping out front of house. She still hides away from strangers, you understand. We all like her, she's a nice little thing, and I want to see her get her money, but you know how hard it is to find work at this time of year and I've heard rumours that there could be a good booking for us coming up. I need you here, Kate, or we'll lose it for sure!*

Kate stared down at his untidy scrawl, her heart sinking. How much longer could she put Kitty's needs above the company's?

Or, to put it more honestly, perhaps, how much longer could she afford to linger here, indulging a senseless passion for a man who could never be hers?

On their return from church the following morning, Alicia announced her intention of paying a call upon her former governess.

'I had promised to visit her just before you arrived, Kitty, but we have been so busy! I feel quite guilty at my neglect for she is an old lady now and doesn't get about much, so she looks forward to having company.'

'Would you like me to accompany you?' Kate suggested.

Alicia shook her carefully coiffured head. 'Lud, child, you would be sadly bored! No, it is kind of you to offer, but I think you would do better to conserve your energies for this afternoon.'

She picked up her reticule and prepared to leave.

'While I am gone perhaps you might like to give some thought to your costume for Lord Redesmere's forthcoming ball? You must try to come to a decision soon, my love, for I dare say every single modiste in Chester will be swamped with orders!'

This parting shot struck gloom into Kate's soul. To allay her despondency, she went to fetch her sketch-pad. She had explained her hesitation in ordering a costume by pretending she didn't know what character to go as, but, in truth, she didn't know if she would still be in Chester when the fancy-dress ball in honour of the Lattimers took place.

Assuming she was able to attend, she certainly couldn't afford to pay Celestine to create a costume for her. She had already spent too much at the dressmakers and the thought of trading further upon Alicia's generosity was abhorrent. She would have to design something for herself and make it up with the help of Mary's clever fingers.

Taking up a position near one of the long windows in the drawing-room, a large elegant apartment which caught the best of the light, Kate was intent upon sketching several ideas which had occurred to her for an inexpensive costume when George, Lady Edgeworth's young footman, came in to tell her that she had a visitor.

For one hopeful moment, Kate wondered if Randal had come to call on her, but it was Alan Hilton who was announced.

'My dear sir, do come in,' Kate invited, abandoning her drawing and rising to her feet at his entrance.

Lady Edgeworth had indulged her taste for ornate furniture

by ordering a pair of crocodile-footed couches, upholstered in a green brocade which matched the silk-panelled walls. They stood facing each other in the middle of the room and Kate sat down on one of them and waved Mr Hilton towards the other.

'Would you care for some refreshment, sir?' she asked, agog with curiosity, but striving to hide it.

The lawyer, who was dressed with conventional neatness in a suit of black broadcloth and his usual wig, looked extremely hot and accepted her offer with grateful alacrity.

They exchanged polite small talk while Kate rang for a jug of cooling lemonade, which was swiftly brought and served.

When he had slaked his thirst and they were alone once more, Mr Hilton turned to the matter which had brought him to Abbey Square.

'I beg your pardon for disturbing you on a Sunday, Miss Nixon, but I have some important news for you,' he said in his precise manner.

'About Mr Gerald Sullivan?' Kate gazed at him expectantly.

'Quite so. I received an answer from him yesterday evening. He declines to come to Chester, I'm afraid.'

Kate folded her hands in her lap in a composed gesture and strove to conceal her glee. 'Did he give any reason for refusing?'

'He states that his present health will not permit him to make the journey.'

'Do you believe him?' Kate asked boldly.

The lawyer cleared his throat. 'I think it is Lord Redesmere who must judge the matter,' he murmured.

Kate smiled sweetly and, putting on her most innocent air, gently pressed him further.

'In my opinion, Miss Nixon, his refusal does not lend credence to his story.' Succumbing to her charm, her visitor confessed his doubts. 'Given the seriousness of his allegation, I would have expected him to make every effort to prove the veracity of his claim.'

He didn't believe Gerald's excuse! Kate's almond-shaped

eyes lit with triumph and it was all she could do to sit calmly while the lawyer continued to expound upon his theory.

'Would you care for some more lemonade, sir?' she asked at length when he ground to a halt.

'No, I thank you.' Mr Hilton stood up. 'Knowing you must be anxious, I wanted to acquaint you with the latest news, but now I will leave you to enjoy the rest of the Sabbath in peace.'

'Does Lord Redesmere know about this?' Kate asked him as she too rose to her feet.

'I sent one of my clerks round to Stanley Place with a note for him last night.'

'Well, thank you for coming in person. It was kind of you to take so much trouble.'

Mr Hilton took the hand she extended to him and shook it warmly. 'Not at all, my dear young lady,' he said, making her a creditable bow.

He declined her offer to show him out and Kate returned to her seat by the window. Picking up her sketch-pad she sat down, but her mind was not on her drawing.

There had been no real need for Hilton to give up his day of rest and call on her in person. A letter would have done as well. And come to think on it, there had been a different note in his voice as he had said farewell, a much warmer, much more respectful note.

Pondering the change in his manner, Kate began to smile.

Early in their acquaintance Randal had mentioned to Kate that Stanley Place had been erected almost thirty years ago and that his uncle had purchased one of the new houses there with his patrimony on the death of his father.

'It is a good address, although the house itself isn't as grand as the Nixon mansion in Vicar's Lane,' he had added in so bland a tone Kate hadn't been sure whether he was baiting her or not.

Kate stared up at the impressive classical façade of Mr Godwin Crawford's house and gulped.

What must Kitty's inheritance be like!

The warmth of Godwin's greeting soon banished this flicker of trepidation.

''Pon rep, Miss Kitty,' he exclaimed, giving her an approving glance. 'You look as cool as a mermaid in that rig. Don't she, nevvy?'

Lord Redesmere was more than happy to endorse this statement and, revelling in the admiration in his eyes, Kate was glad she had taken the trouble to smarten up a pretty but faded pale blue muslin, donated by Alicia for the occasion to save her good clothes from being spoilt. Mary had helped her create the sleeveless over-tunic of filmy aquamarine *mousseline de soie* from a remnant bought cheaply, but to her friend's consternation, Kate had insisted on leaving off both corset and drawers.

A zona to support her bosom, silk stockings, a pair of thin sandals and a wide-brimmed straw sun-hat trimmed in the same material as her tunic completed Kate's summery ensemble and she felt quite comfortable even when they all repaired into the heat of the afternoon sunlight.

It was, she decided, a very attractive garden. Although fairly small, at least by the standards of the gentry, it was well laid out with lawns, shrubs and trees. Even with thirty-odd guests milling around, its clever design prevented it from feeling cramped.

'Come and get your baskets, everyone,' Godwin called out jovially.

He began to hand out the shallow straw containers with the help of a servant. 'Remember, there is a prize for the lady who collects the most strawberries.'

With much laughter his guests dispersed, heading for the strawberry beds, which were scattered throughout the garden.

'A penny for them.'

Kate looked up to see Lord Redesmere watching her.

'You aren't picking fruit,' she accused indignantly, noting his empty hands.

'Neither were you,' he countered with a smile.

Kate admitted it. 'I was daydreaming,' she confessed.

'About what Gerald's dereliction of duty means for you,' Randal continued for her.

'Perhaps.' Kate's generous mouth curved upwards in an involuntary smile.

A sharp stab of desire lanced through Randal. For an instant all he wanted in the world was to kiss those red, parted lips.

Reading his expression, Kate took a hasty step back, but Randal had already regained control of himself.

'Careful!' he warned. 'You'll snag your dress.'

Kate took a deep breath. Suddenly the warm air, scented by strawberries and gillyflowers, seemed stifling!

'Would you like me to fetch you a cold drink?'

'No…no, I'm all right.' Kate didn't want him to go. She wanted to throw herself into his arms, but she wasn't quite that mad…yet!

Tearing her gaze from his tall virile form, she pretended an interest in the strawberries in her basket.

'Actually, if you must know, I was merely thinking how much luckier we ladies are than you gentlemen,' she fibbed. 'You all look so hot in those tight coats and boots.'

Randal laughed. He didn't believe her for a moment, but he admired her pluck! 'Granted you have the advantage of me, Miss Nixon.'

Kate peeped at him through her long eyelashes. Was it her imagination or was there a slight edge to his tone? They had been getting on so well she had allowed herself to forget what Gerald's refusal to identify her must mean to him.

Not daring to ask him exactly what he meant, she tried to divert the conversation into safer channels. 'People seem to be drifting back towards the house. Shall we join them?'

'Running away again, Katharine?'

Kate lifted her brows delicately. 'Why should I feel the need to run from you, my lord?' she countered, throwing his challenge back at him.

Randal made her an exquisite bow. 'I'm delighted to hear that you trust me.'

This time there was no mistaking the mockery in his deep voice, but Kate had the strangest feeling it was directed at himself.

Beneath his banter she sensed the tension in him. His expression was unfathomable and yet she could have sworn there was some sort of conflict within him, something pulling him in opposing directions.

'Do you think I have collected enough strawberries to win a prize?' she asked cheerfully, exhibiting her meagre efforts in the hope that he would laugh and his odd mood would be broken.

To her surprise he didn't answer, but turned and strode away. Stooping, he picked up the basket he had abandoned earlier in the shade of a beech tree and came back to her with it. Gently tipping its heavy contents into her own basket, he said flatly, 'Now you have.'

Kate's black Egyptian eyes widened. 'But that's cheating!' she gasped. 'I can't take yours. I haven't earned them.'

'Then pay me for them.' Calmly Randal removed the basket from her grasp and set it down on the ground.

Kate stared up into his lean bronzed face and felt her heart thud against her breastbone. 'I...I don't think that's a good idea—'

Ignoring her totally insincere protest, Randal drew her into his arms. 'There's no one to see, if that's what is worrying you,' he said softly, a faint note of amusement entering his deep voice.

Kate was feeling much too overwhelmed by the sensations ignited by being so close to him to take exception to this provocative remark. She could feel his body heat and the sharp fresh lemon scent of his cologne suddenly filled her nostrils, banishing the hitherto pervasive aroma of strawberries.

Obeying the urging of primitive instinct, she wound her arms around his neck, the dark blue superfine cloth which stretched smoothly across his shoulders rasping gently against her bare skin. Gazing into his hot, bright eyes, she ran her fingertips upwards to ruffle the short hair edging his nape and felt him shudder.

'What is your price, my lord?' she asked in a throaty little whisper she barely recognised as her own voice.

'One kiss,' Randal answered and took it.

Kate closed her eyes and surrendered to his embrace.

His lips were warm. They caressed hers with thrilling expertise, making the blood sing in her veins. Violent excitement flowered in the pit of her stomach, tensing her muscles and turning her giddy.

Feeling her melt against him, Randal tightened his arms around her slim waist and deepened the kiss. Her soft lips parted beneath his, admitting his tongue into the intimacy of her mouth. She tasted of strawberries.

The touch of his tongue against her own aroused a wild longing in Kate. She clutched at his broad shoulders, pressing herself closer, wanting to feel his strong body with every inch of her own.

Utterly intoxicated by the exquisite pleasure pulsating in dizzying waves along her nerves, she felt devastated when he finally broke off the kiss and lifted his blond head.

Shaken to his soul, Randal stared deep into the midnight depths of her eyes. God, but he had never imagined such passion could be ignited by a single kiss!

'Consider the debt paid, little cousin.' Releasing her as he spoke, he smiled lightly as he forced the words out, determined not to reveal his feelings.

He stepped away from her and Kate swallowed hard, her thoughts whirling as she struggled to find a reply which would hide her utter confusion.

'Randal!'

At the sound of his name, Lord Redesmere turned away with relief to behold a tall, boyishly-slender girl, who came hurrying towards them with both hands outstretched.

'Emma.' He took her hands in his and smiled at her with a warmth that stung Kate's heart. 'I didn't think you were coming.'

'Oh, I am quite recovered from that dreadful journey!' Emma Lattimer laughed, revealing excellent white teeth.

'Let me introduce you to Miss Nixon.'

Kate found herself being regarded by a pair of candid blue eyes.

'How do you do?' Emma held out her hand, a friendly expression on her pretty face. 'I'm so sorry to have missed your arrival. I could scarcely believe it when Randal told me that our long-lost cousin was here in Chester.' She smiled. 'It was such a surprise, but I expect Randal has been making you feel at home.'

Kate almost choked. Struggling to gather her wits, all she could manage to produce was a faint nod of assent.

Luckily, Randal's sister didn't seem to notice anything amiss. 'Uncle Godwin said you were still out here. He asked me to tell you that he was about to judge the strawberries.' She stared at the basket, which lay at Kate's feet. 'Heavens, but you have been working like a Trojan, Miss Nixon!'

Kate blushed.

'Shall we go in?' Randal suggested smoothly, stooping to pick up the basket.

'Oh, yes, let's hurry or we shall miss the prize-giving!' Emma fell into step by Kate's side and, after requesting permission to use her new relative's given name, rattled on in high spirits. 'What a pity you didn't arrive a few weeks ago, Cousin Kitty. You could have attended my wedding and met all the rest of the family.'

'I hope to do so eventually,' Kate murmured, desperately wishing she knew what Randal, who strode along in silence at his sister's side, was thinking.

Emma beamed at her. 'At least I can introduce my husband to you straight away.'

Even in her preoccupied state, Kate noticed the shy but

proud way Emma said husband and felt a pang of memory. She had spoken of Francis in just that manner once!

Her dream hadn't lasted, but Kate found herself hoping Emma's evident happiness would endure. She seemed a very likeable girl and Kate thought that they might have become firm friends if the circumstances had been different.

'Did you know we went to Wales for our honeymoon, Cousin Kitty?' Emma enquired.

'Lady Edgeworth mentioned it,' Kate replied. 'The Northern coast is close, is it not, and I understand it has become a popular destination since Boney's antics put paid to travel on the Continent.'

'Oh, yes, indeed. We found it charming.' Emma began to elaborate on her travels across the border as they walked back to the house.

Listening to her bubbling chatter of ancient castles and romantic mountain views, Kate decided that Emma was much more outgoing than her brother. There was a distinct family resemblance and they shared the same colouring, but it was a lot easier to tell what Emma was thinking.

They reached the house just as a stocky, dark-haired young man came out into the garden, a slightly anxious expression on his pleasant-featured face.

'Matthew!' Emma broke off her discourse and hurried forward, leaving Kate and Randal behind in her haste to reach her suddenly beaming husband.

Alone for the first time since their kiss and knowing that their solitude would be short, Kate risked a glance in Randal's direction and found that he was staring at her, a peculiarly intent expression on his handsome face.

'Do you want me to apologise?'

His directness took Kate's breath away. Surprised into unthinking honesty, she gasped, 'No!'

'Good. Because I don't wish to.' A wicked smile flickered over Randal's face.

'Then why did you offer? Are you worried that I might have

changed my mind about coming to the Hall tomorrow?' Kate challenged, half-irritated, half-amused by his impudence.

'I don't think there is much likelihood of that, is there?' he countered in a lazy drawl that was at odds with the passion glittering in his eyes.

Kate glared at him furiously for an instant and then turned on her heel and stalked off to rejoin Emma, who was beckoning to them.

Fiend seize the man! His presumption deserved a severe set-down. She ought to have flung his wretched invitation back in his face!

Unfortunately, even in the midst of her anger, Kate knew she would find it easier to fly to the moon than give up the chance to spend an entire day with Randal Crawford.

'So you're still set on going, then?' Mary dumped Kate's valise down by the bedchamber door as she spoke, her expression frowning. 'It's not too late to change your mind. I could pack the rest of our stuff in a twinkling and we could be on the next stage north before anyone was the wiser.'

'I can't just run off, Mary!' Kate picked up her hat from the bed and sighed. 'The carriage is expected at the door any minute. It's too late to do other than go ahead with the plans we've already made.'

'You could leave if you wanted to,' Mary insisted stubbornly.

Kate was almost sorry she had shown her Ned's letter.

Mary had taken the news hard. She had been all for leaving last night when the house was quiet. Exhausted after the effort of appearing in good spirits at Godwin's party, Kate had barely had enough energy to persuade her out of the idea.

'You owe Ned more than Lady Alicia.' Mary folded her arms across her ample bosom, eager to continue the argument. 'He's always helped you, Kate. You wouldn't have done so well without his support.'

'I know!' Angrily, Kate sat down at the dressing-table and

tied the ribbons of her bonnet, wrenching them into a lopsided bow.

'Well?' Mary stared at her, her gaze worried.

'I know he wants us back.' Kate turned away from the mirror and shook her head wearily, her annoyance evaporating as she took in Mary's anxious expression. 'But we are only this far away from success.' She gestured with her finger and thumb, miming an inch. 'It would be stupid to give up now.'

'You want to stay because you are dangling after Crawford,' Mary snapped and then regretted it as Kate's exquisite face paled.

'It's all right,' Kate interrupted her muttered apology. 'I know I'm behaving like a idiot.' She gave a forlorn little shrug. 'I'm sorry. I can't seem to help it.'

Mary's expression softened. 'I wish things could be different, lass.'

'I may be lovelorn, but I swear I haven't forgotten my friends.' Kate's tone rallied. 'I won't let Ned and the rest of the company down. I've already written to tell him to send me word the minute he gets that booking and I'll come immediately, no matter what.'

Mary let out a sigh of relief. 'Thank God for that!'

'And you needn't worry that I'll let my feelings give me away while we are at the Hall. I'm well aware of the risks, believe me!' Kate stood up and smoothed down the skirts of her pomona-green travelling costume in a gesture that betrayed her strained nerves.

'Then why torture yourself by going, lass?'

'I hope to use our visit to persuade Redesmere to give his seal of approval to my claim,' Kate answered quietly.

Seeing that her friend looked sceptical, she continued in a more forceful tone. 'Don't you see, Mary? Now that Sullivan has cried off they can't accept his story. Redesmere must concede that there is no further reason for delay. With luck, the whole thing will be settled in a day or two and we shall be able to leave.'

Mary nodded, her expression brightening. 'It might work.' With renewed energy, she set about collecting up the last of Kate's belongings. 'Come on. Or we'll have Lady Edgeworth wanting to know why you are so tardy.'

Grabbing her scent-bottle and thrusting it into the dressing-case Mary held out, Kate closed her mind to the possibility of failure. She had to succeed in convincing Randal, she simply had to! That way, at least one good thing would come out of this whole sorry mess.

Alerted by the sound of approaching carriage wheels, Lord Redesmere came out to meet his guests. His smile of welcome was the first thing Kate saw as she descended from Lady Edgeworth's barouche and her unhappy memories of her last visit were instantly washed away on a tide of happiness.

'Good morning.' Randal stepped forward and kissed each lady's hand in turn.

If she noticed that he lingered somewhat longer over his salutation to her young companion, Lady Edgeworth discreetly ignored this lapse and chattered brightly of how pleased she was to be visiting the Hall again.

'Do come in.' Randal paused to instruct the footmen to take the bags straight up to the rooms which had been allocated to his guests. 'I'm sure you must feel in need of some refreshment.'

Alicia agreed that it had been a hot drive.

The north-facing entrance hall with its stone-flagged floor felt blessedly cool as they stepped inside. Kate, who had been too nervous to take much note of her surroundings last time, noticed a carved heraldic escutcheon set into one of the timber-framed walls. Her attention caught by its bright painted colours, she tried to make it out. There were two golden lions rampant and what looked like a bear standing between them, but she couldn't translate the accompanying motto—*In Bone Foy*—at all.

Curious, she asked Randal what it meant. 'Is it Latin?'

He shook his head. 'Actually, it's Medieval French. It means *In Good Faith*.' He smiled slightly. 'One of my less reputable ancestors was renowned for taking violent revenge on anyone who betrayed his trust.'

A little chill feathered down Kate's spine.

By the time they had moved on to the morning-room and finished a refreshing glass of iced orgeat, Kate's guilty sense of unease had vanished and she was able to take part in the conversation without feeling as if the sword of Damocles was liable to descend upon her head at any minute.

The housekeeper was summoned to show them upstairs to their bedchambers.

'You'll find me in the Long Hall when you are ready to come down,' Randal told them.

Determined not to linger upstairs too long, Kate was none the less enchanted by the ornate squared plaster ceiling and the diamond-leaded windows which gave her room a quaintly old-fashioned air.

She climbed up on to the high, elaborately carved four-poster bed and bounced experimentally. 'It's a great deal more comfortable than it looks,' she exclaimed in delight.

Mary, who was unpacking, was impressed by the Persian rugs scattered over the highly polished oak floorboards and the beautiful silk curtains which matched the flower-patterned bed-hangings.

Taking one look at her friend's face, however, she held her tongue. No sense in ladling on more praise when the silly lass was already halfway bewitched by the place!

Pausing only to run a brush through her hair and exchange her travelling-costume for the white muslin morning-gown with the blue embroidery around the hem, Kate hurried down to the Long Hall, which lay just beyond the morning-room. The open windows overlooked a flower-filled courtyard garden. Kate barely spared it a glance.

'Hello again.' Alone with him for the first time since he had kissed her, Kate discovered her tongue had suddenly tied itself in knots of shyness. She couldn't help remembering how eagerly she had responded to his touch. Did he really like her or did he merely think she was easy game?

Her awkward murmur of greeting brought his lordship instantly to her side.

'You were very quick,' he said, his gaze absorbing her exotic beauty with renewed wonder.

Kate smiled at him, her confidence soaring. When he looked at her like that she felt like singing! 'I am eager for the tour you promised me.'

'I think we must wait for Alicia,' Randal murmured.

Hearing the regret in his tone, Kate undutifully wished Lady Edgeworth at the Devil.

She was sorry for her meanness when Alicia joined them for the older woman's genuine pleasure as they moved through the rooms was obvious. She took an interest in everything Randal showed them and exclaimed aloud in delight several times, even though she had been conducted over the house before.

'Perhaps we should leave the Curio Room for now,' Randal remarked, coming to a halt and drawing out his watch as they completed their examination of the first floor of the house. 'As I thought. It has gone two o'clock. Shall we call a halt and resume later?'

Kate, who was feeling a little overwhelmed by what she had already seen, was quite happy to fall in with this suggestion.

Randal had ordered a nuncheon for his guests and to Kate's surprise it was served out on the terrace of the courtyard garden she had observed earlier.

'What a charming idea,' Alicia remarked, regarding the table which was laid with several light, delicious-looking dishes. 'And we needn't fear for our complexions, Kitty, if we sit over there.'

Kate nodded. The angle of the sun coming over the far wing of the house meant that the table was in shade.

Randal had explained to her how the Hall had been built in 1557 on the site of a former dwelling of the Crawfords. The new house was in the shape of a long central block with two extending wings, forming an inner courtyard. These wings had been considerably reduced in size when restoration and remodelling work had been carried out some twenty years ago.

At the same time, the courtyard had been turned into a wide flagged terrace opening directly on to a small informal garden. A flight of shallow broad steps set into its centre led down to the rest of the grounds. Kate thought it a particularly pretty place with its old stone sundial and sweet-scented roses.

'A very clever notion, my lord,' she said to Randal as they took their places. 'We might almost be enjoying a picnic.'

'I'm glad you approve.' Randal grinned at her. 'It did seem a pity to waste this glorious weather.'

The food was as good as it looked and Kate particularly enjoyed the veal patties, although she eschewed all offers to fill her glass with chilled hock and drank only lemonade.

'Heavens, I don't think I should have eaten quite so much,' Alicia whispered to Kate as they rose from the table. 'I feel quite sleepy!'

Kate, who'd noticed that Lady Edgeworth had also consumed several glasses of wine, hid a smile.

They went indoors again and Randal asked if they would like to resume their tour.

'Would you mind very much if I cried off, dear boy?' Alicia enquired, cutting across Kate's swift acceptance. 'Only I am feeling a little tired and I think I shall take a short nap.'

'I'm sure his lordship would be happy to postpone—' Kate began dutifully, but Lady Edgeworth interrupted her.

'No, don't let me spoil your afternoon, Kitty,' she said firmly. 'I know you are keen to view the Curio Room, but as I have already seen the items it contains there is no need to delay on my behalf.' Turning to Randal, she gave him an apologetic little smile.

Randal reassured her in a calm voice that hid his sudden elation at the prospect of having his elusive heiress all to himself.

After they parted company with Alicia they made their way up to the top of the house and Kate was very conscious of the last time they had been alone together. Her nerves stretched taut and, much as she wished to ignore the butterflies dancing in her stomach, she couldn't summon any light-hearted chatter.

They reached the Gallery, where the exposed timbering revealed the complicated ancient structure of the house in all its glory, and to her relief Randal broke the silence.

'Take care, the roof gets lower from here,' he warned as they walked past the spot where they had ended their earlier exploration. 'I always bang my head whenever I forget to duck.'

'Luckily, I lack your inches,' Kate answered with a grin, some of her tension dissolving as she followed him up a narrow and steep staircase to find herself on a small landing with several doors going off.

Randal pointed to the nearest one and said, 'That's the Confessional. Would you like to see the escape hatch before you view the curios?'

Kate nodded. Over their nuncheon in response to her interest Randal had told her something of the history of the Hall; she knew that, until Sir Joseph Crawford had followed King James II into exile, the Crawfords had been a devout Catholic family and the Hall had possessed its own chapel. This place of worship had been turned into an elegant music-room by his eventual successor, a more pragmatic cousin who decided to reject the Jacobite Cause in 1715. Rewarded by King George with a barony, the new Lord Redesmere had also diplomatically abandoned the Old Faith.

'The Chapel had to be erased, but since the Oratory and Confessional were only small rooms tucked away at the top of the house I dare say my canny ancestor couldn't be bothered with the expense of further alterations,' Randal had commented with wicked accuracy.

The Confessional was completely empty. Dust motes danced in the sunlight as they crossed the bare floorboards.

'Don't you ever use this room?' Kate asked.

A slight smile curved her host's well-cut mouth. 'I believe there was talk of turning it into servants' quarters once upon a time, but no one would sleep here.'

'Because of the ghost, I presume?' Kate suddenly remembered Alicia's comment.

'Of course.' Randal's smile broadened into a grin of amusement at her sceptical tone. 'It is said that during Elizabeth Tudor's reign a priest came in secret to the house to hear confessions and say Mass. Someone betrayed his presence and, caught while trying to escape, the poor man was dragged off to London where he was duly tortured and executed in the usual grisly manner.'

Kate shuddered.

'Whether or not the story is true, it is certain that this whole floor eventually became disused,' Randal continued. 'It wasn't until my father decided to house the treasures he had brought back from his Grand Tour up here that anything was done to restore the neglect.'

'Now watch.' Randal directed his guest's attention to a point on one of the timber cross-beams. He pressed the spot firmly.

Immediately, a section of seemingly normal white-washed wall slid open, exposing the concealed exit.

'You say this leads all the way down to the cellars?' Kate enquired in awe, staring into the dark hole.

Randal nodded, his expression wry. 'I climbed down there once myself as a lad. It's as black as the Devil's cooking pot when the panel is shut and the stairs are so small and twisting that, even with the aid of a candle, I nearly broke my neck several times. I thought it a great adventure, but the danger would have been all too real in Elizabethan England. I'll wager that at least one poor soul was forced to scurry down there in terror of his life!'

Kate's active imagination ignited at his description and she had to suppress a shiver. She wasn't sure she believed in ghosts, but, somehow, she felt she could detect a faint lingering sadness in this small bare room.

'Are you all right? You've turned quite pale.' Randal stared at her anxiously. He had never experienced anything untoward in this room, but Emma disliked it.

'It's nothing.' Kate gave a little shrug and forced herself to smile at him cheerfully.

There was nothing to fear. Her mind was playing tricks on her, translating her own anxieties into a false sensation of past sorrows.

All the same, she felt decidedly better when Randal closed the escape hatch.

'Let's get out of here.' He put his arm around her shoulders and ushered her quickly from the room.

On the landing he withdrew his arm and asked if she wanted to go back downstairs. 'Perhaps you would like to rest for a while?'

Randal cursed himself for a fool. He was wasting a splendid opportunity to put his plan to test her into action, but he couldn't seem to resist the wave of protective tenderness which had swept over him at the sight of her brave attempt to ignore her obvious distress.

Kate, her unease now vanished as rapidly as it had appeared, shook her dark head firmly. 'I appreciate your concern, but there's no need to worry. I'm feeling perfectly all right and I very much want to carry on with our tour.'

Seeing he still looked uncertain, she gave him a saucy grin. 'It isn't very polite, you know, to imply I need a nap like Lady Alicia!'

'I beg your pardon, ma'am!' he replied with a mock solemnity belied by the laughter in his eyes. Crossing the landing in a few swift strides, he flung open the door of the Curio Room with a flourish. 'Let us continue at once!'

Chapter Eight

'Oh, how lovely!' Kate halted in surprise on the threshold.

She had been expecting another small and dark room, but this enormous chamber must run virtually the entire length of the south wing and it was filled with sunlight streaming in through the diamond lights of a vast five-sided bay window.

'Now I see why your father conceived the odd notion of housing his collection up here,' she said with her usual frankness.

Randal was amused. He couldn't remember anyone else making such a comment, although he was sure all of the servants and most of the visitors who had toiled up the endless stairs must have shared the same thought.

'Actually, I think he chose it as much for its privacy as for the space and good light. You see, he was a man who valued solitude.' Randal let out an abrupt chuckle. 'Fortunately, he was not in the habit of collecting large pieces!'

'I thought you said he brought some statues back from Italy?' Kate moved forward, enticed by the objects she could see on display. The room was immaculately clean, she noticed, but very hot.

'Indeed he did. There is a particularly fine Renaissance marble of Apollo in the Knot Garden, which I can show you later if you are interested, but most of his collection, like mine, consists of smaller items.'

He pointed to a red-figured vase placed upon a low granite plinth in the centre of the room. 'This was his most cherished acquisition. He came across it in Athens and paid a small fortune to bring it home.'

Kate moved closer and marvelled at the skill of the ancient artist. Upon the black surface of the amphora he had depicted a dance of youths and maidens with lively vigour.

'They have just been rescued from the Minotaur by Theseus,' Randal explained.

'You can recognise their joy,' Kate agreed, but nervously declined his offer to handle the vase for herself.

'I should be terrified of dropping it,' she admitted frankly.

Randal chuckled. 'Well, how about this instead?' he suggested, indicating a bronze helmet, which Kate guessed correctly to be Roman.

They wandered round the room and, completely fascinated, Kate forgot both her earlier strange unease and the oppressive heat.

'These are lovely.' Some jewellery arranged in a glass case caught her eye. 'Are they very old?'

'Fourteenth-century French.' Randal opened the case and took out a ring which he handed to her. The broad silver band was engraved with lettering, each word separated from the next by a carved heart in which was set a glowing garnet.

'It's beautiful,' Kate exclaimed. 'May I try it on?'

It fitted perfectly. Reluctantly, she took it off again and examined the wording more closely. *A Vila Mon Coeur Gardi Li Mo.* 'What does it mean?'

'Here is my heart, guard it well,' he replied in a voice that wasn't quite level. 'The garnet signifies constancy.'

Her pulse beating too fast, Kate put the ring back and said hastily, 'Where are the Egyptian curios you mentioned?'

'Over here.' Randal indicated the souvenirs of his own travels, which had been arranged at the other end of the room, which was lit by another large window.

Kate was particularly taken with a tiny blue-glazed hippo and a remarkably life-like little polished stone cat complete with a gold nose-ring and earrings.

'Did you inherit your love of collecting from your father?' she asked, gently stroking the smooth curve of the cat's back.

'I suppose I must have done. Certainly, it was one of the very few interests we shared.'

There was a hard edge to his voice and Kate glanced up at him in surprise.

His blue eyes held a hint of bitterness, but as soon as he noticed her regard his sombre expression vanished and he began to tell her an amusing story of how, longing to learn more of Egypt's strange past, he'd persuaded one of the local peasants to show him a tomb belonging to the ancients.

'He thought I was mad, of course. However, it was well known amongst his people that some of these crazy foreign soldiers were interested in old things so, naturally, he demanded a ridiculous fee.'

Randal grinned at the memory. 'I should have haggled harder over the price! Once inside the entrance to the tomb we had to squeeze through narrow passages clogged by sand and boulders, half-choking on the fine dust that rose with our every movement. In some places there was barely enough room to crawl through on our stomachs.'

'It doesn't sound very dignified,' Kate teased.

'It wasn't! I still have the scars from all those sharp pointy stones which dug into me as I wriggled along like a particularly inept worm,' Randal joked. 'In fact, when I finally returned to camp covered in dust and bloody scratches my comrades derived a great deal of amusement from pretending I must have been in a battle! They couldn't believe I had gone to all that trouble just to look inside an empty tomb, for of course it had been robbed of all its contents, though whether in ancient times or more recently I couldn't tell them.'

'But you still thought it worthwhile,' Kate commented, not fooled by his self-mocking laughter.

'Very much so.' All at once his handsome face was serious. 'The want of air for our candles made the light very faint, but there was enough to see the paintings on the walls when we reached the inner chamber. Paintings which must have been created long before Caesar ruled the world.'

Kate's eyes widened at the thought. 'It must have felt strange to look upon something so old!'

Randal smiled at her suddenly. 'Old they may have been, but I shall never forget the brilliant colours or the sheer charm of those painted scenes!'

'Describe what you saw! Please!'

Kate listened eagerly and then exclaimed impulsively, 'I wish I could have seen them!'

Randal stared down into her animated face. 'Do you know, I do believe you would have appreciated their beauty,' he said slowly. 'And that makes you a very unusual girl.'

There was a note of unguarded admiration in his deep voice and Kate blushed, feeling strangely flustered.

In the last hour she had been able to forget all about Kitty and be herself as they laughed and joked examining all these fascinating objects. Now that sense of shared intimacy was swept away and her former nervousness came rushing back as she remembered how he had kissed her in Godwin's garden. Was he going to make improper advances towards her again?

Her heart thumping too fast from a queer mixture of hope and trepidation, Kate gave a little gasp of alarm which she tried to turn into a cough when his hand moved to cover hers where it rested against the smooth stone cat.

'I've never met anyone quite like you before, Katharine.' Randal's clear features softened in a warm smile. 'You have the intelligence and courage to go your own way and that is very rare.'

Kate dropped her gaze, her mouth drying nervously. He

sounded sincere! Perhaps he had finally dismissed his earlier misgivings about her character?

Delight warred with shame as she struggled to master her emotions. 'You mustn't pay me such extravagant compliments,' she whispered at last, still avoiding his gaze.

'Why not?' Randal lifted her hand away from the statuette and held it firmly in his own. 'It is the truth.'

He raised her hand to his lips and pressed a kiss against the soft skin of her inner wrist. 'It's also true I find you very attractive, but I think you already know that.'

Kate swallowed hard, her pulse hammering. She forced herself to look him squarely in the eyes. 'Flirting is a pleasant game, my lord, but I thought we were friends.'

Randal quirked his tawny brows at her. 'I hope we are,' he murmured, refusing to be rebuffed by her severe tone.

'Then I hope you will agree not to overstep the bounds of propriety,' Kate declared with more conviction than she felt. 'You know you ought not to do so.'

'I thought you might like it,' he retorted wickedly.

Remembering her shameless response to his embrace, Kate was rendered speechless for a moment before managing to stumble on. 'My sentiments are hardly the point. We both know it is wrong to behave...oh, you know what I mean!'

She couldn't let him kiss her! If she did, she might not be able to tell him to stop!

To her dismay, he not only retained his hold on her hand, but his long brown fingers began to gently caress hers.

And, somehow, she couldn't quite summon up the strength to pull free!

'Friends ought to be honest with one another,' she rushed on blindly, determined to make him understand that she had not come to the Hall in order to flirt with him. 'If we can't trust each other, our friendship is meaningless!'

The bright blue eyes narrowed as he digested her hasty remarks.

'I stand corrected.' Abruptly, he let her hand go and a *frisson* of alarm shot along Kate's nerves at his sudden frown.

'You remind me of my obligations as a gentleman, but can I trust *you*, sweet Katharine? Just how honest are *you* being with me?'

Kate barely managed to restrain a wince of horror. What a fool she was! Why had she reminded him of his suspicions just when things were going so well?

'There.' Mary secured the last yellow silk rosebud into the upswept pile of gleaming curls atop Kate's head and gave a satisfied nod. 'Exactly how a demure young miss should dress for a quiet country dinner!' She beamed at Kate. 'You'll melt his lordship's resistance for sure tonight!'

Kate stared at her own reflection in the dressing-table glass. Her friend had created the primrose crape evening-gown she was wearing to Kitty's instructions and its simple lines lent her an air of innocent fragility.

'Thank you, Mary.' Kate forced a smile and picking up her fan rose to her feet.

She hadn't told Mary about her stupid *faux pas* this afternoon. It was pointless worrying the older woman, but, as she made her way to the drawing-room, Kate could feel the colour rushing into her cheeks at the embarrassing memory.

She had managed to laugh off Randal's demand for honesty, employing every coquettish trick she knew to turn the conversation into safer channels and, true to his obligations as her host, he had not forced the issue.

But the warmth had died from his eyes and he had brought their tour to a rapid close.

He had politely offered several other forms of entertainment for her amusement, but she had declined and retired to her room. How could she have enjoyed a walk in the gardens or a row on the placid lake when she knew that he must be contemptuous of her beneath his icily controlled demeanour?

Dreading the evening ahead, Kate was glad that Alicia was down before her.

'Kitty, my dear! What an age you have been!' Lady Edgeworth greeted her warmly and, tilting her elaborately becurled head to one side, she surveyed Kate with short-sighted intentness. 'However, the end result was worth the wait, don't you agree, my lord?'

Lord Redesmere, resplendent in a dark evening coat of Scott's making, had risen to his feet at Kate's entrance and now he made a punctilious bow in her direction. 'Miss Nixon.'

Kate dipped an answering curtsy and moved with apparent calm to sit next to Alicia.

'Would you care for a glass of sherry?'

No one hearing the scrupulous civility in his deep voice would ever guess that he thinks me an adventuress, Kate thought to herself, as she quietly refused this offer.

'We were just talking about what stories this old room could relate if it was able to speak,' Lady Edgeworth announced brightly. 'Only imagine, Kitty! We might hear Sir Robert Crawford describe his exploits in repelling the Armada!' She pointed to a rather small and dark portrait hanging near the fireplace. 'That's him over there, isn't it, Randal?'

Lord Redesmere nodded. 'It's supposed to be a very good example of the Carracci school.'

Kate dutifully turned to look at the portrait, but her mind wasn't on art.

What was going on in that wheat-blond head of his? His manner was that of an attentive host as he listened to Alicia rattle on and yet her senses, acutely attuned to his slightest movement, warned her of the tension coiled within his big frame.

The suite of brocaded furniture that graced this elegant room was modern and her chair was comfortable, but Kate felt she might as well have been sitting on a heap of nails as the conversation wore on. Was he deliberately ignoring her or was it merely a coincidence that he was devoting all his energies to answering Alicia, who was extremely interested in the genealogy of local prominent families?

'I remember your Uncle Godwin saying that one of Sir Robert's grandsons fought against the Dutch in the time of King Charles.' Lady Edgeworth was in her element. 'And several other Crawfords have been renowned sailors, have they not?'

'It is something of a family tradition to go into the Navy,' Randal affirmed with a polite smile that hid his boredom. Hellfire, how he wished the dear woman at Jericho!

With Alicia out of the way, he could have it out with that baggage sitting over there looking as if butter wouldn't melt in her mouth! He should have obeyed his instincts this afternoon and to hell with polite obligations!

'Then why did you go into the army?' Kate spoke up boldly, tired of being ignored.

The bright blue gaze turned on her. 'I had my reasons.'

'Won't you share them with us?' invited Kate sweetly.

'My motives can hold no interest for you.' Randal's velvet tones were cold. 'And I make it a point never to satisfy vulgar curiosity.'

Kate took a deep breath and was about to make a blistering retort when she realised that Alicia, who had been startled by his lordship's savage set-down, was staring at the pair of them with puzzled anxiety.

Reining in her annoyance, Kate managed a cool smile. 'Then I shall say no more, sir.'

'Thank you, Miss Nixon.' Mockery infused his smooth reply.

Fortunately for Kate's temper, Blake arrived at that moment to announce that dinner was served.

She barely tasted a mouthful of the exquisite meal that followed. The fine old refectory table that graced the oak panelled dining-room was spread with several of her favourite dishes and a small part of her mind registered the fact that Randal must have gone to the trouble of asking Alicia what she liked best, but she was feeling too angry and upset to appreciate the gesture.

It was all she could do to respond to Alicia's attempts to keep the conversation flowing smoothly!

The second course was brought in. Strawberry fritters, salamangundy, boiled soles, green peas, a glazed gammon, a raised chicken pie and several other assorted dishes were carefully arranged by the footmen under Blake's eagle-eyed supervision.

'Try a little of this whim-wham, my love. It is delightful,' Alicia urged.

Kate accepted a small helping of the rich trifle, but half of it still remained untouched on her plate when the covers were removed and the dessert set upon the table.

'We shall leave you to your port, my lord.' Alicia gave the nod as soon as it was seemly and, glad to abandon the handful of almonds and raisins with which she had been toying, Kate followed her from the room.

Lady Edgeworth managed to contain herself until they reached the drawing-room but, as soon as she sat down, she exclaimed, 'What on earth is the matter, Kitty? Why are you and Randal at daggers' drawn?'

'I don't know what you mean,' Kate answered stiffly.

'Nonsense, child!' For once Lady Edgeworth's amiable tones were sharp. 'Why, I swear neither of you exchanged a word at dinner! I hardly knew where to look!'

'I'm sorry, ma'am.' Kate sat down opposite the older woman, her expression suddenly penitent. 'It was not my intention to embarrass you.'

Alicia reached out and patted her hand. 'I know you would not wish to upset me, my dear,' she said in a much kinder voice.

Guilt seared Kate's soul.

'Now, have the two of you quarrelled?' Alicia's painted chicken-skin fan fluttered with sympathy.

'It wasn't precisely a quarrel,' Kate murmured awkwardly. 'We…we just don't agree about a certain matter.'

Curiosity brightened Lady Edgeworth's hazel eyes and, realising that she was about to be questioned further, Kate quickly stood up.

'I fear I have the headache,' she said hastily. 'If you will excuse me, I won't wait for the tea tray but will retire immediately.'

Alicia sighed. 'Very well, Kitty. Run along if you must. I shall make your excuses to his lordship.'

Relieved to be let off so lightly, Kate fled.

Moonlight flooded the library. Kate set down her candlestick on the large central reading-table and moved towards the nearest bookcase.

Something light and entertaining, that's what she needed.

Intent on scanning the shelves, Kate didn't hear the soft footfall behind her.

Vathek. Maybe William Beckford's renowned oriental tale would distract her restless thoughts. Kate reached up and plucked the leather-bound volume from its place.

'A good choice, if you've a taste for exotic adventure, but not the most soothing of novels, perhaps.'

Kate whirled round. Damn, damn, damn!

Clutching the book to her scantily clad breast, she said in a slightly breathless voice, 'I couldn't sleep. I thought reading a book might help.'

'So I gathered.' Lord Redesmere's tone was dry.

Collecting her scattered wits, Kate drew herself up. 'I didn't think you would object to my borrowing one of your volumes,' she said with crushing hauteur.

A flicker of amusement passed over his regular features and, horribly conscious of her bare feet peeking out from beneath the hem of her lace-trimmed wrapper, Kate stiffened.

Oh, why hadn't she got dressed instead of sneaking down

here in her night-clothes! Not that she had expected to encounter anyone, of course.

Anyway, what was *he* doing wandering about the house long after everyone else had retired for the night? Apart from the fact he had removed the coat and neckcloth he was wearing earlier, he was fully dressed, so she didn't think he could have gone to bed at all.

Perhaps he, too, was unable to sleep.

'Borrow the book, by all means.' Randal set down his own candlestick. 'I hope you'll find it enjoyable.'

'Thank you.' Kate forced a polite half-smile.

It was definitely time to make her exit. 'If you'll excuse me, I'll leave you to make your own selection in peace.'

'I didn't come in here to choose a book.' Randal leant back against the edge of the library-table and folded his arms across his chest.

'Then why are you here?' Kate hoped he wouldn't notice her discreet attempt to edge away.

'I heard a noise and decided to investigate.'

Under his brooding stare Kate felt like a mouse trapped by a cat. 'Well, now you know I'm not a house-breaker I'll say goodnight.'

She gave him a bright smile and stepped forward to move past him.

So quickly that Kate didn't see it coming, his arm shot out to bar her way.

'No! By God, you'll not run off again!' he said in a low growl.

He straightened slowly to his feet and stood towering over her. 'You are not leaving this room until I get to the bottom of this mystery.'

'I haven't the faintest idea of what you are talking about!' Kate strove to ignore the cold prickle of apprehension feathering down her spine. 'Please, let me pass.'

'Stop stalling, my girl!' Before she could divine his intention he snatched the book from her and slammed it down on the table behind him. 'I want some answers. Now!'

'Oh, how dare you!' He was so close that Kate had to tilt her head back to glare up at him. 'You are behaving outrageously!'

'You have that effect on me, sweet Katharine.'

His eyes glittered in the candlelight and Kate suddenly realised two important facts. One was that, with the abrupt removal of the book she had been clutching, her loosely tied wrapper had come open, and, secondly, Randal Crawford was not entirely sober.

'Well, are you going to tell me why you are pretending to be my cousin?'

Kate decided to ignore this belligerent question. Francis had always got very quarrelsome in his cups and it had never paid to argue with him. He had blacked *both* her eyes on one particularly memorable occasion! She didn't think Randal was likely to turn violent, but it seemed safest not to try his temper.

'It is very late, my lord,' she replied softly. 'We can continue this discussion in the morning if you wish, but right now I want to go to bed.'

The bellicose expression on his face faded.

For one endless moment he stared at her in silence and then, reaching out his hand, he trailed one finger gently down her cheek and said softly, 'So do I.'

There was no mistaking his meaning!

Kate sucked in a deep lungful of air and struggled to stay calm. 'I shall ignore that remark, my lord. You are…not yourself.'

'I may be bosky, but I haven't lost my reason.' There was a hint of indignation in Lord Redesmere's voice.

'Of course not,' Kate murmured soothingly. 'However, you may well regret this conversation in the morning.'

'You think it's the brandy talking, don't you?' His mouth curled in a self-mocking smile. 'Maybe you're right, but it don't alter the fact that you are the most desirable woman I've ever met.'

Out of the frying pan and into the fire!

Now what should she do? Kate wondered frantically as his hand shifted its exploration to her hair, which lay loose upon her shoulders.

'Soft as silk.' Randal lifted up one shining sable lock and twined it around his fingers. 'Such beautiful hair.'

His gaze dropped to her bosom, exposed in her low-cut nightgown. In the soft light her skin appeared to gleam like pearl. 'And such a lovely body.'

Kate controlled a prim urge to snatch her wrapper together. She couldn't afford to panic and, besides, it wasn't the first time a man had seen her *en deshabille*, for heaven's sake!

He released her curls, but Kate's relief was short lived.

'You know something,' he confided with a slightly owlish solemnity. 'It's damned hot in here. Why don't we go outside?'

And without further ado he swung her up in his arms and strode out of the library.

'Put me down,' Kate whispered.

'I won't drop you, word of honour.'

He grinned down at her so boyishly that Kate couldn't help laughing, albeit in a slightly hysterical manner.

No, he wouldn't let her fall. His arms were strong, holding her effortlessly. All the same, it could do no harm to slide her own arm around his neck. Just for the sake of steadying herself, of course.

She thought he would head for the front door. Instead he traversed the dark entrance hall with sure-footed ease.

'You must have eyes like a cat,' Kate muttered.

'Blake always bolts the front door. God knows why, but I can't open it and hold you at the same time,' he answered reasonably.

They entered the morning-room. The heavy drapes which curtained the French-window were not drawn and it opened easily to Randal's touch.

'Another of my father's improvements. Never thought it would come in so handy,' Randal remarked cheerfully and carried her out on to the flagged terrace.

Kate thought he would set her on her feet and she couldn't prevent a squeak of surprise when he immediately continued on into the moonlit garden.

'Randal! Where are you going?'

'Thought I'd show you the statues in the Knot Garden.'

'Oh, this is absurd! Put me down now! At once!'

He came to a halt. 'Why? Don't you feel safe?'

Safe! That was the last thing she felt!

How could she feel safe when they were so close that she could see the pulse beating in his throat, could smell the warm clean scent of his skin, could feel the throb of his heart beneath her hand?

It's not him I have to fear, but myself, Kate thought giddily.

He wasn't like Francis. Apart from the fact he could hold his wine a damned sight better than her husband ever had, he had too much honour to hurt a woman.

And too much pride to force an unwilling one.

She could trust him. It was her own desires she had to be wary of!

'Randal, put me down. *Please!*' He was holding her as gently as if she was made of fine porcelain and, dizzy with temptation, it was all Kate could do to resist the longing to lay her cheek against his.

'Very well.' He set her down carefully. 'You can walk if you want to.'

'Thank you!' Kate shook out her creased skirts. 'I am much obliged!'

Unconscious of her sarcasm, Randal made her a slightly unsteady bow. 'Knew you'd like it out here. Much better than frowsting indoors.'

'It's gone midnight!'

'So it is.' He looked faintly surprised at her objection. 'Nice moon, though.'

Kate had to stifle a giggle. Just how much brandy had he consumed? 'Very nice,' she replied patiently, deciding to humour him. 'But it's still dreadfully late and we ought to be getting back.'

She had often wondered what was going on behind his mask of cool reserve. Tonight her wish had been granted. His inhibitions drowned, he was making no attempt to hide his thoughts...or his feelings.

'I don't want to go in.' He caught her hand urgently. 'I want to go for a walk with you.'

Kate hesitated, knowing she ought to insist on going back to the house. Young ladies did not wander about the garden after midnight. Particularly not in their nightgowns!

'It would be wrong of me to stay,' she murmured, but she let her hand remain in his.

'You owe me a stroll in the moonlight.' He smiled at her winningly. 'To make up for refusing me at Lady Massey's.'

Kate dithered. She didn't think he would try to detain her—his anger appeared to have evaporated—but dare she trust herself to behave sensibly?

Taking her silence for consent, he tucked her hand into the crook of his elbow and set off in the direction of the Knot Garden.

'Not going too fast for you, am I?'

Kate shook her head, feeling overwhelmed by her own idiocy. She was behaving recklessly and she knew it!

And yet prudence hadn't served her any better. Her refusal at the Masseys' ball had been prompted by caution. She had hoped to discourage him from pursuing her, but he was a determined man and all her subsequent attempts at coldness had failed miserably.

Her thoughts in a hopeless tangle, Kate gave up the struggle to make sense of her situation and surrendered thankfully to the beauty of the night.

The lightest of breezes stirred the warm, balmy air as they strolled along arm-in-arm and it was so peaceful she could hear a nightingale serenading the moon, which hung like a golden globe in the star-strewn sky. From somewhere nearby there came a waft of honeysuckle. Drinking in its sweet perfume, Kate could feel the tension draining out of her.

Her behaviour might be foolish, but it was a beautiful night! And, besides, the fresh air might help clear Randal's head!

They crossed another well-tended lawn, the short grass tickling Kate's bare feet, and Randal broke the companionable silence. 'Not far now. Just past that big elm.'

They reached this lovely old tree and, in the darkness of its branches, Kate thought she saw something move and instinctively slowed to a halt with a little gasp of uncertainty.

'Don't be alarmed. It's only an owl out hunting,' Randal said cheerfully.

At the sound of his voice the bird flew up out of the tree with a loud screech of annoyance and, its great wings beating against the dark sky, disappeared in the direction of the Park.

Feeling remarkably silly, Kate gave a rueful chuckle. She had lived too long away from the country! 'You must think me a shocking coward,' she murmured in embarrassment.

'On the contrary.' Randal placed his hands firmly upon her shoulders and turned her round to face him. 'I think you are adorable.'

Taken by surprise, Kate looked up into his eyes and, seeing the warm tenderness in their depths, was lost.

Even as he reached out to draw her into his embrace, she was already swaying towards him, drawn by the magnetic pull of an attraction she could no longer resist.

'Katharine. Sweet lovely Katharine.'

His mouth descended on hers with swift eager hunger and, flinging her arms around his neck, Kate responded with equal fervour.

The minutes ticked by unheeded. Deeper and deeper, they kissed, their tongues entwining in a passionately arousing duel. Closer and closer, Kate pressed herself against him, revelling in the feel of his superb body.

Breathless and giddy with desire, they finally broke apart for want of air.

'You taste of brandy,' Kate murmured against his mouth.

He gave a hoarse laugh. 'I beg your pardon, ma'am.'

'I don't mind…kiss me again!'

'Delighted to oblige,' he muttered, his arms tightening about her slim waist.

Their lips met and a fresh wave of desire swept over Kate. The blood drummed wildly in her veins, deafening her to reason, and she made no protest when his hand found her breast and his long skilful fingers began to stroke her nipple though the flimsy barrier of her white lawn nightgown.

A tiny moan of pleasure escaped her and, encouraged by this wanton response, Randal tugged the thin fabric aside to caress her naked flesh.

Once, long ago, she had caught a glimpse of how wonderful making love might be, but that promise had never been fulfilled. Now, vivid sensation searing every nerve-ending, she was discovering that the reality was far beyond anything she had imagined.

Randal lifted his mouth an inch away from hers. 'You are utterly bewitching!' he whispered, checking his sensuous explorations for an instant.

Kate opened her eyes and smiled at him, happiness fizzing in her veins. 'I like your touch.'

He gazed down into her exquisite face. The moonlight had washed her dark eyes with silver and they glowed to rival the stars as she returned his hand to her breast.

Slowly, lost in mutual delight, they sank to the greensward in a tangle of entwined limbs.

Their kisses grew more passionate and a strange yearning flowered in the pit of Kate's stomach. Held thrall in its erotic power, she made no protest when he gently removed her wrapper and pulled her nightgown down to her waist.

'Oh, God, you are so lovely!' His gaze seemed to scorch her

skin. 'I have wanted you from the moment I first laid eyes on you.'

An alarm bell began to ring in Kate's head. She ought to... she must...tell him to stop!

'Randal...oh!'

His head dipped swiftly, his mouth capturing the rosy peak of her breast.

A delicious excitement shot through Kate and she gasped aloud. Slowly, sensuously, his tongue began to lick her nipple.

Tangling her fingers in his thick hair, Kate arched her back with voluptuous pleasure and abandoned thought.

Aeons of delight passed and then, of their own volition, her fingers shifted, searching for his waistcoat.

'What are you doing?' Becoming aware of her efforts, Randal raised his head.

'I want to touch you.' Kate was struggling impatiently to undo the gilt buttons.

A low chuckle escaped him. 'Allow me,' he murmured and ripped the waistcoat open.

'Take it off,' Kate commanded.

Willingly, he obeyed and Kate immediately tugged the edges of his shirt free, sliding her hands inside the crisp white linen to reach his skin.

At the touch of her eager fingers gliding over his chest Randal let out a low groan of satisfaction.

'Wait!' He pulled the shirt over his head and tossed it aside.

Kate gazed at him with frank curiosity. He was very different to Francis! Her late husband's torso had been lean and narrow, his skin pale and hairless.

Experimentally, she slid both hands up over Randal's chest. 'You feel so warm,' she whispered huskily.

His muscles were superbly delineated and a light covering of fine blond hair, glinting in the moonlight, hazed his upper torso. With a little giggle, she rasped it between her fingers. 'It feels lovely, like the softest of furs!'

He laughed shakily. 'I'm glad I meet with your approval, my lady.'

His laughter died as her questing fingers found his flat copper nipples and began to tease them into hardness.

'Do you like this, too?' Kate smiled at him provocatively, revelling in her new-found power.

'It feels wonderful, you little witch!' he muttered thickly, his breathing quickening and, unable to deny his need to kiss her again, he pulled her against him and set his mouth on hers with a swift hungry passion.

Naked flesh against naked flesh. Dizzily, Kate wondered if it was possible to faint from sheer pleasure.

He began to stroke the slender curve of her hip, his hand moving slowly downwards, and then, before Kate had time to realise what was happening, he'd pushed her nightgown out of his way.

Moving in slow circles against her bare thigh, his hand climbed higher.

'Randal, you mustn't—' Kate broke off with a gasp as his hand slid between the cleft of her thighs and found the hot, aching core of her womanhood.

Violent pleasure erupted in the pit of her stomach, leaving her totally breathless. The sensations his skilful fingers were evoking were so intense she couldn't prevent herself writhing against him.

'Katharine. Beautiful Katharine.' Randal muttered her name feverishly. 'Do you want to…are you sure?'

His free hand cupped her buttocks, arching her towards him and, feeling the shaft of his manhood, hard and hot, against her thigh, Kate understood his hoarse question.

Every fibre of her being crying out for fulfilment and unbearably tempted, she struggled to cling on to sanity.

Making love with Randal would change everything! She *couldn't* take the risk!

'Randal, let me go!'

For an instant he continued to hold her close and then, as she began to struggle, he released her immediately.

'Katharine? You're trembling.' Randal stared at her, his expression half-dazed.

Kate scrambled to her feet and with shaking hands began to set her clothes frantically to rights.

The look of utter humiliation on her face, ghostly pale in the moonlight, shocked Randal into complete sobriety and, grabbing his shirt, he stood up. 'I'm sorry,' he muttered gruffly. 'I didn't mean to frighten you.'

Bitterly aware that she was equally to blame, Kate shook her head in a violent gesture. 'There's no need to apologise,' she grated, horrified by her own stupidity.

She should never have let things go so far!

Far from being scared by his passion, her whole body still longed for consummation. Aching with frustration, she supposed she ought to feel grateful for his restraint, but a rebellious part of her mind couldn't help wishing he had paid no heed to her pleas to stop.

Randal winced at the anger in her voice. O God, why had he drunk so much brandy! 'I thought you liked...I mean you seemed to want me to—'

'Oh, don't!' Close to tears, Kate hastily interrupted him. 'Please don't say any more, I beg of you!'

Belatedly realising his clumsy attempt to apologise was only making things worse, Randal ground to a halt.

Silently, he pulled on his shirt and stooped to pick up his waistcoat. A combination of fresh air and shock had cleared the brandy fumes from his head, but his brain was still refusing to function properly.

Appalled by his loss of self-control and unable to think of a smooth remark to ease their mutual embarrassment, he fell back on formality. 'Pray allow me to escort you back to the house.'

His voice was creditably calm, but a muscle flickered at the corner of his well-cut mouth, betraying him.

'I think it would be better if I went on ahead,' Kate replied, crushing the impulse to reach out to him. The bleak self-disgust in his eyes cut her to the quick, but she dare not try to explain that he had done her no wrong.

If she did, her deep longing to confess might overcome her vow to help Kitty!

For an instant she thought he would challenge her decision and then he bowed his fair head. 'As you wish.'

It took all of Kate's determination to walk away from him and not look back.

In spite of her resolve to stay calm Kate could not prevent a flicker of apprehension when Randal asked if he might have a word in private as they rose from the breakfast table the next morning.

'Of course,' she murmured, trying to look unconcerned.

Randal bowed politely to her chaperon. 'Pray excuse us, Lady Alicia.'

Lady Edgeworth nodded, her eyes bright with curiosity.

She is wondering if he wants to make up our quarrel, Kate thought to herself. Sending up a quick prayer that Alicia might be right, she followed Randal into his study.

It was a large room with a fine view of the grounds and it immediately struck Kate as being utterly masculine in character.

Enter ye the lion's den! Swallowing hard to control her nervousness, she tried to appear nonchalant, letting her gaze roam free to examine her surroundings.

It was, she concluded, very much the private domain of the master of the house. The gleaming oak floorboards remained bare and unadorned, but the panelling had been removed and the walls were hung with a dark red silk. The furniture was in the Egyptian mode, recently made popular by the architect Thomas Hope. It was an austere style with its severe rectangular shapes and sparse use of decorative elements such as lion or sphinx paws and ebony, brass and silver inlays. Kate wasn't sure if she admired the style or not, but there was no denying it was impressive.

The most striking feature of the room was a massive rose-wood pedestal writing-table inlaid with brass. Randal took up a position before it and waved her to a chair.

Kate sat down. Taking a deep breath, she smoothed her amber cambric skirts and waited for him to speak.

'I don't want to keep you long. I know it was arranged that you would leave immediately after breakfast, but I cannot let you go without offering you an apology for what happened last night.' Randal's tone was as stiff as his expression. 'My behaviour was not that of a gentleman and I can only ask for your forgiveness.'

'You were tipsy.'

'That's no excuse! I abused my position as your host!' Randal tugged at his immaculately tied neckcloth as if it was strangling him. 'I had no right to drag you out into the garden.'

'I stayed out there with you of my own free will,' Kate said quietly.

'And I betrayed your trust!'

Her heart sinking, Kate attempted a smile. 'You are not the first man I've kissed.'

'I don't doubt it,' Randal replied with a flash of his usual dry humour. 'However, we did more than exchange a kiss or two.' His brief answering smile vanished. 'We both know that I took advantage of your innocence.'

Kate winced. He thought her a virgin and there was no way she could explain he was mistaken without blackening Kitty's reputation.

Aware she was skating on thin ice, Kate decided to adopt an air of sophistication. 'Please do not flay yourself, my lord. What happened last night was indeed regrettable, but since my virtue remains intact I cannot see that it is going to do either of us any good to dwell upon it.'

'You are very generous, ma'am.'

There was a sharp edge in his voice and Kate bit her lip. Heavens, did he think she was always so casual in her favours?

'Forgive me, I didn't mean to sound sarcastic. You *are* behaving with more magnanimity than I deserve.' Randal gave an awkward shrug. 'I am angry with myself.'

'There is no need.' Reassured, Kate gave him a little smile.

'No? I think you would be entirely within your rights to scream at me!'

Last night when they had both come to their senses, it would have been simple for her to lay the blame on his shoulders. He rather thought most women would have done so, shrugging off any responsibility for what happened. She had not taken that easy course, but had behaved with a courage and dignity that had impressed him deeply.

Randal stared down into her upturned face. 'You must wish you had never come here.'

'Well, my visits to the Hall have turned out to be rather eventful,' Kate agreed.

There was a sparkle of mischievous laughter in her dark eyes and, seeing it, Randal's spirits lifted.

His folly, it seemed, was not irreparable!

God knows, he reflected wryly, he deserved censure.

It was rare for him to drink as heavily as he had done last night, but he'd been angry that he'd wasted his carefully engineered opportunity of discovering what she truly felt for him. Failing to find consolation in the bottle of his best French brandy Blake had brought in to him after Alicia had retired, he had been wide awake when he heard a stair creaking.

Curiosity had driven him to investigate.

The sight of her luscious body in that thin nightgown had provoked both desire and a burning need to teach her that he was not to be mocked.

She was an accomplished flirt. Yet at Godwin's strawberry-party he had come close to believing that her liking for him might be sincere.

The only way to find out whether she was playing him for a fool was to take her in his arms once more.

So, not quite as inebriated as he was pretending, he had seized what had seemed a heaven-sent chance to put her to the test and swept her off into the moonlit garden.

He had got more than he had bargained for! Stunned by the warmth of her response, his self-control had splintered into oblivion. Every calculating thought in his head had been swept away on a tide of desire stronger than anything he had ever experienced before.

If she hadn't asked him to stop, he would have taken her there and then on the grass without a single thought for the consequences!

He hadn't cared whether she was an adventuress or an innocent. He had wanted her so much he had been willing to ignore the dictates of honour. Shocked by this realisation, self-disgust had forced him to confront his own feelings and he had spent the rest of the long warm night trying to work out exactly what this beautiful and mysterious woman had come to mean to him.

He desired her of course, but he didn't trust her. Gerald Sullivan had failed to back up his assertions, but his own instincts still insisted something was wrong and she was trying to gull him. Suspicion, annoyance and hurt pride had all demanded revenge!

But when he'd seen that look of humiliation on her face a guilty anguish, not satisfaction, had filled him and he had known that the vengeance he had craved was nothing but Dead Sea fruit.

No matter what lies she had told, he didn't want to hurt her.

Randal had always taken his *amours* lightly. Even in the throes of calf-love, he had been able to laugh at himself. Now for the first time he realised he had met a woman with the power to stir his soul.

'You are very silent, my lord,' Kate ventured at last. 'May I ask if you still want our friendship to continue?'

'I can think of nothing which would please me more,' he replied sincerely.

He might be no nearer to solving her mystery, but at least last night's folly had cleared up one doubt. Whatever else was a lie, she wasn't pretending to like him just to secure his support for her claim to the Nixon fortune!

Chapter Nine

'What do you mean he's going away?' Mary dropped Kate's comb on to the dressing-table, her expression incredulous. 'I thought he was going to sign the papers!'

'Keep your voice down,' Kate begged. 'Lady Alicia will hear you.'

They had returned home to Abbey Square an hour ago and this was the first chance they'd had to talk.

Mary obligingly dropped her voice to a more cautious level. 'Are you telling me he won't give us the money?'

Sinking on to her bed, Kate gestured for Mary to sit in the elbow chair by the window.

'I didn't know anything about this delay, Mary, believe me,' she said wearily. 'I tried to persuade him this morning, as I promised you I would. He started off by agreeing that Gerald's refusal looked bad, but then in the next breath said he couldn't visit the lawyers because he was going away.'

Kate had been stunned. Had she mended their quarrel in vain? 'But where…you never mentioned you were thinking of leaving Chester,' she had murmured in confusion.

'I have been invited to the Prince Regent's celebration of his accession tomorrow evening. It is being held at Carlton House,' he had replied.

Kate thought that Kitty would have known that the eldest

son of poor mad King George had at last achieved his ambition to be appointed Regent earlier that year so she nodded.

'I shall be leaving for London within the hour, not that I particularly wish to attend. Prinny's parties tend to be vulgar at the best of times and with this excuse I should imagine he will excel himself.' Randal tried to make a joke to lighten the suddenly strained atmosphere. 'I dare say it will be all solid gold plate and flowing fountains on the tables at the very least!'

Kate smiled politely in response to this piece of banter. 'I hope you will enjoy the occasion, my lord.'

'Thank you.' Acutely aware of her unspoken disappointment, Randal almost regretted he had accepted the royal invitation.

By all accounts some two thousand guests had been invited and he doubted he would be missed, except for one fact. His father and the Regent had been particular cronies and the Regent had taken a kindly interest in him since his father's death some fourteen months ago. Randal did not desire the Prince's favour, but he knew that it was well meant and he had no wish to appear ungrateful.

'Do you mean to stay in London long?' Kate asked, carefully concealing her dismay.

'A few days only.' Randal gave a crooked grin. 'Alicia would have my head if I failed to return in time for her dress-party.'

Lady Edgeworth had been busy with the arrangements for this party in her goddaughter's honour almost from the moment Kate had set foot in Abbey Square. It was to be held on the twenty-seventh of June and the invitations had already gone out.

'I shall arrange a meeting with Hilton on my return,' Randal had continued smoothly.

Although Kate had tried to discover what he intended to say to the lawyer, he would not be drawn.

'So we are no better off than before we went to the Hall,' Mary stated with a snort of disgust.

Kate sighed. 'I suppose not.'

Unlike Mary, however, she didn't think the trip had been a waste of time. It was a wonderful old house and she had felt so at home there. She couldn't regret going, even after last night's fiasco.

Kate was trying very hard to forget what had happened in that moonlit garden, but she was finding it an impossible task. If she closed her eyes she could still feel the pressure of Randal's body against her own, feel his lips caressing hers...

You have no shame, Kate Devlin, she scolded herself silently.

'We will just have to wait and see what happens when Redesmere returns,' she said hastily, forcing herself to concentrate on the problem at hand. 'Unfortunately, by then this dreadful dress-party will be upon us.'

Kate shook her head, her expression miserable. 'I had hoped we would have been able to give Alicia enough notice to avoid the embarrassment of having to cancel it at the last moment.'

'Aye, she ain't going to be very happy if we lope off with no warning.' Mary frowned thoughtfully. 'I know I said some hard things the other day and I'm still keen to get back to the company, but I reckon it's unfair to leave her in the lurch, 'specially after she's laid out such a lot of blunt on your account.'

'Don't remind me!' Kate groaned.

Kate hadn't wanted a party in her honour, but Alicia was set upon the idea and she hadn't been able to persuade her out of it. The finest food and wines had been ordered, the musicians hired and the servants were already busy spring cleaning the house in preparation for the one hundred and twenty or so guests who were expected to arrive.

Mary sighed gloomily. 'We'll just have to pray that Ned doesn't write saying we're needed until the blasted thing is all over and done with.'

Kate shuddered. After all the lies she had been telling lately, she wasn't in the least bit hopeful that the Almighty would exert Himself on her behalf!

'Did you enjoy yourself in Parkgate, Cousin Kitty?'

'It was most agreeable, thank you.' Kate smiled at Emma Lattimer and handed her a cup of coffee.

It was Lady Edgeworth's regular at-home morning and the Lattimers had joined several other visitors calling in Abbey Square to welcome Alicia and her god-daughter home after their brief holiday.

'I think it was a splendid idea of Lady Alicia's to take you to spend a few days by the sea.' Emma took a sip of her drink. 'Matthew suggested we might do the same before we left. However, I decided that I was sure to be sick of the sight of salt-water by the time we reached Spain!'

Mrs Lattimer's blue eyes were merry with amusement.

Kate chuckled. 'Indeed. Long sea voyages are apt to be boring.'

She knew Emma would assume that she was speaking of her own experience crossing the Atlantic, but as Kitty had described this passage to her in some detail she was not afraid of answering questions.

Parkgate had helped her to relax.

Kate hadn't dared admit to herself that she missed Randal, but in spite of her best efforts she had found herself becoming quiet and withdrawn. Putting her lack of colour and loss of appetite down to the continuing heatwave, Lady Edgeworth prescribed a change of air.

'No, I insist, Kitty dear. There is absolutely no reason for us to remain in Chester and it will restore the roses to your cheeks.'

To Kate's surprise, she had greatly enjoyed their visit to the small Deeside village of Parkgate. It wasn't as fashionable as some of the larger sea-bathing resorts and the entertainments on offer were somewhat sedate, but there were several pleasant walks, a convivial Assembly House and a fine lending-library.

Alicia was delighted with the improvement in her spirits. 'I *knew* Parkgate would do you good, Kitty,' she had exclaimed on the third morning of their stay as they strolled along the Terrace, as the main sea promenade was known.

'You are very kind to me, ma'am.' Kate felt a sudden rush of guilt that made her avert her gaze and stare out quickly at the sparkling waves. 'I'm sure you would rather have stayed at home or, if you had wished for a change of scene, gone to London to attend the Regent's party as so many of the *beau monde* are doing.'

'Nonsense, my love. I have always liked visiting Parkgate. I much prefer it to rackety resorts like Brighton, which is ruined by that riff-raff crowd who toadeat the Prince Regent.' Lady Edgeworth gave a disdainful sniff. 'No, I certainly did not wish to attend his party so you may rest easy upon that score, I assure you!'

Kate murmured a soothing response. It was only recently that she had learnt of her benefactress's disapproval of the Prince Regent. Lady Edgeworth was too worldly-wise to shout her feelings from the rooftops, but she had conceived a dislike of the Prince when he had separated from his wife.

Such want of conduct offended Lady Edgeworth, who had strong views on the sanctity of marriage. She might have been prepared to overlook the Prince's other failings, such as his vanity and his notorious extravagance: she could not approve of a man who was so wrapped up in the pursuit of pleasure that he appeared to have no regard for his wedding vows.

Princess Caroline might have her faults—certainly she was a loud and coarse woman—but she was his legal wife and the mother of his child. Not that he appeared to bother much with visiting his daughter and Kate knew that Lady Edgeworth considered that disgraceful, too.

'May I ask if you have made any plans for next Wednesday Cousin Kitty?'

Emma's voice broke in on Kate's private thoughts and she rapidly abandoned them to answer her.

'I don't believe we have any engagements that day,' she replied, offering Emma a plate of seed cake.

'We were thinking of driving out to Malpas and I wondered if you would care to join us? It is a very pretty little town with many fine old buildings, including a church which Matthew wishes to see.' Emma gave a little chuckle. 'I happened to mention to him that it is the burial place of one of my warlike ancestors, the bold Sir Randal Brereton.'

Kate's ears pricked up. 'I didn't realise that your brother bore an old family name,' she murmured.

'Oh, that's due to my grandfather! Certain names have always cropped up in our family tree, but he decided on a deliberate policy of reviving the old English names when Papa was born. Papa decided to carry on the tradition, much to my sister's disgust I might add!'

A puzzled frown tugged Kate's fine brows together.

'Milly's full name isn't Amelia. It's Mildred.' Emma giggled. 'But don't ever tell her I let the secret out. She hates it!'

Kate grinned. 'My lips are sealed!'

'My own name is an old one, too, but after all the fuss she made, I could never understand why Milly elected to continue the tradition,' Emma continued. 'I suppose naming her son Harold was meant as a memorial to our elder brother, but, then she went on to call her girls Hilda and Edith, poor things.' Becoming aware that Kate was staring at her in surprise, Emma paused. 'Didn't you know? About Harold, I mean?'

'Cousin Randal never mentioned having an elder brother.' Kate took a sip of her own coffee to give herself time to recover from the surprise.

'He died in an accident as a child. I believe Papa was devastated.'

Emma shrugged awkwardly. 'It all happened many years before I was born. However, Papa still disliked anyone speaking of it so all I know is that Harold wandered off out of his governess's sight during a family visit to Scotland. Papa found him. He had taken Randal, who was only three years old, out for a walk and they came across Harold lying at the foot of some rocks. He had fallen and cracked his skull. Emma sighed. 'He'd just had his seventh birthday.'

'How dreadful for your parents,' Kate said quietly. 'I'm so sorry.'

It was a horrid story. No wonder Randal didn't want to revive what must be a disturbing memory by speaking of it.

Emma thanked her for her condolences. 'As you can imagine, it made Papa extremely cautious of our safety. He used to get so cross with Randal when he climbed trees or played daring tricks.' A rueful smile flickered over her neat features. 'We girls learnt that obedience to his strict rules was the easiest way to maintain the peace and to avoid his anger, but Randal often defied him and was regularly beaten for it!'

She took a bite of her cake and Kate gave her time to swallow it before putting a question which had intrigued her for some time.

'Forgive my curiosity, but am I right in thinking that the situation did not really improve when your brother was older?'

Emma hesitated and then, apparently deciding that Kitty's family connection entitled her to an answer, nodded her blonde head. 'They were often at odds. Mama always tried to act as a peacemaker. Her efforts were mostly in vain.' Emma set her plate down. 'Please don't misunderstand me, Cousin Kitty, Papa loved us all, but he was very proud and unbending. Perhaps if he had attempted to understand Randal rather than to demand instant unwavering obedience, Randal might have tried harder to please him.'

A wry smile, uncannily like her brother's, twisted Emma's lips. 'As it was, they had so little in common that their differences always ended in a quarrel!'

'I got that impression from something Randal said,' Kate murmured.

'Papa was particularly angry when Randal announced he wanted to join the army once war was declared in 'ninety-three. He wanted Randal to go up to Oxford, but he might have accepted the idea if Randal had shown any tact. But he completely rejected Papa's alternative suggestion of entering the Navy and was obstinately set on the cavalry. I was very young at the time, but I can still remember the shouting!'

Emma's eyes clouded at the memory of her father's fury.

'Mama pleaded with him, reminding him of his patriotic duty. Even Uncle Godwin tried, but I doubt if Papa would have been persuaded if the Prince Regent hadn't intervened. It was his advice which tipped the balance.' She let out a small ironic chuckle. 'Did you know, Kitty, the Prince always wanted a military career?'

Kate thought it safe to admit this knowledge since it was a widely known fact.

'He was prevented by the King from achieving this ambition so he sympathised with Randal and brought his influence to bear on Papa to buy Randal a cornetcy.' Emma shook her head in mock despair. 'I don't know who was the most upset when he left home to join the Twelfth Light Dragoons. Mama and I cried for days until Papa shouted at us to stop. He was still angry with Randal even when he began to achieve promotion.'

'Did your father never relent?'

'Not really. Oh, he was proud of Randal's success, which was entirely through his own efforts, I might add, since Papa refused to do anything further for him, but he wanted him to come home.' Emma shrugged. 'Papa had a bee in his bonnet about the succession and he wanted Randal to settle down. He was immensely proud of our lineage and I think Harold's untimely death preyed on his mind. Mama told me once that he was worried Randal might be killed before he had fathered an heir.'

Kate nodded understanding. Her own father had suffered from a similar obsession, forcing her mother to undergo endless miscarriages in order to obtain the son he craved. When Kate was fifteen her mother had lost her life in yet another vain attempt to satisfy his ambition. Immediately their year of mourning was up, he had promptly married again.

It had been a very unhappy time for Kate. Well aware of her young stepmother's dislike, she had tried not to resent her father's choice, but Lucy's high-handed behaviour made it impossible. Her father, who had never made any secret of his disappointment that she was not a boy and rarely showed her any affection, soon agreed to Lucy's demands that Kate be sent to stay with her maternal grandmother in Carlisle.

At sixteen Kate hadn't wanted to understand that part of her stepmother's hold over her father was sexual, but even then she had realised that Sir George was besotted by Lucy's abundant fertility. Having already presented him with twin boys a scant nine months after the wedding, Lucy had been increasing again when news of Kate's elopement filtered back to the manor house on the shores of Lake Bassenwaite.

Furious, Sir George had threatened to cut all connection between them unless she returned home immediately. The idea of a life of repentance under Lucy's resentful eye was enough to make Kate refuse, even though her rosy dreams had already begun to tarnish after only a brief taste of marriage.

Her father had carried out his threat. Encouraged by Lucy, he had sent one last message, announcing that he had no wish to acknowledge such an undutiful wretch as his daughter.

You have brought disgrace upon us, he had written. *Do not expect any help from me now or in the future. I want nothing more to do with you. You will not be admitted if you attempt to visit and any letters of yours will be thrown on the fire unopened. The rest of your belongings and your mother's pearls will be packed up and sent to you. Once this is concluded, your name will never be mentioned in this house again.*

Even in the fog of shocked disbelief and dismay which had accompanied the blow of his cold words, Kate had understood one thing very clearly. He had no need of her now that he had sons to take her place.

'Papa expected Randal to sell out when the Peace of Amiens was declared.' Emma's soft voice roused Kate from her unhappy reverie. 'Randal refused. He did come home for a while

when Mama was dying, but he resisted Papa's attempts to persuade him to stay and returned to his regiment after her funeral.'

Emma pulled a face. 'It wasn't until after Walcheren that he
sold out and I can't say that I blame him!'

This odd-sounding name was familiar to Kate. The campaign
to help the Austrians by sending men to the island of Walcheren at the mouth of the Scheldt in the hope of diverting Napoleon's attention away from the Danube had taken place
barely two years ago. It had been a complete disaster!

Kate would have loved to ask Emma to clarify what she
meant. Unfortunately, even as she opened her mouth to do so,
Tom Egerton, another of that morning's callers, bore down on
them with an eager smile and the opportunity for any further
private conversation was lost.

It wasn't until the Lattimers were on the point of leaving
that Kate remembered that she hadn't given Emma an answer
to her invitation. Quickly seeking Alicia's permission, which
was immediately granted, she was able to intercept her friends
in the hallway and tell them that she would be delighted to
accompany them on their outing.

'Excellent, Cousin Kitty,' Matthew Lattimer replied, his
pleasant face breaking into a smile. 'It will give us the chance
to spend a day together before we have to leave Chester.'

'I shall be sorry to see you go,' Kate said and meant it.

Emma smiled at her. 'Let's not think about partings,' she
declared cheerfully. 'We have your party tomorrow night to
look forward to and the ball my brother is giving for us.' She
giggled happily. 'I always wanted to hold a costume ball, but
Papa would never agree to it.'

'I hope you have organised your costume, cousin,' Matthew
chimed in with a grin at his wife.

'It is well in hand, sir,' Kate answered.

'Ah, a lady of decision!' Matthew's grin broadened and
Emma instantly began to assert that she *had* made her mind up

this time and would have done so earlier if he hadn't been so horridly rude about her earlier ideas.

Laughing, Matthew bore her away and, trying to crush her envy of their transparent happiness, Kate returned to her duty at Alicia's side.

Bidden to dine in Abbey Square before the party to celebrate Miss Nixon's debut into society, Lord Redesmere arrived some ten minutes early. Handing his hat and gloves to Thorpe, he strolled into the drawing-room and was rewarded by the sight of the young lady in question standing alone by the marble fireplace.

'You are very prompt, my lord.' Kate held out her hand to him with a dazzling smile.

'My compliments, cousin.' Randal lifted her fingers to his lips. 'You look even more ravishing than usual.'

His brilliant eyes glinted as he absorbed her exquisite appearance. She was wearing a gown he hadn't seen before, a delicate blossom-pink *mousseline-de-soie* with long plaited sleeves and a triple-flounced hem. Her shining curls were dressed *à la Sappho* and she wore the Nixon locket around her slim throat.

He wanted very much to kiss her, but, mindful of what had happened last time, he merely expressed the hope that she had remembered to save him a dance. 'Or I shall be utterly desolate, for I am sure your card is overflowing. You dance so divinely it cannot be otherwise.'

Kate laughed. '*Two* flattering compliments in as many minutes! It is easy to see you have just returned from Court, my lord!' she teased, trying to suppress her elation. His words had been lightly spoken, but his eyes burned with admiration. 'I trust you enjoyed your evening hobnobbing with the Prince?'

'It was…interesting,' Randal replied with a lazy smile.

'Is that all you can say?' Kate demanded indignantly.

In response, Randal laughingly described the occasion, but even as he spoke of the Regent's startling appearance in a field-marshal's uniform he'd designed himself and which was so heavily embroidered in gold that it was rumoured to weigh as much as it cost—a full two hundred pounds—he was aware of a niggling unease.

He had spent some of his time in London in seeking the Hogans, the couple Lydia Ashe had requested to keep an eye on her daughter during the journey from America. After that first stormy meeting in the lawyers' office he had instructed Alan Hilton to try and find the Hogans, knowing that if Gerald Sullivan failed to appear they could provide a positive identification of Kitty. After a great deal of diligent and discreet enquiry, Alan had come up with a lead shortly before he was due to depart for London.

This intelligence had suggested the Hogans might be staying with a relative in Chelsea. Randal had gone to their lodgings. The information was correct, it was the right man and his wife, but then his luck had run out. The couple were away, visiting friends in Norwich, and were not expected to return for at least a week. Their niece had promised to give them his letter.

He believed that the Hogans would agree to help. They were well acquainted with Henry Ashe and would certainly wish to reassure themselves of his stepdaughter's safety. As a further precaution he'd deposited a generous sum in cash with a London lawyer named in his letter to reimburse any expenses they might incur in travelling to Chester.

He ought to have a final answer to the mystery of Kitty's identity before the deadline John Nixon had stipulated in his will ran out on the fifteenth of July, the anniversary of his death.

Should he tell her what he'd done?

Staring down into her enchanting countenance, Randal smothered a curse. Damn it, he had to resist his crazy urge to protect her!

It was madness to think of revealing his information. Duty demanded that he keep all knowledge of the Hogans secret until he could present them to her. Otherwise, if she knew what he was planning, he might lose what common sense told him must be his best chance of finding the real Kitty.

In his heart Randal desperately hoped that his suspicions were wrong and the Hogans would confirm that Katharine was the girl they had escorted to Ireland. Instinct stubbornly insisted that they would denounce her as a liar.

For the thousandth time, he wished that she would tell him the truth.

He wanted to hear it from her own lips before it was too late. Once her deception was uncovered, all hell would break loose! And yet, providing the real Kitty was safe, he wasn't even sure he cared any more that she might turn out to be an adventuress. She fascinated him and, no matter what the answer to the mystery might be, he didn't intend to lose her.

Surely she must know by now that he wanted to help her?

There was only one reason Randal could think of why she would not tell him the truth...and it hurt.

But how could he persuade her to trust him?

'My dear Randal! I didn't realise you had arrived!'

Alicia, splendid in royal blue taffeta and a tiara of sapphires and pearls, came hurrying into the drawing-room and Randal was forced to abandon his speculations.

They were sixteen for dinner and, to Lord Redesmere's disappointment when they took their places at the long polished mahogany board, he was seated too far distant from Katharine to permit easy conversation.

'Your little heiress is looking well tonight.' Godwin Crawford nudged his nephew in the ribs as they rose from their port to rejoin the ladies in the drawing-room for a brief interval before the new influx of guests began to arrive. 'Damme, I wish I were twenty years younger!'

Randal shot him a quizzical look. 'Thought you weren't much in the petticoat line, O revered uncle.'

'I ain't,' his relative returned affably. 'Which ain't to say *she* couldn't tempt me.'

Since he was of the opinion that the lady in question could

tempt a saint, Lord Redesmere sensibly raised no objection whatsoever to this remark.

Kate, engaged in conversation with Mrs Egerton, looked up when the gentlemen entered the room and her gaze was drawn like a magnet to Lord Redesmere's tall figure.

He looked so handsome and distinguished in his dark evening-clothes! None of the other men could hold a candle to him! She wanted to leap up, rush to his side and fling her arms around his neck and kiss him until she was breathless!

Naturally, she did nothing of the sort, and after a few more minutes Alicia signalled to her with a wave of her pearl-encrusted fan.

Gracefully excusing herself, Kate joined her benefactress and they took up their position to receive the rest of the guests. By eleven o'clock the steady stream had dwindled to a trickle and all the reception rooms were crowded.

'I'll wait a little while longer in case anyone else decides to come,' Alicia announced. 'You run along and enjoy yourself.'

Her face aching from so much smiling, Kate gave a little stretch of her stiff back, adjusted the gold net scarf she wore over her arms into more becoming folds and obeyed this command.

The drawing-room was crammed full of people and Kate paused on the threshold. She saw Tom Egerton wave and start towards her, but, luckily, Caroline Legh reached him first.

Kate let out a sigh of relief. In a weak-willed moment yesterday she had given in to his importunings and promised Tom the first quadrille, but she knew it was a mistake to encourage him.

A loud hum of conversation, punctuated by occasional bursts of laughter, filled the warm air. Pinning a bright smile to her lips, Kate moved forward.

'Miss Nixon!'

Waylaid before she had advanced a yard, Kate dipped a curtsy. 'Mr Hewitt. How nice to see you here.'

Her youthful admirer blushed. 'I have been longing to talk to you!'

'Have you?' Kate gave him a playful smile, which made his colour deepen still more. 'Dare I ask why?'

He murmured something inarticulate and, taking pity on his confusion, Kate decided to drop her flirtatious manner and ask after his sister's health. 'I understand that the reason she cannot join us tonight is a sprained ankle. Please give her my best wishes for a speedy recovery.'

'Oh, I will!' he assured her fervently.

'How did Sophy actually hurt herself?' Realising that he was too shy to follow her lead, Kate cast about her for some way to keep the conversation from flagging. 'Lady Edgeworth said something about a riding accident. Is that correct?'

Given this encouragement, he launched into a complicated explanation. Kate allowed him to ramble on, nodding and smiling in all the right places, but, of its own volition, her gaze kept straying beyond the heavily wadded shoulders of his evening-coat in search of another face.

When she found him, her face lit up in an involuntary smile, a smile which so dazzled Jack Hewitt that his interminable monologue faltered and he blurted out what he had been wanting to say all along. 'I say, Miss Nixon, you...you look like an angel in that dress!'

Summoned by the invitation in her eyes, Lord Redesmere strolled over to join them.

Mr Hewitt, who stood in awe of his lordship, immediately clammed up, his face turning the colour of a tomato as he belatedly realised what he'd just said.

Kate watched him insert a finger into his neck-cloth and ease it away. Even the ridiculously high points of his shirt-collar were wilting, though whether that was from the heat or embarrassment she wouldn't have liked to hazard.

'I was just remarking to Mr Hewitt how humid it is this evening,' she said quickly, stepping into the breach. 'I shouldn't wonder if we are in for a storm.'

'Quite possibly.' Impatience glinted in Lord Redesmere's eyes.

'Very...very hot in here,' Mr Hewitt ventured, recovering his nerve a trifle.

'And no doubt you are thirsty, Cousin Katharine?' Randal enquired.

Kate nodded warily. What was he up to? There was a gleam of mischief in his bright blue gaze.

'Did you hear that, Jack?' Randal turned to the younger man with an innocent look that didn't fool Kate for a minute. 'Here is your chance to earn my cousin's undying gratitude.'

Mr Hewitt looked at him blankly.

'By fetching her a glass of something cold,' Randal added *sotto voce*.

'Oh, yes, right!' Jack nodded furiously. Turning back to Kate, he cleared his throat shyly. 'May I procure a cool drink for you, Miss Nixon?'

'Please!' Kate rewarded him with a glowing smile. 'I should love a glass of chilled champagne.'

He nodded eagerly and, excusing himself with a somewhat clumsy bow, rushed off to obey her request.

'Randal!' Kate let out a little chuckle at the way Jack had been so easily dispatched. 'That was underhand of you!'

'Teach him not to bore on,' his lordship retorted brutally.

He held out his arm to her. 'Come. Let me lead you out of this crush.'

Delighted at the prospect of having him to herself for a while, Kate allowed him to escort her through the throng. With relentless efficiency, he forged a path for them towards the long windows where a number of chairs had been placed for those desirous of a little quiet conversation.

'That's better,' Randal exclaimed as they sat down and a fresh breeze from the open window reached them. 'You know, the way the wind is getting up we might be in for a thunderstorm after all.'

'I hope not.' Kate gave a little shudder.

'Scared?' Randal allowed his gaze to roam over her delicious form. 'I didn't think you were scared of anything, Katharine!'

Kate blushed at the teasing warmth in his deep voice.

Idiot! Telling herself to stop behaving like a ninny, Kate lifted her chin at him. 'There are several things I find disturbing,' she murmured sweetly. 'Thunder happens to be one of them, although I would not rank it half as irritating as impertinent questions!'

A crack of laughter escaped his lordship. *'Touché!'* He shook his fair head in a gesture of mock despair. 'Why do I bother attempting to cross swords with you, little cousin?'

'Perhaps you like to live dangerously, my lord,' Kate retorted with a sparkling look.

'Perhaps I do.'

Randal gazed into her dark eyes. God, but he had missed her while he was away! He had found himself longing to hear her contralto voice at the oddest moments. No other woman had the same power to interest, amuse and rouse him. What's more, he no longer cared who knew it!

A pair of chattering young ladies came towards them, plainly meaning to sit down and rest their tightly shod feet. Forgetting her good intentions, Kate glared at them in her most ferocious manner and they retreated with startled haste.

'Oh, dear, I shouldn't have done that!' she exclaimed ruefully, catching sight of Randal's amused glance. 'It was appallingly rude of me!'

'Don't worry. I was about to do the same myself,' he consoled her with a wicked grin.

Kate laughed, a warm throaty sound which caused Lord Redesmere's loins to tighten in response.

'I wish we were back at the Hall,' he said abruptly.

'So do I,' Kate answered honestly before she had time to think.

Randal's brows lifted. 'We could seek out a quiet spot,' he suggested delicately.

Temptation simmered in the air. With a visible effort, Kate conquered her desire to surrender to it.

'I don't think that would be wise.' Her dark ringlets danced reluctant denial.

Silently Randal acknowledged she was right. If they were alone, he wouldn't be able to resist his need to kiss her.

Pulling himself together, he cast about for a safe topic of conversation. 'I understand from my sister that you went to Parkgate while I was in London. Did you enjoy the change of scene?'

Kate confirmed it and was in the middle of an amusing description of her sole attempt to try a healthy sea-bath when Jack Hewitt returned with her champagne.

'Thank you!' She took the glass from him with a grateful smile.

'Didn't you bring me one, Jack?' Randal asked gently.

Mr Hewitt, who was wishing his lordship at the Devil, shook his head. 'Er...I didn't realise you were thirsty, sir,' he muttered in confusion and, embarrassed by his lapse, took a hasty gulp from his own glass.

Lord Redesmere's pained expression achieved a new intensity.

Bowing to the inevitable, Jack sighed. 'I'll go and fetch another glass of champagne, my lord.' He jerked his head at Kate, his expression glum. 'Excuse me, Miss Nixon. I'll be as quick as I can.'

He stalked off, his back bristling with indignation.

Her eyes brimming with amusement, Kate watched the young man retreat. 'Out-manoeuvred, out-gunned and most definitely routed,' she murmured.

'He'll learn to do better when he's older,' Randal remarked with a singular lack of feeling.

Kate opened her mouth to make a saucy retort that his lordship obviously had no need to take lessons in guile and then thought better of it. The subject was too uncomfortably close to home!

A sudden flash of lightning lit up the dark sky beyond the window, drawing their attention.

Observing her alarm, Randal asked if she would like the window closed.

Kate nodded gratefully and, scorning to summon a servant, Lord Redesmere rose to his feet and performed the task with his usual brisk efficiency.

No soon had he sat down again than a loud rumble of thunder made Kate flinch. 'Did Emma tell you that she has invited me on an excursion to Malpas?' she said quickly to distract her mind from the disagreeable weather. 'To visit the church of St Oswald?'

Randal nodded. 'Matthew wants to see the Brereton monument, I believe.' He smiled at Kate. 'The carving is very fine.'

'I'm sure I shall enjoy the outing, but I must own that I am a little puzzled by Mr Lattimer's interest,' Kate acknowledged, taking a sip of her champagne. 'Somehow, he doesn't strike me as a lover of sculpture.'

Randal laughed. 'Matthew is more interested in the story of the muzzled bear.'

'Muzzled bear?' Kate's black brows winged upwards in thought. 'A bear features on your family crest, does it not?'

'Correct. I salute your excellent memory, O learned cousin.'

'Stop teasing and tell me why this bear is important,' Kate said severely, tapping him smartly on the forearm with her folded fan.

Another streak of lightning illuminated the night as Randal obliged. 'The original Brereton crest was a bear. Then one of my remote ancestors, a stalwart knight so it is said, was guilty of excessive ardour in battle. His bold attempt was witnessed by the King, who was displeased by it. ''I shall muzzle that bear,'' he declared and his order duly went out to the College of Heralds.'

A little chuckle escaped Kate. 'A most salutary tale, sir.'

Randal grinned at her. 'I can't promise you it's true, but the chest tomb in St Oswald's does have a muzzled bear carved to lie at Sir Randal's head.'

'And your family is related to the Breretons, hence the bear on your escutcheon.' Kate's generous mouth curled up in a quizzical smile. 'Is your bear muzzled, Randal?'

He shook his head warily.

'I see,' Kate murmured. 'That explains it.'

Knowing it was a trap didn't prevent Lord Redesmere from demanding to know what the deuce she was on about.

'Why, your lack of concern for the conventions, my lord.' Kate widened her eyes innocently at him.

Randal let out a crack of laughter. 'You abominable little wretch! The next thing you'll be telling me is that boldness is an inherited trait!'

They were both still laughing a moment later when Lady Edgeworth came sweeping up to them.

'Kitty, my dear.' Alicia's voice was high-pitched with excitement and she spoke loudly to make herself heard over another roll of thunder. 'I have a surprise for you. Only look who is here!'

Her benefactress was beckoning someone forward. He came closer and Kate started violently. She felt herself turn pale, her thunder-strained nerves jumping with superstitious horror.

'Katharine?'

She ignored Lord Redesmere's urgent undertone and, as if in a nightmare, watched the dandified young man halt in front of her chair and execute an elegant bow.

When he straightened, she saw that his eyes were not a soulful Celtic blue, but merely nondescript grey and her pent-up breath was released in a sudden rush.

What a fool she was! Just because he had a distinct resemblance to her late husband, there was no need to let a stranger rattle her into a panic! To be sure, he had the same slight build and romantically tousled black curls, but on closer inspection he was nowhere near as handsome as Francis had been and was obviously several years younger to boot. Probably no older than twenty-two or three, in fact.

Distance, and her nervous dislike of thunder, had lent him that uncanny likeness to Francis, nothing more!

Draining the contents of her champagne glass to settle her nerves, she summoned up a polite smile. 'Good evening, sir.'

'Is that all the greeting you can spare for me, *mavournin*?' The stranger's voice had a soft Irish lilt.

It sent a cascade of ice down Kate's spine and her fingers clenched convulsively upon the slender stem of her glass as she stared at him in helpless dismay.

Chapter Ten

Lightning streaked across the sky, bringing with it a heavy curtain of rain to drum against the window.

'I take it I am still in the suds, then?' the newcomer continued lightly. He flaunted a charming smile in her direction. 'And here was I hoping you had forgiven us for our lack of welcome, Cousin Kitty.'

'Cousin…Cousin Sean.' Feeling as if she was about to faint, Kate struggled for composure. 'I trust you are in good health?'

'Excellent, thank you, *mavournin*.'

Kate realised that his eyes were fixed upon the locket she wore around her neck and a shiver chilled her spine. He must guess I got it from Kitty, she thought in dismay.

'And before you ask, I can tell you that I left my parents blooming like the roses.' He smiled at her again. 'They charged me to deliver their best regards.'

'How kind.' Kate's tone was sugar-sweet, but her blood was racing with a violent mixture of fear and rage.

How dare this monster turn up here after what he had done!

Sean Sullivan turned to Lady Edgeworth. 'There, now. Didn't I tell you she would be pleased to see me once the first shock was over, Lady Alicia?'

What the devil was he up to? He *must* know she wasn't Kitty!

A light touch on her arm reminded her of Lord Redesmere's presence.

'Are you all right?' he asked in a quiet undertone as Sean loudly assured Alicia of his desire to be Kitty's friend.

Seeing an opportunity to escape, Kate shook her head.

'This storm…' She let her voice trail off piteously.

Right on cue, a particularly loud clap of thunder rent the air and Kate let her empty glass slip from her fingers with an artistic little shriek.

The effect was all she could have hoped for.

Heads turned in their direction and several people came hurrying up.

'Kitty! My love, you are as white as a ghost!' Lady Edgeworth fussed over her charge, patting her hand anxiously.

'Permit me, ma'am, to escort my cousin to her room.' Lord Redesmere's deep voice cut decisively across the babble of comment and advice. 'She will do better if she is allowed to rest quietly until the storm blows itself out.'

'I shall come up with you—'

'Mary will look after me,' Kate interrupted in a faint voice. 'Pray stay with our guests, ma'am, and make my apologies. I don't want my affliction to spoil anyone's enjoyment of the party.'

Alicia hesitated and then nodded her assent.

Randal assisted Kate to rise and put a steadying arm around her waist. 'Lean on me,' he ordered and Kate was only too glad to obey.

'I hope you will feel better soon, Kitty.' Sean Sullivan's voice matched the concerned expression on his narrow face but, as they passed him, Kate glanced up and saw that his grey eyes were filled with anger.

She shuddered and Lord Redesmere's arm tightened around her waist.

'Steady! Don't faint on me, I beg of you!' he commanded with a touch of his usual dry humour.

Their progress was slow, hampered by anxious enquiries and

good wishes for her recovery, but at last they left the reception rooms behind and reached Kate's bedchamber.

Randal announced their presence with an imperious knock and flung open the door.

Mary leapt to her feet in startled dismay as his lordship calmly steered Kate into the room and sat her down on the bed.

'God-a-mercy, what's wrong, lass?' Mary flung down the sewing with which she had been occupied and hurried over to Kate's side.

'The thunderstorm has upset your mistress,' Lord Redesmere replied, giving no indication that he found this greeting in any way untoward. 'See to it that she rests.'

Mary bobbed an obedient curtsy. 'Yes, my lord.'

'Thank you for your help.' Kate judged it safe to speak at last. She had been playing the part of the invalid for all it was worth for fear that he might ask awkward questions. God knows, it was imperative he didn't connect her agitation with Sullivan's arrival! 'I am sorry to be such a nuisance.'

'Nonsense!' Lord Redesmere replied briskly. 'You cannot help being afraid of thunder. My sister Milly is the same. An indomitable woman in all other respects, she hides in cupboards at the first clap, I do assure you.'

Kate permitted her mouth to curve in a brave smile. 'All the same, I fear I may have spoilt the party,' she murmured, vastly relieved that her exaggeration of her own natural fears had succeeded in deflecting his attention.

'On the contrary, you've given them something to talk about.' A hint of amusement lit his lordship's bright gaze.

'I'll come down again if the storm ceases.' Kate made the offer, knowing it was expected.

'I'll send up urgent prayers to Jove asking him to end his thunderbolts.' The warmth in his lordship's voice was marked.

Mary let out a judicious cough.

'Quite right.' Randal bowed elegantly to them both. 'It's time I took my leave.'

As soon as the sound of his footsteps died away Mary demanded to know what was going on.

'Sullivan!' She let out a low whistle. 'Fancy him resembling Francis! And all this thunder, too. No wonder you are feeling shook up, love. Shall I brew you a soothing posset?'

Kate refused this well-meant offer. 'I can't afford the time to have a fit of the vapours,' she commented wryly.

She slid from the bed and went to stand before the fireplace. Staring into the unlit black grate, she muttered, 'What the hell are we going to do, Mary?'

Mary grimaced. 'Damned if I know, lass! Sullivan! Who would have reckoned he'd have the brass neck to show up here after what he did to Kitty?'

Kate looked up and gave a short laugh. 'I strongly suspect that *gentleman* has enough impudence for anything,' she stated, remembering the coldness of those grey eyes. 'I just wish I knew what his game was.'

Mary shook her head in bafflement. 'By rights, he should have denounced you the minute he laid eyes on you.'

'He didn't even seem surprised,' Kate said slowly. 'It was almost as if…Mary, do you think he came here *expecting* to find an imposter?'

Mary rubbed her nose thoughtfully. 'It's possible, I suppose. Leastways, they must have suspected that their plan had gone wrong when Mr Hilton wrote to them asking the old man to come and identify Kitty.'

'Let's try and think this through.' Kate drummed her fingers against the marble mantelpiece. 'The Sullivans must have realised that Kitty, if she had survived, would have had to have had help from someone.'

'Aye, she couldn't have got away on her own. The poor lass was in a terrible state.'

'So, they would wonder who helped her. Now it's likely any respectable citizen fishing Kitty out of the river and hearing her claim her cousin had tried to drown her would have immediately alerted the authorities. Even if Kitty had persuaded

them not to do so, it's odds on that they would have gossiped.'
Kate frowned thoughtfully. 'But there wouldn't have been any
gossip filtering its way up to Ballyhad House because the Gillman Players were the only ones who knew what really happened.'

Mary sat down heavily in the chair by the window. 'You
think that the Sullivans might have guessed Kitty's helpers
weren't locals?'

'It makes sense.' Kate nodded. 'And our playbills were plas-
tered all over town.'

Brushing back a strand of hair from her hot forehead, she
took a deep steadying breath. 'We've got to face the possibility
that Sean knows that the Gillman Players are somehow involved in Kitty's disappearance. If he does, he must also be
aware that we know what he is.'

'Aye, a would-be murderer.'

Mary's eyes met hers across the room and Kate saw her own
fear reflected in her friend's anxious gaze.

The thunderstorm did not abate for several hours, giving
Kate an excuse to avoid returning to the party. However, the
next morning dawned clear, although much cooler than it had
been of late, and she knew that she couldn't hide in her room
for ever.

A confrontation with Sean Sullivan was inevitable.

'I believe he will call on me this morning,' she told Mary
as she finished her ablutions.

'You could pretend you were still feeling ill,' Mary suggested.

Kate shook her dark head. 'I'd as lief get it over.'

She had made poor work of the breakfast Alicia had insisted
on sending up to her bedroom, but she had recovered her nerve.
'At least he can't offer me violence in Alicia's house.' She
gave a wobbly grin. 'Too many witnesses!'

'Don't joke!' Mary whirled from laying Kate's clothes out
on the bed. 'That man is dangerous. We know he's prepared

to commit murder to get at the Nixon fortune. You can't afford to take chances, Kate!'

'I know but, having come this far, I'm not prepared to give up tamely and let him walk off with Kitty's fortune.' Kate threw her towel on to the washstand. 'Don't you see, Mary? By acknowledging me last night Sean has confirmed my claim to be Kitty!'

She began to put on her underclothes. 'He can't turn round and say I'm an imposter after half of Chester heard him call me cousin. He has furnished the final proof and I'm going to demand that the lawyers pay up.'

'Aye, but why did he acknowledge you?' Mary demanded. 'He must have realised it would give you the advantage, unless he is a complete idiot.'

'I don't know,' Kate admitted. She bent to slip on her shoes and the rest of her reply was slightly muffled as she added, 'He must have some scheme in mind.' She straightened up again. 'But I'm not going to let him scare me off.'

Mary sighed. They had argued whether it was safe to stay last night. Then, as now, Kate had worn her stubborn face.

'At least consider my idea of contacting Ned,' Mary urged. 'He ought to be told what's going on and so should Kitty. With any luck she might agree to come out of hiding.'

'Not a chance. Once she knows Sean is here, she'll fly into a panic.'

'Happen, happen not. Don't forget she's had a few weeks to get over the shock of what he did to her. You remember her as a terrified little creature, but I reckon she wouldn't want us to run into danger on her behalf.'

'Maybe you're right, but I don't want to worry her or the others. At least not until I've found out what Sullivan is up to.' Kate wanted to deal with Sean herself. 'This impersonation was my idea. I don't want to drag Ned here to save my bacon. It isn't fair on him.'

'He'd gladly help. You know he's sweet on you.'

'All the more reason then to do it on my own,' Kate retorted tartly.

'You are as stubborn as a mule, Kate Devlin,' Mary exclaimed in exasperation. 'We ought to be packing to leave and you won't even ask a friend for help!'

'I *will* ask Ned if I can't manage to deal with Sullivan on my own, but this mess is of my making and it's up to me to try and sort it out,' Kate answered more quietly. 'Ned's done enough for me already and I won't take advantage of his feelings for me.'

Mary shrugged irritably and picked up the gown from the bed. 'Have it your own way.' She held out the gown to Kate. 'But for God's sake be careful and don't let that Irish bastard get any opportunity to be alone with you.'

'I won't.' Kate laid her hand on Mary's arm and gave it a quick affectionate squeeze. 'I promise.'

She breathed in the fresh scent of newly laundered and ironed cotton as Mary helped her into the jonquil dress and took comfort from its normality. Truth to tell, she wasn't sure she was doing the right thing. Part of her longed to book a ticket on the next coach out of Chester. Playing a brave heroine on stage was one thing, acting the part in real life was quite another!

Mary seemed to think it was folly to stay and fight. Yet she hated the idea of letting the Sullivans win. Hated it almost as much as the thought of inflicting hurt on Randal. And he would be hurt if she suddenly ran away.

The alternative, of course, was to confess that she had lied to him from the start, but she didn't think she had the courage to do that. She couldn't bear to see the warmth fade from his eyes and watch his expression harden in contempt!

Kate stared at her reflection in the glass as Mary put the finishing touches to her hair.

You are an idiot, Kate Devlin, she told herself and went to find Alicia.

'My dear! I didn't think you would be down so soon!' Lady

Edgeworth exclaimed as Kate walked into the morning-room. 'Are you sure you are feeling quite the thing?'

Kate went over to her chair and bent to kiss Alicia's cheek. 'I am perfectly well, thank you, ma'am,' she said, feeling a rush of genuine affection for the older woman. 'And I do hope that my stupid affliction did not embarrass you last night, particularly after all your kind efforts on my behalf.'

'Lud, child, there's no need to apologise!' Alicia shrugged philosophically.

To be sure, she had been disappointed by Kitty's early exit, but otherwise the party had been successful.

'Thank you for your forbearance. I just hope other people will be so understanding,' Kate murmured.

'You are a very popular girl, Kitty, and, at the risk of sounding vulgar, a rich heiress can be forgiven almost any eccentricity.' Alicia gave her a complacent smile.

Delighted that her benefactress was not miffed with her, which she had feared might prove the case, Kate gladly jettisoned her burden of guilt and sat down.

Alicia began to rattle on about who had said what and who had danced with whom at the party.

'By the by, Mr Sullivan said he'd call on us this morning to see how you did,' she announced. She gave Kate a shrewd look. 'I fancy he wishes to mend bridges, but I know you hold him in dislike.'

Kate acknowledged it. 'I want as little as possible to do with him,' she said firmly.

'I understand your sentiments, my love, but I must own I was pleasantly surprised by how he has turned out,' Alicia confessed. 'Gerald brought him over here on a visit some ten or eleven years ago and I thought him a very spoilt child. All I had heard of him since seemed to indicate he had gone on to become an extremely wild young man. However, last night I could not fault his behaviour. He offered me a very pretty apology for turning up without warning and even volunteered to leave, saying he didn't wish to intrude on my party.'

Kate snorted, barely managing to change it into a cough as Alicia turned surprised eyes upon her.

'I can see from your expression that you think me easily pleased, Kitty. But I can assure you he made a good impression upon everyone. Several people remarked upon his charming manners, including the Leghs and the Egertons. Indeed, I overheard Tom asking him if he wished to attend a cock-fight this evening.'

Kate shrugged. 'I do not deny Mr Sullivan has charm, ma'am,' she said. 'However, having experienced the other side of his nature, I have no wish to further the acquaintance.'

'You didn't used to like Lord Redesmere,' Alicia pointed out mildly. 'But you seem to have changed your mind about his character.'

A tide of colour stained the translucent skin which stretched over Kate's high cheekbones. 'I was wrong,' she agreed in a cool little voice.

'Oh, dear, I didn't mean to offend you, Kitty!' Lady Edgeworth fluttered her carefully pampered hands in agitation. 'You do like Randal, don't you?'

Unable to deny it, Kate nodded silently.

'It is very obvious he likes you. Everyone was talking of his partiality last night.' Alicia smoothed her skirts. 'In fact, Lady Massey asked me when the engagement was to be announced.'

Horrified, Kate stared at her.

'Now don't be flying into a pet!' her ladyship advised soothingly. 'You may be sure that I was discreet, but you cannot blame people for speculating when you both appear to get on so well. You are always laughing together and he has a habit of looking at you as if you were a banquet and he a starving man!'

A reluctant laugh escaped Kate's compressed lips.

'I've heard that they are laying bets on a wedding before the summer is out,' Lady Edgeworth added in a low whisper.

Kate took a deep breath. Damn the gossips!

'I value Randal's friendship,' she said tightly. 'But I must repeat that I have no desire for marriage as I hope you will make clear, ma'am, to anyone who has the temerity to ask about my intentions!'

'I shall do my best,' Alicia promised, but her expression revealed that she didn't think her denials would be believed.

A knock at the door interrupted them and Kate forced down her anger as the footman came in, carrying a silver salver.

She hadn't realised that her friendship with Randal had become fuel for loose tongues. It wasn't surprising, she supposed. He was a very eligible bachelor and Kitty's money would always attract attention.

But how was Randal going to feel if everyone started whispering that he'd been jilted once she disappeared back to her real life?

Lady Edgeworth held up the visiting-card which George had brought in. 'Mr Sullivan is here,' she announced. 'Shall we receive him?'

Kate abruptly abandoned her painful speculations and consented with an appearance of calm that belied her racing pulse.

Lady Edgeworth nodded to George and a moment later Kate's *bête noire* was ushered into the room.

He was looking very dashing in a smart tan coat and biscuit-coloured pantaloons and a charming smile lit his narrow face as he bent over Lady Edgeworth's hand in greeting.

'Good day to you, Lady Alicia. A lovely fresh morning, is it not?'

He turned to Kate and bowed once more. 'Cousin Kitty. I hope you are feeling better today.'

'I am, thank you.' Kate inclined her head in acknowledgement, but did not hold out her hand to him.

Annoyance flickered in his grey eyes at the deliberate snub.

Kate didn't care. The idea of him touching her revolted her. Besides, flattery wouldn't work. He would remain her enemy whether she cajoled him or not.

Alicia invited him to be seated and instructed George, who

hovered expectantly awaiting further orders, to bring them refreshments.

'Tell me, Mr Sullivan, do you find Chester much changed? It is many years since your last visit, if I'm not much mistaken.' Alicia launched into a stream of small talk, which left Kate free to examine her supposed cousin more closely.

In full daylight his resemblance to her late husband was less marked. They possessed similar colouring and the same lean frame, but Sean's features were harsher and already marked with evidence of dissipation. The dark circles under his eyes and those tiny broken veins marring his pale skin had been veiled by candlelight. Morning sunshine was less kind.

Too much drink and high-living, Kate concluded. She'd met his type often enough, spoilt young men who made a drunken nuisance of themselves shouting and carrying-on during a performance. If he didn't break his neck trying to lead the hunting-field or win some crazy wager, his good looks would be gone before he reached his thirtieth birthday!

Becoming aware of her gaze upon him, Sean stared back at Kate and his mouth curled into a satisfied little smile.

He thinks he can charm me, Kate realised indignantly. The impudence of the man! Heaven knows what he was up to, but did he really think she would be so stupid as to trust him?

'I'm putting up at the Feathers, in Bridge Street,' Sean informed them when his hostess paused for breath. 'A tolerable kind of place, but I'm not a great one for inns. No home comforts, you see, and it's so difficult to get a good night's sleep.'

Kate exchanged a swift glance with Lady Edgeworth, who gave a tiny shake of her elaborately curled head.

Reassured, Kate was able to dismiss her fear that Alicia might take up his broad hint.

'I dare say you feel the same way, Kitty, since I find you lodging with her ladyship.' If he was disappointed not to be invited to stay in Abbey Square, Sean took care to hide it behind a jovial chuckle.

Kate nodded coolly. 'I prefer to stay with *friends*,' she replied, laying a delicate emphasis on her final word.

'Kitty has made lots of new friends here in Chester,' Alicia broke in quickly. 'We have been inundated with invitations since her arrival.'

'I'm sure she's a *succès fou* and not just because of Grandfather Nixon's money.' He gave Kate one of his charming smiles, but Kate's keen ears detected a note of bitterness behind the compliment.

Kitty had told her that, thanks to their massive debts, there was no money to fulfil Sean's desire to cut a dash in London. Even the pleasures of Dublin, which lay a couple of miles or so to the east of Ballyhad House, were beyond his purse, although apparently Sean didn't let that deter him.

He must think my success could have been his if only the Nabob had left the money to them instead of me. No wonder he resents me. Or rather, he resents Kitty!

Aware that her thoughts were becoming dangerously convoluted, Kate forced herself to pay attention to what Sean was saying.

'I hope you can allocate some time for me in your busy social round, Kitty,' he was continuing in the same pleasant tone. 'One of the reasons I called today was to ask you if you would care to have supper with me one evening soon.'

'My evenings are very full at the moment, I'm afraid,' Kate replied blandly.

'Surely you can spare me an hour or two?' Sean adjusted the set of his striped brocade waistcoat, tugging it down a fraction. 'I know we got off to an unfavourable start, cousin, but, truly, I should like the opportunity to prove I'm not such a bad fellow.'

Kate shrugged lightly, ignoring the look of appeal in Alicia's eyes. 'I do not wish to break prior engagements, sir,' she said sweetly.

The arrival of their refreshments provided a welcome diversion and, to Lady Edgeworth's relief, her goddaughter discarded her provoking behaviour in favour of consuming one of Mrs Hibbert's excellent little drop cakes.

'Will you take another glass of Madeira, sir?' she asked politely, noting her guest had already finished his wine.

Sean accepted, holding his glass out to be refilled with an imperfectly concealed eagerness that confirmed Kate's earlier guess that he might be a toper.

He was just finishing this second glass when George announced the arrival of another visitor.

'Lord Redesmere! Do come in and join us,' Alicia invited.

Randal strolled into the room, his tall elegant figure drawing Kate's gaze like a magnet.

When all the polite formalities were over and he was comfortably settled with a glass of wine, Alicia asked him if he had come to see how Kitty did.

'That was my intention, ma'am, but I see there is no need for me to ask.' He directed one of his lazy smiles in Kate's direction. 'You exceed even your usual good looks this morning, Cousin Kitty.'

Kate coloured slightly as she laughed and thanked him for his compliment. It was lovely to hear him sing her praises, even though she didn't deserve his admiration.

Impulsively, she got up and changed her seat so that she could engage him in a private conversation, leaving Alicia to entertain Sean.

'I had hoped we might go and see Mr Hilton today,' she murmured, keeping her voice low so that the others couldn't hear. 'Now you have your proof of identification.'

Randal was very well aware of it. He had lain awake half the night pondering its implications.

'I should be happy to oblige,' he answered quietly. 'However, Hilton has gone out of town. He won't be back until next week and I want to consult him before we sign the documents.'

Kate's face fell.

'Are you in such a hurry to get the business over and go back to America?'

Every instinct longed to scream denial, but Kate managed to summon a carefree smile. 'I certainly don't want to miss Emma's costume ball,' she replied lightly, evading the question.

Randal decided not to press her for an answer. He sensed that her earlier determination to leave Chester had weakened, but she obviously didn't care to admit it.

Randal wondered if he were a coxcomb to hope he was the attraction which made her want to stay. Her sentiments towards him had certainly changed, just as his own had. Their initial hostility was only a memory now, but how deep did her attraction go?

Uncertain of his own feelings, Randal felt as if he were floundering in a mass of newly discovered thoughts and emotions. Nothing in his previous experience provided a guide to help him find the right path now. Even his instincts, which he had always been able to rely upon, seemed to be letting him down. He could have sworn that she was an adventuress and yet Sullivan had vouched for her.

Last night he had returned to Godwin's house flown with elation. This morning, however, his doubts had come rushing back as he contemplated the idea of giving up his carefree bachelor existence. He was thirty-six years old and set in his ways with a string of meaningless liaisons behind him. What did he know of love?

How, in God's name, did any man know when it was real enough to last a lifetime?

'My costume is all ready and I hope to create a stir!' Kate noticed the lack of focus in his gaze and wondered where his thoughts were drifting.

'Am I to be permitted to know what character you mean to come as?' Recovering from his fit of abstraction, Randal put the question to her with a slight smile.

Kate shook her head. 'It is a secret. I want to surprise you.'

Randal decided against probing further. She was sure to look lovely even if she came as a beggar-maid, but he was rather

oping she might choose to be a nymph and wear a scanty
evealing costume!

'Actually, there's another matter upon which I would like
your opinion,' he announced, hastily curbing his unruly imag-
nation. 'Shall I invite Sullivan to the ball?'

Kate lifted her thin brows delicately at him. 'I would never
presume to dictate your guests, my lord.'

Randal's smile grew broader. The little baggage plainly de-
ested the fellow! 'Can't say I care much for him either,' he
onfided softly. 'All the same, I think I had better do the pretty
r tongues will wag.'

'I thought you didn't care what the gossips said,' Kate re-
narked, her heart thumping painfully against her ribs at this
eminder of the power of scandalmongers.

'I don't as a rule, but as I mentioned to you once before,
ttle cousin, my sisters do.'

'Do you always bow to your sisters' wishes?' Kate asked
rovocatively.

'I find it saves tedious argument to always agree with
women,' he nodded with mock solemnity.

'Fie, sir! I don't believe a word of it!' Kate wanted to whoop
with mirth at the idea of him living under the cat's foot. 'You
ften disagree with me!'

'Ah, but you are a very special woman, Katharine.'

The warmth of his smile brought a blush to her cheeks.

'What nonsense you do talk, my lord!' she alleged hastily,
onscious that the Irishman was straining his ears to discover
hat they were laughing at. 'I dare say that when your mind
set upon something you don't give a fig for accommodating
our sisters.'

'Truth to tell, I usually do my best to oblige them if I can,'
andal protested. His grin faded. 'However, you are correct in
inking that I draw the line at letting them dictate my conduct.'

He paused and Kate allowed her curiosity to appear on her
ace.

'Milly is always on at me to marry. She says it is time I

settled down.' Randal gave a short laugh. 'Mind you, she usually adds the rider that I am getting long in the tooth to find a girl who will put up with my stubborn ways!'

Kate stared at him in frank astonishment. Even shorn of wealth and title, Randal Crawford would still attract women in droves! He was a virile man in the prime of life, not some silly fop or useless weakling. His sister might not be able to see it, but to every other red-blooded female of his acquaintance Lord Redesmere's self-possession and innate air of command were incredibly seductive.

Only a nun could resist the potent appeal of a man whose cool smile acted like a magnet on the senses!

Randal noted her disbelief and, secretly jubilant, explained that in Milly's opinion he had been a bachelor too long. 'She blames my solitary state on my lack of regard for the conventions and informs me that a properly brought-up young lady desires more refinement in a husband.' Randal shrugged his broad shoulders, his expression wry. 'Oh, and my antiquarian interests are another handicap since they must bore all but the most dedicated bluestocking!'

Kate gave vent to a throaty chuckle of amusement. What an idiot his elder sister must be! 'Does Emma agree with this assessment?'

'Not entirely, although she agrees it is time I found myself a bride.'

Randal knew what his sisters would say if he told them that he was contemplating matrimony. The resulting hullabaloo was yet another reason for being absolutely certain of his feelings before he took any action whatsoever!

'I must take my leave of you, cousins.'

Their attention captured by his announcement, Sean Sullivan rose to his feet. 'Are you sure now that you won't have a bit of supper with me, Kitty?' he asked, employing one of his charming smiles.

Kate shook her head. 'I fear I cannot, sir.'

'Then come for a ride with me tomorrow. I'll hire a hack and you can show me Chester.'

Unlike the real Kitty, who was in practice, Kate hadn't ridden on any regular basis since she was sixteen. Her skills were sadly rusty and, although she wasn't afraid of falling off, any clumsiness on her part might appear odd. 'I'm sorry. I don't have a riding habit available.'

'Couldn't you borrow one?' Sean pleaded. When the glossy sable curls shook denial once more he frowned. 'Then why don't I hire a carriage?' he suggested, his voice hardening. 'Surely you can have no objections to taking a short drive with me?'

Kate hesitated. She had no intention of going anywhere with him, but she didn't want to provoke an argument.

'Actually, Sullivan, our cousin has already agreed to come out with me tomorrow,' Randal intervened calmly. 'I am taking her to see the Nixon mansion in Vicar's Lane.'

For an instant anger flared in the grey eyes. 'I see,' said Sean coldly. 'In that case, Kitty, I'll not be troubling you.'

He turned to bid farewell to Lady Edgeworth and then swung round to face Kate once more, a new smile pinned firmly to his lips. 'We still have lots to talk about, *mavournin*. Maybe we can arrange the outing for another day.'

'Of course,' she replied with what she hoped was convincing sincerity.

'I'll count the minutes.' Sean bowed to her with an extravagant flourish.

'Let me escort you to the door, Mr Sullivan,' Lady Edgeworth offered, rising to her feet.

'Much obliged, ma'am!' Sean held out his arm to her with flamboyant gallantry.

She gave Kate a reproving look in passing and Kate had to stifle a sigh. The situation was bad enough without Alicia flying into a pet with her!

'Don't worry.' Lord Redesmere proffered this advice with

an encouraging smile. 'Alicia is no fool. She'll soon see that Sullivan is merely turning up her sweet.'

'Do *you* think I should forgive him?' Kate demanded boldly.

'I would never presume to dictate your conduct, cousin,' he replied wickedly.

Hearing the echo of her own words, Kate laughed. 'I suppose I deserved that! Seriously, though, do you think my refusal to accept his friendship will occasion talk? I don't want to embarrass Alicia.'

'I shouldn't let the thought of gossip deter you if you have decided against the fellow. You are under no obligation to him or his family, although it is clear that he is hoping that you are going to agree to hand over a share of the Nabob's money—'

'I most certainly will not do so!' Kate interrupted indignantly.

Randal hid a smile. He couldn't blame her for feeling angry. Sullivan had himself confirmed her oft-repeated claim that they had treated her with deliberate discourtesy and she had too much spirit to find forgiveness easy, especially when Sean's repentance was so patently insincere.

Lord Redesmere owned himself puzzled by Mr Sullivan. In spite of his flowery compliments, a furious resentment smouldered in those grey eyes whenever they rested on Katharine. Only someone like Alicia who saw good in everyone could fail to spot it. Given the nature of the old Nabob's will, it was understandable that the fellow was bitter, but, somehow, Randal felt there was more to his dislike than a simple grudge.

Maybe his instincts were at fault again, but, all the same, he decided that he would keep an eye on the Irishman.

'Your best course is simply to ignore his blandishments. Once he realises you aren't going to succumb to his charm, he will likely leave Chester,' Randal said with confident assurance that belied his inner uneasiness. 'After all, he cannot force you to change your mind.'

'I have no intention of allowing him to do so,' Kate affirmed and thanked him for his advice.

'Now, assuming you do want to view your grandfather's property, what time shall I call for you tomorrow?' Randal continued briskly.

Glad to leave the subject of Sean Sullivan, Kate discussed the details of their visit, but after Randal had departed she couldn't help wondering if he was right about the Irishman.

His interpretation of Sean's motive for pursuing her made sense. She just hoped his conclusion that Sean would soon give up the pursuit was equally correct!

The Nixon mansion in Vicar's Lane was a handsome brick-built property. Set well back from the road, it possessed a large cobbled courtyard enclosed by iron railings. On each side of the ornate gates were stone-faced carriage houses constructed to resemble lodges.

'Good heavens, it looks like a public hospital!' Kate exclaimed as Lord Redesmere's curricle drew to a halt.

Randal laughed. 'The style is somewhat heavy and severe, I'll grant you, but it was all the crack some fifty years ago.'

Kate, who rather regretted her impulsive frankness, was reassured by the twinkle in his bright gaze. 'Did my grandfather have it built?' she asked, trying to do the necessary sums in her head as a servant came running to open the gates and admit them.

Randal shook his fair head. 'He purchased it from the original owner on his return from India in 1770. I remember him saying once that his future in-laws were very impressed when he showed them where he and his bride would be living.'

Kate knew that John Nixon had made his fortune with the East India Company before retiring at the age of forty with the aim of marrying well and launching himself into society. Alicia's fondness for gossip had also inadvertently revealed that, while he had acquired a well-bred wife, he had failed to gain the acceptance he craved.

'Naturally, his fabulous wealth opened many doors, but he was a very opinionated man,' Alicia had remarked. 'I don't think it was his connection with trade that was held against him so much as the fact that he was too clever and outspoken.' She had sighed heavily. 'It was such a pity your papa did not share his dreams of shining in society for he pinned all his disappointed hopes upon Charles. Indeed, after your parents emigrated, he sold off all his other property and became a positive recluse.'

Kate felt rather sorry for the Nabob. By all accounts he had been a miserable old curmudgeon, but thwarted ambition was a good recipe for bitterness. No wonder he had been so angry with his son when Charles had defied him to marry Lydia!

'Did Hilton explain to you that the bulk of the fortune is tied up in investments and shares?' Randal inquired as he assisted Kate to alight.

She nodded, shaking out the skirts of her amber carriage-dress. 'He told me that there were several fine paintings and some excellent jewellery, but no property other than this house. Apparently, my grandfather didn't care for country life.'

A grin flitted over Randal's handsome features. The old man's strictures on that head were quite unfit for feminine ears! 'No, he didn't. His first wife, your grandmother, persuaded him to buy a very handsome estate out near Llangollen, but he rarely set foot in the place.'

Randal gave instructions to the servant about the care of his horses and then offered Kate his arm.

'Shipping was the Nabob's preferred investment,' he informed her as they began to walk towards the main entrance 'He was very good at picking lucky captains. In his later years he liked talking to them far more than anyone else. He even left generous bequests to several of them.' Randal shrugged 'He could be a difficult man, as I'm sure your mother must have mentioned, but he wasn't the ogre some people make out.'

'I'm sure he wasn't,' Kate said warmly, realising that Randal had been quite fond of his great-uncle.

They reached the flight of steps which led up to the front door and Kate stared at the house, wondering what Kitty would make of it. Three storeys high with rusticated stone at ground level and pedimented gables at either end, it was very grand and impressive, but Kate couldn't like it.

Once inside, her first impression of gloomy grandeur was modified a little by the elegant proportions and beautiful rococo plaster ceilings which graced the principle rooms. The furnishings were magnificent, too, with exquisite crystal chandeliers and fine paintings everywhere.

'In his will your grandfather instructed that the house be kept in perfect readiness for your return,' Randal remarked, running a finger along the shelf of the ornate rose-coloured marble mantelpiece which graced the drawing-room.

He held his finger up and Kate saw that it was free from dust.

'I believe he hoped you would make your home here.'

Kate recoiled. 'I should hate to do so!' she exclaimed, shaking her head so vigorously that one of her glossy sable curls became unpinned. 'All this cold stiff formality would give me the vapours!'

Randal chuckled. 'I must confess it isn't to my taste either. However, you could always throw everything out and start again if you wished to live here.'

'It isn't a condition I have to fulfil in order to receive my inheritance, is it?'

A prickle of anxiety raised a cold sweat along Kate's spine. Had she misunderstood the terms of the will?

'Don't look so alarmed, Katharine. You are free to do whatever you wish with this house. There is nothing to stop you selling it the minute the ink is dry on Hilton's papers.'

Lord Redesmere's faintly amused expression faded. 'Or you could keep it while you make up your mind what you are going to do next.'

Kate barely managed to restrain a guilty shudder. She was beginning to wish she had never come to view this…this mausoleum! The very act of doing so brought home to her the enormity of what she was doing.

Stop it, Kate Devlin! What does it matter how much money this house is worth! Your deception isn't hurting anyone. The Nabob *wanted* his fortune to go to Kitty. Randal doesn't need it and the Sullivans certainly don't deserve a penny.

A tense little silence fell while Kate struggled with her guilty conscience.

Randal took a step towards her. '*Have* you decided your next move?'

Kate swallowed hard. 'Not…not really,' she faltered, unwilling to admit how desperately she needed the money.

The original plan concocted between Ned, Kitty and herself was to demand that all the money which could be quickly realised be handed over to her. Once they had it in their possession, she and Mary would immediately rejoin the company. Kitty would then have the necessary funds to pay Kate for her efforts and buy herself a passage home.

When she was safely back in Amherst, Kitty intended to send further instructions to the lawyers.

'But that can wait,' Ned had asserted. 'Your first priority, Kate, is to squeeze as much rhino as you can out of them once you've signed those papers.'

Kate had blithely agreed, never realising how embarrassing the task would turn out to be. Randal, Alicia, Mr Hilton—they had all been mere names to her then. Now they were real people and she knew that her behaviour would disappoint and hurt them. They would think her a grasping harpy, but time was running out…

Randal moved closer. His eyes glittered. 'Have you ever thought of staying in England?' he demanded abruptly.

Kate gasped. 'I…I cannot. I must return to America very soon.' She dropped her gaze to avoid meeting his eyes and began to pleat the edge of her silk shawl with nervous fingers. 'My mother expects me home once the business of my legacy is concluded.'

'I'm sure she would understand if you told her you wished

to stay in Chester while you considered your options.' Randal halted in front of her. 'Postpone your departure! Please!'

Kate shook her head and the lock of hair that had been loosened earlier tumbled down her neck. 'I don't think that would be sensible,' she whispered, refusing to look up.

Randal took her chin in his long fingers and gently tilted her head up so that she was forced to meet his gaze. 'Shall I let you into a secret?' he said softly.

Kate's eyes widened in surprise at this unexpected question and he smiled down at her with a tenderness that made her heart start thumping wildly.

'I'm nervous, too, sweetheart.' Randal's hand moved to caress the pure line of her jaw. 'I feel as if I were standing at the edge of a precipice, not knowing whether to jump or not. Down below is a sea of dreams holding all that I ever wanted from life, but the idea of stepping out into the unknown makes me hesitate and cling on to what I've already got, even though it no longer satisfies me.'

His eyes burned into hers. 'You see, falling in love is dangerous.'

The breath seemed to catch in Kate's throat. 'Are you…are you saying what I think you are saying?' she faltered.

'Aye.' He began to wind the loose curl around his finger. 'I'm caught in your spell.'

He paused, his lips only inches away from her own and, dizzy with excitement, Kate could hardly breathe. She longed for him to kiss her!

'I want you to stay, but I don't know if I have the right to ask. We barely know one another…' There was a tremor of uncertainty in his deep voice which Kate had never heard before.

He paused. 'Your company makes me happy,' he continued simply. A tiny choke of laughter escaped him. 'To be absolutely honest, my dear Miss Nixon, whenever you are near me all I want to do is take you in my arms and make love to you!'

His smile fading, Randal released her lock of hair. 'However, we could be letting our mutual attraction overrule our common sense.' His mouth twisted into a wry grimace. 'Or maybe I'm just a hopeless coward who doesn't deserve you.'

'I don't think you are a coward.' Kate lifted up her arms and wound them around his neck. 'It takes courage to face one's doubts.'

An impulse to confess the depth of her own feelings rose in Kate. She crushed it ruthlessly. Far from being in a position where she could return Randal's honesty, she was about to desert him. Exposing him to malicious gossip was bad enough. Telling him that she loved him would make her abrupt departure seem even more base.

It was much too late to try and persuade him that she didn't care a rap for him. All she could hope for was to soften the eventual blow to his pride. He was on the verge of falling in love with her in earnest and much as she longed to encourage him it wasn't fair. He would get over her far more quickly if he thought she had been merely indulging in an indiscreet flirtation.

'You are right,' she agreed in a light-hearted tone. 'It is too soon to be sure of our feelings. It would be easy for us to pretend that everything is going to be wonderful, but dreams don't always last.' She gave an airy laugh. 'Reality has a nasty habit of intruding and love can fade into oblivion if it isn't strong enough to withstand the knocks that everyday life can dish out.'

'You sound as if you have been in love before.' A pang of totally irrational jealousy shot through Randal and his arms tightened instinctively around her slim waist.

'I thought I was.' Kate shrugged lightly, inwardly cursing his acute perception. 'It didn't last, but the aftermath was quite amazingly painful. So, you see, I *do* know what you are trying to say.'

'And you don't mind?' His bright gaze was dubious. 'We both know what is expected of a gentleman. A little light flirting is acceptable, playing fast and loose with a lady's affections is not.'

'Are you only playing with me, Randal?' Kate couldn't resist asking.

'You must know I'm not!' he declared hoarsely and, before Kate could prevent him, swooped to capture her mouth in a passionate kiss.

Chapter Eleven

Knowing she ought to resist was no help at all. The embers of erotic excitement, which smouldered whenever he was near, flared up into a devouring flame, burning away Kate's good resolutions in an instant.

To Randal's delight, she clung to him, kissing him back with a fervour that was as unladylike as it was welcome. Her lips parted eagerly beneath his and her little tongue darted to entangle with his own. The blood roared in his veins as she pressed closer, her fingers burying themselves in the hair at his nape.

Her gloriously wanton response had an inevitable effect and feeling himself harden, Randal pulled away a little, breaking off the kiss.

'Say you will stay.' He whispered the words hoarsely into her ear. 'At least for a while longer!'

'I promise you I won't leave until I have to.' Kate clung tighter, a desperate urgency filling her.

She didn't want to leave him! It would break her heart, but if she stayed and he discovered the truth his illusions would be shattered in a far worse manner.

'Then I won't ask for more.'

She looked so lovely smiling up at him that Randal couldn't deny his need to kiss her again, but even as he bent his fair head he knew he had to take care. He had let passion bring them within a hair's breadth of dishonour once before and he knew it would be unfair on them both to ignite that dangerous conflagration again.

Much as he longed to caress her beautiful willing body, he would have to resist!

Instead, he contented himself with showering a rain of tender little kisses upon her upturned face. From brow to eyelid, from cheek to the tip of her nose and to her mouth again in one last slow and lingering kiss, his lips bestowed a gentle benediction.

'Did anyone ever tell you that you kiss beautifully, Lord Redesmere?' Kate trailed her fingers across his broad shoulders with a tiny sigh of satisfaction.

'I ought not to kiss you at all without a formal declaration of my intentions,' Randal murmured ruefully.

'Why?' Kate demanded with a pert look. 'How can anyone find out whether they suit unless they practise first?'

He gave a choked laugh. 'You have somewhat unusual views, ma'am!' He stroked a wisp of stray hair from her brow. 'I don't think your chaperon would approve!'

'Maybe not, but I've always thought it rather unfair that a man must declare himself before his kisses are considered proper,' Kate announced with a wicked grin. 'Ladies are allowed to be fickle. Why can't a man admit he might not be sure? It's not a crime to want to be certain of one's feelings. Marriage is for life, after all.'

'Marriage?' Randal released her abruptly and stepped back a pace.

Kate blushed vividly. 'I'm…I'm sorry,' she stammered, mentally damning her own stupidity. 'I had no right to mention marriage—'

'You have every right!' Randal's expression revealed his disquiet as he interrupted her. 'Marriage is the usual outcome for two people in our situation. It's perfectly natural you should wonder if my intentions are honourable.'

'After what happened at the Hall, I think I already know that you are a man of honour,' Kate said quietly, abandoning her flirtatious manner. 'I do not believe you would use my feelings to take advantage of me.'

'As usual, you are more than generous, cousin.' A tinge of colour warmed Randal's sun-bronzed skin at the reminder of his earlier folly. God knows, he had wanted her so much that night he would have counted honour well lost!

'We both know I behaved badly,' he said gruffly. 'But I promise you I will never lose my head in such a manner again. I want you to be able to trust me!'

She nodded, too full of guilty remorse to offer him any re-assurance.

Unnerved by her silence, Lord Redesmere plunged on. 'I do not wish to deceive you, Katharine. You know I find you extremely attractive, but I have always fought shy of marriage.'

It was true, but it was not the whole truth.

How could he explain that he was waiting for the Hogans to appear? Given that Sean Sullivan had confirmed her identity his procrastination seemed absurd and yet his instinct still insisted that something was wrong.

To complicate matters still further, he had promised his father that he would carry on their line and the debt he owed him demanded that he choose a suitable bride.

Honour compelled him to act with caution and listen to the warning voice in his head.

'I don't want to promise you something I can't deliver,' he said carefully, adding with genuine sincerity, 'As far as I'm concerned only an absolute bast…only an absolute rogue would abuse a woman's trust by coldly feigning a love he did not feel in order to secure a conquest.'

Kate flinched away from the memories his words unwittingly conjured up.

Seeing his look of concern, she shook off the past and swiftly summoned up a sophisticated smile. 'I certainly don't expect you to make me an offer just because we have exchanged a few kisses!' She put one hand on his arm in a gesture of reassurance. 'No matter what convention decrees, I think that would be stupid. Too many people rush into marriage and then regret it.'

Randal laid his hand over hers. 'I was worried you might feel insulted if I told you that I didn't yet know the depth of my feelings for you,' he said, a note of rueful apology in his deep voice. 'But when you began to talk of going home I couldn't keep silent any longer.'

'Why should I be offended? I am used to plain speaking, remember?' Kate spun away from him and, planting both hands on her hips, tilted her chin at him, her expression full of mock indignation. 'Furthermore, I'll have you know, sir, that one of the qualities I value most in a man is honesty. Give me unvarnished candour rather than Spanish coin any day!'

'Then you are happy to let things remain as they are, sweetheart?' Randal held out his hands to her, finally convinced that she had accepted his excuses without resentment. 'Is friendship enough for now?'

'Of course.' Kate reached out to clasp his hands in her own.

He cared enough to be honest with her. It was more than she deserved!

On emerging from St Peter's the following morning Kate was accosted by Mr Sean Sullivan.

'I thought I'd attend Morning Service here,' he explained breezily. 'Someone told me that the sermons were always excellent.'

Thinking it more likely that someone had told him it was Lady Edgeworth's regular habit to worship at St Peter's, Kate gave him an acid smile. 'I hope you found this morning's text instructive, sir,' she murmured and had the malicious satisfaction of seeing him colour up.

The sermon had been based upon the first letter of St Paul to Timothy 6:10. Kate thought it singularly appropriate in the circumstances.

Alicia frowned at her. The love of money is the root of all evil, indeed! Really, the child could be most provoking!

'Pray do not tease your cousin, Kitty,' she said with unwonted severity.

'I'm sure Mr Sullivan knows I am only funning, ma'am,' Kate replied sweetly.

Sean quickly concurred. 'Sure now, Lady Alicia. I can take a joke,' he laughed.

He turned back to Kate. 'I won't deny I was piqued to discover Grandfather Nixon had played favourites, but I assure you I'm over my disappointment now. All I want is for us to be friends, Kitty. I don't begrudge you a penny of the old man's fortune.'

How she managed not to spit in his eye Kate didn't know. Of all the liars!

Aware of Alicia's anxious gaze, Kate reined in her temper. Quarrelling with this trickster would lower her in the older woman's estimation and she needed Lady Edgeworth's continuing good-will.

'That is kind of you, Cousin Sean.' Kate employed her most brilliant smile. 'If you are prepared to let bygones be bygones, why, then I shall do the same!'

This reply won her a delighted response from both her hearers, but Kate's patience was tried when Alicia then went on to invite Sullivan to join them for dinner that evening.

'I'd love to, dear lady, but I'm already promised to Lord Redesmere.'

Kate gave a tiny start of surprise, which she quickly disguised by fussing with her parasol.

Randal hadn't said anything to her about inviting Sean to dinner. How odd! She thought he didn't like the Irishman.

She abandoned her speculations just in time to hear Sean accept Alicia's invitation to join them on their forthcoming visit to the theatre.

'Is that all right with you, cousin?' he added with a solicitude that grated on Kate's nerves. 'I don't want to push in where I'm not wanted.'

Kate summoned up a smile. 'I'm sure your company will add to our enjoyment, cousin.'

The compliment nearly choked her, but she was damned if she would give him the satisfaction of wrong-footing her in front of Alicia.

Kate's determination was sorely tested over the next two days. Sean Sullivan haunted Abbey Square and she was forced to resort to the excuse of a sick headache to avoid driving out with him.

'I swear I'll throw something at him if he asks me out again,' she told Mary crossly as she dressed for the trip to the theatre on Tuesday evening.

'Here, let me do that for you.' Mary took the Nixon gold locket from Kate's impatient fingers. 'You'll break that fine chain, tugging at it like that.'

She fastened the clasp and stood back to admire her young friend's appearance. As usual, Kate looked lovely in that prim-rose crape, but her dark eyes were shadowed with strain.

'Bear up, lass. Sullivan is a pain in the backside, but he can't do us any harm. Mr Hilton is home the day after tomorrow. Once those papers are signed, Sullivan can go whistle.'

Kate nodded, her expression lightening. 'You're right, Mary. I am being silly to let him rattle me. It's probably what he wants!'

Kate was still puzzled by the Irishman's behaviour. He was busy making friends with all of Lady Edgeworth's acquaintance and was already a popular figure. The city's Summer Music Festival had begun, quickening the pace of social events, and she kept bumping into him everywhere she went. When she questioned Alicia, her benefactress had admitted he had asked for a list of their engagements. There was nothing Kate could do to prevent him haunting her. She would just have to put up with it.

Damn the man! Why couldn't it be Randal who was her escort tonight? She hadn't seen him since their visit to the Nixon mansion and she missed him desperately. However, he had mentioned that he hoped to see her at the theatre, which was something to look forward to in what promised to be an otherwise difficult evening.

Sir Richard Fitton, whom Alicia had also invited to share her box, arrived with commendable punctuality and the three of them set out for Northgate Street, where Sean Sullivan was to meet them at the entrance to the theatre.

The dark-haired Irishman was already waiting when they reached the playhouse and he greeted them effusively.

They made their way to Lady Edgeworth's box and Sean paraded a great fuss of seeing Kate settled. Listening to his flowery compliments, Kate wondered what was going on in his head. Alicia believed he wanted to make amends, but Kate would sooner believe that pigs could fly.

Trying to ignore his irritating attentions, Kate stared about her with interest. As usual, the theatre was over-hot from all the lights and the press of bodies which filled the crowded benches and boxes. A familiar smell of candle-grease, sweat and stage-paint wafted up to her from the stage and Kate felt a pang of nostalgia. She ought not to have come! Simply being here was unsettling her nerves!

Up to now she had managed to avoid visiting Chester's Theatre Royal, although she had been curious to see it. Alicia had told her that it was housed in the reconstructed old Wool Hall, once part of the medieval St Nicholas Chapel. The exterior was something of a hotchpotch, but the auditorium was smart enough with space for a proper orchestra and plenty of gold paint everywhere. Handsome wrought-iron chandeliers provided illumination and there were fancy red curtains draping the stage.

In fact, it was a better theatre than most of the places she had played in, apart from the one in York. Backstage, it was probably another story. Managers never cared if actors suffered inconvenience and green-rooms were always shabby in her experience, although she had heard that things were better in the big London theatres. Not that the Gillman Players aimed so high. They played the provinces, with occasional forays to Ireland when Ned managed to secure a booking.

She lent over the edge of the box, scanning the audience for Randal, but could catch no glimpse of his tall figure.

'Take care, *mavournin*. You'll do yourself an injury, so you will.'

Much you'd care, Kate thought, withering him with a look. Then, remembering, she forced her lips to curve sweetly. 'Oh, pray do hush now, cousin! See, here comes the prompter with his staff. They are about to begin!' she exclaimed in her best girlish tones.

He nodded obediently and sat back in his seat as the prompter struck the floor with his staff three times and the curtain rose to reveal a cleverly painted backcloth showing the interior of a noble house.

The programme began with a popular song and then a couple performing a Highland Reel before moving on to a short recitation given by a pretty actress. The main item on the playbill was *The Fatal Marriage*, a tragedy by Southerne, which had been made popular by Mrs Siddons. Kate had attempted the part, but she did not consider tragedy to be her forte and the sufferings of the heroine, Isabella, were too long-winded for her taste.

The plot began to unwind. To Kate's disgust, the actress playing Isabella was trying to copy Sarah Siddons's high-flown style, but her voice lacked authority and her gestures seemed petulant rather than tragic. When she completely misjudged one move and almost stumbled into one of the oil-bath footlights which brightened the stage, Kate gave up.

Her wandering attention soon succumbed to anxiety over the problem of extricating herself from Chester without hurting anyone and she twisted restlessly in her seat.

'Can you not see as well as you might, Miss Nixon? Perhaps you would like to exchange seats with me?'

Kate shook her head at Sir Richard. 'Thank you, sir. It is kind of you to ask, but I am quite comfortable,' she whispered back, resolving to stop fidgeting.

She was glad when the interval arrived.

'Would you care for a stroll to stretch your legs, Kitty?' Sean enquired.

When she refused he announced he would go alone and excused himself. Kate continued to scan the other boxes and the pit. After a few moments Lady Alicia suggested they adjourn to the coffee-room.

'I am not thirsty, ma'am,' Kate declared, still hoping that Randal was here and would pay their box a visit.

'I'm not sure we should leave you on your own.' Her benefactress cast a doubtful glance at Sir Richard.

'I dare say Miss Nixon will be all right for a few moments,' he said in his gentle voice.

'Of course I will.' Kate smiled at him gratefully.

After a little more persuasion Lady Edgeworth was convinced and Sir Richard escorted her out of the box.

They hadn't been gone more than a pair of minutes when Kate's attention was caught by the sound of a quiet knock. She jumped up to open the door, thinking it might be Lord Redesmere.

A burly man dressed in working-clothes stood there. 'You Miss Nixon?'

Kate nodded.

'Message for you. There's someone who would like a word with you.'

Kate's fine brows lifted in surprise and the man hastily thrust a folded sheet of paper at her. 'Gentleman told me to give you this.'

Kate unfolded the note and let out a gasp.

It read: *Meet me downstairs.*

'Shall I take you to meet him, miss, or not? Said he needed an answer quick.'

Beneath the single line of writing was a bold *R*. Kate stared at it in consternation. Something must be wrong for Randal to approach her in this hole-in-the corner fashion!

'Very well.' Kate followed the man out into the corridor. Moving at a purposeful speed, he led her through the old building, taking bewildering shortcuts which confirmed her guess that he was probably one of the stagehands.

'Right.' They came to a halt in a temporarily deserted corridor on what Kate concluded must be the ground-floor. 'Through there, miss.' Her escort pointed to a door. 'He's waiting for you in the alleyway.'

'He's *outside*?'

The man shrugged, an embarrassed expression on his face. 'Said he wanted to talk to you private-like,' he muttered. 'It's up to you what you do, miss, but I've got to get back to work and I can't leave this door open. More than my job's worth.'

Good God, he thinks it is a romantic assignation!

Kate squashed her unseemly mirth and began to fish in her reticule for a coin.

'No need for that, miss.' The workman hurried to unlock the door. 'Gentleman already paid me.' He held it open for her. 'Good luck!'

Kate went through and found herself in a narrow stone passageway. The door immediately slammed shut and she heard the bolts ram home.

It was very gloomy, but she could see a tall male figure, dressed in a dark suit of clothes with his hat pulled well down waiting near the end of the passage. He was carrying a cloak over one arm and had his back towards her.

'Randal!'

At her approach the figure turned in her direction and, even as her surprised brain registered his black mask, he flung the cloak he carried over her head.

* * *

'May I come in, Cousin Kitty? Lady Alicia said you were allowed to have visitors today, but if you are tired I could come back later.'

Kate sat up against her pillows and signalled Emma Lattimer to enter the bedroom. 'Don't go,' she begged, waving her visitor towards the elbow chair by the window. 'There is nothing wrong with me, save boredom, but Alicia won't let me get up.'

Emma sat down and stripped off her gloves. 'I must say you look better than I expected. From what Randal said I thought you would be a mass of cuts and bruises.'

Kate gave an abrupt laugh. 'My bruises are in an unmentionable spot! But, yes, I'm all right.'

'Are these flowers from Randal?' Emma enquired, pointing to the exquisite bouquet of summer blooms which decorated the little drum-top table near her chair. 'He said he had called to ask after your health.'

Kate nodded. 'What exactly did your brother tell you?' she asked cautiously.

'Well, I didn't swallow the polite fiction he tried to feed me, if that's what you mean,' Emma declared with a touch of indignation. 'I knew you wouldn't cry off from our trip to Malpas for a mere toothache so I went to see him yesterday and wormed the truth out of him.' She gave a shudder. 'It must have been a terrifying experience!'

'It was.' Kate's tone was grim.

'Randal said you had no idea who your attacker was?'

Kate shook her head.

She was lying, of course. She had a very good idea of who had attacked her, but she couldn't prove it.

Sean Sullivan was behind that attack or she was a Dutchwoman. But why had Randal been there so conveniently on hand to rescue her?

At the time Kate had been too relieved to question his presence. She would have thanked the Devil himself for getting her out of that scrape, but she'd had two days to lie here thinking about what had happened and a cold chill settled on her heart whenever she tried to explain Lord Redesmere's presence in the Rows that night.

Blinded by the cloak Sean had tossed over her, Kate had struggled to free herself from his strong grip. The heavy cloth muffled her cries and hampered her arms, making it easy for him to snatch her up and fling her over his shoulder like a sack of turnips.

Half-choking for want of air and jolted uncomfortably against his back as he hurried along, Kate fought off panic. She couldn't tell which way they were heading, but she knew she had to get free quickly. The Theatre Royal wasn't far away from the Rows, which were unlit and notoriously dangerous at night. Respectable people kept well clear, leaving the area to footpads, drunkards and ne'er-do-wells. Even if she managed to scream for help, it was unlikely anyone would interfere.

Sean had attempted murder once already. Let him get her to a quiet spot and her fate would be sealed!

She could hear him panting. She was slim and didn't weigh much, but her frantic wriggling was making it difficult for him to carry her. He stopped. Kate thought at first it was so he could catch his breath and then his arm came up and it dawned on her he was going to try to knock her senseless.

She jerked her head away at the last second and he missed, his fist crashing into her shoulder instead. The blow was painful, but Kate scarcely noticed it. He was dragging her into a more upright position, probably to make the task of rendering her unconscious easier, but the movement was causing the edge of the cloak to work loose, freeing part of her face.

Gulping in air, Kate immediately twisted her head and bit his ear lobe, sinking her teeth into his flesh with a desperate, savage fury.

He let out a startled shriek of pain and, in pushing her away, dropped her.

Kate landed heavily on her bottom, spat out blood and struggled to scramble free of the cloak.

'Bitch!' His hand flew to his injured ear.

Before she could regain her feet he sprang towards her, his fist upraised and Kate screamed at the top of her well-trained lungs.

A loud sound of booted footsteps running in their direction answered her cry.

Sean's head jerked up. He hesitated for an instant and then, realising how close the stranger was, let out an explosive curse.

Snatching up his cloak, he whirled and fled.

'Let me help you.' Her rescuer skidded to a halt beside her and extended a hand to assist Kate to her feet.

'Randal!' It was too dark to make him out clearly, but his voice was unmistakable. 'What…what are you doing here?'

'I was on my way to the theatre. When I saw that fellow behaving so suspiciously I couldn't resist an urge to play the knight errant.' Lord Redesmere shrugged lightly.

'Not that I realised you were the particular damsel in distress,' he continued in the same insouciant tone. 'I shall be fascinated to hear how you came to be in such a predicament, but I think we had better leave explanations for later.' He placed a supportive arm around her shoulders. 'This is not a healthy place to linger at this hour.'

He had taken her home, ignoring her protest that Alicia would be frantic.

'You can't go back to the theatre. You are in no fit state to be seen,' he had pointed out with brutal logic.

Kate gasped and he had added in a kinder voice, 'Don't worry. I'll inform them of what has happened.'

When they reached Abbey Square he had handed her over to the care of Mary, who was summoned by a visibly distressed Thorpe. Feeling close to tears herself, Kate had allowed Mary to fuss over her. Put to bed with soothing compresses and a hot posset, the shock had worn off sufficiently for her brain to start working again by the time Alicia returned home.

'Kitty, my dear! Whatever happened?'

'It was my own stupid fault,' Kate murmured and launched into the story she had decided to tell of how deciding she fancied a breath of air, she had impulsively stepped outside the theatre.

'Then I heard a cry for help coming from the alleyway and without stopping to think I ran towards the sound. It was a trap, of course.' She sighed artistically. 'That footpad must have seen me and decided I was easy game. He got away with both my reticule and my gold locket.'

The Nixon locket had indeed disappeared. Kate thought the chain must have snapped during her struggles to free herself and she felt terribly guilty about losing it.

'You poor girl! Thank goodness Lord Redesmere was on hand to rescue you!' Dabbing at her eyes, which were overflowing with sympathy, Alicia quite forgot to scold her charge for being so independent.

To ward off further enquiries Kate had pretended to feel ill, but her ploy backfired on her when Alicia ordered that she remain in bed.

'She says that I may get up for your costume ball tomorrow night. *If* I rest quietly until then,' she informed Emma with a doleful sigh.

'Then I had better go away and leave you in peace,' Emma chuckled.

'Aren't you going to tell me about your trip to Malpas?' Kate demanded.

Emma was happy to oblige, but they had only been chatting for a few more minutes before Alicia came to tap on the door with instructions that it was time for Kitty's nap.

When Emma had gone Kate lay back with a thoughtful expression. She was sure she could trust her friend to be discreet about the attack, but discretion alone wasn't going to solve the problems besetting her.

Alicia's insistence on her remaining in bed meant that she had not been able to sign those all-important papers yesterday. She had pleaded with Alicia to summon Mr Hilton, but her benefactress had refused.

She had also turned Randal away, merely promising to convey his flowers and good wishes to Kitty.

Kate could have screamed in frustration.

'As soon as you are allowed up, you'll have to demand the money,' Mary had advised anxiously. 'We've got to get out of here. It's as plain as the nose on my face that you are in danger so long as that villain is on the loose.'

Kate had nodded. Sean was bound to try again.

She was furious with herself for falling for his trick. It had been stupid of her to assume that the note had come from Randal!

Gossip and her own behaviour must have convinced the Irishman of her attraction to Lord Redesmere and he had used her susceptibility to lure her away from the safe companionship of her friends. Like a fool, she had rushed into his trap.

Worse, she dare not denounce him and he knew it!

Well, he would be laughing on the other side of his face now! Kate smiled grimly. She hoped her bite had poisoned him!

Still, she was going to have to be very careful. He was getting desperate and she couldn't hope to avoid him completely. Until those papers were safely signed every minute spent in his company would be fraught with danger.

A little chill feathered down her spine.

For that matter, just how safe was she in the company of the man she loved?

Kate shifted uneasily against her pillows, trying to flick the thought away, but, once again, it stubbornly persisted.

She had once angrily declared to Mary that Randal Crawford was probably in league with the Sullivans. She had long since dismissed the idea as ridiculous, but during these last two days it had come back to haunt her.

He said he didn't like Sean but he had invited him to dinner. Such civility, like the invitation to Emma's ball, could be excused on the grounds of their distant connection, but Alicia had mentioned that Lord Redesmere had taken Sean along to his club. Jack Hewitt had also seen them together at a prize-fight on Saturday evening.

Try as she might to dismiss these events as unimportant, Kate was uneasy. Was it just a stroke of luck that Randal had been on hand to save her the other night? She felt terrible for doubting him, but his explanation lacked conviction. For heaven's sake, it was a very odd route for him to take to the theatre!

Kate bit her lip, struggling to ward off a sense of panic. She *must* be mistaken! She could trust Randal, of course she could.

It *had* to be a coincidence that Mr Hilton had departed town just when she was about to sign the papers. The alternative was too horrible to contemplate!

Ablaze with lights, Crawford Hall put Kate in mind of an enchanted castle in a fairy tale. As she stepped down from Alicia's carriage and made her way inside the house, the illusion was strengthened. Everywhere she looked cavaliers and knights, shepherdesses and queens, Romans and more Tudors than she could count abounded.

To her intense satisfaction, she didn't spot anyone wearing a costume similar to her own.

'Kitty!' Her hostess, dressed with lavish splendour as Queen Elizabeth in a silver farthingale and red wig, greeted her with a pleased cry. 'Oh, doesn't she look lovely, Matthew!'

Lieutenant Lattimer, who might have stepped out of the frame of one of the Hilliard miniatures kept in the Library, nodded speechlessly.

Kate smiled at him and turned to greet the man on Emma's other side. 'Good evening, Randal,' she said, lowering her painted eyelids demurely.

For a moment, like his brother-in-law, Lord Redesmere seemed to have lost the power of speech. Recovering, he made her a flawless bow.

'Greetings, "my serpent of old Nile".'

Recognising the quotation, Kate laughed in delight. 'I cannot

claim to be Cleopatra, sir. I ask only to be taken for one of her
subjects.'

'And you have succeeded brilliantly.'

Quickly turning to his sister, who was now welcoming Lady
Edgeworth, stately in hooped petticoats and a towering pow-
dered wig, Randal murmured a few words. Then, offering Kate
his arm, he led her swiftly away.

'You are deserting your post, my lord.'

'It's Emma and Matthew's party.' He smiled lazily at her.
'Let them do the honours. I want to be with the most beautiful
Egyptian lady I have ever seen.'

The approval in his eyes warmed Kate's heart and more than
made up for the hours spent in concocting her outfit...and Alicia's disapproval!

'You cannot wear that!' she had shrieked when Kate had
finally let her into the secret of her costume earlier that evening.
'It's indecent!'

'Dear Godmama, it is no more revealing than a nymph's
costume,' Kate had declared laughingly. 'Please, please don't
say no or I shall have to stay at home since I haven't got
another outfit to wear.'

'You are scarcely wearing *that* one!' Lady Edgeworth retorted waspishly.

However, as she didn't want her charge to miss what promised to be the most glittering event of the summer, she'd reluctantly swallowed her objections.

Alicia had high hopes for this evening. Let Randal see the
child looking so incredibly lovely and he was bound to declare
himself! Besides, she consoled herself, everyone knew that costume balls were an occasion when daring behaviour was acceptable, particularly if the perpetrator was a rich heiress.

'She even lent me these bracelets.' Kate confided the anec-
dote to her host, indicating the two wide gilded bracelets or-
namented with turquoise with which she had adorned her upper
arms.

Randal stared at them. The gold gleamed softly against her

bare arms and he experienced a fierce desire to reach out and touch her ivory-tinted skin.

Her shapely shoulders were also revealed almost in their entirety, save for the two broad straps which held up her dress. Made of dark red gauze, it was cut low and straight across her breasts and fell in a slim sheath to just above her ankles. It was obvious she was wearing very little beneath it for, when she moved, the material was sheer enough to hint at her voluptuous curves.

Thin gold sandals exposed her equally bare feet and she wore an intricate necklace shaped like a gold collar studded with large blue stones, which he thought must be glass. Matching earrings dangled from her dainty ears. They provided a very dramatic effect, particularly when combined with that long blue feathered fan she carried.

Her new hairstyle was also striking. Dressed *à la Egyptienne*, her sable locks had been brushed smoothly back and caught with a gold comb high at the back of her head, but instead of curls, a myriad of tiny plaits cascaded to graze her shoulders. A row of blue beads, looping above her ears from the comb, hung horizontally across her forehead.

They drew attention to her long slanting eyes, which looked more exotic than ever since she had outlined them with some black paint and dusted a gold powder over the lids. She had also reddened her wide full mouth.

Shocking, provocative...and utterly seductive! She looked good enough to eat!

His opinion was evidently shared by most of the men present and, to his annoyance, she was instantly besieged by admirers clamouring to dance with her.

'Remember you are promised to me for the next cotillion,' he said, struggling to keep jealousy out of his voice as he reluctantly acknowledged Jack Hewitt's prior claim.

'How could I forget?' Her eyes sparkled teasingly at him. 'You might cut off my head!'

Since a sensible wish to avoid an uncomfortable costume

had led him to dress in the plain attire of a Roundhead soldier, her sally made him laugh as he released her.

Watching her glide away on Jack's arm, his smile faded and he said softly, 'Oh, but I can think of much better things to do with you, my little Egyptian!'

Honour be damned! He wasn't going to delay any longer for the Hogans. Whatever else she was, she had the manners of a lady and his father's ghost would have to find comfort in that!

'I'm not sure we should be doing this.' Kate's voice trembled slightly as she watched Randal unbuckle the broadsword which added a lethal veracity to his Ironside captain's uniform.

'You said you didn't want to dance.' Randal shed his buff leather coat and cast it carelessly over the back of a chair.

'I know, but if anyone were to come in—'

'My study is strictly off limits,' he interrupted. 'No one will disturb us here.'

Kate remained by the door, which he had closed firmly behind them a moment ago. The candelabrum he'd placed on the rosewood desk lit the room's quiet darkness.

She thought he must be able to hear the wild banging of her heart. Now clad only in a pair of breeches and a white linen shirt, his tall strong body was arousing a devastating reaction in her.

Was it only yesterday she had doubted him? Overwhelmed by his virility, she could barely breathe and yet in some befuddled corner of her brain a warning voice was shrieking.

'All the same, I think we should go back,' she murmured, her fingers playing nervously with the feathers of her fan.

Randal walked over to her and firmly removed it from her frantic grip. 'What are you afraid of, Katharine?' he asked, laying it aside. 'Yourself or me?'

He began to slide one of the straps down off her shoulder.

Kate gasped. 'I'm not afraid of anything!' she exclaimed hotly, pushing her strap back up.

'Then kiss me,' he challenged with a lazy smile.

'No!'

'I'll wager I could make you change your mind.' He ran one fingertip lightly along her bare collarbone.

'Coxcomb!' Kate retorted unsteadily.

'Am I?'

He drew her slowly into his arms, giving her every chance to withdraw. Deafened by the pounding of her own heart, Kate watched his mouth come closer and closer...and then his lips found hers in a long, slow and thrillingly expert caress.

Stars exploded behind her closed eyelids and, just as he had predicted, her resistance melted.

'You see?' A gleam of triumph lit his brilliant gaze. 'You cannot help yourself any more than I can. We were made for each other, sweetheart.'

Dizzy with passion Kate broke away from him. He was right, but she couldn't let sensuality blind her! 'I won't bed with you! It would be wrong!'

'You think I asked you here to *seduce* you?'

Suddenly realising that his voice was full of amusement, Kate hesitated. Had she read too much into his actions? 'I...I, oh, damn it, Randal, what am I supposed to think with you stripping off the minute we were over the threshold!'

He let out a shout of laughter. 'That jacket is very heavy and I'm hot, you goose.'

A flood of colour washed into Kate's face as he added wickedly, 'However, if you've a mind to sample my poor skills, I should very much enjoy playing Antony to your Cleopatra.'

Feeling a complete fool, Kate glared up at him. 'Don't flatter yourself that I wore this costume to please you,' she snapped, lying through her teeth.

'I'm sorry. I thought you knew you could trust me not to take advantage of our privacy,' he apologised.

Kate supposed she did. 'It was unfair of you to tease me,' she muttered, wishing it was possible for both of them to forget all restraints.

'You looked so adorably shocked when I started to undress

that I couldn't resist the temptation to do so,' he confessed with a grin.

His smile faded. 'However, you are right to suspect my motives for seeking a chance to be alone with you tonight.'

Kate felt the colour drain rapidly from her cheeks. 'What... what do you mean?' she faltered.

'I haven't been completely honest with you, sweetheart. In fact, there's something I must tell you. I ought to have confessed earlier, but I've been putting the moment off.' His expression hardened. 'It won't wait any longer.'

Kate stared up at him, her head whirling. *He* hadn't been honest?

Seeing her confusion, Randal guided her towards the leather-upholstered couch which stood opposite his desk and gently pulled her down to sit next to him. Holding both her hands in his, he said quietly, 'Honour demands that I tell you about Walcheren.'

Kate blinked in surprise. 'I know you took part in that campaign,' she replied uncertainly.

'I suppose Emma told you?' A slight frown touched his brow.

'She didn't say much,' Kate asserted quickly, not wishing him to think they had been gossiping about him.

Randal nodded and, taking a deep breath, said evenly, 'She knows I don't like talking about it. You see, I caught the infamous fever.'

Kate's eyes widened. She had read all about this dreadful affliction in the news-sheets at the time. The low-lying ground of Walcheren island bred a malignant ague which had devastated the entire army. The effects were so bad that the campaign had to be called off.

'Only five men in my company escaped it, but I was luckier than most. I survived.' Randal shrugged. 'Not that I appreciated my good fortune at the time. I was shivering and shaking so hard I thought my teeth would snap into pieces.'

Kate had heard that the ague fits came thick and fast, several

n a day and every one was followed by high fever and a thirst
o intense it felt as if the throat was on fire. Afterwards the
victim was left utterly exhausted.

'We landed back in Ramsgate in mid-September. Thousands
of sick and dying men.' Randal shook his head at the memory.
My father came to fetch me home. I don't remember much of
he journey, I was delirious most of the time. The doctors told
im that I would die.'

His well-cut mouth twisted. 'My father wouldn't listen. He
scoured the country for a cure until he found a doctor who
reated me with infusions of Peruvian bark. The method seemed
o work, although I think it was my father's prayers which
ulled me through.'

Kate nodded, thinking privately that his recovery probably
ad more to do with his own stamina and determination.

'It was weeks before I could even get out of bed, but the
oll was heaviest on my father. The anxiety had aged him and
is heart was weak.'

'And you felt guilty?'

'Aye. He had never wanted me to join the army.' A muscle
witched by Randal's well-cut mouth. 'When he asked me to
esign my commission, I did not think I had the right to refuse.
owed him my life.'

Indignation rose in Kate. 'That's blackmail!'

Randal agreed. 'However, I could see his point. He'd lost
y brother and he'd nearly lost me and possessing an heir
iattered a great deal to him.' He shrugged. 'Truth to tell, I
ound that I didn't mind leaving the army as much as I thought
would. Maybe I'd been a soldier too long. Certainly, the bun-
ling at Walcheren had opened my eyes to the stupidities of
ar.'

He gave her a crooked smile. 'I'd had a good run. It was
me I settled down to my responsibilities at home. These days
m happy to follow Lord Wellington's success in the Peninsula
om my armchair.'

Kate sensed that his loss went deeper than he was willing to admit. However, he wasn't the kind of man to sit around bemoaning his lot. Instead he had forged a new life for himself, learning to manage his estates and pursuing his academic interests.

'Did your decision to take the honourable course bring you any closer to your father?' she asked curiously.

Randal gave her a sharp look, but he did not deny that a rift had existed. 'It was too late for us to become friends,' he admitted. 'But at least I had the satisfaction of knowing he died content.'

'I am honoured you chose to confide in me, Randal,' Kate said in a quiet voice. 'But I'm afraid I don't really understand why you thought it necessary to do so.'

His grip tightened on her hands. 'I suffered another attack six months ago and the doctors told me that it could recur again.'

The disgust in his voice told Kate that, like most strong healthy males, he had no patience with his own illness and saw it as a humiliating weakness, but before she could utter a word of reassurance he was continuing in the same rapid tone.

'My health is otherwise good and I have every intention of living to a ripe old age, but you ought to know what you are letting yourself in for if you take me on.'

Kate went very still.

'Sweetheart, do you understand what I'm saying?' Randal's gaze held hers intently. 'The other night when I saw you in danger I *knew* I couldn't live without you! I love you and want you by my side always!'

Kate swallowed hard. Dear God, what had she done to deserve this torment! Like Tantalus of old, what she desired most in the world was within her reach, but she couldn't grasp it.

'I'm aware we agreed to wait until we knew each other better, but I need to know if there's some hope for me.' He continuing silence brought a puzzled look to his face and then a humorous smile lit his bright blue eyes. 'Ah, I see I shall have to do the thing properly!'

In a quick movement he dropped to one knee before her.

'My dearest love, will you do me the honour of becoming my wife?'

His beloved promptly burst into tears.

'Please go away!'

Abandoning his attempts to comfort her, Randal asked if she wanted him to send Alicia to her.

'No!' Kate mopped her eyes with the handkerchief he'd given her and then in a quieter voice added, 'I don't want anyone. I just want to be left alone!'

'Don't you mean to give me an answer, sweetheart?' he asked gently.

'I'm sorry, but I can't think straight right now,' she gasped, choking on another half-hysterical sob.

'Then I shall wait until you are ready.' The expression on Lord Redesmere's face revealed that he longed to say more, but, after dropping a light kiss upon her bowed head, he withdrew.

Kate knew that he was puzzled by her behaviour and she suspected she had hurt his feelings into the bargain. An aching sense of deep regret filled her.

She hadn't dreamt that he would actually ask her to marry him. For a single brief second joy had blazed in her heart.

The knowledge that she must leave him had extinguished it.

She would have to refuse his offer, of course. What he would think of her when she then grabbed Kitty's money and ran off sent fresh tears pouring down her face.

At length she grew calmer and was able to creep from the study and make her way up the rear staircase which lay close by. Randal had invited several guests, including herself and Lady Edgeworth, to stay overnight and she had been given the same bedchamber in which she had slept on her last visit.

To her immense relief she didn't meet anyone on her way there.

The room was empty. Kate realised that Mary must be in

the servants' hall enjoying the festive atmosphere. However, there was sufficient water in the ewer on the washstand for her to cool her hot cheeks and remove the streaks of eye paint which had run when she'd wept.

She had the necessary cosmetics with her and she quickly repaired the damage to her *maquillage* before tidying her hair and applying a little more perfume.

Her mirror reflected a calm face, which hid her inner turmoil. There was no further excuse to linger.

Kate steeled herself to open the door and stepped into the corridor.

'You took your time.'

She gazed in dismay at the blue-satin-clad Cavalier who lounged against the wall outside her room.

He straightened, unfolding his crossed arms, and as he approached Kate could smell the aroma of gin on his breath.

'Still, the improvement was worth the wait. Been crying, have you?'

'Keep away from me or I'll scream!'

His eyebrows climbed up to the fringe of his heavy becurled periwig. 'Why so unfriendly, Cousin Kitty?'

'You know why, Sullivan,' Kate retorted.

'All I want is a little chat, *mavournin*.'

'Get out of my way!'

To her surprise, he obligingly flattened himself against the wall.

Her flesh creeping, Kate stalked past him.

'I am thinking you should listen to me.' His voice followed her. 'What I've got to say is to your advantage, Mrs Devlin.'

Chapter Twelve

Slowly Kate turned round. 'How did you find out who I was?' she asked flatly, not wasting time on denials.

'I saw you a couple of years ago at the theatre in Limerick. You were playing the part of Viola in *Twelfth Night*. I thought you a handsome piece!' A sneering smile curved Sean's mouth. When I first arrived in England I wasn't sure if you were the same woman or not. For a common actress you ape the part of a lady to perfection.'

Kate ignored the insult.

'I knew you were an imposter, of course,' he continued in the same patronising tone. 'Then last Sunday I suddenly remembered seeing a handbill in Dublin puffing off the Gillman Players. Once my memory had been jogged I recognised you at once.'

He started to pull something from the deep pocket of his coat and Kate stiffened in alarm until she saw that it wasn't a weapon.

'That's how you got this, isn't it?' Sean dangled the Nixon locket in front of her. 'You helped that silly little bitch escape the river.' His eyes narrowed. 'I was sure she would drown!'

Kate resisted the temptation to try and snatch the locket from him. 'Air trapped in her skirts kept her afloat,' she informed him coolly.

'I should have made sure she was dead before she went into the water.'

The look of revulsion on Kate's face made him laugh. 'Squeamish, eh? Well, at least that answers my next question. I did wonder whether you might have finished the job before presenting yourself here, but I suppose you left her alive.'

'I don't believe in violence,' Kate replied cautiously.

'So, she's gone into hiding somewhere.' A frown twisted his petulant mouth. 'Do you know where she is now?'

'I helped her get to Dublin in exchange for the locket,' Kate lied. 'I don't know what became of her after that.'

To her surprise Sean shrugged. 'No matter. I can deal with her if she turns up here.'

Misliking the feral expression burgeoning in his light eyes, Kate tried to wrest control of the conversation. 'Why didn't you denounce me when you realised who I was?' she demanded boldly.

He looked at her as if she were stupid. 'Why should I want to do that? You are my ticket to a fortune, Cousin Kitty.'

A cold dread shivered down Kate's spine. 'You can't imagine I would *cooperate* with you!' she exclaimed in accents of disgust.

'I did wonder if I could make you trust me enough to accept an offer of marriage.'

Her expression revealed that he had been right to abandon hopes of charming her.

He laughed unpleasantly. 'My parents put pressure on Kitty to wed me. You're a damned sight more attractive, but, all in all, I will be happy to settle for the money.'

'I won't give you a penny of it,' Kate said tersely.

'Sure now it's very greedy of you to want to keep it all *mavournin*.'

Kate opened her mouth to protest and then realised that to do so would betray her knowledge of Kitty's whereabouts. She had to let him go on thinking she was acting from the same corrupt motives which drove his own pursuit.

'Especially when you've got your eye on Redesmere. Now don't poker up, Mrs Devlin. Anyone can see you're sweet on him...or his money, but I'm not out to spoil your game. You can have him for all I care so long as you hand over half of Kitty's inheritance.' His feral smile reappeared. 'I'd say it was a fair bargain. Pay Pa and me to keep silent and you get half of the old man's money and a rich husband if you can catch him.' His smile deepened. 'I'll warrant you that Redesmere won't suspect a thing. Your past and your involvement in defrauding Kitty will be our little secret.'

Kate clasped her hands tightly together to stop them trembling. 'Really? It had occurred to me once or twice that his lordship might be in league with you and your family.'

Astonishment flickered over Sean's face. 'Redesmere? What maggot put that idea into your head? He's too damned honest! Besides, why should we want to join forces with him? He's the one who stands to inherit if Kitty fails to register her claim.'

Randal was innocent! Struggling to keep her expression dispassionate, Kate pointed out that Gerald would automatically receive £10,000 in that case.

'A mere bagatelle when we could be sharing the whole lot with you.' Sean grinned. 'This way all of us win.'

Kate laughed shortly. 'You'd start blackmailing me the minute you'd wasted your share of the old Nabob's money!'

'I might,' he conceded. His thin lips twisted into a sneer. 'It's a risk you'll have to take if you want Redesmere.'

Sean knew that it was his own acknowledgement of her claim to be Kitty Nixon which had secured her Redesmere's support and paved the way for a brilliant marriage. Luckily, he still had a lever to force her obedience. She was trying to hide it, but he recognized that she was scared witless of Redesmere finding out she was an actress.

'Well, what do you say, Mrs Devlin?' Sean played idly with the locket, dropping it into his coat pocket and lifting it out again. 'Do you want to go to prison or do we have a bargain?'

Kate hesitated, thinking quickly. She had no intention of

cooperating with Sean, but he would wreck everything unless she pretended to accept his vile proposal.

'Promise me you will leave Kitty alone.' It was only too easy to inject a faltering note into her voice. 'I can't consent to murder.'

'I swear it.' Sean made a showy gesture of laying his free hand across his heart.

Kate wondered if she dare try any more delaying tactics, but, seeing the impatience in his cold eyes, decided there was no sense in annoying him.

'Very well. I agree to your demands. You may call on me in Abbey Square after I have signed the papers.'

Kate started to turn, eager to get away.

'Won't you shake on it, *mavournin*?' Sean stepped closer. One hand was still casually thrust into his pocket, but he held his other out to her in the universal gesture of goodwill.

Realising that she had to make him trust her, Kate swallowed her revulsion and smilingly extended her hand.

'Ah, nevvy!' Emerging onto the courtyard terrace, Godwin Crawford hailed his nephew, who was staring moodily out into the darkened garden. 'Have you seen Kitty?'

Randal turned to face him, his abstracted expression sharpening. 'Why?'

'She was promised to me for this dance.' Godwin shrugged. 'That fellow Sullivan was asking after her, too. However, she seems to have disappeared.'

Randal stiffened.

'Is something wrong?'

'I don't know. But I intend to find out.'

'Do you want me to come—?'

'No. Please stay and entertain our guests.' Randal flashed him a brief smile and strode away before his surprised uncle could protest.

Several ladies sought his company as he quickly scanned the rooms for any sign of his elusive heiress. Adroitly side-stepping their entreaties, Randal excused himself. Reaching the main staircase he rapidly mounted to the first floor. To his dismay, Katharine's room was empty.

A nameless anxiety clawed at his heart.

Should he find Emma and ask her to check the room which had been designated the ladies' cloakroom for the evening? Or would that be as fruitless as he suspected it might be to seek out Mary?

Katharine had been upset, but surely there was no reason for her to avoid him? Or did she really think he would pester her like that fool Sullivan?

Randal's mind slammed back to the night of Alicia's dress-party. Katharine had hidden herself away on that occasion, too.

His thoughts whirling, Randal began to search the other rooms along the corridor. They were all deserted and his uneasiness escalated.

Could it be Sullivan she was trying to elude? Of a surety, she disliked the fellow, but why did his instinct insist that she was afraid of the Irishman?

A monstrous suspicion made Randal draw in a sharp breath. Hellfire, if only he had caught a proper look at the rogue who had attacked her!

Something blue lying on the floor just inside the entrance to the Gallery caught his attention and, distracted, it took Randal a moment to realise what he was staring at was a feathered fan.

He picked it up and stood for an instant, turning it over in his hand, his gaze unfocused. Then, with an inaudible curse, he hurried towards the steep staircase which led up to the top floor of the house.

The cold kiss of the knife blade at her throat urged Kate on. 'There now, that's better!' Sean kicked the door of the Confessional shut behind him and, ordering her to set down the lantern which he had forced her to carry, smiled smugly at Kate. 'I knew we'd manage those stairs if you cooperated.'

Kate's eyes glared at him over the silken gag which silenced the angry curses she longed to hurl at him.

Her suspicions lulled, he'd been too quick for her.

When she had held out her hand he had yanked her hard against him and threatened her with the dagger he'd whipped out of its concealment in his pocket. Thrusting a silk handkerchief into her mouth, he'd bundled her into the Gallery where earlier he had hidden a lantern. Then, with the knife at her throat and her arm twisted up behind her back, he had forced her up the stairs.

'You see, I don't trust you to keep your word, *mavournin*,' Sean said conversationally, pushing her further into the small bare room. 'You might succeed in finding a way to keep the money all to yourself and cheat us.'

Kate's brows flew up in eloquent scorn.

Sean halted, an ugly expression flickering for an instant across his thin features. 'Think what you like of me, but I'll have the last laugh.'

Kate stiffened, the pain in her arm forgotten as the import of his words sank in.

Amusement danced in the cold grey eyes. 'Aye, I'm afraid I'm going to have to kill you, Mrs Devlin. The world believes you to be Kitty Nixon and I need your corpse as proof that my snivelling little cousin is dead.'

He laughed. 'I hoped to lure you outside and drown you in the lake—a fitting solution, don't you agree? But I soon realised I'd never be able to smuggle you through the crowd downstairs. Then I remembered the priest's escape hatch and thought of the perfect *tragic accident* for you.'

Releasing Kate's arm, but still keeping the knife at her throat, Sean indicated the concealed exit. 'Pa brought me here on a visit when I was a boy. Lord Cedric took us on a tour of his infernal curios. They bored me senseless, but this was different.'

His feral smile appeared, more frightening than ever in the shadowy light. 'The next day I made Emma show me exactly

how it worked. She didn't want to, but after a bit of ah…
persuasion…she did as she was told.'

Kate watched helplessly as he pressed the release mechanism
and the panel slid open.

A waft of cold dank air entered the room, releasing the same
emanation of ancient misery which Kate had sensed once before. She forced herself to ignore it and concentrate on what
Sean was saying.

'There'll be a hue and cry when you go missing, of course.
Even Kitty might turn up to find out what's going on.' Sean
giggled spitefully. 'Naturally, everyone will assume *she* is the
imposter. By the time the confusion is cleared up, it'll be too
late!'

The deadline for Kitty to claim her fortune expired next
week. Frustration boiled in Kate, overcoming her fear, and she
strove desperately to think of some way of outwitting him.

Thank God, he was enjoying himself too much to make a
quick end of her!

'Now, would you like me to knock you senseless before I
send you to meet your Maker?' A malicious parody of solicitude infused her tormentor's tone. 'I dare say you'll break your
neck straight off, but then again they might not think to search
the cellars for days…'

In spite of herself, Kate couldn't help shuddering as his voice
trailed off suggestively.

Her reaction made Sean laugh gleefully. 'It was a mistake
to bite me, eh, *mavournin*!'

He was laughing so hard that the pressure at her throat slack-
ened and, seizing her chance, Kate lashed out, forcing the blade
away. At the same time she kicked him as violently as she
could on the shin.

He staggered. 'You little—'

Kate hared for the door, but before she could snatch it open
Sean grabbed her and, in spite of the frantic flailing of her fists
as she tried to fend him off, managed to drag her towards the
priest's-hole.

The door crashed back on its hinges and a voice of thunder roared, 'Let her go!'

His mouth gaping in astonishment, Sean swung round to behold Lord Redesmere standing in the open doorway, sword in hand. Taking advantage of his surprise, Kate wrenched free.

'Get behind me, Katharine.' Randal gave the order with a cool calm as Sean unsheathed the Cavalier's rapier he wore at his hip.

Kate obeyed and watched in horror as Randal advanced and the two blades met with a hiss of steel. Sean had a speed and skill which alarmed her until she realised that he had met a master of the art.

Randal, who had the longer reach, wove a net of flashing steel around his opponent, driving him back relentlessly and Kate saw Sean's confidence give way to panic. Sweat dripped down his face and he was gasping for breath as he attempted ever more desperate flanconades.

'Give this up, Sullivan.' Randal parried the attacking thrusts with a cool ease.

Too hard-pressed to have breath left to reply, Sean scowled and launched another onslaught.

Once more the broadsword smashed his rapier aside.

Sean stepped back abruptly. 'All right,' he panted. 'You win.'

'Drop your sword.'

The rapier clattered to the floor.

'Now move away.'

Sean obeyed and Kate sagged with relief against the wall behind her.

'Are you all right, Katharine?' Half-turning in her direction, Randal shot her a worried glance.

Kate was struggling to remove the gag from her mouth. Out of the corner of her eye she saw Sean's hand slip furtively into his pocket.

'Watch out, Randal!'

For one terrible moment Kate thought her hoarse cry of

alarm had been too late as Sean lunged and the dagger bit into Randal's chest.

Then the room became a sudden storm of flailing arms and legs. In the dim light, shadows flickered like crazed giants across the white-washed walls.

The dagger went flying, skittering to the floorboards, and Kate darted to pick it up. Retreating from the fray, she waited, ready to use it if necessary.

Randal's fist crashed into Sean's jaw. He tumbled backwards and, as suddenly as it had begun, the fight was over.

Randal stared down at the unconscious figure at his feet. Sean had landed right by the escape hatch. An overwhelming desire to kick his body down into the dark depths tensed Randal's muscles.

'Don't!' Kate hurried to lay a restraining hand on his shoulder. 'He's not worth staining your honour.'

Randal laid his hand over hers in silent acknowledgement.

'I knew something was wrong!'

They both looked up to see Godwin hurrying into the room.

Mr Crawford held up the candlestick he carried and surveyed the Irishman with an expression of disgust. 'I suppose he was after the inheritance?'

Randal nodded. 'He wanted Kitty Nixon dead.'

'For the sake of the family we had best hush up this scandal.' Godwin glanced at Kate. 'That is, if you have no objections, my dear?'

Kate shook her head. Sean deserved imprisonment, but the cost was too high.

'I'll see to it that he doesn't get off scot-free,' Randal said grimly.

His great-uncle had introduced him to several of his sea captains. One of them owed him a favour. Working his passage before the mast on the long voyage to India might make the Irishman think Newgate preferable!

Content to leave the matter in his nephew's capable hands,

Godwin nodded. 'Why don't you escort Kitty back downstairs? I'll keep an eye on this rogue until Matthew gets here.'

Randal's brows lifted in enquiry.

'I told him to follow me if I didn't report back in a few minutes.' Godwin suddenly chuckled. 'Jupiter, but Emma will throw a fit! Not one of us doing the pretty at her cherished party!'

'Most improper,' Randal agreed drily and, accepting the candlestick Godwin proffered, ushered Kate out.

Eager to escape, Kate hurried down the narrow stairs. Another light came bobbing along the darkened Gallery towards them and after a few words of explanation Randal let his brother-in-law proceed upstairs while they went in the opposite direction.

Outside Kate's room Randal halted. 'How are you feeling, sweetheart?' He touched her cheek gently.

'I'm all right.' Kate attempted a smile. 'He didn't hurt me.'

'I must go and reassure Emma,' Randal said reluctantly. 'If I don't put in an appearance soon, people are going to start wondering what is going on.'

Kate reached out and brushed her fingers across the deep gash over his heart where the thick leather of his uniform coat had turned Sean's blade. 'What will you tell her if she asks about this?'

He shrugged lightly. 'Merely that Sean and I were indulging in a foolish re-enactment of the Civil War.'

A full explanation of how he had come by his bruised knuckles would have to wait for a more appropriate time.

Kate nodded her understanding. They had to try and prevent damaging gossip.

'Shall I send Mary to you?'

One of Kate's hands flew instinctively to her hair. She probably looked as dishevelled as she felt, she decided, accepting the offer gratefully.

'Let me take this. You don't want to alarm her.'

To Kate's astonishment she realised she was still clutching

Sean's dagger in her other hand. With a gasp of revulsion she released it into his waiting palm.

For all her horrified expression Randal sensed that she would have had no hesitation in using the blade in their defence. Most women would have fainted long since, but she had shown exemplary courage.

'A stiff brandy might help.'

Kate agreed. He was right, she could feel herself beginning to tremble with reaction.

But the nightmare wasn't over yet.

'I'll send a bottle up with Mary.' He lifted her hand to his lips and kissed it softly. 'Don't come down. I'll make your excuses and we can talk in the morning.'

'Wait!' Kate laid an urgent hand on his arm as he turned to go. 'There's something I must tell you.'

Randal eyed her in concern. She was shaking like an autumn leaf!

'You saved my life tonight. I don't want to go on lying to you any longer.' Kate spoke in a rapid harsh voice, the words tumbling over themselves as she struggled to get them out. 'Even if you hate me for it, you deserve to know the truth.' She took a deep breath and, sending up a silent prayer for forgiveness for breaking her vow, blurted, 'You were right. I am not Kitty Nixon, I'm an imposter.'

He smiled at her crookedly. 'I know.'

Shock left Kate bereft of words; before she could recover, they heard footsteps.

'Randal!' Emma was hurrying towards them as fast as her heavy skirts allowed. 'Where have you been? You've got to come! Now!'

In a flurry of agitation she grabbed Randal's arm. 'I don't understand a word of what that man is saying, but you must get rid of him!'

Randal cast a look of incomprehension at Kate.

His sister stamped her foot. 'He is threatening to make a scene!'

Seeing she was ready to dissolve into hysterics, Randal put aside his desire to wring her neck. 'Very well, but this had better be important,' he growled with a quick nod of apology to Kate.

Emma headed for the rear stairs and he followed.

Realising that the unwelcome visitor must have been tucked away to keep him from the guests, curiosity drew Kate to peer down the stairwell. Two couples stood in the small hallway which gave access to the west entrance and several rooms on this side of the house. She didn't recognise the middle-aged man and woman, but a loud gasp escaped her at the sight of the younger pair.

'Ned! Kitty!' Kate hurtled down the stairs and flung herself at Ned Gillman's thick-set form.

'Kate! Thank God you are safe!' His truculent frown fading, Ned caught her in a bear-hug. 'Mary wrote to tell me that Sullivan was here in Chester. We've been so worried about you!'

Kate smiled at him mistily. 'Thank you for coming.' She turned to the thin-faced girl at his side. 'Both of you.'

'As soon as we heard about Sean I knew I couldn't stay in hiding any longer.' Kitty Nixon's soft voice was filled with determination. 'I have come to claim my inheritance in person.'

'Will someone please tell me what is going on?' Emma demanded loudly in tones of angry bewilderment. 'Who on earth are all these people and what are they doing here?'

Randal stepped forward, and gesturing his outraged sister to silence, took charge of the situation.

'Mr and Mrs Hogan, I presume?' The respectably clad couple nodded. 'I am Redesmere. My apologies for this unusual reception.' He bowed to them elegantly. 'May I ask you to accompany me to my study where I shall furnish you with an explanation?'

They nodded again and he turned to Emma. 'Please escort our other guests up to the privacy of your sitting-room, my dear. I am sure our cousin Miss Nixon—' here he inclined his head at Kitty '—and her friends will be happy to explain.'

Emma's mouth had dropped open in astonishment. She stared at Kate and then at Kitty. 'What…? Oh, very well!'

In his study Randal questioned the Hogans and then, pushing aside his latest letter from Thomas Young discussing their exchange of ideas on translating the demotic text of the Rosetta stone to make more room on his desk, he quickly wrote out a statement declaring formal recognition of Kitty.

They signed it and he thanked them for their help.

'Won't you accept our hospitality for the night?' he asked, willing to give up his own bedchamber for their use.

'Nay, my lord. You've a house full and we've already taken rooms at the George in Malpas,' said Mr Hogan, shaking his grey head and rising to his feet.

His wife, a little dumpling of a woman against her husband's broad inches, added her apologies for disturbing his lordship's party. 'We had intended to visit you tomorrow and then we spied Kitty and Mr Gillman in the inn-yard asking for directions to the Hall. Once Kitty told us what had happened we realised that haste was required and came at once in the hope of preventing mischief.'

'I am thankful you did, ma'am.'

'You seem to have managed very well without our help, my lord.' There was a twinkle in her eyes. 'But I'm glad we could be of service to Kitty.'

Randal showed them out, promising to convey their farewells to his cousin, who would doubtless wish to call upon them before they left Cheshire.

After quickly checking that the ball was continuing to survive his absence, he hurried up to the pretty sitting-room which adjoined his sister's bedchamber.

'Ah, come and join us, my boy!' Godwin hailed him.

Accepting the glass of brandy Matthew handed him, Randal raised his eyebrows at his brother-in-law.

'It's all right. Blake is keeping watch,' Matthew murmured quietly.

Randal nodded and went over to speak to Kitty.

Kate watched them, a bitter pain rousing her from her dazed state.

She had taken little part in enlightening Emma and the others, letting Ned and Kitty explain how, after her rescue from the river, they had smuggled Kitty back to England with them and how Ned's chance remark on their sharing the same name and colouring had sparked Kate's impulsive offer to impersonate the heiress.

Countless questions had followed, but to her surprise Kate had seen admiration, not censure, dawn in their eyes.

Kitty now broke off her conversation with Randal. 'I would like to propose a toast,' she announced with a new-found confidence which delighted Kate.

Mary had been right. Kitty had recovered her nerve. There was no need to worry about her any longer.

'To Kate Devlin and the Gillman Players.' Kitty raised her glass. 'Without their help I would have lost both my inheritance and my life.'

Kate blushed. Sensing Randal's gaze on her, she avoided his eyes.

'To think Sean could be so wicked!' Emma shook her bewigged head. She was finding it hard to take in. Her new friend was an actress! What was funny was that she looked more of a lady than the real Kitty who, though no doubt an admirable girl, had chipped nails, a frightful hairstyle and an abominably dowdy taste in dress!

She smiled a little awkwardly at Kate, trying to convey her continuing support. 'You are very brave, Mrs Devlin.'

'Indeed, I take my hat off to you, ma'am! You had us all properly fooled!' Matthew Lattimer exclaimed, coming forward to refill her glass.

Knowing that he was wrong, a shiver prickled down Kate's

spine. How in God's name had Randal discovered her secret? And when?

She covered the top of her glass. 'No more for me, Lieutenant.' An apologetic smile trembled on her lips. 'I think I shall seek my bed.'

'Me, too,' Kitty declared. 'It's been a long day.'

Since all the guest bedrooms were taken, Kate had suggested she and Kitty share a room while Ned had professed his willingness to accept a bed anywhere a corner could be found.

'Don't worry about me, Mrs Lattimer. I can sleep in the servants' hall or over the stables,' he'd said cheerfully.

Emma's calm acceptance of this offer had forcibly reminded Kate of Ned's status. He was an actor, not a gentleman!

And now she was no longer a lady!

She rose to her feet, suddenly too weary to face the implications of Kitty's return.

Randal came forward to escort them to the door. He willed Katharine to look up at him, but she was still avoiding his gaze.

'Will you warn my godmother of my arrival, sir?' Kitty asked. 'I do not want to spoil the ball for her, but I fear my sudden appearance in the morning may come as a shock.'

Kate paled. She had forgotten about Alicia!

'I shall speak to her before she retires,' Randal promised.

Behind him, he could hear the others making preparations to return downstairs, Emma murmuring about neglected guests.

Randal didn't give a tinker's curse. All he wanted to do was to have things out with Katharine!

But the exhaustion in her great dark eyes stilled his tongue.

'Come and give me a kiss, my dear,' Lady Edgeworth commanded. 'I cannot say that I am pleased that you did not see fit to trust me, but my goddaughter has explained everything and I understand your reasons.'

Her heart lightening, Kate crossed the room to where Alicia resided upon a chaise longue.

'Thank you, ma'am,' she murmured, obeying her ladyship's command. 'It grieved me to deceive you.'

Alicia, who, although she had arisen at an unusually early hour, was still *en deshabille*, waved her to a chair.

Kate sat down. 'I intend to repay all the monies you have laid out on my behalf—' she began nervously, but Alicia let out a snort of outrage.

'Nonsense, child! I enjoyed having your company so do not prattle of owing me anything.' Alicia fixed her with a stern look. 'Besides, what you did for Kitty must earn my eternal gratitude and a very poor way of showing it I would have to take your shillings.'

A smile lit her plump face. 'Let us call it quits, my dear, and say no more about it!'

Kate nodded and, feeling overwhelmed by Alicia's unexpected generosity, had to struggle to prevent the tears which stung her eyelids from falling.

Lady Edgeworth saw her distress but wisely said nothing, inviting her instead to help herself to a cup of chocolate from the pot which her maid had brought up earlier.

Stilling her shaking hands by sheer willpower, Kate poured the rich dark liquid and sipped it gratefully. She had been far too tense to eat any breakfast and, while Kitty had been closeted earlier with her godmother, she had paced the bedroom in a turmoil of guilty apprehension.

'I don't know why you are fretting,' Mary had grumbled. 'If her ladyship can't see we did everything for the best, then to hell with her!'

It wasn't so simple. A part of Kate knew she was worrying about what Alicia might say to mask her greater concern about Randal's reaction.

Mary had reported he was busy with his guests, and he would have to do something about Sean who, presumably, was still being held prisoner up on the top floor, but Kate knew that Randal would seek her out the minute he was free.

The thought terrified her!

'So, my dear, will you tell me a little about yourself?' Alicia asked when she judged that her visitor had recovered her composure.

Kate obliged, confining her remarks to her recent experiences with the Gillman Players.

If she was disappointed by this reticence, Alicia took care not to show it, remarking instead that Kitty intended to return to America as soon as possible.

'She tells me she is homesick,' Alicia said sadly. 'Not that I can blame her for not wishing to remain in Chester. It would be very awkward!'

Kitty had announced that nothing would induce her to try and take up the place which Kate had carved out in society. 'I have no wish to become an object of gossip, Godmama,' she'd said. 'I shall remain quietly hidden until the legal process is completed and I can leave.'

Kate nodded, setting aside her empty cup. Kitty had confided in her last night.

'I believe she has also persuaded Mr Gillman to take your company to America?'

'Apparently, English actors are all the rage over there, ma'am.'

Stunned at first by this proposal, Kate now believed it had several merits. The booking Ned had such hopes for had come to nothing and, as usual, it would be hard to find profitable work until the autumn. Kitty had assured them that American audiences would welcome them, pointing out that several other companies had made a success of such ventures.

What's more, Kitty wanted to pay everyone's passage as a mark of her gratitude. The Gillman Players had nothing to lose.

And, as Mary had bluntly observed, the change of scene would help Kate put the last two months behind her.

Kate rose to go. 'Goodbye, ma'am, and thank you for all your kindness.'

'I shall miss you, my dear,' Alicia said truthfully.

A deep sigh escaped her when the bedroom door closed behind Kate.

She would have loved to see her young friend the mistress of this house, but last night's revelations had destroyed that hope.

Randal Crawford might be careless of convention, but marry an actress? Surely not!

'Are you sure you will be all right?' Emma Lattimer was frowning. 'I don't like leaving you on your own in a place like this.'

Kate smiled reassuringly. 'I've put up at inns which were far less respectable.'

'I'm sorry,' Emma muttered, exchanging a strained glance with her husband. 'I keep forgetting you aren't Kitty.'

Kate managed to summon a cheerful smile and thanked them for allowing her to drive back to Chester with them.

'I don't know what Randal is going to say when he finds—'

Matthew nudged his wife to tactful silence. 'Come and say goodbye before you leave, won't you, Mrs Devlin?'

'Oh, yes! Do come and see us before we sail on Thursday.'

Kate promised to call and the Lattimers took their leave.

Untying her bonnet, Kate threw it on the bed, which looked hard. In fact, the whole room seemed very spartan.

Idiot! What did she expect? Her days of luxury were over! Tomorrow it would all be over.

'Randal has sent a message summoning the lawyers to meet me here tomorrow morning,' Kitty had told her on her return from Lady Edgeworth's bedchamber. 'They are to bring my grandfather's strong-box, so I will be able to pay you and Mary.' She'd beamed at Kate. 'I am sure my cousin will have no objection to you all remaining here until then.'

Gritting her teeth, Kate had agreed, but as the morning had worn on without any sign of Randal her strained nerves had given way.

'I've asked Emma for a ride,' she had told Mary tersely. 'I'll put up at the Bear in Lower Bridge Street tonight and you and Ned can meet me there tomorrow after Kitty has handed over the money. I'll take the small valise. Will you bring the rest of my things?'

Mary had nodded and Kate held out a hastily scribbled letter. 'Can you give this to Lord Redesmere?'

'Are you sure, lass?'

Kate nodded grimly. There was nothing left to say except goodbye.

He hadn't known she was an actress when he had asked her to marry him. Her running away would save them both embarrassment.

Don't mope, she now told herself sternly. In a few weeks you will be on your way to America and all this will seem like a dream.

Blinking away her tears, she forced herself to ring for the chambermaid. For sure, she would feel better when she had washed and changed—her pomona-green travelling costume was abominably dusty!

The maid took a long time to answer the bell. 'Sorry, miss, we're right busy,' she muttered in a harassed tone before rushing off again.

Kate decided to tidy her hair while she was waiting and had just unpinned her curls when a knock came at the door.

'Come in,' she called, pleasantly surprised that the hot water she had asked for had arrived so quickly.

'Why did you run away, sweetheart?'

The brush fell from her nerveless fingers as Kate whirled round from the mirror.

'I…I…you shouldn't have followed me. Please go away!'

'You haven't given me an answer yet.' Randal closed the door and set his hat and driving gloves down calmly.

Kate stared at him, her heart thudding wildly. She had thought she would never see him again! 'You know it is impossible!'

He raised his brows at her. 'I thought you loved me.'

Kate drew in a shaking breath. Oh, God, why was he torturing her like this?

'Well? I told you that I loved you and wanted you for my wife. Don't I at least deserve to know whether my feelings are reciprocated?' His appearance of calm could not disguise the faint tremor in Randal's voice. 'Or maybe you don't care enough to take the risk of marrying a man who might turn into a fever-wrecked cripple one day?'

'How can you say such a thing!' Kate's precarious self-control splintered. 'What happened at Walcheren isn't important to me because I don't mind whether you get ill or not! You'll still be the same man and I'll still love you!' Her eyes glittered with unshed tears. 'Of course I want to marry you!'

'That's all I needed to hear.'

In two strides he crossed the little room and gathered her into his arms.

'Don't ever run away from me again,' he said thickly and set his mouth on hers.

The kiss was long and deep, igniting a familiar flame of longing in Kate, but when he lifted his fair head she struggled for sanity.

'Randal!' Placing her hands flat against the lapels of his blue superfine coat, she held him off. 'I cannot marry you. I am an actress!'

'You are also the daughter of Sir George Redcliffe.'

Kate's eyes widened. 'I suppose Mary told you?'

He nodded. 'She told me everything.'

'You aren't disgusted?' Kate whispered.

'Only with your relatives.'

The Redcliffes were an old Cumbrian family of good lineage and modest fortune, but her father's behaviour was monstrous. Almost as bad, her frivolous grandmother, whose careless neglect had allowed Devlin to pursue his courtship, had refused Katharine succour for fear that the baronet would refuse to settle her continual gaming debts.

'They deserve nothing but contempt for the way they behaved. I think you well shot of them!'

A shaky smile curved Kate's lips. She might have known he wouldn't take the conventional view of elopement! 'I can't imagine you abandoning Emma in a like case,' she murmured.

'Indeed I would not!' he replied forcefully.

She had been an innocent sixteen-year-old desperate for affection, easy prey for a cruel rogue who had hoped to gain access to Sir George's money. Sadly, she had paid a bitter price for her mistake!

'Now we have disposed of that objection, may I ask if you are ashamed of having had to work for your living?'

'No!' Kate hesitated. 'Well, not now, although I was at first,' she admitted honestly.

'You *didn't* want to go on stage?'

Hearing the surprise in his voice, Kate gave a rueful little laugh. 'I may have been foolishly enamoured of an actor, but I wasn't actually stage-struck. No, it was Francis who insisted on my becoming an actress.'

'You don't have to tell me if you'd rather—'

Kate shook her head, making her loosened hair ripple over her shoulders. 'I don't want any more secrets between us,' she said in a slightly unsteady voice.

At his quick nod of understanding, she was encouraged to continue. 'On my seventeenth birthday Francis asked me to elope with him over the border to Gretna. I thought it the most romantic thing! It didn't matter to me that he was poor and from a different *milieu*. He was kind and gentle and he swore he loved me.'

Kate had been so happy she had ignored her guilt about running away and blithely refused to think of the future.

'Then my father cast me off and Francis's attitude changed overnight.' She gave an awkward little shrug. 'I hadn't realised, you see, that he was only pretending to be in love with me.'

Randal's arms tightened around her protectively, rage against the dead man burning in his heart.

'Francis had left his previous company in order to arrange our elopement. It took his last penny and, Papa having failed his expectations, we were on the point of being thrown out of our lodgings when the Gillman Players arrived in Carlisle.'

Ned had agreed to take Francis on and Kate, in a state of shocked bewilderment at her new circumstances and intimidated by her husband's foul mood, soon discovered that she was expected to earn her keep by helping with the numerous small tasks that went on backstage. She had barely adjusted to this situation when Betsy, one of the younger actresses, sprained her ankle and Francis had curtly informed her that she would have to take her place.

'I…I can't stand up there in front of all those people!' Kate had gasped in affronted fright.

'Too proud, eh? Actors not good enough for you, I suppose.' The black frown she had come to fear descended on Francis's good-looking face.

'No…no, but—'

'You're no better than the rest of us now, Miss High and Mighty!' Francis had snarled at her. 'And I won't drag a useless dead-weight around with me! Either you'll do as I say or, by God, I'll throw you out!'

So, terrified of his anger, Kate had obeyed and to her surprise, once she had overcome her initial nerves, she had begun to enjoy her new employment.

'Oddly enough, in the end Francis became jealous of my success and forbade me to take any of the larger roles,' she murmured with a rueful chuckle.

Not wishing to upset her, Randal swallowed his rage at Devlin's vile behaviour and tried to match her light tone. 'I told you once before that I approved of honest toil so there's another obstacle vanquished. Which, since you've no objection to my person, means there is nothing to stop us getting wed.'

'Not everyone is as liberal-minded as yourself, my lord.'

Randal traced the curve of her smiling mouth with the tip

of his finger. 'You let me worry about the gossips,' he commanded.

A quick glance about him revealed that the little room boasted but one chair so he led her to the bed and sat down beside her.

'It would be foolish to deny that your impersonation of Kitty won't raise a few eyebrows,' he said, taking her hands in his. 'However, with the support of Lady Edgeworth I intend to put it about that Kitty was too shy to claim her inheritance and you were a friend doing her a favour. We will present it as nothing more than a silly prank which went too far.'

'Do you think people will believe your explanation?' Kate asked anxiously.

'There is no reason for them to doubt me.' Randal paused. 'I am curious, though. Why did you take such a risk for someone who was almost a stranger to you? Surely, it wasn't just for the money?'

Mary had told him of her fervent wish to rid herself of debt, and she had spirit enough for any bold venture, but the penalties for forgery and fraud were extremely severe.

'I felt sorry for her,' Kate answered simply. 'You see, I knew what it was like to feel alone and afraid.'

Randal smiled at her warmly. 'I intend to see to it that you never have to feel that way again, my brave darling.'

Kate's heartbeat increased, leaving her feeling giddy. 'Truly, I didn't think there was much risk,' she protested in a slightly breathless voice. 'If I had known Sullivan had written to you, I wouldn't have dared come to Chester.'

Randal's smile broadened. 'I'm glad you did,' he said, reaching out to stroke her hair.

The ardent glitter in his eyes made Kate colour up.

'You mustn't worry,' he murmured, taking pity on her blushes and returning to the subject under discussion. 'Our profuse apologies should soothe any ruffled feathers and, with luck, it will soon be just a piece of girlish foolishness, forgotten once fresher tidbits become news.'

'But what about the rest of it, Randal? Even if you introduce me as a baronet's daughter, someone still might recognise me.' Kate shivered. 'Sean did.'

Randal squeezed her hands gently. 'Do you think I hadn't thought of that possibility, you goose? It is a risk we will have to take. If the worse comes to the worse, we shall brazen it out.' He smiled at her. 'I am not without influence, you know.'

Kate nodded slowly.

'What's more, I intend to see to it that we have powerful allies. Lady Massey likes you. With your permission, I shall tell her and a few select others a carefully edited version of the truth.' A wicked grin suddenly split his handsome face. 'A well-bred widow forced to earn her own crust who foils the dastardly villain and saves the day. You'll be a heroine, sweetheart.'

A tiny tendril of hope began to unfurl in Kate's heart.

'Do you really think they will accept me?'

He nodded confidently. 'You are of their world and, besides, even the highest sticklers like my sister Milly acknowledge certain actresses to be respectable.'

'Like Mrs Siddons, you mean?' Kate met his gaze thoughtfully. 'Well, my reputation is as unblemished as hers at any rate.'

Randal was honest enough to admit to himself that he was glad Kate had taken no lovers since her husband's death.

'But it is your character, the unique essence which makes you yourself, and not your past, which is important to me,' he avowed quietly and, remembering that he hadn't even known her real name when he had asked her to marry him, Kate joyfully realised he spoke the truth.

'Last night you repaid my faith in you by confessing you were an imposter, trusting me just as I'd always hoped you would. Now I know the whole story, it further vindicates my belief in your integrity.' He bent forward and kissed her cheek tenderly. 'I admire your courage, my love, and I'm sure others will, too.'

Kate blinked away tears of happiness.

Taking a tiny box from the pocket of his coat, Randal flipped the lid open and held it out to her. 'We can get you something else if you prefer, but I thought you might like to wear this as a token of our betrothal.'

'Oh, Randal!' Kate stared down at the beautiful poesy ring from his father's collection and the garnets twinkled like fire as her eyes misted afresh.

Here is my heart... He slipped it on to her finger and she flung her arms around his neck and kissed him with all the love and passion that burned in her soul.

Desire exploded in them both. Breathless and giddy, they sank back on to the bed and for one endless moment the world was lost, drowned in a sea of pleasure.

'No, my dearest love, no!' Fighting temptation, Randal broke off the kiss. 'Not like this! Not in these drab surroundings where we may be disturbed at any moment!'

He propped himself up on one elbow and smiled down into her puzzled face. 'You deserve better.'

Devlin had treated her badly. He wanted to show her that lovemaking could be different, wanted to make their first time special for her.

'Let's wait for our wedding night, eh, sweetheart?'

Much as she desired him, Kate realised he was right. It was going to be difficult facing the world she had hoodwinked. Knowing that any lewd speculations about their relationship were unfounded would bolster her confidence.

'Come on!' Randal sprang to his feet. 'It's time we got you round to Abbey Square.'

Kate scrambled from the bed. 'Lady Alicia is willing to take me back?' A delighted expression lit up her face.

'She suggested it. She also suggested I might like to call upon the Bishop while you are unpacking.' He grinned at her baffled expression. 'To arrange for a special license, my love. You do want to marry me as soon as possible, I hope?'

Kate nodded enthusiastically.

'Good. Then we can be married before Emma sails for Spain.' Randal took her hands in his own, laughter in his brilliant blue eyes. 'When I left her, Alicia was blissfully devising arrangements for the ceremony, subject to your approval, of course.'

'Should you mind if I invited Mary and Ned?' Kate experienced a stab of guilt. Ned was expecting her to go with them to America! 'I feel as if I am letting them down by leaving the company so abruptly.'

'Of course you may invite them and anyone else you wish.' He smiled reassuringly at her. 'They are your friends, I'm sure they will understand your decision and be happy for you.' He looked deep into her eyes. 'It's time for you to return to your own world, Katharine. You belong here with me, not with them.'

Kate's face lost its frown of concern and she smiled back at him.

He was right. She would miss everyone in the company, but they would survive without her. Many theatres were already closing for the summer, which would enable Ned to find an actress to replace her and, with Kitty's help, she felt certain they would achieve success in America.

'Time to go,' Randal said firmly, rousing her from her speculations. 'I'll collect your belongings while you attend to your hair.'

Kate began to bundle up her curls into a high knot. 'What of Sullivan?' she asked out of reluctant curiosity, pushing home the final hairpin.

'You needn't worry. I've taken care of him.' Randal picked up her valise, placing it on the bed. 'He won't bother us again.'

'Why did you suspect him?' Kate dropped her hairbrush into the valise. 'He was always so agreeable.'

'When he thought himself unobserved, his eyes filled with anger when they rested upon you.' Randal shrugged. 'It made me decide to keep a watch on him.'

'So that's why you invited him to dinner and were friendly

towards him!' Remembering her absurd suspicions, Kate was ashamed.

'Aye, but I slipped up that night at the theatre. I spotted him heading backstage as I arrived and meant to follow him, but I was waylaid by Mrs Egerton, who kept me talking. He'd vanished by the time I escaped her, but when I went to seek you your box was empty, although I soon discovered that Alicia was present. Eventually, I wondered if you had stepped outside for a breath of air.'

Randal remembered the unease which had assailed him when he couldn't find her. Then he'd caught a glimpse of a man running in the distance with a strange bundle slung over his shoulder.

Instinct had prompted him to follow, thank God!

'I never saw his face that night. If I had—'

'Don't let's dwell on it,' Kate interrupted with a shudder.

'As you wish, sweetheart.'

Kate closed the valise. There was something else that had to be said before she could forget the past.

'You haven't uttered a word of reproach,' her voice trembled. 'But I want you to know that I am ashamed about all the lies I told you.'

'Kitty might have died without your help,' he reminded her. 'Certainly, she would have lost her fortune.' He adjusted the set of his elegant waistcoat a trifle diffidently. 'Beside, I have to confess that I wasn't always above board in my dealings with you.'

He quickly explained how he had persuaded Alan Hilton to enjoy a few days out of town. 'And I contacted the Hogans in secret.'

Kate grinned. 'The end justifies the means,' she murmured, suddenly feeling better.

'We would never have met if you hadn't embarked upon this crazy scheme,' he agreed, smiling back at her.

'I hadn't thought of that!' Kate laughed and picking up her bonnet put it on.

Randal took the valise and ushered her towards the door.

'Randal!' Kate came to an abrupt halt. 'You still haven't told me! *How* did you know I wasn't Kitty? I thought Sean's acknowledgement had convinced you!'

He grinned at her. 'Remember you informed me at our first meeting that Kitty possetted all down my new coat at her christening?'

Startled, Kate nodded.

'Well, my old nurse whisked the pair of us off to the nursery to be cleaned up. I was very indignant at the time, I can tell you! Maybe that's what fixed the memory in my mind, although it became buried later. I suppose it was responsible for my instinct insisting that you were an imposter, but it wasn't until last night when you wore that skimpy Egyptian costume that it finally resurfaced and I realised why you couldn't be Kitty.'

Putting down the valise, Randal turned to face Kate squarely.

'You see, sweetheart, Kitty has a large strawberry mark just here.' His fingertip gently touched Kate's left breast. 'I saw it when Nurse changed her clothes.' Amusement glinted in his eyes. 'It would show in any low-cut gown, but your lovely skin is unmarked.'

Kate's lips parted in astonishment. No wonder Kitty favoured such modest necklines!

'''O what a tangled web we weave,''' she chuckled.

'''When first we practise to deceive!''' Randal finished the quote from *Marmion* for her. 'But your deception was masterly my love. If it hadn't been for that nagging memory, I would have been fooled like all the rest.'

He lifted her hand to his lips and kissed it. 'I think you are an excellent actress, Mrs Devlin. I just hope you won't miss the stage too much.'

Kate shook her head firmly. 'My ambitions lie in another direction, sir.'

One tawny brow rose in enquiry.

Kate wound her arms around his neck and lifted her smiling

ace to his. 'I want to make you such a good wife that even your sister Milly will approve of me.'

'If she doesn't, the Devil can fly away with her!' Lord Redesmere declared promptly and bent to kiss his beloved's waiting lips.

* * * * *

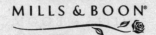

MILLS & BOON®

Makes any time special

**Enjoy a romantic novel from
Mills & Boon®**

Presents...™   *Enchanted*™   TEMPTATION.

Historical Romance™   ✚ **MEDICAL ROMANCE**™

MAT

FREE!

2 Books
and a surprise gift!

We would like to take this opportunity to thank you for reading this Mills & Boon® book by offering you the chance to take TWO more specially selected titles from the Historical Romance™ series absolutely FREE! We're also making this offer to introduce you to the benefits of the Reader Service™—

  ★ FREE home delivery
  ★ FREE gifts and competitions
  ★ FREE monthly Newsletter
  ★ Books available before they're in the shops
  ★ Exclusive Reader Service discounts

Accepting these FREE books and gift places you under no obligation to buy; you may cancel at any time, even after receiving your free shipment. Simply complete your details below and return the entire page to the address below. *You don't even need a stamp!*

YES! Please send me 2 free Historical Romance books and a surprise gift. I understand that unless you hear from me, I will receive 4 superb new titles every month for just £2.99 each, postage and packing free. I am under no obligation to purchase any books and may cancel my subscription at any time. The free books and gift will be mine to keep in any case.

HOEB

Ms/Mrs/Miss/Mr ....Initials................................
BLOCK CAPITALS PLEASE

Surname..

Address..

....

....Postcode ....

Send this whole page to:
UK: The Reader Service, FREEPOST CN81, Croydon, CR9 3WZ
EIRE: The Reader Service, PO Box 4546, Kilcock, County Kildare (stamp required)

Offer not valid to current Reader Service subscribers to this series. We reserve the right to refuse an application and applicants must be aged 18 years or over. Only one application per household. Terms and prices subject to change without notice. Offer expires 30th November 2000. As a result of this application, you may receive further offers from Harlequin Mills & Boon Limited and other carefully selected companies. If you would prefer not to share in this opportunity please write to The Data Manager at the address above.

Mills & Boon® is a registered trademark owned by Harlequin Mills & Boon Limited.
Historical Romance™ is being used as a trademark.